PRAISE FOR THE NOVELS OF

Whitney Gaskell

. . ..

WHEN YOU LEAST EXPECT IT

"Gaskell's novel depicts the fear and heartbreak that accompanies infertility with an emotional adeptness that few other authors could produce."
                                    —Night Owl Reviews

"*When You Least Expect It* is a book once you start, you will not put down until the last page is read."
                                    —Me, My Book, and the Couch

"Competently done and appropriately affirmative."
                                    —Publishers Weekly

"*When You Least Expect It* is clever, poignant, and refreshing. The crisp writing, smart voice, and strong dialogue make it a fast-paced, engrossing read. Gaskell's latest is hard to put down!"
                                    —Jane Porter, author of *Easy on the Eyes*

"With her signature wit, charm, and irresistible voice, Whitney Gaskell knocks it out of the park with this emotional powerhouse of a novel about—above all things—hope."

—Melissa Senate, author of *The Secret of Joy*

"Whitney Gaskell has so much talent it makes me want to throw myself through a plate glass window. I loved *When You Least Expect It*. Whitney brings us through all the heartache and triumph of the adoption process with relatable characters, memorable scenes, and much needed humor."

—Kim Gruenenfelder, author of *Misery Loves Cabernet*

GOOD LUCK

"Money doesn't buy happiness, but you'll have a blast reading along as Lucy (with her $87 million) learns that lesson."

—*Redbook*

"Gaskell has crafted an emotional roller coaster of a novel. The highs are funny and furious, and the lows will tug at readers' heartstrings as they relish this superb tale of the slings and arrows of outrageous fortune." —*Booklist* (starred review)

"Frothy wish-fulfillment fantasy." —*Publishers Weekly*

MOMMY TRACKED

"There are few periods more challenging for women than the pre-school years, and this compassionate novel captures that time in all its endearing, slovenly, enchanting glory."

—*BookPage*

"An excellent read . . . Gaskell has so many fine points in this book, it was hard to put it down."   —*Coffee Time Romance*

"[This book] celebrates motherhood, marriage, and friendship with humor and vibrant insight."   —*Publishers Weekly*

"Poignant, funny, and peppered with snappy dialogue, *Mommy Tracked* is a great addition to the friendship book list, which includes *Waiting to Exhale*, *The Circle of Five*, and *The Dirty Girls Social Club*."   —*Booklist*

"It's like reading a really juicy grown-up Judy Blume book."

—WackyMommy

"Filled with humor, charm, and richly developed characters."

—Fresh Fiction

"A laugh-out-loud, witty view of motherhood."

—*Romantic Times*

TRUE LOVE (AND OTHER LIES)

"Funny, romantic . . . an entertaining read with all the right stuff."
                                                  —Romance Reviews Today

"A hilarious story about love and friendships . . . A compelling, thought-provoking and nevertheless entertaining book . . . breezy, delightful, and well worth reading."
                                                  —The Best Reviews

"Witty, honest, and refreshingly fun."   —Roundtable Reviews

PUSHING 30

"Feisty, poignant, sexy, and packed with delicious comedy."
                                    —Sue Margolis, author of *Forget Me Knot*

"A breezy romp."   —*The Miami Herald*

"A sprightly debut . . . breezy prose, sharp wit . . . a delightful romantic comedy heroine."   —*Publishers Weekly*

"Gaskell takes a familiar 'oh-no' chicklit theme and turns it sprightly on its ear. . . . What sets *Pushing 30* apart from others in the genre is Gaskell's sharp writing and skillful handling of many plot strands as it weaves into a cohesive, thoroughly satisfying read."   —*Pittsburgh Post-Gazette*

ALSO BY *Whitney Gaskell*

Pushing 30

True Love (and Other Lies)

She, Myself & I

Testing Kate

Mommy Tracked

Good Luck

When You Least Expect It

Table for Seven

BANTAM BOOKS
NEW YORK

Table for Seven

A NOVEL

Whitney Gaskell

A Bantam Books Trade Paperback Original

Copyright © 2013 by Whitney Gaskell

Excerpt from *When You Least Expect It*
copyright © 2010 by Whitney Gaskell

Published in the United States by Bantam Books,
an imprint of The Random House Publishing Group,
a division of Random House, Inc., New York.

BANTAM BOOKS and the rooster colophon are
registered trademarks of Random House, Inc.

LIBRARY OF CONGRESS CATALOGING-IN-PUBLICATION DATA

Gaskell, Whitney.
Table for seven : a novel / Whitney Gaskell.
pages cm
ISBN 978-0-553-38628-8
eBook ISBN 978-0-345-53577-1
1. New Year—Fiction. 2. Dinners and dining—Fiction.
3. Clubs—Fiction. 4. Friendship—Fiction. I. Title.
PS3607.A7854.T33 2012
813'.6—dc23   2011044940

Printed in the United States of America

www.bantamdell.com

9 8 7 6 5 4 3 2 1

Book design by Barbara M. Bachman

for Sam

Table for Seven

january

. . . .

TEQUILA SHRIMP

ARUGULA, FENNEL, AND ORANGE SALAD

SEARED SCALLOPS WITH BUTTER SAUCE
OVER TARRAGON RICE

CHEESE PLATE

WHITE CHOCOLATE–RASPBERRY
CRÈME BRÛLÉE TARTLETS

*F*RAN WAS THE ONE who first suggested a New Year's Eve dinner party. But it was Will's idea to serve a different course every hour, on the hour, counting down to midnight.

"Then, for the last course, we can have something like cherries jubilee, which we'll light up at the stroke of midnight," Will said.

"Cherries jubilee?" Fran repeated doubtfully. Cherries jubilee reminded her of fusty country club dining rooms, the sort that were always decorated in shades of mauve and served the food buffet-style, with carving stations where thick slabs of chewy, flavorless roast beef were hacked off for each diner.

"Or something else that we can serve flambé," Will said. "Bananas Foster? Baked Alaska?"

"What's this sudden fascination with desserts that are on fire?" Fran asked, paging through *The French Laundry Cookbook*. A few of the pages were stained with what looked like splattered olive oil. Fran had a habit of propping cookbooks too close to the stove when she cooked.

"Just think: The clock strikes midnight, it's the first minute of the New Year, and we celebrate by turning off all the lights and serving a flaming dessert."

"I was thinking more along the lines of white chocolate–raspberry crème brûlée tartlets," Fran said. "But I like the idea of serving a course every hour, on the hour. Do you think that would be hard to pull off?"

"I'll help," Will said, sealing this promise with a chaste kiss on Fran's cheek. Then, whistling cheerily, he headed off to the garage to continue work on his latest combat robot, leaving Fran to plan everything herself.

Fran paged through her extensive collection of cookbooks, looking for inspiration, while she considered the guest list. Jaime and Mark Wexler. Audrey, obviously, although she was going to be defensive if she was the only single person at a party of couples. Fran tried to think of any other single people she knew—and if it was a man, it couldn't be someone Audrey suspected Fran was trying to set her up with, another area on which her best friend was ridiculously touchy—and then she thought of her next-door neighbor Leland McCullogh. He was a widower in his seventies—which meant he was about thirty years older than the others—but Leland was witty and charming and would make an excellent addition to the dinner party.

Fran stood and padded barefoot to the garage, where Will sat hunched in concentration over his workbench.

"What do you think of inviting the Wexlers, Audrey, and Leland from next door to our New Year's Eve dinner party? Six is a good number, right?" Fran asked.

Will didn't give any indication that he had heard her.

"Will?" Fran said.

"Hmm?" Will said, still not looking up.

"I started a grease fire in the kitchen. The house is going up in flames. What should I do?" Fran asked.

"The fire extinguisher is right over there," Will said, waving vaguely toward the shelving that lined the back wall of the garage. "See? I'm not ignoring you."

"Very convincing," Fran said. "What do you think of the guest list?"

"Sounds fine," Will said. He picked up a hunk of metal—

part of his latest combat robot, Fran assumed, although Will's creations always looked more like metal boxes than C-3PO—and secured it in a vise.

"Can you think of anyone else we should invite?" Fran asked.

"Nope." Will picked up a screwdriver and held it over the robot like a surgeon contemplating his first cut.

Fran waited a beat or two, but Will didn't give any indication that he was going to join the conversation they were having. She turned.

"Coop," Will said.

"What?" Fran turned back.

"Coop," Will said again. "Didn't I tell you? He's in town."

"Wait. What? Coop's here? In *our* town?" Fran asked. An image of Coop—sexy Coop with his tanned face and pale gray eyes, the hair on his arms bleached white from hours spent out on his boat—flashed through her thoughts.

"Yes," Will said. "I thought I told you."

"No," Fran said. "What's he doing here?"

"He's living here. He rented an apartment on the beach."

"Okay, put down the screwdriver, and start from the beginning," Fran said.

Will looked up, blinked at her, and set the screwdriver down on his workbench.

"Coop's living here," he said again.

"Yes, you said that. Now I want to hear the rest of it. What is Coop doing here? When did he move here? Why haven't you told me about this before?" Fran asked.

"He's editing some film he's working on. I think it has something to do with coastal tides. They shot it up near Nova Scotia. He said it was freezing, and that he was glad to be back in Florida," Will said.

"I can imagine. But why is he here in Ocean Falls? What happened to Miami?"

"He sold his condo before he left for the shoot, so he decided to rent up here while he's in postproduction. I thought I told you all of this," Will added, looking longingly at his robot.

"No," Fran said. "You didn't. How long is he in town for?"

"No idea. Indefinitely, I think."

"We should have him over."

"That's what I was suggesting. Invite him to the dinner party."

"You think?"

"Sure, why not?"

"Wouldn't he think a dinner party was boring and suburban?"

"No way. We're hip and cool," Will said. *But that was just it,* Fran thought. They were not hip and cool. They didn't live in Brooklyn, and have tattoos, and name their children Fifi or Zola. Will was a city planner, Fran was a physical therapist, and they spent their weekends grocery shopping, mowing the lawn, and chauffeuring their two daughters to soccer and dance practices. "What about Audrey?"

"What about her?"

"If we invite her and we invite Coop, she'll jump to the conclusion that I'm trying to set her up with him," Fran said.

"That's because you're always trying to set her up."

"No, I'm not."

"The last time we were at the grocery store, you accosted some guy in the deli meat line—"

"I did not accost him!"

"—and asked him if he would be interested in going out with Audrey," Will finished.

"He wasn't a stranger. His son was on the same soccer team as Rory, back when they were little. I just couldn't remember his name. We all called him Cute Single Dad Guy," Fran said.

"Except now he's married," Will said.

"How was I supposed to know that? I haven't seen the man in five years," Fran said.

"He was wearing a wedding band."

"Whatever. Anyway, Audrey needs a little push to get back out there. Ryan's been gone for, what, seven years now?"

"Wow, has it been that long?"

"Yeah, it has. Remember? Iris was in first grade, and so was at school, but Rory was just a toddler. I had the hardest time finding a babysitter to watch her while we went to the funeral."

"I don't remember that," Will said.

"I do. Anyway, she's been alone for a long time. Long enough."

"Maybe Audrey's not ready for another relationship. You can't prescribe how long a person is allowed to grieve for."

"Yes, I can. Seven years is objectively too long. If you died, I'd give it a year, tops, before I started dating," Fran said.

"Wow, a whole year? I'm touched," Will said.

"What do we do about Coop and Audrey?"

"Why do we have to do anything about them? We invite them both, and if Audrey doesn't want to come because there's a single man there, that's her choice. Unless . . . wait." Will held up one hand. "I just had the most brilliant idea."

"Uh-oh," Fran said.

"No, wait for it. We tell Audrey that Coop is gay."

Fran blinked, nonplussed. "Why would we do that?"

"Because that way Audrey won't think she's being set up. And it will be an excellent way to get back at Coop for telling Kelly Feinstein that I lost both testicles in a freak BB gun accident so she'd go out with him instead of me," Will said.

"What? When did that happen?" Fran asked.

"Tenth grade. But it's never too late for payback," Will said.

"I don't know," Fran said. "Won't Audrey be able to tell he's not gay?"

"How would she?"

"Coop is just very . . ." Fran stopped. She could feel her cheeks go warm.

"Very what?"

Adjectives that could be applied to Coop began flashing through Fran's thoughts. *Hilarious. Flirtatious. Incredibly sexy.*

"Heterosexual," Fran said.

"No, trust me, she'll never figure it out." Will was eyeing his robot with impatience.

"Should I call Coop? Or do you want to?"

"Sure. Whatever you want," Will said, his screwdriver again hovering in the air, ready to get to work.

Sensing that she was losing his attention, Fran went back into the house.

Coop, she thought. It had been a long time since she'd thought about him. There had been a time when she'd thought about Coop too much. And one day, back when she and Will were first married, when something had almost happened between them.

They'd been out on Coop's boat—he always seemed to have a boat, even back then, when they were in their twenties and still had to scrounge for beer money—and it must have been summer or early fall, because Fran remembered that it had been hot. So hot everyone had stripped down to their bathing suits, and both Will and Coop's date—he'd dated so many women over the years that Fran couldn't remember this one's name or even what she'd looked like—had drifted off, lulled to sleep by the combination of sun, alcohol, and the gentle rocking of the boat.

While the others napped, Fran and Coop hung out in the stern of the boat, chatting lazily. Fran could still remember that she'd been wearing a turquoise bikini—this was back in the pre-child days, when she'd had the figure to carry off a two-piece—and her long, curly hair was loose around her shoulders. Coop had suddenly leaned over and fingered one of her corkscrew ringlets, drawing it out and then letting it spring back. It usually annoyed her when anyone did that, but Coop's touch had been incredibly erotic. Fran—who had never once considered cheating on Will—suddenly found herself holding her breath, hoping beyond hope that Coop would move even closer, that he would lean forward, that his lips would touch against hers. . . .

But instead, Coop sat back and gazed at her with knowing gray-blue eyes. Coop's features, taken apart, were all wrong—the planes of his cheeks were too sharp, the jaw was too prominent, the nose was too long, the lips too thin. But put together, it all worked.

It was the sort of face you never tired of looking at, Fran thought.

"It's too bad Will met you first," Coop said quietly. "You're really more my type than his."

Despite the skittering leap her heart took at those words, Fran had laughed. "I didn't know you had a type. There seems to be quite a bit of variety in the women you date."

"True. But I've always had a soft spot for smart asses. And for women with blue eyes and dark hair. Especially long, curly hair," Coop said softly.

Fran's smile slipped away, and the joke she would usually have made stuck in her throat. Her hair, which she'd always considered one of the great annoyances of her life, with its unruly curls that never looked good in a ponytail, suddenly made her feel beautiful. Sexy. Desirable. She and Coop just sat there, gazing at each other, possibility humming between them.

Will had woken up then, stretching and sighing. And just like that, the spell was broken. Coop leaned back on his elbows, away from Fran.

Will sat up, blinking in the sunlight. "Anyone want to go for a swim?" he called out.

Fran watched as Will and Coop jumped overboard together, plunging into the aquamarine water and bobbing up a few moments later. They'd called to her to join them, along with the nameless girlfriend, who had also woken up by then, but both women had demurred. The girlfriend said she wanted to work on her tan, while Fran knew that the salt water would cause her mascara to run and her hair to puff and frizz. She didn't want Coop to see her looking waterlogged, her nose red, her hair bedraggled. She wanted him to think of her as the sexy girl in the blue bikini, the girl with the blue eyes and dark curls.

Nothing ever happened again between them. Fran had both hoped and feared that it would, had even wondered for a time if she'd made a mistake marrying Will. But Coop went back to treating her with a teasing affection that, while yes, was definitely flirtatious, never crossed any lines. And after a while, Fran began to wonder if she'd imagined the whole thing, that it was just some harmless flirting on a warm summer's day.

And now, Fran thought, after fourteen years and two children, all traces of that girl in the blue bikini had disappeared. She wondered what Coop thought of her now that she was forty with tired eyes and a body that had never bounced back from childbirth, before realizing that of course he wouldn't think of her. At some point, somewhere along the way to middle age, Fran had become invisible.

"DO YOU NEED HELP bringing in the groceries?" Mark asked. He sat at the kitchen table, one leg thrown casually over the other, iPhone in hand.

"No, this is the last of it," Jaime said, as she heaved a green recyclable grocery bag up onto the Carrara marble countertop. "Where are the kids?"

"Playroom," Mark said, his eyes on his phone.

Jaime could hear the distant sound of a Thomas the Train DVD. She pressed her lips together. Their children—Logan, three, and Ava, nearly two—were already far too familiar with the genre of animated talking trains. Every time Mark was home alone with the kids, he planted them in front of the television set.

"When was the last time you checked on them?" she asked.

"A few minutes ago," Mark said vaguely, still scrolling through his messages.

Jaime headed to the playroom, just a short hallway down from the kitchen. Logan sat on the floor in front of the television, his eyes fixed on the screen, where Thomas the Tank Engine was getting a lecture from Sir Topham Hatt on the merits of being useful. Ava was curled up on the blue denim slip-covered sofa, her eyelashes curled down over rounded cheeks and her mouth slack with sleep.

"You okay, sweetheart?" she asked.

Logan, transfixed by the television, didn't answer.

"You can finish this episode, but then we're going to turn off the TV," Jaime said.

Logan didn't give any indication that he had heard her, and Jaime was reminded of his father. *Is the addiction to electronic gadgets genetic?* she wondered. *Or learned?* Either way, she might as well take advantage of the lull to put the groceries away.

When she returned to the kitchen, Mark hadn't moved. Jaime turned her attention to the groceries, a job for which she had a well-planned system. Frozen groceries were put away first, of course, then refrigerated items. Cans were neatly stacked in their cupboard, arranged by size. She had once organized her canned goods in alphabetical order—an approach that had worked well in the spice cabinet—but hadn't liked the way it looked, tiny containers of tomato paste dwarfed by hulking cans of imported tomatoes.

Finally—and this was her favorite part—Jaime decanted the remaining groceries into their specially designated containers. Pasta went into glass jars with hinged lids. Dish soap was poured into a tall blue bottle next to the sink. Sea salt went into a porcelain saltcellar she had found in an antiques store in Palm Beach. Sugar and flour were stored in glossy stainless steel canisters on the highest pantry shelf. Powdered laundry detergent went in a large white tin box that Jaime had stenciled "laundry soap" along one side in a swirly blue font.

She opened the pantry door to retrieve the pasta jars and then stopped, blinking at the mess. A box of cookies sat opened and unsealed. Where it came from, Jaime had no idea; she never purchased anything that contained partially hydrogenated oils. A crumpled bag of Doritos lay on its side, also opened, with the top folded loosely down and not a bag clip in sight. Boxes of crackers and cereal were no longer neatly lined up, but all askew, as though someone had pulled out every single box and then shoved them carelessly back in. The glass lid to the canister that contained the almonds was gone. Jaime looked down and saw it on the floor.

"Doritos?" Jaime said. "Oreos?"

Mark raised his hand. "Guilty."

"When did you start eating junk food?"

"I didn't. Emily was hungry when I picked her up, so I sent her into the store with a twenty while I took a business call. What you see there is the result of a twelve-year-old grocery shopping without supervision," Mark said, still not looking up from his iPhone.

Emily was Mark's daughter from his first marriage. And, as Jaime had learned in the four years she and Mark had been married, the problem with being the second wife—especially when your husband shared a child with his former wife—was that the first family never really went away. Mark's ex-wife, Libby, called and texted him all the time, keeping Mark apprised of every last detail of Emily's life. This constant contact had only gotten worse since Emily had begun to show real promise as a tennis prodigy. Mark—already a tennis enthusiast—was obsessed. He was at the courts nearly every day, chauffeuring Emily back and forth to her lessons, consulting with coaches, spending more time and money than seemed possible nurturing her talent.

"She made a mess," Jaime said, bending over to pick up the lid to the almond jar. It was cracked.

"Don't worry, I'll get her to clean it up," Mark said. Then, raising his voice, he said, "Emily! Come down here."

"What? Why?" a muffled voice called back from the general direction of the living room.

"I'd like to speak to you, that's why," Mark called back. He rolled his eyes at Jaime. "And just think, the teen years are still ahead of us."

Emily strolled into the kitchen. She was very thin, with fair hair caught back in a ponytail and her mother's dark, shrewd eyes. "What's up?"

"I need you to—wait." Mark's phone beeped, and he stopped to peer down at the new text he'd received. "What's this? Why is Coach Sarah putting you with Savannah for the doubles draw at the tournament this weekend?"

Emily shrugged. "I don't know. It's stupid, right? Savannah can't even hit a backhand."

"She's not a strong enough partner for you," Mark said.

"Yeah, but Savannah, like, cried after she lost at the tournament last weekend. I think Sarah thought it would give her, I don't know, confidence or something to put her with me." Emily shook her head with disgust. "It's, like, totally ridiculous."

"It's not your job to give Savannah confidence," Mark said.

"I know, right? I totally told Coach Sarah that. She said something stupid about making sacrifices for the team," Emily said, rolling her eyes. She rested her hands on her narrow hips, and tossed her ponytail back.

Jaime often marveled at her stepdaughter's self-confidence. She herself had been painfully shy at the same age, and would never have had the nerve to challenge an authority figure.

"I think Savannah should just give up tennis and take up volleyball or something," Emily said.

"I thought you and Savannah were friends," Jaime said.

Mark and Emily both turned incredulous faces toward Jaime. They looked so much alike at that moment—the high foreheads, the square chins, the matching expressions—that Jaime almost laughed.

"So?" Emily said.

Jaime suddenly felt tired, and lost enthusiasm for the conversation. "Please don't put food back into the pantry without making sure it's sealed," she said.

Emily's expression turned stormy. Jaime could almost see a bubble caption appearing over her stepdaughter's head that read, YOU ARE NOT MY MOTHER.

"I don't want to get bugs," Jaime said, trying—and failing—to sound calm and not at all defensive.

"I folded the bag over," Emily said.

"I know. And that's great. But once you do, just put a bag clip on. I keep them right here in this drawer," Jaime said, opening the drawer nearest the pantry to show her.

"You're so, like, anal," Emily muttered.

"Emily," Mark started, without hearing Emily's snide remark.

Jaime turned to him, relieved that her husband was stepping in. Technically, she had every right to chastise Emily for rude behavior. But in practice, doing so typically caused small conflicts to erupt into larger dramas. *You're not my mother* was in fact a frequent retort. And it was hard to argue the point. Jaime was not Emily's mother. What was more, Emily had never asked for her parents to divorce, or for her father to remarry, or for two younger half-siblings to be born. Jaime had some sympathy for her stepdaughter's ever present resentment.

Some.

"I'm going to talk to Sarah. If she's not going to assign you a partner you can win with, I think we'll pull you from the doubles draw, and have you just play singles," Mark continued.

Jaime stared at her husband. Had he completely missed how rude Emily had just been to her?

"I think Coach Sarah will be really annoyed if I do that," Emily said.

"Too bad. I don't want your ranking to be affected, which it might be if you're forced to play with Savannah," Mark said.

"Mark," Jaime said.

"Yeah, but Coach doesn't like it when one of us says we don't want to play with someone she puts us with. She says it's bad sportsmanship or something," Emily said.

Jaime's temper rose, filling her throat, causing her to almost choke on her husband's name. "Mark!"

Mark finally looked up, surprised at the sharpness of her tone. "What's up, babe?"

"Emily just called me anal," Jaime said, hating that she sounded like she was ten years old and tattling to the teacher.

"She did?" Mark asked. He looked at Emily. "Did you call Jaime anal?"

As if I would lie about it, Jaime thought, now so furious her stomach curdled and her mouth tasted sour. *Is that what he thinks? That I would make up stories of Emily behaving badly, just to drive a wedge between them?*

Emily shrugged one shoulder, and studied her nail cuticles.

"Emily, apologize to your stepmother," Mark instructed.

"Sorry," Emily muttered, still not looking up from her nails.

It wasn't a heartfelt apology. In fact, it barely counted as an apology at all, as it was made under duress. But Mark seemed satisfied.

"I'll talk to Coach Sarah," he said. "I'll work it out with her. Don't worry."

"Thanks, Daddy," Emily said. She walked over to the pantry, retrieved the bag of Doritos, and fished out a handful of chips.

Jaime wondered if she really saw a triumphant smile flash across her stepdaughter's face, or if she had just imagined it. Jaime opened a drawer, took out a bag clip, and set it pointedly on the counter. Then she turned and strode out of the kitchen toward the playroom, determined to get Logan away from *Thomas the Tank Engine* before his mind atrophied into Jell-O.

AUDREY DICKINSON CONSIDERED TURNING her car around and heading home. At one point, she put her indicator on, and pulled into the center turn lane. Then, reminding herself she couldn't just not show up to a dinner party she had said she'd attend, she turned her indicator off, and pulled back out into traffic.

She hated New Year's Eve. None of the holidays were particularly easy to get through, but New Year's was the very worst. Everyone was always desperate to prove that they were having a good time but no one ever really did. Audrey had given up on going out for New Year's Eve years ago, even before Ryan's . . . well. Even before he had died. In fact, her reluctance to do anything on New Year's Eve other than sit on the couch, wearing sweats and eating bad Chinese takeout straight from the boxes, used to drive Ryan crazy. He would celebrate an average Tuesday, or a night that a professional athletic team was playing a game, with three vodka martinis. A holiday that was actually dedicated to drinking to excess was not something he'd ever miss out on.

And now Audrey was stuck going to a New Year's Eve party, when what she really wanted to do was stay home and snuggle up on the couch. Maybe with a dog. If she had a dog.

I need to get a dog, Audrey thought. *That could be my solution to all holiday invites. Thanks, I'd love to, but I have to stay home with my dog.*

Audrey was still thinking about her imaginary dog—*An Irish wolfhound? An English bulldog? A pug?*—when she pulled up in front of the Parrishes' small, Spanish-style house. Twinkle lights circled the trunks of the palm trees and a huge Christmas wreath hung on the door. Audrey climbed out of her car, and then reached back in for the cheese and olive plate and bottle of red wine she'd brought.

Here goes nothing, she thought. *And I am absolutely not staying until midnight.*

Audrey rang the bell. A few beats later, Fran opened the door.

"Happy New Year!" Fran said, hugging Audrey awkwardly over the plate and bottle. Fran's cheeks were flushed and she was wearing a red and white striped apron decorated with a felt Santa.

"Happy New Year," Audrey said. She handed Fran the wine. "I brought a cheese plate, too."

"Will will be thrilled. His personal motto is *You can never have enough cheese,*" Fran said. "I gave him a wheel of Maytag blue cheese for Christmas, and it nearly brought him to tears. Come on in. Everyone's back in the kitchen."

"Who is everyone exactly?" Audrey asked.

"You know Jaime and Mark, right? They're here. And our next-door neighbor Leland."

I knew it, Audrey thought. *I knew it, I knew it.*

"Fran," Audrey said. "Please tell me this is not a set up."

"It's not, I swear!"

"I've told you about a thousand times that I don't want you to play matchmaker for me," Audrey said.

"Leland is seventy-one and walks with a cane," Fran said. "I've told you about him before. He's the one who makes those amazing oatmeal cookies."

"Oh, right, I remember. But I thought there were going to be seven of us," Audrey said.

"I also invited Will's friend Coop, but he'd already made other plans," Fran said.

Audrey looked at her, eyebrows raised.

"I wasn't trying to set you up with him, either," Fran said. She played with the silver heart hanging on a chain around her neck. "Coop is gay."

"Oh," Audrey said, mollified. "Okay. Sorry. I didn't mean to jump all over you."

"No worries. Come on back to the kitchen. I tried to get everyone to go into the living room where it's more comfortable, but they won't budge."

"Maybe they just want to keep you company while you cook," Audrey suggested, following Fran down the short front hall. "Or maybe it's that the act of food preparation is nurturing, so it makes people feel good to be around it."

"Well, prepare to be nurtured," Fran said. "I have five courses planned."

The Parrish kitchen was bright—Fran had painted the walls orange in an effort to draw attention away from the dated white laminate cupboards—and filled with the smells of dinner preparation. Will stood at the counter, also wearing an apron—his was green, with KISS THE COOK emblazoned across the front—chopping parsley.

"Audrey, hey," Will said, opening his arms. Will was balding, with a round, pink-cheeked face. He had kind brown eyes, an easy smile, and sideburns that he wore too long.

"Hi," she said, accepting his hug and peck on the cheek.

"Do you know everyone? Mark and Jaime?"

"Hi, Jaime. Hey, Mark," Audrey said, smiling at the couple standing at the counter, both holding glasses of red wine. They were both tall and lean with fair hair and very white teeth, and probably could have passed as siblings. Audrey remembered Fran telling her once that Jaime had all of her body hair lasered off. Audrey eyed Jaime's arms. They did look suspiciously smooth.

"Hi, Audrey. I love your dress," Jaime said, leaning forward and kissing the air over Audrey's right cheek.

"Thanks," Audrey said.

"And this is our neighbor Leland," Fran said.

Audrey turned to smile at an elderly man who was dressed jauntily in a blue blazer with gold buttons and a red handkerchief tucked in the front pocket. He was stooped and wizened, and reminded Audrey of a turtle who had escaped from his shell. He held out his hand and Audrey shook it gently. "Hello, I'm Audrey."

"Leland McCullogh. A pleasure to meet you," he said. His grip was surprisingly firm.

"Nice to meet you, too," Audrey said, taking an instant liking to the elderly man. "I've heard a lot about you from Fran and Will."

"None of it is true," Leland said solemnly. "Except the part about my secret elopement with Elizabeth Taylor."

"What's this about Elizabeth Taylor?" Fran asked, handing Audrey a glass of wine.

"I never told you about her? Never mind. You don't need to know all of my secrets," Leland said, winking at Audrey, who laughed.

"You're really serving five courses? I'm impressed. What are we having?" Audrey asked.

"All sorts of delicious things. We're going to serve a course every hour, on the hour, until midnight," Fran said.

Audrey managed to suppress a sigh. So much for her hope to be safely at home, in bed, before the New Year's Eve ball dropped.

"That's very ambitious," Audrey said. "Can I do anything to help?"

"No, that's okay. Will's making his famous tequila shrimp for our eight o'clock course, and then we'll be having an arugula, fennel, and orange salad for the nine o'clock salad course, which I'm just finishing now. The scallops will cook quickly, so I won't start them until after we have our salads," Fran said.

"Yum, I love scallops," Audrey said, wondering if this meant they wouldn't be eating anything substantial until ten o'clock. She helped herself to a cracker and cheese from the plate she had brought. "Where are the girls?"

"Iris is at our house babysitting," Jaime said.

"And Rory is upstairs," Fran said.

"No, I'm not," Rory said, appearing in the kitchen. She smiled shyly, showing off a mouthful of neon green braces.

"Hi, Rory," Audrey said.

"Hey. Mom, can I watch *Terminator*?" Rory asked.

"Didn't you watch that last night?" Fran asked distractedly, as she whisked salad dressing in a Pyrex measuring cup.

"No. I watched *Terminator Salvation*. It's the newest one. Now I need the backstory," Rory said.

"You don't think those movies are scary?" Jaime asked.

Rory shook her head.

"Rory has a special affinity for action movies. Especially if they involve blood, gore, and high-speed chases," Will explained.

Rory fixed herself a plate of cheese and crackers, added three olives, and then scampered out of the room.

"She is such a cutie pie," Audrey said.

"We're enjoying her while we can," Fran said. "If she's anything like Iris, she'll turn surly and uncommunicative in about two and a half years."

Jaime glanced to make sure that Rory was gone, and then leaned forward slightly in the time-honored posture with which all good gossip is shared. "Did you hear about Allison and Michael Hart?"

"No, what about them?" Fran asked, pouring Leland more white wine.

"Are you trying to get me drunk?" Leland asked.

"Absolutely," Fran said.

"Why do I know her name?" Audrey asked.

"Because we live in a small town," Fran said, pouring some wine into a glass and thrusting it at Audrey. "I've known Allison forever. Rory was in Music Babies with Josh Hart. How do you know Allison, Jaime?"

"She works out at my gym," Jaime said. "We have the same trainer."

"Who's your trainer? I've been thinking of going to one. I seriously need to firm up," Fran said.

"Dina Martin," Jaime said. "She also runs a boot camp that meets at the beach a few mornings a week. Lots of squats and lunges. Hard, but great for your rear end."

Will and Mark exchanged an exasperated look.

"How did we go from Allison Hart to squats and lunges at the beach?" Will asked.

"That's nothing. We're probably going to have to hear about a dress someone bought or how many calories there are in that block of cheese before we get to the good gossip," Mark said.

"Mark! That is so sexist!" Jaime said, looking indignant. "Although," she continued, turning back to Fran and Audrey, "there is supposed to be a great post-Christmas sale going on at Nordstrom right now. Have either of you been?"

"Wait, don't change the subject. I want to hear about Allison and Michael," Fran said.

"I want to hear more about the squats and lunges you ladies are doing on the beach in bikinis," Will said.

"We don't wear bikinis while we work out," Jaime said.

"Don't ruin it for me," Will said.

"Anyway," Jaime said, leaning forward again, and lowering her voice to a loud whisper. "Allison and Michael are getting divorced. Apparently, Allison was having an affair with one of the fathers at her kids' school. At least, that's the gossip. She claims that nothing happened, and that she and Michael split up because they'd grown apart."

"Wow," Fran said. "Her kids go to St. Andrew's, right? I wonder which dad it was?"

"The rumor is that it was Joe O'Keefe, but so far that's unconfirmed," Jaime said.

"Unconfirmed? What, are you suddenly a reporter?" Mark teased her.

Jaime shrugged, unrepentant. "I just don't want to spread a rumor."

"Isn't that exactly what you're doing?" Mark asked.

Jaime's mouth thinned into a line. "Okay, fine, I won't say any more."

"No, tell us the rest. What do your unconfirmed sources tell you?" Will asked.

Jaime glanced at her husband, but Mark just shrugged and drank his wine. "Apparently Allison and Joe were flirting pretty intensely at the St. Andrew's ball. And I saw them at the gym a few times," Jaime said.

"What, they were there together?" Fran asked.

"No, I don't think they went there together. But when I saw them they were talking in a way that just seemed . . . intimate. Like they were close. Very close. And Allison was very affectionate," Jaime said.

"Allison's like that, though. She can't talk to you without touching your arm or stroking your hand," Fran said. "But Joe O'Keefe? I don't know. He doesn't strike me as being the sort of guy you'd leave a marriage for."

"Not your type?" Will asked, nudging his wife affectionately.

Fran shook her head. "He wears man jewelry," she said.

"Never a good look," Jaime agreed.

"Man jewelry? Like watches and wedding bands?" Mark asked.

"No. I'm talking gold chain necklaces. And those awful chunky link bracelets. And pinky rings," Fran explained.

"Good God. It sounds like you're describing a Vegas mobster," Mark said.

"Yes, exactly. Also, Joe wears black button-down shirts," Fran said.

"Ick," Jaime said.

"A guy gets dinged for a black button-down? Wow, you women are tough," Mark said. "Poor Joe."

"I'd feel more sorry for him if he didn't wear so much cologne," Fran said.

"Or cheat on his wife," Jaime added.

"His wife is a client at my spa," Audrey said, feeling a pang for the quiet, pretty brunette with the quick smile.

"Don't say anything to her," Jaime said quickly. "Like I said, I'm not one hundred percent sure he was the one she was having an affair with."

"Of course not," Audrey said, wondering if Jaime thought she intended to interrogate Melissa O'Keefe about the state of her marriage the next time she came in for a pedicure, and feeling mildly insulted by the insinuation.

"I wonder how Allison and Michael's kids are taking it," Fran said. "Josh is eleven, like Rory, which means Sidney must be what? Nine?"

Jaime nodded. "Allison said the kids are taking it all in stride, and that they just want her to be happy."

At this, Jaime and Fran exchanged a dark look.

"What?" Audrey asked. Her childlessness rarely bothered her, but sometimes, when she was around mothers, they would do this—communicate with a knowing raised-eyebrow look, as though they were speaking in a silent code you only got the key to after a period of gestation.

"Children would always rather their parents stay married than be happy," Jaime said. "I mean, I suppose if there was some sort of domestic abuse going on, that might be a different story. Otherwise, there isn't a nine-year-old out there who would want her parents to get divorced just so her mom could be happy."

"I think that might be an overstatement," Audrey said, taking a sip of her white wine. It tasted thin and overly sweet. She set her wineglass down on the counter, and wondered if she could covertly switch to red without first finishing the white.

"No, it's true," Fran said. "I know the girls could care less if I'm happy or not. It would never occur to them to care. Children are terribly self-centered."

"What if the parents are fighting all the time? I would think that, at least in some cases, the children would be relieved to have that end," Audrey said. Will picked up the bottle of white wine and gestured to her glass. Audrey shook her head, and held her hand over the top of the glass. "No more for me, thanks."

"Do you like the wine? My guy at the wine store recommended it," Will said.

"You have a wine store guy?" Audrey asked.

"Yes. He's great. He looks like a biker—shaggy beard, covered in tattoos—but he never steers me wrong," Will said.

"I was devastated when my parents divorced," Jaime said suddenly. "They didn't fight—at least not in front of my brothers and me—but looking back, I don't think they'd been in love for years by then. At the time, all I knew was that my life was being turned upside down. Having to spend weekends at my father's depressing apartment, my mother dating again, every holiday becoming a power struggle between them. I never felt . . . safe." Everyone fell silent at this admission, and Jaime flushed. She waved her hand. "Never mind me. I didn't mean to kill the party."

"You? Never," Will said, pouring her another glass of

wine. "If it weren't for you and Fran, I wouldn't have known that I need to get rid of my black button-down shirts and gold necklaces."

"Please. Like I would ever allow you to leave the house like that," Fran said. She looked at the clock. "It's almost time for the first course."

"Do you need any help?" Audrey asked.

"No, not at all. Just take a seat," Fran said, gesturing toward the small dining room just off the kitchen.

"And prepare to be amazed," Will added. "My tequila shrimp has won awards."

"No, it hasn't," Fran said.

"It should," Will said with a shrug. "Let's eat."

WILL'S SHRIMP DISH WAS delicious, as was the salad course, but by the time the scallops were served, it was already ten o'clock, and everyone had consumed too much wine and not enough food. Audrey was starting to feel light-headed, and happily accepted the plate of seared scallops Fran passed to her. The scallops were swimming in a butter sauce, and nestled next to a mound of tarragon-scented rice.

"Yum," Audrey said.

"That smells so good it must be fattening," Jaime commented, taking a sip of water.

"Like that's something you have to worry about," Fran said, setting down the last of the plates, while Will refreshed everyone's water and wine. "Does everybody have everything they need?"

The scallops were amazing—tender and perfectly complemented by the delicate sauce. There was a lull in the conversation as everyone ate.

"Fran, you have outdone yourself," Leland said. "What a lovely meal."

"Absolutely wonderful," Mark said.

Fran looked flushed but pleased. "Would anyone like more scallops?"

Jaime leaned back in her chair, sighing with contentment, one hand resting on her flat stomach. "I couldn't eat another bite."

"We still have two courses to go," Will reminded her.

Jaime groaned. "I should have paced myself. I'm going to start off the New Year twenty pounds heavier."

"This is a treat for me. It's the first time I've been out on New Year's Eve since my wife died," Leland said.

Audrey turned to the older man. "I was just thinking the same thing on my way over here. I'm a widow," she added, although the word still felt awkward on her tongue even after seven years.

Leland's face creased with distress, and Audrey instantly regretted her words. Why was she bringing up Ryan now? And at a party?

"I'm so sorry. You're too young to already be widowed," Leland said.

"A car accident," Audrey said. Then, anxious to change the subject, she asked, "What did you and your wife used to do on New Year's Eve?"

"We always got dressed up and went out dancing," Leland said.

"That sounds like fun," Jaime chimed in.

"Oh, it was. Penny loved to dance. Me, I have no rhythm, but she was a natural. But she would have loved this, too," Leland said, indicating the remnants of their dinner with a sweep of his hand. "She always adored throwing dinner parties."

"I do, too," Jaime said. "I was just thinking we should get together like this more often."

"We definitely should," Will said, helping himself to more wine.

"Why don't we?" Fran asked. "I was just reading an article in a cooking magazine about how popular dinner party clubs have become."

"Dinner party clubs?" Mark echoed. "That sounds very official. Would we get to wear a fez like the Shriners?"

"It's like a book club, only instead of discussing a book each month, you have a group of friends over for dinner. Everyone takes a turn hosting," Fran said.

"Eating in is the new eating out?" Will suggested.

"I love this idea," Jaime said. "Count us in."

"How would it work? Would it just be the six of us?" Mark asked.

"I'm not sure. Should we invite one more couple?" Fran said. Her eyes cut to Audrey. "Or it wouldn't have to necessarily be another couple."

Audrey pointed a finger at her friend. "No matchmaking. You promised." She turned to Leland. "Fran is forever trying to set me up, and she has the absolute worst taste in men."

"Hey now," Will said.

"Other than you, of course," Audrey said.

Fran held her hands up. "I promise. No more set ups. So should we keep it to just us? What do you all think?"

"How about the Ferrers?" Jaime suggested.

"Absolutely not," Fran and Will said together.

Jaime looked bemused. "What's wrong with the Ferrers? Christine's a sweetheart."

"Yes, Christine is lovely. But Adam's an ass," Fran said.

"Is he? I've never really talked to him. I usually see Christine on her own. We take yoga together. What's wrong with him?" Jaime asked.

"Me, me, me," Will said.

"You?" Jaime repeated. Her forehead wrinkled with confusion. "You're what's wrong with him?"

"Adam's a narcissist. Everything is always about him. What *he* likes to do, the music *he* likes to listen to, whatever hobby *he's* currently into. He's incapable of having a conversation that doesn't focus on him. And God forbid that you should ever disagree with him," Fran said.

"And did you know that he went to Yale?" Will said.

"No, I didn't. Why? Is Yale a bad thing?" Jaime asked.

"No, but it proves that you've never really talked to him. Because if you had, you would have known that Adam went to Yale," Will said.

"Seriously. I've known Adam Ferrer for ten years, and even after all this time, he still makes a point to tell me he went to Yale every single time I see him," Fran said.

"Oh, the Yale guy!" Mark snapped his fingers. "Now I know who you're talking about. He's sort of short, with a thick neck and mostly bald?"

"Hey, watch it. There's nothing wrong with being bald," Will said. "In fact, I have it on good authority that my style is going to be all the rage six months from now. I like to call it the 'Friar Tuck.' Just wait, you'll see George Clooney shaving his head to imitate the male-pattern baldness that I come by naturally."

"Just keep telling yourself that, honey," Fran said, reaching over to pat his hand. "I think we should come up with a name for our dinner party club. Any ideas?"

"How about the Hungry, Hungry Hippos?" Mark suggested.

"How much have you had to drink?" Jaime asked him.

"Not nearly enough," Mark said. He grabbed the wine bottle and poured himself a healthy amount. "I need to let out my inner hedonist. You're driving us home."

"The Hedonists! That's what we can call ourselves," Will said.

"No way," Fran said. "That's the name of that naked resort."

"Come again?" Mark asked. "A naked resort? I want to hear more about that."

"You know. It's one of those all-inclusive resorts in Jamaica, only everyone walks around naked," Fran said.

"Ick," Jaime said. "Because I so want to lie down on a chaise longue that some guy has rubbed his naked, hairy ass all over."

"Okay, that's out. We absolutely do not want a club name that conjures up images of naked, hairy man asses," Will said, leaning back in his chair and crossing an ankle over one knee.

"How about the Home Chefs?" Jaime suggested.

"That sounds like a line of kitchenware," Fran said.

"You're right," Jaime conceded. "I'm terrible at coming up with names. Ask Mark. It took me forever to decide on the kids' names."

"There will be six of us, right? Why don't we call it the Table for Six Club?" Fran suggested.

"I sort of like it," Mark said.

"Me, too," Jaime said.

"I think we have a name," Will said. He raised his wineglass in a toast. "To the Table for Six Club."

"The Table for Six Club," the others chimed in, clinking together their glasses.

The doorbell rang. Everyone looked at one another in surprise.

"Christmas carolers?" Mark suggested.

"A week after Christmas?" Jaime said.

"Christmas carolers with poor calendaring skills?" Will said.

"I'll go see who it is," Fran said, starting to stand. She looked unsteady, and swayed for a moment before catching the back of her chair.

"Wait, you stay put. I'll go," Audrey said.

"I'm fine," Fran protested.

"Honey, you're drunk," Will said. He grinned. "As am I."

"It's these bottomless wineglasses," Mark said, inspecting his as though it were a strange artifact. "Every time I empty it, it magically refills itself."

"Why doesn't Audrey seem drunk?" Fran asked.

"I switched to water over an hour ago," Audrey said, patting Fran's shoulder as she passed by. "I'll be right back."

Audrey left the room with some relief. It felt good to stand after so many hours of sitting, and she arched her back, stretching the muscles. She fumbled momentarily with the dead bolt and then opened the front door. There, standing on the front porch, was a tall, rangy man with broad shoulders. His face was tan, and his fair hair was short. His features weren't handsome—his pale eyes drooped at the outer edges and were lined, and his nose looked like it might have been broken at some point. But the overall effect was surprisingly sexy.

He blinked at her. "You're not Fran."

Audrey smiled. "No. I'm not." She held out her hand. "I'm Audrey Dickinson."

He shook her hand. His hands were large, and the palms were calloused. "Nice to meet you, Audrey Dickinson. I'm Coop."

Ah, Audrey thought. *Will's gay friend.* She was a little surprised—Coop didn't seem gay. She could have sworn that his eyes flickered toward her cleavage for a moment.

"Just Coop?" Audrey asked.

"Preston Cooper." Coop grimaced. "I still haven't forgiven my parents for that. But I suppose it could have been worse."

"True. They could have named you something really weird, like Phoenix or Dweezil," Audrey said.

Coop grinned. "I always thought that if you're going to have an unusual name, it should be something really cool. Like, I don't know"—he pondered this for a moment—"Spike?"

Audrey wrinkled her nose.

"No? How about d'Artagnan?" Coop suggested.

"D'Artagnan? Isn't that one of the Three Musketeers?"

"Yes. It has a certain swashbuckling charm, don't you think? And it's much more manly than Athos or Porthos."

"Much more manly," Audrey agreed. "Come on in. Everyone's in the dining room. You missed the main course."

"I'm only stopping by for a few minutes. I just left one party and am headed toward another. But I thought I'd swing by and say hello," Coop said, stepping inside.

Audrey remembered Fran telling her at some point that Coop directed oceanographic documentaries. It was funny, she thought, that in all the times Fran and Will had mentioned Coop over the years, they'd never said anything about his sexual orientation. Anyway, it was too bad he hadn't been able to make it for dinner. He would have been an interesting addition to the group. More interesting than Jaime's bore of a husband.

"Who's here?" Fran asked, appearing in the hallway. Her eyes were too bright, but she had discarded her heels and was now standing steadily in her bare feet. "Coop! I can't believe you made it!"

Fran flung herself in Coop's arms, and when she pulled away, her face was flushed. "Come in and say hi to everyone," she said, taking Coop's hand and pulling him into the dining room.

Audrey trailed after them. Fran introduced Coop to the rest of the guests, while Will found him a chair and poured him a glass of wine.

"I really can't stay," Coop said. "Although it looks like I missed quite a meal."

"You did. Everything was wonderful. Fran is a fabulous chef," Leland said.

"I know she is," Coop said, throwing an affectionate arm around Fran's shoulders.

"We were just talking about making this a regular event," Will said. "Forming a monthly dinner party club."

"Coop, you totally have to join," Fran said.

Coop looked skeptical. "What exactly would it entail?"

"We'll get together once a month and take turns hosting," Jaime explained.

"I'd have to cook?" Coop asked.

"I'll help you when it's your turn," Fran said. "Come on, you have to join us. It will be so much more fun with you there."

"Should we take that the wrong way?" Mark asked.

"I don't know if I'll be able to make it every month,"

Coop said. "I'm looking at taking another filming trip in the next few months."

"That's okay. You can come when you're in town," Fran said.

"You might as well go along with it," Will said to Coop. "You know how Fran is. When she gets an idea into her head, resistance is futile."

"She is persistent," Coop agreed, patting Fran's shoulder.

"Just do what I do. Nod and say, 'Yes, dear,' " Will said, demonstrating his beleaguered husband nod.

"Will, cut it out," Fran said, her tone suddenly sharp.

"It's okay, I already know better than to argue with you," Coop said. "I'm in. But I'm going to hold you to your promise to help me when it's my turn."

Fran grinned at him. "You've got it. I'll be your sous chef."

"No, I'll be your sous chef," Coop said, squeezing her arm.

"Why does that sounds vaguely dirty?" Mark asked.

"Because Coop's the one saying it," Will said. "What did we say the name of our dinner party club was going to be?"

"Table for Six," Jaime said.

"Now we're seven," Will said. He raised his glass. "Let's try this toast thing again. To the Table for Seven Dinner Party Club."

february

. . ..

WARM GOAT CHEESE SALAD WITH
PEARS AND WALNUTS

INDIVIDUAL FILETS EN CROÛTE

PARSLEY LEAF POTATOES

ASPARAGUS

CHOCOLATE POTS DE CRÈME

*J*AIME STOOD IN HER kitchen, whisking bittersweet chocolate into a mixture of milk and cream, which had been brought to a simmer and removed from the heat. As she stirred, waiting for the finely chopped chocolate to melt, she wondered if Mark was having an affair.

She didn't have any definitive proof. There hadn't been any of the clichéd signs, like lipstick marks on his shirt collars or unexplained late-night phone calls. And she couldn't imagine where he would find the time or energy. Between work and home and the hours he logged at the tennis club with Emily, how could Mark possibly fit a mistress into his schedule?

Even so, she had a nagging feeling that something was up. Mark had been so distant lately. Even more so than usual. And then there was his damn iPhone fixation. He always claimed he was checking work emails, but Jaime had her doubts. She'd even stolen a look at his messaging history in the hopes that it would give her some insight into what was going on. But the texts there were mostly work related, with a few from Libby, Mark's ex-wife, about Emily's schedule. This was not in itself enough evidence to prove his innocence—Mark was smart enough to delete anything damning.

Once the chocolate had melted evenly, Jaime whisked together eggs and sugar in a glass bowl until the mixture turned a pale yellow. Then she stirred the eggs and sugar into the chocolate, and set the custard aside to cool.

As she wiped down the countertops and put away the ingredients, she wondered why the thought of Mark having an affair didn't upset her more. Shouldn't it make her feel sick and queasy? Or move her to rage? Instead, the idea just made her tired. If he was having an affair—if she found out for sure—she'd have to do something about it. Take a stand. It might even lead to a divorce, to selling the house, to dividing up their time with the children. At the very least, they'd probably end up in couple's therapy, which was truly a grim prospect. The last thing she wanted to do was spend an hour every week dissecting the problems in her marriage in front of a stranger. Who had the time or energy?

Jaime got out seven of the set of eight vintage pink Spode custard cups she'd found on eBay. They were lovely, complete with double handles, covers, and saucers, and were perfect for the chocolate pots de crème she was serving for the dessert course at the first official meeting of the Table for Seven Dinner Party Club. She poured an equal amount of the chocolate mixture into each cup, lined them up on a rectangular Pyrex baking dish, and placed it in the Sub-Zero refrigerator.

The front door opened, and Mark's voice called out, "Hey, where is everyone?"

"In the kitchen," Jaime called back.

Mark was dressed for tennis, wearing a navy blue sweatshirt over gym shorts. His hair was damp and his cheeks were flushed.

"Hi," he said, brushing his lips against her cheek. He smelled of sweat and fresh air.

"Hey," Jaime said.

"Where are the kids?" Mark asked.

Jaime looked pointedly at the clock. It was after eight. "They've been in bed for over an hour."

"Emily's practice ran late," Mark said.

"I figured as much," Jaime said. Then she wondered—not for the first time—if he was seeing someone at the tennis club. There were certainly enough attractive women hanging around there, all showing off their tanned legs in short skirts. But she had a hard time believing that Mark would choose to flirt with another woman while Emily was nearby. His daughter was very sharp and very perceptive—she'd catch on quickly if something was up.

If Mark heard the edge in her voice, he ignored it. "Sarah was working on speed drills with the kids," he said. "I think Emily needs to do more of that. She gets lazy with her footwork."

"Mmm," Jaime said, as she mentally reviewed her to-do list for the dinner party. She scanned the recipe for the salad to see if any portion of it could be completed ahead of time. Baby greens tossed with pears and a vinaigrette, then topped with slices of pan-fried goat cheese. Maybe she could whisk up the vinaigrette now. The main course of filets en croûte— filet mignon covered with a sautéed mushroom mixture and Gorgonzola cheese, then wrapped in puff pastry—was already prepared and chilling in the refrigerator. There would be plenty of time to finish the rest of the salad, the asparagus, and the potatoes tomorrow afternoon.

"What is all this?" Mark asked, running his finger over the dribble of chocolate left in the saucepan and sticking it in his mouth. "Pudding?"

"Chocolate pots de crème," Jaime corrected him.

"It's delicious. Is it ready to eat?"

"No, it's setting in the fridge. And don't even think of eating one. It's dessert for tomorrow night," Jaime said.

Mark looked at her blankly. "Tomorrow night?" he asked.

"Please tell me you're joking," Jaime said. "Please tell me you didn't forget."

"Okay. I didn't forget," Mark said. He hesitated. "Um, what exactly am I supposed to have not forgotten?"

"Our dinner party. Remember? The Table for Seven Club? It's our turn to host," Jaime said.

"That's tomorrow night?" Mark asked.

Jaime stared at him. He couldn't possibly have forgotten, could he? She had talked of little else for at least a week.

"What time are people coming over? Emily has a tournament down in Boca. I'm not sure what time we'll get back," Mark continued.

"Mark, come on. You *have* to be back in time. We're hosting," Jaime said through clenched teeth. She rubbed her jaw, trying to make the muscles relax. Her dentist had warned her that she was damaging her teeth by grinding them. He'd fitted her with a night guard to wear while she slept— apparently she was stressed out even then—but during the day she had to make a conscious effort to unclench.

Mark finally seemed to register the edge in her voice.

"Don't worry, honey, I'll work something out. Maybe Libby can take Emily to the tournament," he said, although he looked doubtful.

"Emily has a tournament every other weekend. Can't she skip this one?" Jaime said.

"I'd rather she didn't. It's a Designated."

"What's that?" Jaime asked, instantly regretting the question. She didn't care if it was Wimbledon. The damn tournament was not going to ruin her dinner party.

Jaime had spent the entire day getting the dining room ready—ironing the linen tablecloth, setting out her set of Spode Camilla china, putting fresh candles in her two antique silver candelabras. Tomorrow, she'd add a vase of flowers, perhaps white orchids.

"It's a special tournament for higher-ranked juniors," Mark said. He went on in more detail, but Jaime started to tune him out.

I need to make sure there are enough guest towels in the downstairs bath, she thought. *And I need to make sure the wineglasses are all spot-free. And what causes the spots anyway? Is it hard water residue?*

". . . It will be a good challenge for her," Mark finally concluded.

Jaime took a deep breath and exhaled slowly before she spoke. Past experience had taught her it was better to keep her temper in check around Mark. As soon as she started getting snappish, he'd get defensive and contrary. Knowing this actually made her even angrier, but right now she wanted to get her way more than she wanted to have a fight.

"Maybe she could catch a ride down with one of her friends," Jaime suggested.

"That's a possibility. Or I could drive her down, and then find her a ride back," Mark said.

"I was really hoping you'd be around tomorrow to help out," Jaime said.

"Help out with what? You know I can't cook. Well, not anything you'd want to serve to our friends."

"No, I'll do the cooking," Jaime said quickly. "But I could use some help getting the house ready."

"Didn't Mary come today?" Mark asked.

Jaime nodded, struggling to keep a grip on her patience. "Yes, she cleaned today. But you know the kids will start dragging their toys out, and it will have to be tidied up before our guests arrive. And you said you were going to cut back the hedges. The front walk is turning into a jungle. Besides, isn't it Libby's weekend to have Emily, anyway?"

As soon as the words were out of her mouth, Jaime regretted them. Mark's face closed and his eyes turned stony. He always got annoyed if Jaime offered even the mildest comment about how he and Libby parented Emily.

"She's my daughter all the time, not just on the weekends," Mark would say, as if that were the end of any conversation.

But what about us? Jaime wanted to say. *What about Logan and Ava? Aren't they your children, too?* Mark didn't spend nearly as much time with his younger children as he spent at the tennis courts with Emily.

"I'll call the lawn care company in the morning. They can come take care of any landscaping that needs to be done. And I'm taking Emily to the tournament, but I'll ask one of the other parents to give her a ride home. I'll be back in plenty of time for the dinner party, I promise," Mark said. He kissed her on the forehead, clearly believing that these solutions ended the need to discuss the matter further. "Have you eaten yet?"

"I ate with the kids, but there's chicken and pasta in the fridge," Jaime said, turning back to her recipes.

Maybe instead of a dinner party club, I should start a second wives' club, she thought. *The only problem is that it would have* to be a club of one, because I don't know any other second wives. I was the only one foolish enough to make that mistake.

"HOW DOES THIS LOOK?" Fran asked.

Will and Rory looked up from the remote-controlled combat robot they were building. It was a Rammer, and was about the size of a canister vacuum. In fact, the very first robot he'd ever built had been made from a canister vacuum, which Fran was still annoyed about, as it had been her vacuum and practically new. This Rammer was low to the ground, with six wheels and a heavy casing. It was a totally new design for Will, who normally preferred to compete with spinning robots, right up until his last Spinner—nicknamed Freddy—had been mercilessly crushed against the arena wall by a Rammer built by two teenagers from Orlando. After that, Will started to see the wisdom in competing with a heavy-duty bot. Today's project was to mount the wheels onto their axles. The parts were scattered along the workbench Will had built along one side of the garage. Will and Rory sat perched on high stools to work.

Will blinked at his wife, who was wearing a black-ribbed sweater over a dark denim skirt and low black heels.

"It seems like overkill for movie night," Will said.

"No, it's for tomorrow. To wear to the dinner party."

"You're pre-dressing?"

"I'm trying to decide what I'm going to wear."

Will decided this must be one of those odd womanly behaviors that he was never going to understand, and was therefore better off not asking too many questions. "It's fine."

"Fine?" Fran made a face. "I don't want to look *fine*. I want to look pretty."

"It's very nice," Will said.

"Nice isn't any better than fine."

"You look great. Don't you think, Rory?" Will asked, hoping his daughter would bail him out.

Rory scrutinized her mother. "I think the sweater is too tight. It shows your stomach."

Fran clutched her stomach. "Seriously?"

Rory nodded.

"Then why did you tell me it looks good?" Fran asked Will accusingly.

He shrugged. "I like it."

"I swear, I have nothing to wear. I'm going to have to go shopping tomorrow," Fran said. She turned and stalked back into the house.

Will looked at Rory.

"What?" Rory said. "I had to tell her the truth if you weren't going to. And I was nicer about it than Iris would have been. She would have told Mom she looked fat."

"That's true," Will said. Iris had recently become incapable of saying anything nice to anyone and was especially nasty to her mother and younger sister. "Where is your sister, anyway?"

"Babysitting," Rory said.

"Again?"

"She's saving up for some ceramic iron thingy," Rory said.

"She's saving up for an iron? You mean, like, to iron her clothes with?" Will asked, completely bewildered. "What's wrong with the iron we have in the laundry room?"

Rory laughed. "No, not for clothes. It's an iron for her hair. You know, to make it straight."

"Why would Iris want to straighten her hair with an iron?" Will asked. Iris had inherited Fran's beautiful dark corkscrew curls. He'd always been glad one of the girls had lucked out. Rory had straight hair so baby fine, barrettes and ponytail elastics slid right out of it.

"She hates it. She says that curly hair makes your face look fat." Rory turned her attention back to the battle bot and began sifting through a pile of bolts. "It's so stupid. I'm never going to bother with that girly stuff."

Will remembered with a pang Iris saying almost exactly the same thing when she was Rory's age. Just a few years earlier, Iris had been more tomboy than girly-girl, always climbing trees and playing soccer and helping him in the workshop. He tried to remember the last time she'd been in the garage. Months? No, longer. It had been over a year, at least. He glanced at Rory, who was intent on the workbench, distractedly pushing her blue wire-frame glasses back up onto the bridge of her nose, and wondered how much longer she'd be willing to hang out with him out here, building fighting robots, talking about upcoming competitions. Rory was still young enough to lack the self-consciousness that made the teen years such hell. Sometimes Will would catch her breaking into a dance for no reason at all, throwing her skinny arms around and shaking her head, lost in rhythmic abandon. The sight never failed to fill him with joy.

Will gave Rory a one-armed hug, which she tolerated for exactly three seconds before wiggling free.

"Come on, Dad. I want to get the front wheels mounted before we watch the movie," she said.

"Then we'd better get to work," Will said, smiling at her.

COOP GRADUALLY BECAME AWARE of a wet, rough tongue licking his cheek. He opened one eye. His dog, Bear—who was a mutt of undetermined parentage—continued to give his face a bath.

"Knock it off." Coop groaned and pushed the dog away. Bear didn't seem offended. He sat, panting happily, smiling his doggy smile.

Coop sat up on the couch, stretching. The muscles in his back made an odd popping noise. When had he gotten so creaky? Lately, it seemed that there was always something aching somewhere on his body. Today's lower back pain was courtesy of some work he'd done on his boat that morning—the water pump had been on the fritz—before taking it out on the water.

"What time is it?" Coop asked aloud. Since Bear didn't seem prepared to answer him, Coop glanced at the digital clock on the cable box. 6:07. "Oh, no."

Coop leapt to his feet, trying to ignore the twinge of protest from his back. He was due at the dinner party at 6:30. Between the morning of work, the day spent out in the sun, and the beer he'd had with lunch, he'd sacked out on the couch when he came back from the marina and had managed to oversleep.

"Why did I ever agree to go to this thing?" he muttered as he headed to the bathroom. The last thing he wanted to do was spend a Saturday night eating dinner at somebody's house with a bunch of people he didn't know, save for Will and Fran.

It was all Fran's fault, he decided. He'd never been able to say no to her. She was a force of nature. They really should ship her off to the Middle East, he thought ruefully. She'd have the Israelis and Palestinians squared away in no time.

Twenty-five minutes later, he was showered, shaved, and dressed in a crisply ironed white shirt tucked into his favorite faded jeans. He stopped at the liquor store down the street from his waterfront condo, purchased two bottles of Taittinger champagne and drove fifteen minutes inland to the address he'd scribbled on the back of a receipt. Mark and Jaime lived in a looming white house with a carefully manicured front lawn and a huge silver Lexus SUV parked ostentatiously in the tile-paved driveway.

Coop sighed. It was going to be a long night.

He climbed out of his white pickup and headed to the front door without bothering to lock the truck. The neighborhood didn't strike him as a hotbed of crime. He made his way up the walk to the front door—which was flanked with two tall black urns, each containing a leafy palm tree—and rang the bell. A moment later, he heard the clacking of high heels against hard floors and then the door was opened by an attractive woman with a thin, gym-toned body and stick-straight blond hair whom he'd met briefly at the Parrishes' New Year's Eve party.

"Hi," she said. She smiled, displaying professionally bleached teeth, and held out a hand. "It's nice to see you again. I'm Jaime, by the way."

"I remember. Nice to see you again." Coop juggled the champagne bottles so that he could shake her hand, which was thin and cold. Then, he held up the bottles. "These are for you."

"Thank you," Jaime said, looking with delight at the bottles. "What a treat."

"An apology for my lateness," Coop said.

Jaime shook her head. "No need for apologies. In fact, you beat my husband home. Come on into the living room, everyone's in there. What can I get you to drink?"

"Do you have whiskey?" Coop asked as he followed Jaime

across the foyer. He took advantage of his position to admire the curve of her bottom. If she was logging time at the gym it was definitely paying off, he thought. It was too bad she had a husband. Coop had never been interested in the drama of extramarital entanglements.

"Yes, of course. How would you like it?" Jaime asked. She led him into a large living room tastefully decorated in shades of cream and beige. There was a small knot of people gathered there, including Fran and Will.

"Straight up," Coop said. "I'm easy like that."

He grinned again, although out of respect for Jaime's marital status, he was careful not to use his most dazzling smile, which had on many occasions caused women to tear off their clothes and throw themselves at him.

"Just give me one minute," Jaime said and headed over to a bar just off the living room.

Fran looked up. "Coop!" she called out and bounded over to him. Her long curly hair was loose around her shoulders and she held a wineglass in one hand. "I was starting to think you'd ditched us!"

"Would I do that?" he asked, kissing her cheek.

"Of course you would," she said. "You're thoroughly unreliable, and you know it."

"Hey, guy," Will said, slapping his shoulder. "Good to see you."

"You, too," Coop said, grinning at his friend.

"Coop, do you remember Leland?" Fran asked, gesturing to an elderly man who was sitting in a cream jacquard arm chair. It was impossible to tell his age. He could be a hard-living seventy-five or a ninety-year-old with excellent genes. Either way, he looked fragile and shrunken, and his face was a web of lines. Still, his eyes were a sharp, bright blue and he seemed alert.

"I would get up, but it would take so long you'd grow bored waiting for me," Leland said, gesturing to the curved cane resting against the chair.

"Then, I'll come to you," Coop said. He stepped forward to shake Leland's hand. "And please, call me Coop."

"And this is Audrey, who you also met on New Year's," Fran said.

Coop turned. Audrey had glossy dark hair cut into a short angled bob that showed off a long, graceful neck. Her smile reached her brown eyes, causing faint laugh lines to appear at the corners.

Coop pointed at her. "You were on door duty and said I was lucky not to have been named Phoenix," he said.

"Good memory," Audrey said. She was wearing very high heels and dark red lipstick, a combination Coop was very much in favor of.

Coop covertly checked for a ring on her fourth finger. There wasn't one. The evening was looking up, he decided. This time when he smiled, he didn't hold back—he went for the full dazzling effect. Strangely, Audrey didn't swoon or throw her bra at him.

"Fran told me you make nature documentaries," Audrey said. "That sounds fascinating. How did you get started in it?"

"In the most ass backward way possible," Coop admitted. "When I was fresh out of college, I took a job with a small company down in the Keys that ran boat tours taking tourists out for dives. One day, a production company was looking for some qualified divers to help out with a film they were making about shipwrecks off Key Largo, and they hired me on. I liked the work and managed to talk my way into a permanent spot with the production company."

"Coop can talk his way into just about anything," Fran interjected.

"Is that so?" Audrey said, shooting Coop a smile that was encouragingly flirtatious. He accepted the glass of whiskey Jaime handed him.

"Thank you," he said.

"You're welcome. Leland, can I get you a refill?" Jaime asked.

"The answer to that question is always an emphatic yes," Leland said, holding out his glass. Jaime laughed and took his empty tumbler from him.

"Jaime, do you need any help?" Fran asked.

"There's a cheese tray and a plate of gougères in the kitchen. Would you mind bringing them out?" Jaime asked.

"Sure thing," Fran said.

Once they were alone, Coop leaned toward Audrey. "What in the world are gougères?" he murmured.

She smiled. "I was just about to ask you the same thing."

"I guess we'll have to wait and see."

"You were saying, about your job—you worked your way up to directing?" Audrey asked.

"Basically." Coop nodded. "Directing, and now producing, too. We just wrapped filming a piece about the effects of the coastal tide on marine life off the coast of Nova Scotia."

"Wow. That sounds fascinating," Audrey said.

"And what do you do?" Coop asked Audrey.

"I own a day spa."

"Sounds very Zen," Coop said.

"I hope it's relaxing for my patrons. But, no, I don't think the actual running of a business is ever very Zen," Audrey said.

"Do you have many male clients?" Coop asked, leaning a bit closer toward Audrey so that his arm brushed against hers. She didn't move away. Another good sign, he thought.

"Absolutely," Audrey said, nodding enthusiastically. "It's actually a growth area in the industry that I'm hoping to capitalize on. In fact, quite a few of my regular clients are gay guys."

Coop blinked, confused by this non sequitur.

Audrey continued. "I've introduced a few men to the joys of manicures. They were resistant at first, but now they're hooked. In fact, one of my clients keeps telling me I should advertise them as our *man*-icures. Emphasis on the man part." Audrey tilted her head and scrutinized him. "Actually, you'd really like him. His name is Ron." Then she smiled and shook her head. "No, never mind, forget I said anything. I'm as bad as Fran."

"As bad as Fran?" Coop repeated, his brow wrinkling. He had a feeling he was missing something. But before he could ask Audrey what she meant, Will clapped a hand on his shoulder again.

"When are we going to go fishing?" Will asked.

"Haven't you gotten your own boat yet?" Coop asked. Audrey had turned to talk to Jaime and Leland.

"No way. A wise man once told me that owning a boat was an expensive, time-consuming pain in the ass, and that I'd be much better off finding a friend with a boat and then bribing him to take me out on it," Will said.

"What wise man?" Coop said.

"Some drunk guy I met in a bar down in the Keys. I think he was about twelve hours into a bender." Will shrugged. "But the advice was still solid."

"Would either of you care for a blue cheese gougère?" Fran asked, appearing beside them with a silver tray piled with what looked like cream puffs.

"At long last, a solution to the gougère mystery," Coop said, helping himself to one. It was a bit like a cream puff in texture, although it was savory, not sweet, and didn't have a cream-filled middle. "Mmm."

"I'll set them down right here next to you," Fran said.

"I knew there was a reason I liked you," Coop teased her. Fran grinned at him, and then turned to join the conversation Audrey and Jaime were having about the best place in town to buy seafood.

Coop observed the women for a few moments. Audrey was calm and still, especially standing next to Fran, whose hands moved frenetically while she talked, constantly threatening to spill the contents of her wineglass. Jaime seemed tense. Her fingers played nervously at the diamond charm she wore around her neck on a gold chain, and she kept glancing back over her shoulder, as though looking for someone. The mystery of just who she was looking for was solved when a tall, lean man wearing a Lacoste polo shirt, khaki shorts, and sneakers strode in and said, "Hello, everyone, sorry I'm late."

"Hi, Mark," Fran said, as Mark leaned down to kiss her cheek.

"Emily won the tournament," Mark announced proudly.

"Good for her!" Fran said.

"Way to go, Emily," Will said, shaking Mark's hand. "Where is she?"

"I dropped her off at her mom's house. She wanted to show Libby her trophy. It's nearly as tall as she is," Mark said.

Coop noticed that as everyone greeted Mark and repeated words of congratulations about Emily's big win, Jaime remained silent. And when Mark reached her and tried to slip a hand around her waist, she stepped away, out of his reach. Unfazed, Mark turned to Coop.

"Mark Wexler," he said, holding out his hand for Coop to shake. "You look familiar."

"We met at Fran and Will's house," Coop said, remembering that Mark had been pretty drunk that night.

"That's right. Sorry I'm late. My daughter was in a tennis tournament today. I couldn't bring myself to leave while she was winning," Mark said.

"I just got here myself," Coop said.

"And you've already got a drink, I see. Good. I could use one of those." Mark glanced around. "Although I'd better not ask Jaime to get me one. She'd probably dump it over my head. I'm in the doghouse for being late."

Coop merely raised his eyebrows. Listening to spouses complain about each other had to rate near the top on his list of least favorite conversations. But he was saved from having to hear any further details by Jaime saying, "Now that we're all here, let's move into the dining room. The first course is ready."

There was a stir of activity. Will leaned down to help Leland out of his chair. Those who had empty glasses set them on the bar. Fran continued to talk to Audrey and Jaime, her hands moving constantly, as they turned to head into the dining room, just off the living room. Coop followed closely behind them, still holding his whiskey. He wanted to make sure that he got to the table in time to claim a seat next to Audrey.

AUDREY WAS ENJOYING HERSELF more than she thought she would. She ate the excellent warm goat cheese salad Jaime had made, sipped a very good glass of red wine, and for once she didn't mind being seated between the only two single men present at dinner. Coop was flirtatious and attentive, obviously the sort of gay man who truly liked women. And Leland was a hoot.

"Everything tastes better when you add bacon," Leland announced.

"Everything?" Will asked. "That can't be true. There must be some foods that clash with it."

"No such thing," Leland said. "I'll go so far as to say that you can't name a food that isn't improved by bacon."

Will smiled mischievously. "Care to make a small wager on that?"

"Look out," Mark said. "Dinner party smack talk."

"You're on," Leland said, pointing a finger at Will. "How much are we betting?"

Will considered this. "I'm in for five dollars," he said.

"High stakes gambling," Mark said.

"It's a deal," Leland said. "Go ahead. Name something that is not improved by the addition of bacon." He sat back and waited, while Will thought.

"Beets?" Fran suggested.

"No helping him," Leland admonished her. "And besides, a roasted beet salad would be delicious with bacon bits."

"How about cauliflower?" Will said.

"Steamed cauliflower topped with cheese sauce and sprinkled with bacon," Leland said.

"This isn't fair," Will complained. "Whatever food I name, you'll just announce that it's improved by bacon. We need an impartial judge."

"I am a judge," Leland said. "Or at least, I was a judge."

"For all we know, you spent your entire tenure on the bench on the take," Will teased.

A grin split across Leland's wizened face. "I'll never tell," he said.

"I'll be the judge," Fran said. "Or am I disqualified because I'm married to one of the players?"

"You are," Will said. "But only because you'd be biased in Leland's favor."

"Have Coop do it, then," Fran suggested.

Will gave his oldest friend a sideways look. "Coop will probably favor Leland, too."

Coop held up his hands. "I'm as impartial as they come. Should I take an oath on a package of bacon?"

"That won't be necessary. You look trustworthy," Leland said. "Are you stumped, Will?"

"Not a chance. How about chocolate?" Will said.

"I think they actually make chocolate and bacon candy bars. One of Emily's friends at the tennis club had one. She said it was pretty good," Mark said.

"Peanut butter," Will said.

"Mmm, I used to love peanut butter and bacon sandwiches when I was a kid," Fran said. "I'd have one for breakfast every Saturday morning."

"If you can't help me, you can't help Leland," Will said.

"Sorry, honey," Fran said. "But I'm starting to think Leland is right."

"Spinach," Will said, sounding less certain.

"That's easy. I make a wonderful spinach salad with golden raisins and hot bacon dressing. It's delicious. Although not as delicious as this," Leland said, raising a courtly fork to Jaime in appreciation for her starter. Jaime smiled her thanks back at him.

"Pizza," Will said uncertainly. "No forget that. I've had bacon on pizza. Crap. I can't think of anything."

"Are you admitting defeat?" Leland asked.

"Not a chance, old man," Will said. "Just give me a minute to think."

"Should I help him out?" Coop murmured in Audrey's ear.

She turned to him, smiling broadly. "You'd better not. You may be impeached and stripped of your judgeship."

"You're right. I can't risk losing my power," Coop said. He leaned closer to Audrey and inhaled.

She leaned back and laughed. "Are you sniffing me?"

"You smell good," Coop said. "What is that?"

"I don't know. What are you smelling? My perfume?"

"No, although I like that, too. This is something else. Rosemary?" Coop asked.

"My shampoo has rosemary in it," Audrey said. "You have a good nose."

"One of my many talents," Coop said, touching her arm lightly.

He really is a flirt, Audrey thought. She'd known other gay men who liked to flirt with women. It was funny, though—if Fran hadn't told her that Coop was gay, Audrey would have assumed he was straight. She could have sworn she was getting an interested vibe off him.

Good God. How pathetic am I? Audrey thought. *I'm actually starting to imagine that openly gay men are attracted me. Maybe Fran's right, maybe it is time I started dating.*

"Isn't that what they call the people who develop perfumes? Aren't they called *noses*?" Audrey said.

"Is that right? Maybe I should change careers. It's probably easier than traveling for two thirds of the year," Coop said. When he smiled, his gray-blue eyes crinkled up at the corners.

He's really quite sexy in a rugged sort of way, Audrey thought. His face was interesting, if not handsome, and he was in terrific shape. It was annoying—and so clichéd—that he should be gay. He was easily the most interesting man she'd met in ages.

"But probably not as glamorous," she said.

"That's true. Then again, who needs glamour when you have my natural charm and good looks," Coop said, grinning devilishly.

Audrey laughed. "And so modest, too."

"I think modesty is overrated," Coop said.

"And do your boyfriends agree?"

"Milk!" Will said triumphantly. "Bacon-flavored milk would be disgusting. Am I right?"

"You're right. That is disgusting," Jaime said. "In fact, it's something I'd rather not think about when I'm eating my dinner."

"I would drink bacon-flavored milk," Leland said stubbornly.

"I don't know, Leland, I think he might have pulled it off," Fran said. "Coop? What's your verdict?"

But Coop was no longer paying attention to the bacon conversation. Instead, he was staring at Audrey. "Boyfriends? Wait. Do you think I'm gay?"

Audrey looked at Fran in alarm. "Wasn't I supposed to say anything?" She looked back at Coop and laid a hand on his arm. "I'm so sorry. I assumed you were . . . out."

Will had just taken a sip of wine, so when he started to laugh, it came out as a hiccup that quickly turned into a cough. Mark pounded him on the back, hard enough to make Will splutter. "Ack. Jesus, Mark, have you been lifting weights?"

"What exactly did you tell her, Will?" Coop asked.

"I feel like I'm missing something," Audrey said. "Am I missing something?"

"For starters, I'm not gay," Cooper said dryly.

Will had finally stopped coughing, but now he was laughing so hard, his eyes were watering. Mark, amused at his mirth, grinned. Fran just rolled her eyes.

"You're not gay?" Audrey asked. She looked from Coop to Fran and then back at Coop again. "Then why did Fran tell me you were?"

"Fran told you that?" It was his turn to look at Fran, his eyebrows arched.

"It was Will's idea," Fran said. "Although I'll admit I may have had a teeny-tiny role in spreading the misinformation."

"Maybe I should forget the individual filets en croûte and pop some popcorn instead," Jaime remarked.

Audrey placed her hands on the table in front of her, palms down, fingers spread. "Fran. Why did you tell me that Coop was gay?"

"Yes, Fran, we'd both like an answer to that question," Coop said.

Fran looked at Will for help, but he was too busy chortling and helping himself to another glass of wine. She sighed, pushed her curls back from her face, and, turning to Audrey, said, "If you'd known there was a single, heterosexual man invited, you'd have assumed I was trying to set you up."

"What am I, chopped liver?" Leland asked.

"I'm sorry. It was stupid," Fran said sheepishly. "And, again, it was all Will's idea."

"I think it's hilarious," Will said, still giggling.

Audrey felt her cheeks flush hot but she didn't want to throw a hissy fit right in the middle of a dinner party. Revenge would have to wait. Instead, she drew in a deep breath and tried to regain her composure.

"You must have spent most of this evening incredibly confused by my conversation," Audrey said to Coop.

"It certainly explains why you spent so much time trying to sell me on your *man*-icures idea," Coop said. "I thought you were oddly excited about that."

"Is this the anti–set up? Put two single people together, and then try to make sure they're not attracted to each other?" Mark asked.

It was Fran's turn to flush pink. "No, of course not," she said.

"If so, it didn't work," Coop said.

Audrey felt her pulse kick up a notch. Was Coop saying that he *was* attracted to her?

"No, there was a flaw in Fran's plan. She should have told you something that would turn you off Audrey," Mark said.

"Like telling you that I'm gay, too," Audrey said.

All of the men at the table—with the exception of Leland, who was listening to the conversation with a puzzled expression—exchanged raised-eyebrow looks.

"Oh, please. That would just have made him that much more interested," Fran said.

"Why are men so intrigued by lesbianism?" Jaime asked.

"Oh, we're talking about lesbians now?" Leland asked with interest. "I've never fully understood how that works."

"*Well*," Will said, leaning forward, clearly about to hold forth on the subject. But Fran whacked him on the shoulder before he could continue.

"Don't start," she warned him.

"No, what Fran should have told Coop is that Audrey is one of those incredibly needy women who insist that her boyfriend check in with her four to five times a day," Mark said, twirling his wineglass in one hand.

"Every man's biggest fear, right after Glenn Close in *Fatal Attraction*," Jaime said, rolling her eyes. She stood and began clearing the salad plates.

"No, it's really one and the same. The bunny-boiling is just clinginess taken to the extreme," Mark said.

Audrey noted that Mark wasn't making any move toward helping his wife clear the dishes. It also hadn't escaped her attention that he hadn't managed to make it home before his dinner guests arrived. Which meant, of course, that Jaime had done all of the work. And the dinner party had clearly been a lot of work—everything from the table settings to the food to the wine had been just so.

What a jerk, she thought. Occasionally, Audrey wondered if it had been a mistake to swear off ever marrying again. Then she saw how some of her friends' husbands behaved, and it just reinforced the wisdom of her decision.

She stood and began collecting dishes. Jaime flapped a hand at her and said, "It's okay, I've got this."

Audrey smiled at her. "No, let me help. I just spent the last hour trying to set up Coop with a handsome architect who has a standing weekly appointment for a massage. I need to take a few minutes to regain my composure."

"And here I thought you were trying to talk me into hiring that guy," Coop said. "Which was really confusing because I rent my condo."

Everyone laughed, and then Will said, "Leland, you owe me a fiver." He held out a hand. "Bacon-flavored milk."

"I don't think we've had an official ruling on that," Leland said.

As the conversation swung back to its previous bacon theme, Audrey followed Jaime into the kitchen, dishware balanced in her hands.

"Wow, it's gorgeous in here," Audrey said, glancing around admiringly at the soaring glass-fronted cupboards and professional-grade appliances. "Like something out of a magazine."

"Thanks," Jaime said with obvious pleasure. "I'm really happy with how the remodel came out. It's exactly what I wanted."

Audrey wondered if, for Jaime, the nice kitchen made up for the less-than-helpful husband. It wouldn't be a trade-off she'd willingly make, but, then, other people's marriages and how they worked were always hard to figure out.

"What can I do to help?" Audrey asked.

"Nothing at the moment. But it would be great if you could help me carry the plates out," Jaime said. She leaned over to open the oven door, and, using a red silicone oven mitt, pulled out a pan of perfectly browned individual filets en croûte. The puff pastry exteriors were decorated with tiny pastry leaves. Audrey wondered how long it had taken Jaime to assemble such a complicated entrée, and how she'd managed it with two toddlers running around.

"Where are your kids?" Audrey asked, leaning back on the kitchen counter.

"They're in the playroom with Iris," Jaime said. "Fran dropped her off earlier this afternoon so she could help me out. She's been a lifesaver."

"Does Iris babysit for you often?"

Jaime nodded. "Yes, she's great with the kids. And I think Fran likes it that babysitting keeps Iris from going out with her friends. Speaking of Fran . . . just how angry are you?"

"Do I seem mad?"

"Actually, no," Jaime said. She spread spiky stalks of asparagus on a rimmed pan, doused them with olive oil, and then slid the pan under the broiler.

"Good. Then I'm hiding it well. I have every intention of killing Fran. I just didn't want to ruin your dinner party with bloodshed," Audrey said.

"I appreciate that," Jaime said. "And I hope I can show similar restraint."

"Is everything okay?" Audrey asked tentatively. She and Jaime had known each other for a few years through Fran, but they had never been confidantes.

Jaime smiled mechanically, masking whatever anger she might have been feeling. "Yes, fine, I was just kidding. I think everything's about ready. Can you hand me that stack of plates there? And could you open another bottle of wine?"

"Here you go," Audrey said, handing the plates to Jaime before turning her attention to the wine. Jaime obviously didn't want to talk about whatever was going on with Mark, and Audrey had no intention of pressing the issue. She respected a person's right to keep her troubles private.

"I THINK IT WENT well. What do you think?" Jaime said later that night when their guests had left into the chilly February night and she and Mark were lying in their black four-poster bed.

Jaime was making notes about the dinner party in an orange leather-bound notebook. She always made a habit of this after they entertained—what was served, who attended, notes on what she might do differently.

The orchids were a bit too delicate looking. Also, taller candlesticks, so the guests can see each other better, she wrote.

"Hmm?" Mark asked. He was, as usual, fixated on his iPhone.

Jaime tapped her pen against the notebook. She thought the dinner party had been a success overall. Everyone seemed to like the food, although she worried that the filets had been just a touch overdone and thought that maybe the potatoes were just slightly underdone.

"Did you think the potatoes were underdone?" she asked Mark.

"Maybe a little," he said.

"Really? Do you think anyone noticed?" Jaime asked.

Mark continued to stare at his iPhone. Then he looked up, as if only just realizing she'd been speaking to him. Jaime wondered who he thought she was talking to, considering they were alone in their bedroom.

"The potatoes," Jaime repeated. "You thought they were underdone?"

"No, they were great. Everything was great. You outdid yourself," Mark said. He patted her hand, and then turned his attention back to the iPhone.

Jaime sighed and rolled away. The potatoes *were* underdone, she decided, and made a note of it. The chocolate pots de crème—each served with a dollop of freshly whipped cream—had been a huge hit. Will, especially, had loved his, scraping his spoon against the bottom of the pudding cup to make sure he got up every last bit.

Pots de crème were the perfect dessert, Jaime wrote. *Simple but elegant.*

"Do you think Will and Fran have the happiest marriage of anyone we know?" she asked.

There was another long pause. Jaime was just wondering if Mark had tuned her out again, when he said, "I don't know, really. It's hard to tell about someone else's marriage."

"But do you get the sense that they're really happy together?" Jaime persisted. "I would say that they're comfortable with each other. But I don't get the sense that they're still madly in love."

Mark put down his iPhone and glanced at Jaime over the top of his horn-rimmed readers. He hadn't worn glasses until recently, and even now insisted that he didn't really need them. But Jaime had noticed that he'd taken to wearing them more often while reading, at least while he was home.

"They've been married for, what, twelve years?" he said.

"Something like that," Jaime said.

"I think it's unrealistic for any married couple to still seem madly in love after that much time."

"That's not true," Jaime said. "Leland told me that he was married for forty-years, and I could tell he adored his late wife."

Mark shrugged. "I think that's the exception, not the norm."

"What do you think other people think about our marriage?"

"Who knows?" Mark said. "And, really, who cares?"

"I care," Jaime said.

"I meant, who cares what anyone else thinks about us?

People can think what they want to think. We have no control over that," Mark said. His iPhone dinged, and, like Pavlov's dog, Mark immediately turned his attention back to it.

Jaime set her notebook down on the nightstand, and then rolled over on her side, her back to her husband. How long had it been since she and Mark had made love, she wondered. A few weeks? Longer? Over a month?

That was worrying.

Although, Jaime had to admit, at first she had been grateful that her husband's libido had taken a nosedive shortly after Ava's birth. Her days were spent with one or both children in her arms, picking up their warm, solid bodies, their small hands always reaching out to grab on to her shirt or a lock of her hair. By the time she fell into bed each night, the last thing she wanted was to have anyone else touch her, even her husband.

But a month or more? Jaime felt a prickle of unease. That was a long time to go without sex, even for a couple with two small children. Was this further evidence that Mark might be having an affair? And if he was, was it because she'd been sexually inaccessible to him? Or was it the other way around—had he lost interest in her because he'd found someone else? A swooping, sickly feeling spread through her stomach.

This can't go on, she thought. *We need to fix this. I need to fix this.*

Jaime rolled back toward Mark, intent on doing *something*. They needed to talk. Or no, forget talking, she'd just seduce him. But Mark's eyes were closed, and his breathing had deepened, so that he was snoring softly on each exhale. His iPhone was still clasped in his hands. For a moment, Jaime considered taking the phone gently out of his hands and sliding his reading glasses off his face. But for some reason she wasn't quite sure of, she instead rolled back over, turned off her bedside table lamp, and closed her eyes.

"ARE YOU TALKING TO me?" Fran asked when Audrey answered the phone.

"No," Audrey said.

"Will you at least listen while I apologize?" Fran said.

There was a pause. Fran wondered if Audrey was so mad, she'd actually hung up.

"Are you there?" Fran asked.

"I'm waiting for my apology," Audrey said.

"Oh good, I'm glad you didn't hang up. I'm sorry I told you Coop is gay," Fran said.

"And that you humiliated me?"

"You weren't humiliated, were you?"

"Of course I was humiliated. I spent the entire evening trying to talk a straight man into having a homosexual relationship with one of my spa clients," Audrey exclaimed.

"Well, yes, I can see how that would be slightly embarrassing."

"I'm still not clear why you lied about his sexuality in the first place."

"I didn't want you to think it was a set up. I know how you feel about that."

"Are you really going to take the position that you lied to me in order to spare my feelings?" Audrey asked.

"No," Fran said. She smiled. "Well, yes, sort of. It was Will's idea, I swear. Back when I wanted to invite both you and Coop to our New Year's Eve party. I told Will you'd think it was a set up, so he said to tell you that Coop was gay. It all seems so stupid now."

"Yes," Audrey agreed. "Very, very stupid."

"I know." Fran sighed. "It was all part of some weird revenge plan Will had cooked up. Something to do with Coop telling a girl that Will only had one testicle."

"Will only has one testicle?"

"No, he has two."

"I'm confused."

"It's not important," Fran said.

"Except for my public humiliation."

"Right. And just so you know, I would never have tried to set you up with Coop."

"Why not?" Audrey asked. "You try to set me up with everyone."

"I can't see the two of you together. You're a much more serious person than he is."

"Serious? That makes me sound like a drip."

"No, not at all. It's more that he's never serious about anything. And besides, you're a go-out-to-a-nice-restaurant-in-heels kind of woman. Coop is more of a beer-and-chips-on-the-boat kind of guy," Fran said.

She was sitting on the living-room couch, her bare feet tucked up beneath her, a worn purple chenille pillow clutched to her chest. She'd always thought the purple had been a mistake, a discordant note in a room that was dominated by heavy brown leather sofas and an ugly sage green rug they'd gotten on sale years ago.

I want to live in an all-white room, Fran thought. Tailored sofas with crisp white slipcovers. One of those furry white rugs. Maybe a small punch of orange here or there, a pillow or a small round stool. Modern and stark and completely impractical for a family that liked to lounge in front of the television with their bare feet up on the furniture.

Fran looked down and noticed a smear of something—it looked like chocolate—on the pillow. She sighed and put it to one side.

"I don't know. I thought Coop was interesting," Audrey said thoughtfully.

Fran's attention snapped back to their conversation. "You think he's interesting?"

"Sure. How often do you meet someone who directs oceanographic documentaries?"

"But he's not at all your type," Fran said.

"Do I have a type?"

"I don't know, do you?"

"Hmm," Audrey said. "I've always liked Jeff Goldblum."

"The actor."

"Mmm."

"Really?"

"You don't think he's attractive?"

"No, not really. And is he a type?"

"He could be a type. Funny, dark hair, sexy glasses."

"I guess. Nothing like Coop, though."

"No," Audrey agreed. "But I never said I was interested in Coop. I said I thought he was interesting. Big difference. Besides, Coop seemed full of himself."

Fran tried to ignore the trickle of relief she felt at these words. "Yeah, he can be. And when it comes to women, he has a short attention span. He's had a lot of girlfriends."

"Really?"

"Yes. A *lot* of girlfriends," Fran said again. "We need to find you someone who's ready to settle down."

There was a huff of impatience on the other end of the phone.

"First of all, as I've told you about five hundred times, I

don't want you to find me anyone. And second of all, why do you assume that I would only be interested in someone who wants to settle down? Maybe I want to sleep around. Sow my wild oats. Have wild sex with anonymous strangers."

"Mmm. That sounds exciting."

"Really? You think so? Because I think it sounds exhausting," Audrey said. "The entire idea of dating is exhausting."

"Speaking as someone who has been in a relationship with the same person forever, I think it sounds like fun."

"Please. And first dates are the worst. They're so awkward. You spend the evening trading boring bits of information back and forth, while the entire time you're making constant superficial judgments. Like, why did he choose to wear a T-shirt and flip-flops on the first date? Does he have bad taste, or just not care about making a good first impression? And you know he's making the same sort of judgments about you. Thinking that your breasts are too small or your ass is too big. It's all too hideous. I've tried it, and frankly, I'd rather just be alone than go through it again."

"But what about those amazing first dates? The ones where you have that great immediate connection, and you're both leaning forward across the table, wanting to know everything about the other person there is to know. Even the minor stuff, like whether they like licorice or if they played an instrument when they were a kid," Fran said dreamily. "And the entire time, there's this energy vibrating between you, so that every time your arms brush up against each other, you feel a shock of excitement."

"You," Audrey said severely, "have been reading too many romance novels. It's completely warped your memory. First dates are dreadful. Or maybe it's just me. I think I'm missing the romance gene."

"Don't be ridiculous. You've been married."

"What does that prove? Dating, love, romance, whatever you want to call it, might just be one of those things that some people are good at, and some people aren't. Besides, when was the last time you went on a first date?"

Fran tried to remember. Her last first date had been with Will. "I was twenty-one," she said.

"There you go. Trust me, a first date with a forty-year-old is completely different," Audrey said. "First, you have to hear all about his career—how great he is at what he does, how everyone he has to deal with at work is an asshole, his future plans for being even more wildly successful than he already is. This takes up a good ninety percent of the evening. Then, maybe, if you're very lucky, your date will stop talking about himself long enough to ask you a question or two about what you do for a living. And then, after about five minutes of barely listening to you, he'll wrench the conversation back to himself, usually at this point introducing the subject of past relationships. If he's the angry, bitter sort, he'll start complaining about what a bitch his ex is. If he's not, he'll go on and on about how his ex is a beautiful person who changed his life for the better, but they just reached a point where they realized they'd be better off without each other, but don't worry, they are still the best of friends. Which always makes me wonder if the guy is really just auditioning to be my future ex-boyfriend. Like I should be all reassured that someday he'll be telling some other woman he's on a first date with that I have a beautiful soul. And then he picks up the check—"

"Wait," Fran interrupted. "I thought men always wanted to split checks these days."

"No, never. In fact, I think that's a lie circulated by men, so that women will be so grateful that they're not being asked to pony up for the bill, they won't mind that they just spent the last ninety minutes listening to how grueling it is to run an optometry practice," Audrey said. "Anyway, then once dinner is over, there's the whole good-night-kiss debacle."

"See, that's where you lose me. First kisses are amazing," Fran said.

"With someone you like, maybe. Someone you're attracted to. But those are few and far between. News flash: Good kissers are few and far between. Most grown men are terrible at it," Audrey said. "I think it's laziness. Or lack of practice. Mostly I try to get out with a handshake. Maybe a cheek peck."

"This is so depressing. I have such fond pre-marriage memories of spending hours and hours kissing boyfriends. Of being in a haze of lust and losing all track of time," Fran said dreamily, cuddling the ugly purple pillow closer.

"Get a grip. It's nothing like that at our age," Audrey said. "Which is why I have no interest in dating anyone at the moment. So please stop trying to set me up."

"I told you, I really wasn't trying to set you up with Coop."

"How about this? No more trying to set me up, *and* no more telling me that the men you don't want to set me up with are gay," Audrey said. "Is that specific enough?"

"That's pretty specific," Fran said.

"Good," Audrey said.

"Are you still coming to next month's dinner party club?" Fran asked hopefully. "It's going to be at our house."

"Didn't you just host last month?"

"That wasn't an official Table for Seven dinner party. Tell me you're coming."

Audrey hesitated.

"Audrey?"

"I'll be there," Audrey said with a sigh.

Fran couldn't be sure, but she thought it sounded like Audrey was smiling.

march

.. ..

CHOPPED SALAD

CABERNET-BRAISED SHORT RIBS WITH
MIXED HERB GREMOLATA

GORGONZOLA POLENTA

LEMONY GREEN BEANS

MIXED BERRY TART

*W*HAT ARE YOU DOING?"

Will started at the sound of Fran's voice. He looked up sheepishly at his wife, feeling like a kid who'd been caught sneaking a peek at his dad's dirty magazines. Of course, he was doing nothing of the kind. He had simply taken advantage of his wife and daughters' absence—Fran had taken Rory to her soccer game, and they'd dropped off Iris at the mall on their way—to spend ten minutes making some needed adjustments to his new Rammer bot.

"What happened to Rory's soccer game?" Will asked.

"It got rained out," Fran said.

"It's raining?" Will looked out the garage-door window. The panes were streaked with water. "I hadn't noticed. Anyway, I thought soccer players were supposed to be tough and play through extreme weather conditions. The ref called the game over a little rain?"

"First of all, it's thundering and lightning out." As if to prove her point, a loud explosion of thunder rumbled just then. "And second, Rory is eleven, and the coaches are all parent volunteers. No one wants to stand out on the field in the middle of a storm."

Will shook his head sadly. "No wonder kids these days are so soft."

"You're deliberately avoiding my question," Fran said.

This was true. Will was avoiding her question. Mostly because he knew the direction the conversation was headed.

Fran had been on a home improvement kick lately. It had something to do with the upcoming dinner party they were hosting, and, Will suspected, anxiety on Fran's part that their home was nowhere near the showplace that Mark and Jaime's house was. So far, her list of chores for him—which she insisted on calling a Honey-Do list just to annoy him—included painting the living room, replacing the faucet in the half bath, and installing a new kitchen countertop.

"A new countertop?" Will read aloud when she handed him the list. Or, more accurately, the first version of the list. It had grown extensively since then, as Fran found more and more home improvement projects. Pictures that required hanging. Carpets that needed steam-cleaning. A pergola that had to be built in the garden. "I don't think I'm qualified to put in a new countertop."

"You build robots that fight other robots. I'm sure a countertop will be easy in comparison," Fran had said breezily.

Fran's nickname among her family growing up was the Drill Sergeant, or Sarge for short. It was a personality mixture of bossiness and steely-eyed determination that she would get her way, no matter what. Will had devised a number of coping methods over the years. Usually, he just gave in, which was easier than being steamrolled into submission. Other times, when—like now—what Fran wanted was infeasible, he opted for gentle persuasion with a mild passive-aggressive chaser.

Using this strategy, Will had been trying to whittle down the list to a manageable size. The pergola was too big a project to start, he'd explained. There was no way he'd be able to finish it in time for the dinner party. And even if he could figure out how to install a countertop, they simply couldn't afford to buy one now. But he'd been slowly chipping away at the rest of the list, or at least those items that he couldn't talk his way out of. This morning's project had been to re-paint the living room. Fran had bustled off to the Home Depot first thing, returning with paint, rollers, brushes, paint trays, and blue tape.

"If you paint, I'll take Rory to soccer," she'd bargained.

Will had agreed, although in truth, he liked going to Rory's soccer games. It gave him a kick to see how focused his youngest became out on the field. She was fast, too, the way she darted in and hooked the ball away from larger, older girls.

But just when he had finished moving all of the furniture into the center of the room and taping off the trim, and was about to pour the paint—an unremarkable shade of white that the paint manufacturer called "Crescent Moon"—he'd decided his new battle robot—nicknamed Iggy by Rory—needed a lighter casing to help with mobility. Will figured he could sneak in a few minutes' at his workbench and still have plenty of time to get the painting done before his family re-turned home. But he hadn't counted on the rain.

Will now considered giving a smart-ass answer to Fran's question. *I'm baking a blueberry pie,* or, *I'm contemplating the unbearable lightness of being.* But Fran didn't seem like she was in a very jokey mood at the moment, so he decided to go with the truth instead.

"I'm reworking Iggy's outer casing," Will said.

"What I meant was, why aren't you painting?" Fran asked.

"I was just taking a short break," Will said. "Don't worry, I'll get it done. The living room will be painted by the end of the day. You have my word."

"It's not just painting the living room! The dinner party is next weekend. This is our last chance to get everything on the list taken care of," Fran said. "I was just looking at the front hedges, and I think they're practically dead. We're going to have to dig them up and replace them."

Will contemplated how he would fit this new chore—which sounded simple enough, but would almost certainly entail hours of dirty, sweaty, back-straining work—into a weekend that he was already scheduled to spend painting and steam-cleaning all of the carpets in the house. It was time to take a stand.

"There's no way I'm going to have the time to tackle the front shrubs," he said, shaking his head with what he hoped looked like regret. "Not with everything else you want me to do."

"It's not what I want done," Fran said. "It's what needs to be done."

Will didn't agree. The living room certainly didn't *need* to be repainted. Although Fran might have a point when it came to the carpets, which had been in the house when they bought it and were now worn and tatty.

"Honey, these are our friends who are coming over. The house doesn't have to be perfect."

It was the wrong thing to say. Fran's face hardened into the stubborn expression.

"Yes, it does," she said. "I want everything to look nice."

"It *will* look nice. But I don't think you should get so worked up about this," he said, convinced that Jaime's perfectionist insanity was rubbing off on Fran.

"I'm doing all of the shopping and the planning and the cooking," Fran said. "The least you can do is help with everything else. There's no way I can get it all done on my own."

Will stood and went to his wife, wrapping his arms around her waist. "It'll be fine," he said soothingly. "Don't worry, we'll get the house shaped up and you're an amazing cook. It's going to be a great night."

Fran turned, moving out of his embrace. "Maybe I can dig up the hedges myself," she said. "Do you have a shovel in here?"

IT WAS STILL EARLY—too early to be awake, he could tell from the weak light just beginning to stream in through the blinds—when Coop woke up. The girl lying beside him had insisted on spending the night, and Coop never slept well when he had to share his bed. And this girl—*wait*. What was her name again? Mena? Mindy? Coop felt a surge of panic. He didn't want to be *that* guy, the one who couldn't remember the names of the women he brought home. Then, with a surge of relief, Coop remembered. *Misha*. That was her name. He remembered mentioning, when he'd first been introduced to her the night before at a wine tasting, that he'd heard Misha was Mikhail Baryshnikov's nickname. She'd looked at him blankly.

"The Russian ballet dancer?" he'd said. "He was also in that movie *White Nights*. Although that might have been before your time."

"I know who you're talking about," Misha's friend had said. Coop also couldn't recall the friend's name, but as he hadn't slept with her, he felt no guilt about this. "He was on *Sex and the City*. He was Carrie's boyfriend. The old guy who asked her to move to Paris with him."

"Oh," Misha had said, comprehension dawning on her pretty face. "I know who you mean. That guy's a ballerina?"

Perhaps Coop hadn't used his best judgment when he took her home with him. She was awfully young, still in her twenties. She taught kindergarten, she'd said. He'd imagined her wearing a full-skirted dress, reading a picture book aloud to her class, while they stared up at her with wide eyes and slack mouths, riveted by the goings-on of Peter Rabbit. And even though this was as nonsexual an image as possible, the picture had charmed him, and he'd spent the rest of the evening at her side as they compared the finish on a selection of Chilean wines. The more wine they tasted, the less it seemed to matter that she wasn't much of a conversationalist—her topics of interest focused heavily on who the current contestants of some reality dancing show were and whether or not two Hollywood stars were really dating or if it was all just a publicity stunt—and the more he admired her long, shiny dark hair and shapely legs.

The sex had been fine, although once it was over Coop felt nothing more than a sense of weariness and the beginning of a red wine–induced headache. Now he wondered how long she'd stay. Some women bolted, while others hung around, lingering over coffee and dropping hints about going out to brunch together.

Misha showed signs of life. She stretched and sighed, and then sat up.

"Good morning," Coop said.

"Hi," she said. "What time is it?"

Coop checked the clock by his bed. "Ten to seven."

Misha threw her legs over the side of the bed and padded off to the bathroom, where she proceeded to spend an inordinate amount of time. When she finally emerged, she was wearing Coop's bathrobe. She plopped down on the edge of the bed and turned to face him, leaning back on her arms.

"God, I was so wasted last night," she said conversationally.

"Oh, yeah?" Coop said.

She nodded her head enthusiastically. "I haven't been that drunk since the Kappa Spring Fling last year."

This information clanked around in Coop's head—still rusty from too much wine and too little sleep—for a few beats before it dawned on him what she was saying.

"Spring Fling?" he repeated. "Kappa? What's that? It sounds like a sorority."

Misha nodded. For someone who claimed to have been "so wasted" the night before, she was looking offensively bright eyed and chipper. "Kappa Kappa Gamma," Misha said. "University of Florida."

Coop stared at her. "Please tell me you're not still in college," he said.

Misha laughed and tossed her hair back. Coop noticed that she played with her hair a lot. She was constantly stroking it or twisting it around one finger. "Of course not."

Thank God, Coop thought.

"I graduated last year," Misha continued.

"Which would make you, what . . . twenty-four? Twenty-five?" he asked hopefully. Maybe she had been on one of those six-year plans.

"Twenty-three," Misha said.

Twenty-three. He had brought home a twenty-three-year-old girl, fresh out of college. Popular culture instructed that this should give him a rush, that it was proof he was still virile. But instead it just made Coop feel old and even more tired.

"Why? How old are you?" Misha asked.

She had very large, very round eyes, set wide on her face. Coop had spent the night before trying to figure out who Misha reminded him of—an old girlfriend, maybe, or a movie actress. But suddenly it hit him—she looked like Veronica from the old *Archie* comics. He opened his mouth to tell her this, but then decided against it. She had probably never heard of the *Archie* comics. It was probably before her time. Hell, it was before his time.

"I'm forty-five," Coop said.

Misha's mouth dropped open and her eyes grew even wider. "Are you *serious?*" she asked.

Coop wasn't sure if her disbelief was flattering or not. He nodded, warily.

"God, you're so *old,*" she said.

Okay, definitely not flattering.

"I've never been with someone so old before," Misha continued. "I mean, you're practically as old as my *father.*"

"Thanks for that. I have to say, I'm really enjoying this conversation," Coop said.

But Misha wasn't listening to him. Instead, she'd hopped off the bed again and was rummaging through her purse. He had a momentary flash of hope—maybe she was so horrified, she would turn into a bolter—only to have it dashed a moment later, when he saw she was just retrieving her phone. She returned to the bed, sitting cross-legged, and began to tap on the phone at lightning speed.

"What are you doing?" Coop asked.

"Texting Marissa. She's not going to believe that I just had sex with someone who's forty-five," Misha said. She paused. "Or maybe I should just tweet it. I haven't had anything good to tweet in ages."

"You're going to tweet that we had sex?" Coop asked. He had a vague idea that this had something to do with posting messages on the Internet. "Are you sure that's a good idea?"

Misha nodded happily. "Yeah, this is great." She hit another rapid succession of buttons on the phone, and then looked up at him. "I'm starving. Do you want to go get breakfast? I can tweet that, too."

AFTER WORK, FRAN STOPPED by Uncorked to browse through their selection of Cabernet Sauvignons. She'd decided she wanted to make short ribs for the dinner party club, and the recipe she'd selected called for two bottles of Cabernet, which the ribs braised in for several hours.

What was the rule about cooking with wine? Fran tried to remember. Were you supposed to use wine you would serve with dinner, or was it okay to use the cheap stuff? Someone tapped her on the shoulder. She looked up, and her heart gave a lurch.

"Hey there," Coop said, leaning over to kiss her cheek. "Mmm, you smell good."

Fran felt a thrill of excitement. *He thinks I smell good,* she thought. She wondered if his lips had actually lingered on her cheek, or if she was just imagining it.

Even though Coop looked tired and hadn't shaved that morning, he still managed to look sexy. Fran suddenly pictured pressing her lips against his neck, which was smooth and deeply tanned. This mental image caused her to flush a deep, hot red.

This is ridiculous, Fran thought. *I'm suddenly forty going on fourteen.*

"Hi!" Fran said, hoping Coop didn't notice how flustered she was. "What are you doing here?"

"Probably the same thing you are—buying wine for your dinner party," Coop said. "Your email said we're having short ribs, right?"

Fran nodded. "I'm braising them in Cabernet," she said. "So I thought I should probably serve a Cabernet to go along with the meal."

"Good thinking." Coop looked over the selection of wines, and grabbed a bottle that the wine store was advertising as having received a ninety-three rating from *Wine Spectator*. "I'll bring two of these, as an extra backup for you."

"Thanks, that's so nice of you," Fran gushed.

Then she looked at the price tag, and her heart sank. The wine Coop had selected cost nearly fifty dollars a bottle. Will would kill her if she spent that much, especially since she had planned to buy four bottles of red, along with a couple bottles of white, in case someone didn't drink red. But if she went with the thirteen-dollar bottle she had been about to put in her cart, it would look like she was being cheap, especially in comparison to the wine Coop would be bringing.

"This Chilean Cabernet is excellent. Have you tried it?" Coop asked, pointing at a bottle priced at fifteen dollars. "It was featured at a wine tasting I went to last night, and I really liked it."

"I've never tried it." Fran picked up the bottle and examined the label. "Do you think it will pair well with short ribs?"

Coop nodded. "It's perfect."

Fran felt a rush of gratitude as she loaded four bottles of the Cabernet into her cart, next to the two bottles of Chardonnay she'd already selected. She had a feeling that Coop was steering her toward the less expensive wine because he knew she and Will were on a tight budget. But he'd done so in a way that didn't make her feel small. He was such a good guy, Fran thought, with a rush of affection.

"Thanks," Fran said, squeezing his arm.

"No problem." Coop grinned down at her, which caused Fran's heart to start skittering around again. "How's Will doing?" he asked.

"Will? He's fine." She shrugged. "You know Will. Same as always."

"He knows there's going to have to be payback, right?" Coop said.

"For what?" Fran asked. Then, remembering the last dinner party, she said, "Oh, you mean for the whole telling-Audrey-that-you're-gay thing?"

Coop nodded. "That was a serious violation of the Guy Rules."

"Guy Rules?" Fran rolled her eyes. "Please tell me you're not serious. Besides, I'm the one who actually told her."

"But I know he was the one behind the lie," Coop said, undermining his statement with another grin. "Don't worry. I won't cause any permanent damage to him."

"I'll tell him to be on his guard," Fran said. "Did you have fun at the dinner party?"

"Sure. What's the story with your friend Audrey?" Coop asked. Fran thought that he posed this question with the sort of casual tone that belied a deeper interest, and, instantly, jealousy snaked through her.

"What about her?" Fran asked, turning to inspect a cooler with a display of gourmet food. Olives, cheeses, pâtés. She picked up a wheel of brie and placed it in her cart. She'd slather it with raspberry preserves then bake it wrapped inside puff pastry, and serve it with drinks before dinner.

"She seemed nice. Very smart," Coop said.

Fran nodded. "She is both of those things," she said. She might not love the direction this conversation was going in, but even so, she wouldn't—couldn't—run Audrey down. Besides, it should hardly be a surprise that Coop would be interested in Audrey. She was attractive, elegant, and smart.

Far more attractive than me, Fran thought ruefully. *And single. And not married to his best friend.*

"She said she runs a day spa," Coop said.

Fran nodded again. She selected a box of wheat crackers from the display on top of the cooler and wished she had changed out of her work scrubs and rubber clogs. She could have at least put on some lip gloss. Audrey never left the house with a bare face and tangled hair.

When did my personal grooming standards become so lax? Fran wondered.

"Why are you making me dig for information? Come on, give me the scoop on her," Coop said, sounding exasperated.

"What do you want to know exactly?" Fran asked, resigning herself to the conversation.

"I didn't notice a wedding ring. Is she single?"

"Yes. She was married once, but her husband died," Fran said.

"Really?" Coop's eyebrows shot up. "What's the story there?"

"It was a car accident. Seven years ago," Fran said, remembering that awful week. Audrey's early morning call from the hospital, her voice hollow with shock. Accompanying Audrey to the funeral home. Sitting in the rocking chair, holding a four-year-old Rory and weeping into her baby fine hair, as she couldn't break down in front of Audrey. "It was pretty horrible, actually."

"That's too bad," Coop said. Then, after an appropriate pause, he said, "She's not involved with anyone now?"

Fran looked at him directly for the first time since the

conversation had started off on this Audrey tangent. "No," she said. "She's dated a bit over the years, but she's never met the right person. In fact, she's convinced that there's no such thing. At least, not since Ryan."

Coop nodded thoughtfully. "What was he like?"

"Who, Ryan? He was great. Funny, smart, the sort of guy everyone likes," Fran said.

"So she was married to Mr. Perfect?"

Fran exhaled a short laugh. "He was definitely not perfect. Ryan drank. A lot."

"Had he been drinking the night he died?" Coop asked.

"Probably," Fran said. "His car hit the side of an overpass on I-95. It was late, and there was a bad storm that night, but knowing Ryan, I've always assumed he'd been drinking. Audrey has never said much about it to me. She's very protective of him. Of his memory."

"I wouldn't think many alcoholics have happy marriages," Coop said.

"I wouldn't, either," Fran said. "And I don't know that their marriage was necessarily that happy. But haven't you ever noticed that sometimes when a person dies, the people mourning them start rewriting history? I've seen it with some friends who've lost their parents. I had one friend whose mother was emotionally abusive to her throughout her childhood, but once the mother died, my friend kept going on and on about some trip they took to New York City when she was little, and how her mother took her to tea at the Plaza like Eloise."

"Eloise?" Coop asked.

"You've never heard of Eloise? It's a picture book about a little girl who lives in the Plaza Hotel with her dog, Weenie. Anyway, my friend had this one good memory of her mother—seriously one good memory in thirty-eight years of being her daughter—but it's the one she clung to," Fran said. She shrugged. "I guess it's a way of protecting yourself from the pain."

"The pain of the loss?" Coop said.

"Yes, partly. And partly from the pain that whatever went wrong in your relationship, whatever it was that was screwed up, can't ever be changed. It's over." Fran looked in the cooler again, picking up a container of mixed olives. "Do you like olives?"

"What?" Coop seemed caught off guard by the sudden change of topic. "No, I can't stand olives."

"Really? I never knew that about you," Fran said, putting the olives back. She was glad she'd jettisoned her original menu, which had included lamb chops piled with goat cheese, chopped tomatoes, and olives. It was delicious—Fran had made it for Easter dinner the previous year—but she ultimately decided it was too simple for the dinner party club.

"What can I say? I'm a man of mystery," Coop said, grinning down at her again.

"An enigma wrapped in a riddle," Fran said.

"Actually, I'm not," Coop admitted. "Pretty much what you see is what you get with me."

"And that's why we love you," Fran said, squeezing his arm.

JAIME SAT AT THE kitchen table with a pile of green netting, a coil of wire, and assorted craft materials set out in front of her. She was planning a Peter Pan and Tinker Bell party for Ava's second birthday. All of the children from Ava's play group were invited, along with a select few children from her Music Babies class (although not Aidan, who once bashed Ava over the head with a maraca, and had the reputation of being a biter). Jaime was making a set of fairy wings for each of the little girls and felt Peter Pan hats for the boys.

She was just finishing up her fifth set of tulle wings—not bad for an afternoon's work, considering she had to keep stopping to assist Logan, who was building a complicated train track in the playroom, or Ava, who was ignoring the wooden puzzles and basket of board books Jaime had set out in favor of playing with the Tupperware—when she heard the front door open.

"Hello? Is anyone home?"

Jaime tensed.

Mark's ex-wife, Libby, had—yet again—walked right into their house without bothering to knock.

Sure, she was dropping Emily off. But still. It was one of those touchy blended family issues. God, Jaime hated the word *blended,* as though the people involved were a fruit shake. Their house was Emily's home, or, at least, her second home. So of course Emily had her own room and her own key, and she was free to come and go as she pleased. But sometimes, like today, when her mother was with her, it meant that Libby also felt free to breeze in, unannounced. It was, Jaime thought, completely inappropriate. Not to mention incredibly annoying.

"I'm back here," Jaime said, getting to her feet.

"Mommy, up," Ava demanded.

Jaime obligingly scooped her up and headed out to meet Libby and Emily. Maybe if she was quick, she could intercept Libby in the hallway.

"Hello, Jaime. Hi, Ava," Libby said, smiling brightly at the little girl, her head tilted to one side.

Libby was short and curvy, with short dark hair and very tan skin. She was attractive, but not beautiful, Jaime had always thought with a certain amount of satisfaction.

"Hi," Jaime said, smiling back with equal wattage.

"Hey, Jaime," Emily said. She was wearing a navy blue tennis dress, and had her pink backpack slung over one shoulder. She came over and dropped a kiss on her half-sister's head. "Hi, Ava. I like your bow. I'm starving. Is there anything to eat?"

Emily headed back toward the kitchen. Libby followed her, not waiting for an invitation. Jaime swallowed a sigh.

"What's going on here?" Libby asked, her eyebrows arched, as she looked at the piles of fairy wings and green tulle.

"Ava's birthday party is next weekend. We're having a Peter Pan themed party for her," Jaime said.

"Cool," Emily said, picking up a set of the wings. "Can I help?"

Jaime smiled at her stepdaughter. "You really want to? I'd love that," she said.

"You're going to an awful lot of work for a bunch of two-year-olds, aren't you?" Libby said with a laugh. "It's not like Ava will remember it when she's older."

Jaime's teeth clenched. That sounded like something Mark would say. In fact, it was exactly what Mark had said when she began planning the party. What was so wrong with wanting to make their daughter's birthday special? And even if Ava didn't remember it, she'd see the pictures, which were certain to be adorable.

"Did you have a lesson this morning, Emily?" Jaime asked.

"No, I have one this afternoon," Emily said.

"You do?" Jaime asked and wondered why Mark hadn't mentioned this to her. "Does your dad know?"

"Yep." Emily grabbed an apple out of the fruit bowl and bit into it. "He's taking me. We're going to go early and hit for a while before my lesson."

Jaime had been hoping Mark would hang out with the kids for a few hours, so she could run errands. She wanted to go to the mall and look for something to wear to the dinner party that evening, and she'd also promised Fran she'd swing by the fish store to pick up a container of smoked fish dip. And she couldn't put off a Target run for one more day—they were running dangerously low on paper towels, toilet paper, and laundry detergent. If Mark took off to the tennis club with Emily, it would scupper her plans. She could just about make it through Target with Ava and Logan, as long as she got one of the huge, tank-like carts that sat two kids and were impossible to steer, but there was no way she could go clothes shopping with a two- and three-year-old in tow. The last time she'd brought Logan to the mall, he'd crawled out under the dressing room door, just as Jaime was trying on a strapless dress. She'd had to chase after him into the store, barefoot and unzipped, holding the dress up around her.

"He didn't mention anything about it to me. Your dad's at the gym right now, and when he gets back, I have some errands to run," Jaime said, making sure to keep her voice pleasantly neutral.

"Emily needs to get the extra practice time in. She has a big tournament next weekend." Libby smoothed a hand over Emily's head. "Mark knows. He and I talked about it last night."

Jaime tried to swallow back her irritation. Libby just assumed that Emily's tennis was going to trump all other plans for the weekend. But that was Libby. She was just so self-centered, so sure that she'd get her way at all times.

"Yes, but apparently Mark forgot to talk about it with *me*," Jaime said evenly. She shifted Ava to her right hip.

Libby flashed her a conspiratorial smile. "I know how that goes. Mark was the same way when we were married. I swear, that man is incapable of keeping track of his schedule."

Jaime refused to be drawn in. "Yes, well, we'll figure it out when he gets back from the gym."

"I have to go to the tennis club. I have a lesson with Coach Sarah at two. I can't just *not* show up," Emily said. Ever since Emily had turned twelve, it seemed she was incapable of saying anything without that snotty edge to her voice, Jaime thought.

"Emily's right," Libby said. "She shouldn't have to miss out on her lesson just because you and Mark haven't communicated well."

"You won't miss your lesson," Jaime said. It took considerable effort to keep her voice calm. "But I don't know if your dad will have time to hit with you before your lesson."

"But he promised!" Emily said.

"Emily, why don't you go see what Logan is doing," Libby suggested.

"He's in the playroom," Jaime said.

"Let me guess. Trains?" Emily said. Jaime nodded, and Emily rolled her eyes in affectionate exasperation. "Come on, Ava, let's go find Logan."

Ava was happy enough to be transferred from her mother's arms to Emily's—both of the little ones adored their big sister—and the two of them set off for the playroom.

Once they were alone, Libby turned to Jaime and, lowering her voice, said, "I didn't want to say anything about it in front of her, but you should know Emily has been having a hard time lately."

"Why? What's wrong?" Jaime asked, instantly concerned as all of the problems that plagued young girls flashed through her thoughts. Mean girls, eating disorders, school-work pressures.

"She's been having a crisis in confidence ever since her tournament in Fort Lauderdale last weekend. She lost to a girl she's always beaten in the past, and now she's convinced that she's not training hard enough."

Tennis, Jaime thought. *It's always tennis.*

"It was just one match. She wins all the time," Jaime said.

"A lot of the kids she plays against are homeschooled so they can spend more time training. Emily wants to do that, too," Libby said.

"You're going to homeschool Em?" Jaime asked, surprised. Somehow she couldn't picture Libby as a teacher. And although Libby didn't really work—she didn't need to—she did occupy some sort of position at her family's company that involved frequent trips to the headquarters in Tampa.

"I need to talk to Mark about it," Libby said. "Obviously, I couldn't do it on my own. He'd have to be on board."

"Wait, you want *Mark* to homeschool?" Jaime asked. She shook her head. "He'd never take the time off work. He's at the office so much as it is, we barely see him."

As soon as the words were out of her mouth, Jaime wished she could cut her tongue out. She was a big believer in always putting on a good front with everyone, and this was even more important when it came to her husband's ex-wife.

"We'll figure something out. Emily could always go to his office, and do her studying there," Libby said smoothly.

Jaime knew that when Libby said *we'll figure something out,* she meant herself and Mark. They wouldn't ask for Jaime's input, even when it came to this sort of big decision, one that would certainly affect Jaime and the two younger children.

But before Jaime could say anything, before she could assert herself, Libby glanced at her watch and said, "It's already eleven-thirty? I have to run. I have a lunch date."

"A date? Are you seeing someone?" Jaime asked.

Libby smiled and her dark eyes sparkled. "There is someone I've been seeing quite a lot of lately."

"Anyone I know?"

"Believe it or not, he's my dentist. Wes Thompson. Do you know him?"

Jaime shook her head. "Did he ask you out while he was examining your teeth?"

Libby laughed. "No. I ran into him at the produce section. He asked for help picking out a melon."

"A likely story," Jaime said, grinning despite herself. At times, she could almost imagine that, under different circumstances, she and Libby might have been friends. Almost.

"I know, right? I bet he was just hanging out there, waiting for someone he could use his melon line on," Libby said. "I'll have to tease him about that." She shouldered her large, calfskin bag. "Tell Mark I'll call him later. We need to go over Emily's upcoming tournament schedule. I can take her to the tournament in Tampa, but I need him to cover Jacksonville in two weeks and Miami at the end of the month."

"Jacksonville in two weeks," Jaime repeated, as though

she were committing it to memory. When in truth, she was reeling from the sudden announcement that Mark would be away for two of the next four weekends. And that she wasn't even hearing it from Mark himself, but from his ex-wife.

"I HOPE I'M NOT too early," Audrey said when Fran opened the door on the night of the dinner party. "Wow, you look great! Is that a new dress?"

Fran flushed with pleasure and did a little twirl, showing off her red knit dress. "You like? I was worried it might be too low-cut."

"No way." Audrey gave Fran a kiss on the cheek, and held up a foil-covered plate. "I brought blue cheese stuffed dates wrapped in bacon. I thought Leland would like them."

"You're sweet. I'm sure he'll love them," Fran said, taking the plate from her. "Come back to the kitchen and keep me company while I cook. Do you want some wine?"

"Do you have to ask?" Audrey replied, following her friend back to the kitchen. The Parrishes' house was small but cozy. Photos of the girls framed in black lined the hallway, a pair of pink sequined flip-flops had been abandoned by the front door, pencil lines marking the girls' heights decorated the kitchen door frame. Audrey felt a small pang. She had never been one to pine for a baby, had never even been completely convinced that she wanted to be a mother. And she and Ryan hadn't been anywhere close to starting a family when he died. But now and again, it would hit her how much she might be missing out on.

Audrey tried to shake off these maudlin thoughts. *You're here to have fun tonight,* she told herself sternly.

She accepted a glass of red wine from Fran and sat down

on one of the bar stools lined up in front of the kitchen counter.

"Can I do anything to help?" Audrey asked.

"No, I've got it under control. I just have to finish chopping the chopped salad," Fran said. "What's going on with you?"

"Nothing new," Audrey said. She studied Fran as she took a sip of wine. "Have you lost weight?"

"A little. I've started going to the gym again," Fran said.

"You look fantastic," Audrey said.

"Thanks." Fran smiled at her friend and picked up a large chef's knife. She began chopping a head of radicchio into a fine dice, stopping occasionally to scoop the chopped lettuce into a large wooden salad bowl. "Do you like the wine? I ran into Coop yesterday at the wine store, and he recommended it."

"Is Coop a wine connoisseur?" Audrey asked.

Fran nodded. "He's not one of those guys who go around with their own personal tasting cups and insist on gargling every wine they try. But, yeah, he's pretty knowledgeable about wine. Food, too."

"That surprises me," Audrey said.

"Why?"

"I'm not sure," Audrey said, with a half-shrug. "I guess I saw him as more of a beer and boats sort of a guy."

"He is. He's both, really. I think that's what makes him so interesting," Fran said. She dumped the last of the chopped radicchio into the salad bowl and turned her attention to chopping butter lettuce. "You can't really pigeonhole him."

Audrey eyed her friend suspiciously. "I thought you weren't going to try to set me up with Coop," she said.

Fran looked up from her lettuce-chopping, surprised. "I'm not."

"Uh-huh. Then why are you talking him up to me?"

"I wasn't talking him up. I was just making conversation," Fran said. She seemed flustered and began chopping the lettuce with more vigor than was strictly necessary.

"What's up with you?" Audrey asked, taking another sip of wine.

"Nothing's up," Fran said.

"Hey, Audrey," Will said, wandering into the room. He was wearing a short-sleeve shirt in a lurid Hawaiian print. He ambled over to give Audrey a kiss on the cheek.

"Hey," Audrey said, smiling at Will with affection. "No tequila shrimp tonight? I was hoping you'd make your award-winning recipe again."

"Minus the award part," Fran said.

"Did you like them last time?" Will asked, looking pleased.

"I loved them," Audrey said.

"Fran wanted to try out a new menu tonight. I did make the dessert, though. It's a four-berry tart. The original recipe was for a three-berry tart, but I added blackberries. Because that's how I roll," Will said with a modest shrug.

"Wow, you really know how to live on the edge," Audrey teased. The doorbell rang.

"Can you get that?" Fran asked.

"Sure thing," Will said. A moment later, he returned with Jaime in tow.

"Hi," Jaime said brightly. She handed Fran a bottle of white wine with a big red bow tied around the neck.

"Thank you," Fran said, accepting it and a quick hug. "Where's Mark?"

"He's running late as usual. I decided not to wait for him," Jaime said briefly, and then turned to give Audrey an air kiss. "Hi, there. I don't want to get lip gloss on you."

"What's Mark doing? Work emergency?" Audrey asked, although even as she asked, she couldn't think of what sort of emergency a commercial litigator would have on a Saturday evening.

"No, he was at the tennis club hitting with Emily, and they lost track of time. I talked to him on my way over here. He's going to stop at the house, shower, and then he'll be over," Jaime said. She glanced at Fran. "He said to send his apologies, and please not to wait for him to eat."

She spoke lightly, but she looked strained.

"No worries. Leland and Coop aren't here yet, anyway. Whoops, maybe I spoke too soon," Fran said, as the doorbell rang again.

"I'll get it," Will said. "Will you pour Jaime a glass of wine?"

"Sure thing. Red or white?" Fran asked.

"I'll start with white, please," Jaime said.

Fran retrieved a bottle of Chardonnay out of the fridge, as Will ushered Leland and Coop into the now crowded kitchen. Audrey smiled and joined in with the chorus of hellos, although she felt awkward seeing Coop again. He, however, didn't seem to share her embarrassment. He walked up to her and patted her on the shoulder.

"If it isn't my gay matchmaker," Coop said with a grin.

Audrey could feel her cheeks flaming. "I sort of hoped we could pretend that entire evening never happened," she said.

"Are you kidding? Never," Coop said.

Will and Fran hustled around, making sure everyone

had a glass of wine—or, in Leland's case, a scotch on the rocks.

"So what else has Franny told you about me? Is there anything else I need to set the record straight on?" Coop asked. He spoke softly leaning forward, so that his mouth was inches from her ear. Audrey could feel her entire body go warm and boneless.

Am I attracted to him? she wondered. *Oh, my God, what if I am?*

It was a truly terrible thought. It was the last thing she needed in her life. A dog, maybe. A boyfriend, definitely not. Even that word—*boyfriend*—made Audrey feel itchy. She and romance were not a good mix. It wasn't as though she hadn't tried—she'd been married, after all. And look how *that* had turned out. She'd chosen a dysfunctional alcoholic as her life partner.

Okay. Don't Panic, Audrey told herself. Maybe Coop would reveal some sort of intolerable bad habit—like chewing with his mouth open, or picking at his fingernails at the table—and she'd be so turned off she wouldn't have to worry about how incredibly aware she suddenly was of his presence.

WILL THOUGHT THE EVENING was going well. Everyone seemed to be enjoying themselves. Leland was clearly thrilled to have been seated between Fran and Jaime, and was basking in their joint attention. Audrey and Coop were chatting quietly over their salads, and Will, having seen his friend in action before, could tell Coop was interested. It was harder to tell with Audrey. She'd always kept her emotions contained.

Mark showed up just as they were sitting down at the table, looking fresh from the shower, his hair still damp.

"Hey, man," Mark said, shaking Will's hand. "Sorry, I'm late."

"No problem," Will said. He glanced at his watch and was surprised to see it was already eight. The two glasses of red wine he'd consumed before dinner had made him pleasantly light-headed.

"Sorry, Fran," Mark said, leaning down to kiss Fran's cheek.

"I'm not the one you're in trouble with," Fran said, nodding to Jaime.

Will didn't think Jaime seemed particularly angry. She looked serenely composed, her head tilted to one side as she listened to Leland recount a story of a criminal trial he'd presided over, where the defendant—who was defending himself—had attempted to file a motion entitled "Motion to Request that the Prosecutor Go Fuck Himself."

"What did you say?" Jaime asked. Mark leaned over to kiss his wife's cheek. She didn't turn away, Will noticed, but she also didn't seem overly enthusiastic to see him.

"I denied the motion on the grounds that what it requested was physically impossible," Leland said, and everyone laughed.

"Mark, would you like some wine?" Fran asked, as he sat in the empty seat between her and Coop.

"Yes, please," Mark said. Fran filled his wineglass, while Jaime passed him the salad and a basket of warm rolls infused with rosemary. "I just saw Iris at our house. She was reading Logan a story and acting out all of the characters with different voices. He was mesmerized."

"She's glad to have the work. She was saving up for a straightening iron, but I told her she should really put the money toward the new laptop she keeps insisting she needs. She's coming around to the idea," Fran said. "Actually, I'm proud of her. I think it's a sign that she might really be maturing."

"Laptop? Is that what she told you? And you believed her?" Mark said. He took a sip of the wine. "This is good. What is it?"

Will glanced up, meeting his wife's eyes.

"What do you mean, is that what she told us?" Will asked.

"Mark," Jaime said warningly.

"Wasn't I supposed to say anything?" Mark asked.

"Okay, you two, spill," Fran said.

Will knew that, like him, his wife was running through a mental list of all of the ways a teenage girl could get into trouble with too much spending money. Drugs. Tattoos. Body piercings.

Mark shrugged. "It's not such a big deal. She just mentioned she bought some sunglasses today."

Will relaxed. Sunglasses were infinitely preferable to body piercings. He glanced back at his wife, but she was still frowning.

"What kind of sunglasses?" Fran asked.

"No idea," Mark said.

Fran looked to Jaime.

"Okay, they were pretty expensive," Jaime admitted.

"How expensive?" Fran asked.

"She got them at Nordstrom. They're Oliver Peoples," Jaime said, as though this explained everything. Will assumed she was talking about a brand, but he'd never heard of it. One look at his wife, however, told him that she had. Her cheeks had suddenly flushed a dark red, and her eyes were narrowed.

"How much did she spend on them?" Fran asked.

Jaime hesitated. "I really think you should talk to Iris about this. I feel like I'm tattling on her."

"Seriously, Jaime. How much did she spend?" Fran insisted, using her Sarge voice that Will knew all too well. Jaime might as well give in now, he thought. Resistance was futile.

Jaime looked down at her plate. "I think she said they were around four hundred," she said.

"Four hundred what? Pesos?" Will asked, blinking with confusion. Sunglasses did not cost four hundred dollars. They cost twenty dollars at Target.

"What? Did you know she was planning on buying them?" Fran exclaimed.

Will was pretty sure that it wasn't good dinner party etiquette to interrogate your guests about extravagant purchases your daughter bought with the babysitting money they had paid her.

"Hon, why don't we deal with this later. It's really something we should be discussing with Iris," Will said gently.

Fran looked at him, and, after taking a deep breath and visibly unclenching, she nodded.

"You're right. I'm sorry, Jaime. I didn't mean to jump all over you like that," Fran said.

"It's okay," Jaime said. "I'm already dreading Ava's teen years, and she's not quite two."

"Be afraid. Be very afraid," Fran said darkly. "Practically overnight, Iris has transformed from the sweetest, most helpful, most courteous girl you would ever meet into a demon from hell, complete with retractable horns and a forked tongue."

"She's always very polite with me, and she's great with the kids," Jaime said.

"So, she's saving the bad attitude for when she's home? I'm not sure if that makes me feel better or worse," Fran said.

"It's better. At least when she's home, she spends most of her time locked in her room, and only emerges at mealtimes to snarl at us," Will said.

Fran shook her head. "Four hundred dollars on sunglasses. I'm going to kill her. Then I'm going to make her take them back."

"Do you have children?" Jaime asked Leland.

He nodded. "Two sons. One is an attorney with the Justice Department. He lives just outside of D.C. with his wife and seventeen-year-old fraternal twins. A boy and a girl," Leland said proudly. "And my younger son is an architect in Ohio. He's married, too, but no kids, although I think that's just a matter of time."

"I don't think I could have handled twins," Fran said. She shot Coop a look. "And don't make the easy joke, Coop."

"Why are you picking on me? Mark's the one smirking," Coop said. He looked at Audrey, raising one eyebrow. "And just for the record, I've never dated twins."

"And on that note," Fran said, standing, "I'll get the main course."

DESPITE FEELING PLEASANTLY CONTENT from the excellent dinner and accompanying wine, Coop was on edge.

He couldn't figure Audrey out. Was she interested in him

or not? His opinion on the matter kept vacillating from course to course. Over the salad, she had been chatty and made lots of eye contact. But then she ignored him during the main course, choosing instead to chat with Will about the battle bot he was building. Coop was stuck listening to Mark drone on and on about some upcoming tennis tournament his daughter was playing in, which pretty much cemented Coop's opinion that Mark was a bore. Just when the evening was starting to feel flat and tedious, and Coop was trying to conjure up a good excuse to leave early, Fran brought out coffee and a mixed berry tart topped with whipped cream.

"I know, no coffee for you, Coop," Fran said, as she set out mugs for everyone else.

"You don't drink coffee?" Audrey asked, turning back to Coop for the first time in an hour.

"Nope," Coop said. "Not a coffee fan."

"You strike me as more of a tea man. I can see you sipping a cup of Earl Grey," Audrey said, flashing him a smile.

"Really?" Coop asked, taking a bite of his tart. It was good—the crust was buttery and the berries were just the right mixture of sweet and sour.

"No, not really. You're too rugged for tea. I'd have guessed that you were not only a coffee drinker, but that you preferred it strong and dark. Preferably drunk out of a tin cup, like a cowboy," Audrey said.

Oh ho, Coop thought. *And we're back to the flirting.*

"Is this the point where I'm supposed to break out my John Wayne impression?" Coop asked.

"Sure, I'd love to hear it," Audrey said.

"We all would," Will said.

"Thanks, man. Way to put me on the spot," Coop said, nodding to Will.

"Hey, you're the one who offered," Audrey said, her eyes shining.

Definitely flirtatious, Coop thought. *Not that I should be surprised. It was only a matter of time before I won her over.*

He waited until everyone was leaving—Jaime had told Iris that she and Mark would be home by ten-thirty, Leland was looking sleepy—to make his move. He rested a hand on Audrey's arm and, smiling his most charming smile, said, "Can I walk you out to your car?"

Audrey seemed surprised, but said, "Sure."

The farewells at the door took a while, with all of the women promising to call one another the next day, and Fran urging Mark to walk Leland home, which Leland was vigorously protesting the need for. Coop had to wait for the group to clear off before he finally had the chance to get Audrey alone.

"The short ribs were great," he said.

"They were amazing. Fran's always been an amazing cook," Audrey agreed. She stopped in front of a silver Honda Accord parked at the curb. "This is me."

She hesitated and looked up at Coop. *This is it,* he thought. *She's hoping I'm going to kiss her.* He leaned one hip against her car and shot her his sexiest grin.

"How would you like to have dinner with me sometime?" Coop asked, keeping his voice low and warmly intimate. "Just the two of us, I mean."

"Thanks, but I don't think so," she said. She pressed her key ring remote, and the Accord unlocked with a loud click.

Coop blinked. "What? Why not?"

Audrey walked around and opened the driver's door.

"I don't think it's a good idea," she said.

"Why not?" Coop asked again.

"You're just sort of . . . ," Audrey began and then stopped. "Look, there's no point in getting into it. I don't want to hurt your feelings."

"Now you have to tell me," Coop said. "You can't just leave it at that. 'I don't want to hurt your feelings.' I mean, what the hell is that?"

"See, you're already getting defensive," Audrey said.

"Yeah, imagine that," Coop said. "Just tell me. What's the problem?"

"Okay, fine." Audrey sighed. "You're just . . . well . . . you just seem really full of yourself."

"Really full of myself," Coop repeated.

"Self-centered," Audrey said.

"Self-centered?"

"I don't want to sound mean, but I get the feeling you think you're God's gift to women."

"God's gift to women?" Coop said, wondering why it was that whenever people said they didn't want to be mean, it was a lead-in to saying something really, really mean.

"Are you going to just keep repeating everything I say?" Audrey asked. She crossed her arms, her keys still dangling from one hand.

"I just don't know where you're getting this from. I'm a good guy," Coop said, thinking, *Aren't I?*

"I'm sure you are. I just don't think we're a good fit," Audrey said soothingly. "And I really should get going. Have a good rest of your night."

Coop stared after her as she disappeared into the car, her words ringing in his ears. *Full of himself? Self-centered?* Okay, maybe he was self-*confident*. Which could possibly read as cocky. But he certainly didn't think he was God's gift to women. That was laughable.

The engine started, and then, a moment later, the passenger side window rolled down.

"Hey, Coop?" Audrey called out.

"Yeah?" Coop was wary, wondering what was coming next. Would she tell him he had an annoying laugh? Or insult the size of his penis?

"I can't drive while you're leaning on my car," she said.

"Oh, right." Coop straightened and stepped back to the sidewalk. "I didn't realize I was."

"Good night again," Audrey said.

"Good night," Coop replied. But she was already pulling away, and there was a good chance she hadn't heard him.

april

· · ··

WATERCRESS VICHYSSOISE

S & M CHICKEN

CHEESE AND BACON POTATOES

CREAMED SPINACH

COCONUT LAYER CAKE

*W*ILL SOMETIMES WONDERED IF sons would have been easier than daughters.

"I hate you," Iris had screamed on the day after the dinner party, when Fran informed her that she'd have to return the four-hundred-dollar sunglasses.

"That sort of language is unacceptable, young lady," Fran had said.

But Iris had simply turned and run upstairs to her room, slamming her door.

Will turned to Fran. "Young lady?"

"I know." Fran sighed. "I sound like my mother. In fact, it's entirely possible that I've morphed into my mother, as horrific a thought as that is."

Will had to agree. Fran's mother, Inga, was a dour, disapproving woman. Her great ambition in life had been to be an opera singer, but an unexpected pregnancy—followed by a hasty marriage—stymied her career plans. Inga never recovered from this disappointment and set about running her household with a humorless, absolute authority.

"Are you going after Iris?" Will asked. In their family, the role of disciplinarian had always fallen to Fran. It was the way they'd always done things. He took out the garbage every Monday and Thursday morning, and Fran grounded the girls. But, to Will's surprise, Fran threw up her hands and shook her head.

"I can't deal with her anymore," Fran said.

"Don't you think we should talk to her about her behavior?" Will asked. When he said *we*, he really meant *you*. But he was pretty sure Fran got that.

"What's the point? She's been hideous for months. I don't think a stern talking-to is going to turn her around now," Fran said. She turned on the kitchen faucet, filled the sink with warm, soapy water, and began to wash the wineglasses from the night before.

Will looked at his wife. "Are you okay?"

"I'm fine. I just don't see why I'm always the one who has to deal with Iris. You heard her. She hates me. I think it's time for you to be the bad guy for once."

Will did not like the sound of this. He didn't want to be the bad guy, and he certainly didn't want Iris to start hating him, too. It was vastly preferable to be the fun, easygoing parent. But he had a feeling this was not an argument Fran would find persuasive. At least, not in her current mood.

"Okay, I'll talk to her, but I still need your input. How about . . ." Will hesitated, trying to think. "No cellphone for a week?"

"I vote for sending her off to a convent. Is that still a viable option these days? Can you send an unwilling daughter off to the nuns?"

"No, I don't think the nuns want to deal with back-talking teenagers. Plus we're not Catholic, so there's that," Will said. He hesitated, hoping for a last minute reprieve. "You really want me to go talk to her?"

"Yes," Fran said, rinsing dish soap off a glass.

Will headed upstairs, moving slowly in case Fran suddenly remembered she was far more competent at handling these sorts of parenting issues and stopped him. But she didn't.

The door to Iris's room, the first on the right, was closed. Will knocked.

"Go away!" Iris shouted, her voice muffled through the door.

Will knocked again. "It's me," he said.

"Dad?" There was a pause and then the door opened. Iris's face was puffy and splotched with red. "I thought you were Mom."

"May I come in?" Will asked politely. He always hesitated entering either of his daughters' rooms without express permission.

"Sure," Iris said.

He opened the door. Iris sat cross-legged on her bed, a fuzzy, purple, heart-shaped pillow clutched in her arms.

"I'm not taking the sunglasses back. I couldn't even if I wanted to, and I don't." Iris's chin rose up stubbornly.

"Why can't you take them back?"

"Store policy. They don't accept returns."

Will wondered if this was really true. Iris was not above lying to get her own way. This was why Fran should have been the one to come up and deal with talking to Iris. She probably knew the return policy of every store in the mall.

"Your mother really doesn't think you should keep the glasses," Will said, in an attempt to invoke Fran's greater authority.

"God, I hate her! Why does she have to control everything in my life?"

"First of all, I agree with your mother," Will said, thinking that he probably should have led with that. "Those glasses are too expensive."

"But it was my money! I earned it!"

"And that's something you should be proud of. I think it's

great that you've been working hard and saving your earnings. And you certainly should have some freedom to spend your money as you want. But you have to exercise good judgment," Will said.

"Everyone at school wears those glasses," Iris retorted.

"I find that hard to believe," Will said.

"It's true! Hayley has a pair just like the ones I bought!"

Actually, this Will did believe. Hayley Adams was spoiled rotten. The major drawback of sending the girls to private school—along with the staggering tuition—was that nearly all of their classmates came from privileged backgrounds and had lifestyles he and Fran could never provide for their daughters. The girls' friends were always going off on expensive vacations or spending time in second homes in places like Nantucket or Mackinac Island. Iris and Hayley had taken riding lessons together, right up until Hayley had gotten her first horse. Iris had been impossible to live with for weeks afterward—she cried constantly about how unfair it was that she couldn't have a horse—and finally gave up riding altogether.

"We've talked about this before. You're going to constantly meet people who are richer than you, or who have nicer cars or clothes than you. You'll also meet plenty of people who are prettier, and smarter, and more talented," Will said.

Iris gaped at him. "Is this your idea of a pep talk?"

"The point is you can't expend your energy being jealous. There's no point," Will said.

"So basically, you think I'm dumb and ugly on top of being poor? Thanks a lot!" Iris burst into tears again and flopped down on her stomach, burying her face in her pillow.

Will blinked. He'd been trying to teach Iris a life lesson that he'd always found invaluable.

"Of course I don't think you're dumb or ugly," Will said. "I was just trying to explain that jealousy is a useless emotion."

"Just go away," Iris said, her voice muffled.

Will patted Iris on her shoulder. Her sobs grew louder, more dramatic, and less believable. Finally, Will gave up and left her to her tantrum. As he left her room, he closed the door gently behind him.

That went well, he thought. *Only a matter of time before I get a Father of the Year award.*

Downstairs, Fran had finished washing the glasses and was getting out leftover short ribs to reheat for dinner. This perked Will up—short ribs were always better on the second day. He wondered if there was any polenta left. Sometimes Fran shaped leftover polenta into a log, chilled it, and then sliced it into pale yellow disks which she fried in olive oil. His stomach gave a rumble of anticipation.

"Did she agree to take the sunglasses back?" Fran asked.

"What?" Will had been distracted by thoughts of fried polenta. "Oh. She said she can't."

"Can't?"

"The store she bought them from has a no-return policy."

"Please tell me you didn't fall for that," Fran said, fixing him with a bold stare. "She bought them at Nordstrom. Of course they accept returns."

"They do?"

"Of course they do!"

"How was I supposed to know?" Will asked, stung. "You know how manipulative Iris can be."

Fran snorted. "The understatement of the year. You didn't tell her she can keep them, did you?"

"No, I wouldn't do that," Will said, trying to remember if he had. No. He definitely hadn't said that. Instead, he'd told her that she was stupid and ugly. He wondered if he should mention this to Fran, but then decided against it. His wife was in an odd mood. "But she's going to be impossible to live with if we make her take them back."

"So? She's not exactly a delight to live with now," Fran said.

"I did tell her that she should have some latitude to buy things with the money she earns," Will said.

Fran looked up from the leftovers she'd been arranging on the counter. "Why on earth would you tell her that?"

"We want her to have some free will," Will said mildly. "But I also told her she'd have to make better choices."

Fran lifted her arms and then let them fall, slapping her thighs in irritation. "You just completely undermined me."

Will blinked. "How did that undermine you?"

"Because I told her she had to put the money in a savings account, and that from now on she'd have to talk to one of us before she spent it. It's not just the sunglasses. I don't want her frittering her money away on makeup or clothes, either," Fran said, tearing plastic wrap off a Pyrex dish with more force than necessary.

"You did? When did you tell her that?"

"You were standing right there!"

"I was?" Will tried to remember back to the conversation that ended with Iris storming out of the room, yelling that she hated Fran. It had gotten a bit repetitive at one point— Fran telling Iris she would be returning the sunglasses, Iris's insistence that she never had anything nice—and so his mind had wandered to Iggy the Rammer bot and the problems he was still having with its mobility.

"Jesus, Will!" Fran turned away.

"I'm sorry. I didn't hear that bit. But, look—Iris thinks that we're trying to control her. That's not a good dynamic to get into with a teenage girl," Will said gently.

"We should just stand back and let her make stupid decisions?"

"To a point, yes. If she spends all of her money on lipstick or bathing suits or overpriced sunglasses, and then doesn't have money to get something else she wants, well, that's a good lesson for her to learn," Will said.

"Now you think she should keep the sunglasses?" Fran shook her head in disgust, and then shrugged, as though her earlier burst of anger had sapped away all of her energy. "Fine. Do whatever you want. You can be the good guy who lets her keep the glasses. I'll continue in my role as the evil witch who makes her life miserable."

"Come on, don't be like that. It's not you versus me. We're a team. I just don't think it should be us versus her, either," Will said, stepping forward, and resting his hand on Fran's shoulder.

"I'm not making it us versus her. *She* is. That's part of what being a teenager is. We set boundaries and she tests them. If we give in on this, it's just going to teach her that if she tantrums long enough, she'll eventually get her own way," Fran said.

"It might. But maybe we could explain to her that we'll trust her judgment more, but she'll have to live with the consequences of her behavior. It could help dial back the hostilities," Will said.

Fran sighed and shrugged. "Okay, fine. We might as well

try another approach with her. God knows the current one hasn't been working."

Will smiled at her and rubbed her shoulder. But Fran just frowned down at the short ribs, and said, "Do you think this is enough for dinner? I thought there were more ribs than this. Oh, well. Rory would probably rather have a hot dog anyway."

Fran moved away from him and began rummaging in the fridge again. And even though Will had prevailed—and, he thought, had done so with a well-reasoned position—the fact that Fran gave in so quickly made him uneasy.

THE TENNIS CLUB WAS bustling with activity. Kids wearing sweat-wicking T-shirts and baseball hats milled around, while their parents trailed after them, clutching bottles of water and containers of sunscreen. Bleachers had been set up courtside and people were queued up at the concession stand to buy hamburgers and grilled chicken sandwiches.

Emily was playing singles on one of the center courts—"The show court," Mark had said proudly—and was already up one set over a taller, older girl. Wearing her long hair back in two ponytails, reminiscent of a young Chris Evert, Emily looked fiercely determined. Her small face was set in concentration and she didn't pay any attention to the crowd that had gathered to watch her.

Jaime watched as much of her stepdaughter's match as she could, although she spent most of her time chasing after Logan, who—unlike his younger sister—refused to sit still on the bleachers. Instead, he kept taking off in one direction and then another, running as fast as his chubby legs could carry him. At one point, he ran right onto Emily's court. Luckily, he timed this for when the girls were taking a water break and changing sides. Still, Mark—who was sitting next to Emily's coach, Sarah, in the front row of the bleachers—was not pleased.

"Jaime," he hissed, "can't you keep him under control?"

Jaime had to swallow her scalding retort. Libby was sitting just two rows behind Mark, looking coolly chic dressed in all white with her eyes hidden behind huge tortoiseshell sunglasses and obviously listening to every word. Jaime pasted a smile on her face and smoothed back Logan's hair.

"He's just feeling extra wiggly today. I'm going to take him back behind the clubhouse and let him run off some of his energy," Jaime said brightly, handing Ava to Mark. She took Logan's hand firmly in hers and retreated, not letting go of him until they were a safe distance away from the courts. A group of boys around Emily's age were kicking a soccer ball back and forth in a grassy area, and Logan scooted closer to them, mesmerized.

This was exactly the reason she hadn't wanted to bring the kids to the tournament today, Jaime thought. She knew she'd end up spending the entire time chasing around after one or another of them and would hardly get to watch Emily play. Plus, Ava's naptime was in less than an hour, and she always got cranky when she didn't have her rest. If she started fussing while Em was still playing, Mark would get annoyed.

Well, let him be annoyed, Jaime thought. *He's the one who insisted that the whole family should be here to cheer Emily on.* It was nice in theory, but just not practical when you had a two- and three-year-old in tow. They should have booked a sitter and come on their own, as Jaime had suggested. They could even have stretched it into a real date and had dinner afterward.

Logan turned again and ran smack into a woman who was wearing a white tennis skirt and holding a clipboard in one hand and a Diet Coke in the other. She looked down at him in surprise.

"Hello, small person," she said.

Logan—who wasn't really shy but occasionally liked to pretend that he was—ducked his head and didn't answer.

"Sorry about that," Jaime said, reaching forward to take Logan's hand in hers again.

"No problem." The woman smiled at Jaime. She had brown shoulder-length hair and was very tan with very white teeth. "I'm Becky."

"Hi, I'm Jaime. Oh, wait, Becky? You're the one who runs the club, right?"

"Yes, although on a chaotic day like today, I don't know if I should admit to it," Becky said with a laugh. "Do you have a child playing? This little guy looks young to be competing."

One of the problems of being a stepparent was that there wasn't a great way to introduce yourself. Thanks to an entire genre of Disney movies, the very term *stepmother* was tainted. Cinderella's stepmother enslaved her, forcing her to cook and clean and wait on her stepsisters. Snow White's stepmother attempted to murder her with a poisoned apple. In fact, you rarely even heard *stepmother* without *evil* smack in front of it.

"His older sister is playing," Jaime said. "Emily Wexler."

"You're Emily's little brother?" Becky smiled at Logan, who had apparently forgotten about pretending to be shy.

He held up a faded yellow tennis ball he'd found deserted under the bleachers.

"Look, a ball," he said, holding it up to her.

"Very nice," Becky said. Then, turning back to Jaime, she said, "You must be Emily's stepmom."

Stepmom. Okay, I can live with that, Jaime thought. It sounded nicer, friendlier than stepmother.

"Yes, I'm Jaime," Jaime said, squeezing Logan's hand to prevent him from running off again.

"How's Emily doing?" Becky asked.

"Last I checked, she was ahead. But this guy keeps racing off on me, so I haven't had a chance to watch as much as I'd like," Jaime said.

"Her game has really been coming along. I know Sarah's been pleased with her," Becky said.

"That's good to hear. Emily works really hard," Jaime said.

"It helps that she has such dedicated parents. Both Mark and Libby are very supportive, which is nice to see. Sometimes, once there's a divorce, the parents aren't so good about putting their child's interests ahead of their own grievances," Becky said.

Jaime nodded. Libby frequently got under Mark's skin. He was always much happier communicating with her via text messaging or email rather than talking to her on the phone. But, it was true, both Mark and Libby worked hard to keep any differences they might have hidden from Emily.

"And I know that Emily must appreciate having you and her little brother and sister out cheering her on today," Becky continued, smiling at Jaime.

Jaime felt instantly contrite for her earlier irritation with

Mark over his insistence that the whole family attend the tournament that day. That was the whole point, to cheer Emily on. And of course it would make Emily feel good to know that they were all there for her.

"I'm going to try to catch the end of the match," Jaime said. She looked down at Logan. "Come on, buddy. We're going to go cheer your big sister on."

"Have fun," Becky said with a wave.

Jaime picked up Logan and set him on her hip—which he normally hated, but was now sufficiently tired that he didn't fight her—and backtracked to Emily's court. She didn't join Mark on the bleachers, but instead stood to one side, swaying gently to soothe Logan. This had an almost magical effect on him. The head resting on her shoulder instantly grew heavy, and his thumb disappeared into his mouth.

Emily's opponent served a ball to her, and Emily crushed it back with a stinging forehand. The other girl just barely got to it, popping it up over the net. Emily smashed an overhead past her. The crowd cheered. Jaime wanted to cheer, too, but was afraid she'd wake the now dozing Logan, so instead she raised one hand in a fist pump, before looking over at Mark to see if he was pleased.

Ava was snuggled up on Mark's lap. She was awake, but rubbing her eyes and looked like she might doze off at any moment. But Mark wasn't looking back at Jaime, or even out at Emily. Instead, he was leaning toward Sarah, listening intently to whatever she was saying. Sarah was gazing back up at him, her eyes bright, her young face animated. As she spoke she reached out and lightly touched Mark's arm.

Jaime felt a knife-sharp flash of realization, followed by an even deeper throb of anger.

Sarah.

Was it possible Mark was having an affair with Emily's tennis coach? Jaime wondered, before quickly realizing that it was a stupid question—of course, it was possible. Anything was possible. Sarah was pretty—young and fit, with shiny dark hair that fell down her toned back.

The far more important question for Jaime to consider: *Was it true?*

COOP SAT IN THE SMALL, cramped editing studio, going over footage of migrating gray seals.

In the three weeks that had passed since the last meeting of the dinner party club, Coop had put Audrey firmly out of mind. She clearly had issues of her own that she was dealing with. It wasn't anything for him to worry about.

His cellphone rang.

He clicked the answer button. "This is Coop."

"Hey, Coop, it's Julia Britton. You called last week? I was out of town and only just got the message."

"Hey, Julia. Thanks for calling me back," Coop said.

"I have to say, I was surprised to get your phone call," Julia said.

"Why's that?"

Julia let out a short bark of laughter. "Are you serious? The last time I saw you, you promised me you'd call me the next day."

Coop's heart sank, and he rested his head on his hand, the palm spread out over his forehead. "Did I call you?"

"No. You didn't."

Damn. He had been afraid of that. But at this point, it was hardly surprising. He'd decided to disprove Audrey's accusations by calling old girlfriends—or, at least, women he had gone out with—for reassurance that he was really a good guy. Gallant, thoughtful, a good time. Instead, he found himself hitting up against a wall of seriously pissed-off women, most of whom relished the opportunity to tell him off. Apparently, the majority of them also thought that he was selfish and egotistical, not that he'd been given much of a chance to talk about it in-depth with any of them. After he'd been called a bastard four times and a prick twice, he'd given up. Unfortunately, he'd left a few messages—for Julia and others—and was still having to deal with the returned calls.

"I'm sorry," Coop said automatically. He tried to remember how many times he and Julia had gone out. Three? Four?

"You should be," Julia said. "I thought we had a nice time together."

"We did," Coop said. Probably. To be honest, he couldn't really remember. Not exactly. But he usually had a good time. And he remembered liking Julia. Just apparently not enough to call her again.

"Actually, you ended up doing me a favor," Julia said.

Coop perked up. She didn't sound particularly angry. And she hadn't called him an asshole. At least, not yet.

"How so?"

"I was really upset for a while after you blew me off, so I decided to take some time off from dating. I started training for a marathon, which is something I'd always wanted to do. My gym was sponsoring a training group for marathon runners, so I signed up for it and ended up meeting my fiancé there," Julia explained. "So really, in a weird way, my engagement is all thanks to you."

"Does that mean I'm invited to the wedding?" Coop asked.

Julia laughed, this time sounding genuinely amused. "No. But maybe we'll say a toast in your honor," she said. "Why'd you call? I assume it wasn't to ask me out again, fourteen months after our last date."

"No," Coop admitted. "But there is something I want to ask you."

He hadn't gotten this far in any of his conversations with the women he'd contacted. But Julia was decidedly less hostile than any of the others. *What the hell,* he thought. Might as well see what she says.

"Shoot," Julia said.

"When we went out, you didn't think I was full of myself, did you?"

"Yes," Julia said.

"You don't have to answer right away. You can think about it for a few minutes."

"I don't have to think about it. You were really full of yourself," Julia said.

"Then why did you go out with me in the first place?" Coop asked.

"Good question," Julia said. She laughed.

She had a nice laugh, Coop thought. A low, intimate chuckle that was really quite sexy. Coop found himself wishing he had called her again.

"You were also very charming. We had fun together," Julia said. "Like I said, I was really disappointed when I didn't hear from you."

"I'm sorry."

"You don't have to keep saying that."

"But it's true."

"Why the call? Are you having a crisis of conscience?"

"Not exactly." Coop hesitated. "A woman I was interested in turned me down and told me it was because I'm too full of myself. I wanted a second opinion."

Julia laughed her sexy laugh again. "I guess you came to the wrong woman for that."

"No, I appreciate your candor," Coop said. "And if things don't work out with your fiancé . . ."

"They will," Julia said. "But thanks for the offer. You've officially made my day."

After he got off the phone with Julia, Coop found he was having a hard time concentrating on the footage he was supposed to be editing. Was it true? Was he cocky? Maybe. But was that necessarily such a bad thing? He was basically a good guy in all the ways that mattered. He'd never killed anyone, didn't take drugs, and had excellent personal hygiene.

An unbidden image of Audrey flitted through his thoughts again, before Coop had a chance to dismiss her with an irritated shrug of his shoulders. A neurotic widow was the last thing he needed in his life right now.

AUDREY LAUGHED OUT LOUD when she read Leland's email containing the menu for his upcoming dinner party.

"S and M chicken?" she said aloud.

"Excuse me?" Lisa asked from the doorway of Audrey's office. Lisa was the receptionist at the Seawind Day Spa. She was young and pretty and not very bright. But what she lacked in intelligence, she made up for in dependability. Plus the customers liked her.

Audrey glanced up. "Oh, nothing. Just a funny email. What's up?"

"The mail arrived," Lisa said, handing over a packet of envelopes.

"Thanks," Audrey said. Audrey shuffled through the mail quickly. Bills, bills, and more bills. Nothing that needed immediate attention. She put the stack in her in-box.

"The new mailman is so cute," Lisa said, sitting down in the spare chair without being invited. Audrey had to stifle a sigh. She'd told Lisa over and over again that she had to stay up at the front reception desk, even if there wasn't anyone there. You never knew when someone might stop in to set up an appointment or buy a gift card. And Lisa would always nod enthusiastically, say she completely understood, and then drift away from her post again at the first opportunity.

"I hadn't noticed," Audrey said.

"Really? He's got amazing legs. Very muscular calves," Lisa said dreamily. "But he's not as cute as Marco."

"Who's Marco?"

"Our UPS guy," Lisa said, giving Audrey an odd look. "You don't know the delivery guys?"

"I'm not usually at the front desk when they come," Audrey said. She could have added, *That's your job,* but didn't want to sound bitchy. Besides, she had to admit, ever since Lisa had started working at the spa seven months earlier, there had been a definite step up in the quality of their deliveries. Packages used to get dumped by the front door; now they were all carefully hand-delivered to the pretty young receptionist.

"You should be. I bet Marco would really like you. He's more your age than mine anyway," Lisa said.

Ouch, Audrey thought. And why did everyone keep trying to set her up?

"Thanks, but no thanks. Marco and all of his fellow delivery men are all yours," Audrey said. She turned back to her computer, hoping Lisa would take the hint and leave.

She didn't. Instead, Lisa giggled and said, "I don't think my boyfriend would like that."

Ugh, Audrey thought. *I walked right into that one.*

Lisa's boyfriend, Jared, was a relatively new addition to her life—they'd only been dating for a few weeks—and Lisa was completely besotted. She required no encouragement to discuss him at length. Audrey had been forced to endure long, in-depth conversations about every word Jared spoke, every gesture he made. And since Audrey's impression of Jared—based on a single meeting when he picked Lisa up from work one night—was that he had the personality and intelligence of a Labrador retriever, she found these discussions beyond tedious.

"I should get back to . . ." Audrey gestured to her laptop.

"Last night, Jared asked me if I'd drive down to Key West with him," Lisa announced. She stretched her arms over her head, looking smugly content. "What do you think of that?"

"It sounds like fun," Audrey said, although in truth, she hated Key West and all of its tacky, touristy trappings.

"No, I mean what do you think it means?" Lisa said, leaning forward.

"If I were going to take a wild guess, I'd say I think it means he'd like to go to Key West. And that he'd like you to accompany him," Audrey said.

"You don't think it means he's ready to get serious?" Lisa asked.

"I have no idea. I don't know Jared well enough to say," Audrey said. Thankfully, the bell on the front door to the spa jingled just then. "You'd better get up front. Someone just came in."

Lisa reluctantly got to her feet and clumped out of the office on four-inch platform heel sandals. She was back a moment later.

"It's for you," Lisa said.

"Really? Okay, I'll be right there."

Lisa didn't move. She stood at the door, her eyes gleaming expectantly.

"What?" Audrey asked.

"It's a guy," Lisa said. "A really cute guy. Actually," she said, lowering her voice, "he's not cute so much as he is sexy. Like, really, *really* sexy."

Audrey had to stop herself from rolling her eyes. "Did you ask him what he wants to see me about?"

"No, I forgot," Lisa said, without a hint of apology in her voice. "I'll go tell him you're coming."

Lisa turned and clattered off again, before Audrey had a chance to ask her to find out what the man wanted or perhaps get his business card. Audrey closed her email and stood, shaking her head. She was going to have to have yet another talk with Lisa about her professional duties.

She headed out of her office, took a left, and walked down the short hallway to the doorway that led into the reception area. Then she stopped dead.

"Hey, there," Coop said.

He was leaning against the counter, propped up by one arm. Lisa was sitting in her chair, watching him with an avid sort of interest that Jared would most certainly not approve of.

"Oh. Hello. Can I help you?" Audrey said. She clasped her hands together, knowing she looked and sounded stiff, but not sure what she was supposed to do. Why was he here? Hadn't she made it clear that she wasn't interested in him?

"Actually, yes," Coop said, grinning lazily at her.

Audrey knew that the smile was meant to be sexy—and, in truth, it was—but the fact that he *knew* it was sexy just irritated her. It was exactly why she'd turned him down when he asked her out. His ego was out of control. She folded her arms and waited.

"I'm interested in signing up for one of your treatments," Coop said.

Audrey's eyebrows shot up. "*You* want a spa treatment?" she asked.

"That's right," Coop said. He shrugged. "But I've never done this before, so I need some guidance."

"Lisa would be more than happy to help you select a treatment and make an appointment for you," Audrey said smoothly.

Lisa nodded enthusiastically. "Sure," she said.

"I appreciate that," Coop said, flashing his smile in Lisa's direction. "But Audrey here was telling me all about the spa treatments she's developed especially for her male clients, and I was hoping to get some of her seasoned advice."

Smug bastard, Audrey thought, flushing. He was bringing up that night just to embarrass her. And *seasoned* advice? It made her sound geriatric.

Lisa's head was bobbing up and down. "Actually, Audrey knows a lot more about all of the procedures and stuff than I do. I'm just the receptionist," she confessed.

"Of course. How can I help?" Audrey asked smoothly.

Coop grinned at Audrey again and said, "What do you recommend?"

Audrey ran down the various treatments the spa offered, pointless as it seemed. He was surely going to opt for a massage. It was practically the only service straight men came to the spa for. This thought reminded her again of when she'd made a fool of herself trying to talk Coop into a *man*-icure. She could feel heat staining her cheeks, and knew by Coop's deepening grin that he'd noticed.

That's it, Audrey thought. *He asked for it.*

"Why don't you just leave yourself in my hands?" Audrey suggested.

"I like the sound of that," Coop said flirtatiously.

"Lisa, show Coop back to Farrah's station," Audrey said.

Lisa looked confused. "Farrah?" she said.

"That's right," Audrey said. "She has an opening for an m/p."

Lisa looked from Audrey to Coop and back to Audrey again. "But I wouldn't think . . . ," she tried again. Then, catching the quelling expression on her boss's face, Lisa shrugged helplessly, stood, and said, "Come right this way. Would you like some ice water with lemon in it?"

"I never say no to ice water with lemon," Coop drawled.

Audrey smiled, while fantasizing about kicking him in the shin with the pointy toe of her four-inch pumps. "Farrah will take good care of you," she promised.

Lisa led Coop away. Audrey went behind the desk and busied herself checking the appointment schedule again, while she waited for Lisa to come back. When the younger woman returned, she looked perplexed.

"Are you sure about this? He doesn't strike me as the sort of guy who'd want a mani-pedi. He looks more like the massage type."

"I'm sure," Audrey said. "Is Farrah with him?"

"Yes. She was just getting started with the manicure. He seemed a little confused when she told him to put his hand in the bowl of warm water, but he went along with it."

"Good," Audrey said with satisfaction. That would teach Coop not to play games with her. What was he thinking bothering her at work like this? Hadn't she made it perfectly clear that she wasn't interested when he asked her out to dinner? She had obviously been right about him. He *was* cocky, so much so that he obviously couldn't *conceive* of any woman rejecting him.

"Where do you know him from?" Lisa asked, interrupting her thoughts.

"What?" Audrey glanced up. "Oh. We have mutual friends."

Lisa smiled coyly. "You know that he's into you, right?"

Audrey's pulse gave a quick, nervous jump. "No, he's not. Not really."

"He totally is," Lisa said with relish.

"Why do you say that?" Audrey asked, although the conversation was starting to make her feel like a teenage girl with a crush on the star of her high school lacrosse team.

"I could tell by the way he was looking at you. And he obviously came into the spa to see you," Lisa said.

Audrey realized that this had officially become a conversation she didn't want to have with her airheaded, twenty-two-year-old employee. "I'll be in my office," she said, turning away.

But once she was back at her desk, staring at her computer screen and futilely trying to make sense of the payroll, Audrey realized that Coop's presence in the spa was making it impossible for her to concentrate.

Audrey's eyes fell on a cardboard box full of organic face creams she'd stashed in the corner of her office. She'd been meaning to make room for them on the bamboo display shelving that lined the entrance to the spa. It was just the sort of mindless busywork she could manage in her current state, she decided, and grabbing the box, headed back out of her office. But instead of taking the shorter route straight to the front, she hooked left and then right, so that she'd loop past Farrah's station, tucked back next to the massage room. She hadn't planned to spy on Coop, but once she was up and moving, she couldn't help herself.

I'll walk briskly past them and just sneak a peek, Audrey decided.

But the sight that met her eyes stopped her in her tracks.

Coop was sitting in one of the two raised pedicure chairs, his faded jeans rolled up to his shins and his feet soaking in soapy water. Farrah—short and round, with hennaed hair and tattooed arms—was sitting at his feet, looking up adoringly at him. Coop grinned when he saw Audrey.

"Having fun?" she asked.

"I had never had my nails buffed before. I feel like one of those mob guys in the movies," Coop said. He held up his hands to show her his nails, which did look especially clean and shiny.

"Mob guys get manicures?" Audrey asked.

"Apparently. At least, Hollywood's version of the mob. The wiseguys are always getting manicures, and those hot towel shaves and massages," Coop said.

"And this is behavior you want to emulate?" Audrey asked, her eyebrows arching high. She shifted the box of face creams to her left hip.

"Fuggedaboutit," Coop said in a throaty voice, waving one manicured hand around.

Farrah giggled and held up a towel. "Give me one foot," she said.

Coop obliged, lifting one tanned foot out of the water. Farrah toweled it off and then began rubbing it with exfoliant cream. Coop laughed and squirmed.

"That tickles," Coop said.

"It smoothes your skin," she explained. "You don't want to have nasty scaly patches on your feet, do you?"

"I don't know. Do I?"

"No, you don't," Farrah purred, clearly deeply infatuated.

"I'll leave you to your pedicure," Audrey said.

"No, don't go," Coop said. "Keep me company."

Audrey hesitated. *Just go,* she told herself. *Don't feed into his ego.*

"There's an empty seat right here. We can have a lemon water together," Coop said temptingly, gesturing toward the empty pedicure station. Even though Farrah was the only nail technician on staff, Audrey had opted to put in a double pedicure station when she opened the spa, which allowed girlfriends or a mother and daughter pair to get pedicures together.

"I guess I have a minute," Audrey said, setting the box down in a corner.

"Okay, put that foot back in the water, and give me your other foot," Farrah instructed Coop, as Audrey climbed somewhat tentatively up onto the pedicure chair. It wasn't the easiest task to manage in four-inch heels.

"Did you see Leland's email with the menu for the next dinner party club?" Audrey asked.

"No. What's he serving?"

"Something called S and M chicken," Audrey said. She smiled. "What on earth does that mean?"

Coop laughed. "Let me guess—bacon is somehow involved."

Audrey nodded. "I definitely remember bacon being well represented on the menu."

Farrah wrinkled her nose. "Gross," she said.

Coop looked down at her in surprise. "You don't like bacon?"

"I'm a vegetarian," Farrah said.

"I guess I'll just have to eat extra meat for you," Coop teased.

Audrey expected Farrah to get huffy. She was the sort of vegetarian who made pointed comments about "food with faces" while eating with non-vegetarians. When Audrey took her staff out for a holiday lunch the previous December, Farrah made gagging sounds when Lisa ordered a cheeseburger, and a fight nearly broke out at the table. But, apparently, it was a different story when the gentle teasing came from an attractive man, for Farrah just giggled and began rubbing Coop's foot with a pumice stone.

"Do mafia guys get pedicures, too?" Audrey asked.

"Somehow I doubt it. It's not very manly, is it?" Coop said. He shot Audrey a sideways grin. "But something tells me that you knew that when you suggested this."

"I just thought you'd enjoy it."

"I am enjoying it," Coop said. He wiggled his toes. "And, after all, what man doesn't want to have pretty feet? All of the guys at the editing studio will be so jealous."

Audrey couldn't help laughing. Coop was being a good sport, she'd have to give him that.

"Tell me more about the movie you're working on," she said, kicking off her heels, and tucking one foot underneath her leg. "You said it was about the effect of tidal waters on migrating sea animals, right?"

FRAN BALANCED THE POTTED orchid in her left hand and rang Leland's doorbell with her right. A few minutes passed before Leland came to the door—he moved slowly these days, which worried Fran—but when he saw her, he beamed.

"What a nice surprise," Leland said. He was wearing a crisp white apron over his golf shirt and khaki shorts. His bulldog, Winston, sniffed in Fran's direction, before sitting down with a deep sigh, as though the effort of walking to the door was too much to bear. "Come in, come in."

"You look like you're busy," Fran said, hesitating. She bent over to pet Winston on his white head. In return, he snorted and slobbered into her hand. "I'm just here to drop off this orchid for you. They were having a sale on them today at the farmers' market. Isn't it pretty?"

"It is. Thank you," Leland said, taking the orchid. "But you have to come in. I was just about to make lunch. No, no refusals, I insist."

"Are you all ready for tonight?" Fran asked, as she followed Leland, Winston at his heels, back to the kitchen. Most of the interior was still painted the boring beige shade the builder had slapped on. But the kitchen was the one room Leland had put his imprint on. The kitchen walls were a sunny yellow, and all of the cabinets had been painted a crisp glossy white. A framed poster of Picasso's *Petite Fleurs* hung on one wall. Winston hopped into his basket, circled three times, lay down, and was instantly asleep.

"I was just putting the finishing touches on my dessert," Leland said, setting the orchid down in the middle of the oak pedestal table.

"It looks amazing," Fran said, admiring the towering coconut layer cake rising up from a glass cake stand. "A real showstopper."

"Baking has always been my favorite of the culinary arts. There's something so magical about it. You mix together ordinary ingredients—butter, sugar, flour, and eggs—and somehow they transform into something special," Leland said.

"I think you missed your calling. You could have been a master pastry chef," Fran said. She perched on one of the tall wooden stools lined up in front of the island.

"Would you like a glass of wine?" Leland asked.

Fran glanced at the clock. "It's only eleven-thirty," she said.

"So? If we were French, we'd have consumed a whole bottle before lunch even started," Leland said.

"That's true. And it is a Saturday," Fran said. "What the hell, why not? I'm easily persuaded."

Leland uncorked a bottle of Sauvignon Blanc and poured them each a glass.

"Yum," Fran said, taking a sip.

"It will go well with our lunch," Leland said. He opened the refrigerator and began pulling out eggs, spinach, cold red potatoes, and, of course, bacon.

"You really don't have to cook for me. You are hosting a dinner party tonight, after all," Fran said. "Better yet, why don't you sit down and let me cook lunch?"

"No, let me enjoy cooking for a beautiful lady. It happens all too rarely these days. Just keep me company," Leland said. Brandishing a large chef's knife, he began to dice the bacon. And it will give us a chance to talk."

"Uh-oh," Fran said. "Am I in trouble?"

"You? Never. It's only that I've noticed you haven't seemed yourself lately."

"Really? How so?"

"You've seemed distracted. And your gardenias need watering. It's not like you to neglect them," Leland said.

"I guess I have been a little distracted," Fran said. She twirled the wineglass in her hand. "When I'm at work, I'm thinking about the girls or what needs doing around the house. And when I'm at home, I'm thinking about work, I can't seem to settle to anything."

Fran didn't add that the one constant in her otherwise scattered thoughts was Coop. Ever since the day she'd seen him in the wine store, she hadn't been able to stop thinking about him. She knew it was stupid to obsess—Coop clearly wasn't interested in her, and besides, there was the not-insignificant detail that she was married. And yet, it was out of her control. She found her mind wandering throughout the day, imagining scenarios in which she and Coop might bump into each other. Feeling his lips grazing over her cheek as he kissed her in greeting. Picturing herself touching his arm lightly as they spoke.

If she was feeling particularly fanciful, these daydreams would spin into increasingly outlandish scenarios. Coop confessing his attraction to her. A hastily arranged assignation. And, once there, ripping each other's clothes off . . .

No, Fran thought. *Stop it.* She wondered if she was having a midlife crisis, or if it could possibly be some sort of hormonal imbalance.

She and Coop had always flirted with each other. Why, after all these years, was her imagination getting carried away? And to such X-rated places? Had there always been an attraction between them that she was just now noticing? Or had it come about recently? Maybe it had to do with the decline of her marriage. These days, she and Will were like roommates—companionable and comfortable and utterly passionless. Fran had tolerated the situation for years, assuming it was where all couples ended up eventually, and that on balance, it was all right.

Except that now, suddenly, it wasn't.

"It happens. You just have to be careful," Leland said. He transferred the bacon and what looked like minced shallots into a hot skillet, where the mixture began to sizzle at once.

Fran looked up, startled, wondering if he'd been reading her thoughts. Did he mean she had to be careful about Coop? Dear God, had she been so obvious? Then she remembered the last thing she'd said out loud was that she'd been distracted lately.

That's an understatement, Fran thought.

"Careful, how?" Fran asked.

"You don't want to spend so much time worrying about life that you miss out on it while it's happening," Leland said, stirring the bacon with a heat-proof spatula. He looked up from his work and smiled wryly. The network of lines on his face creased like a paper fan. "I sound like an old fart, don't I?"

"Never," Fran said. "And you're absolutely right. I've been in my head too often lately. I need to be more present."

She meant what she said. And yet, the fantasies about Coop—of kissing Coop, feeling his arms around her, the imagined lovemaking—were irresistible. She was too addicted to them to give them up. It was like jelly beans—as long as they were in reach, she was incapable of not eating them. The only solution was to never keep them in the house. But what did you do when the thing you were addicted to existed inside your own thoughts?

Leland used a slotted spoon to scoop the sizzling bacon and shallot mixture onto a plate lined with paper towels, and poured the bacon grease into a Pyrex measuring cup. Then he measured two tablespoons of the bacon fat back into the hot frying pan and dumped in the chopped cold red potatoes.

"That smells delicious," Fran said. "And very fattening."

"Nonsense. A little bacon grease never hurt anyone. And besides, you could use some fattening up. You look like you've lost weight."

"I have," Fran said proudly. "But on purpose. The last thing I want is to get fat again."

"I've never understood why modern women are so obsessed with being thin. You all want to look like little boys, with no curves," Leland said, stirring the potatoes as they browned to keep them from sticking to the bottom of the frying pan.

"Not quite," Fran said. "We want to be stick thin, but with large breasts and round bums. That's the ideal."

"Your ideal is something that doesn't occur in nature. At least not very often," Leland said.

"And that's what plastic surgery is for," Fran said.

Leland shook his head and made a tutting sound. "In my day, women weren't afraid to look like women. And men always prefer curves to bones."

"Didn't Scarlett O'Hara have a sixteen inch waist?" Fran teased.

Leland pointed his spatula at her. "I may be old, but Scarlett O'Hara was before my time, thank you very much," he said.

Fran grinned back at him. She took another sip of her wine and felt herself relax for the first time in days. Leland finished browning the potatoes and moved them to a small serving dish. He salted and peppered the potatoes, and tossed them with a bit of white vinegar. He added more bacon

grease to the pan—"More grease?" Fran exclaimed—and, ignoring her, dropped diced garlic into the fat. After the garlic
had sautéed for less than a minute, Leland tossed several
large handfuls of baby spinach into the pan. Once the spinach had wilted, he divided it between two plates and then
spooned the potatoes over it. Fran's mouth was starting to
water.

"That looks fantastic," she said.

"One last step," Leland said. He added yet another tablespoon of fat to the pan—Fran was starting to lose track of
just how much grease was going into this dish—and then
cracked two eggs into it. He fried the eggs and slid one on to
each plate, settling them on top of the potatoes. Moving
slowly and carefully, he set one plate in front of Fran and one
on the counter next to her, and got out silverware, napkins,
a bottle of hot sauce, and the wine bottle.

"This looks like a truly decadent lunch," Fran said.

"My mother used to make a version of it to use up leftover potatoes," Leland said, settling on the stool next to
Fran's. "The spinach is my own addition, though. I thought
it would make the dish healthier."

"Right. Because the addition of spinach cancels out the
four gallons of bacon grease," Fran teased.

They each doused their eggs with hot sauce, and then,
following Leland's lead, Fran cut into her egg so that the hot
yolk ran into the potatoes. She took a forkful, making sure to
get a bit of each ingredient in the bite, and tasted it.

"Wow. These are seriously the best fried potatoes I've
ever had," she said, pointing to the dish with the tines of her
fork. "How is it that something so simple can taste so good?"

"It's the bacon. I told you, it makes everything taste better," Leland said.

"When you're right, you're right," Fran said, taking another, larger bite. She glanced at Winston, who was still asleep in his basket. "Does Winston always snore like that?"

"Yes. He snores louder than my wife used to," Leland said.

As if he'd been listening, Winston let out a particularly loud, snarfling sigh.

Fran laughed. "Your wife did not snore like that."

"She did! It was awful, used to drive me crazy. But you want to know the funny thing? After she died, I found I couldn't sleep without her. The room was too quiet. I did some research on what dog breeds had snoring problems and English bulldogs were at the top of the list. So I got Winston here," Leland said. His face creased with concern. "Fran, are you all right?"

Fran nodded and smiled, dabbing at the hot tears that had started leaking out of her eyes.

"That's a beautiful story," she said, sniffling.

"I don't know about that. If my wife were here, she'd be furious I was telling people that she snored," Leland said, chuckling and shaking his head.

Fran touched his arm. "Somehow I don't think she would be angry at all," she said.

"TO THE THIRD MEETING of the Table for Seven Dinner Party Club," Leland said, raising his glass.

"Cheers," the others chorused, also raising their glasses and clinking them together.

"Everything looks absolutely lovely, Leland," Fran said.

"Yes, it does," Audrey said admiringly. Leland had set a

classically elegant table—a starched white tablecloth, silver candlesticks, a crystal bowl filled with pink peonies. The chilled vichyssoise, served in shallow china bowls, was a pretty pale green.

Audrey risked a covert glance at Coop, who was sitting just to her right and looking particularly sexy tonight— tanned and relaxed, and wearing a blue oxford shirt with the sleeves rolled up. She had to admit—even if it was just to herself—that he'd been in her thoughts ever since he'd come into the spa. Coop had been chatting across the table with Will and was smiling at something Will had said. Suddenly his pale eyes cut toward Audrey, and her heart lurched in response. Audrey quickly looked away and back at Fran, who was saying, "Inquiring minds want to know, Leland—what exactly is S and M chicken?"

"I wondered about that, too," Jaime said, smiling.

"What's this about S and M chicken?" Mark asked, raising his eyebrows. He leaned toward Audrey and murmured flirtatiously, "These dinner parties are finally getting interesting."

Audrey smiled politely. She'd never taken to Mark. He always reminded her of the male love interest in a Jane Austen novel, the sort who is superficially charming and handsome, but turns out to be a cad in the end, leaving the heroine free to fall in love with the boring, more honorable gentleman.

"It's a recipe I borrowed from Julia Child," Leland said. "Although I took some liberty with the name."

"How do you make it?" Fran asked.

"To quote Ms. Child, you start with a 'fine, fresh chicken.' You slather it with butter, making sure to get some of the butter up under the skin. Then you stuff a lemon and some herbs up inside the chicken, and tie its legs closed," Leland said. He winked at Jaime. "The recipe sounded so naughty, I decided to rename it S and M Chicken."

Everyone laughed. Spoons were lifted and the soup tasted—*excellent,* Audrey thought, *cool and refreshing, the perfect first course.* Crusty bread nestled in a napkin-lined basket was passed around next.

"Coop, you are officially Rory's hero," Will said. "She was thrilled with the snapper she caught."

"So was I. I made a beurre blanc sauce to go with it. It was delicious," Fran said.

"You took Rory fishing?" Audrey asked Coop. She tried to picture this and was surprised that she easily could. Coop seemed like the kind of guy who'd get along well with kids.

Coop shrugged. "It was the least I could do. She is my goddaughter, after all."

"No, she isn't," Fran said.

"She isn't?" Coop asked, his brow wrinkling in confusion.

"No. Iris is your goddaughter," Fran said, starting to laugh.

"You really should keep that straight," Audrey said.

"I knew it was one of the two. And I invited them both to go fishing, but Iris wasn't interested," Coop said.

"Iris isn't interested in anything other than going to the mall and texting her friends. When I try to talk to her, she just grunts at me," Fran said. She took a sip of wine. "Ah, the joys of living with a teenage daughter."

"It was nice of you to take Rory out," Audrey said, feeling almost shy as she glanced at Coop under lowered lashes.

Coop shrugged and smiled. "It was my pleasure, even if she isn't my goddaughter."

"Actually, Rory's my goddaughter," Audrey said, taking another spoonful of soup.

"Really? If Iris is my goddaughter and Rory is your god-daughter, does that mean you and I are related?" Coop asked.

"No," Audrey said, smiling at him. "It doesn't work that way."

Mark, who was sitting to Audrey's left, tapped her arm to get her attention. "Have you been seeing anyone, Audrey?" he asked.

Audrey cringed. She didn't have to look to know that Coop's eyes were still on her. Why on earth was Jaime's annoying husband asking her such a personal question at a dinner party? Thankfully, Jaime came to the rescue.

"Mark! You're not supposed to ask single people that question," Jaime said.

Mark looked at his wife blankly. "Why not?"

"Because it's rude and intrusive. And you're putting Audrey on the spot," Jaime said. "Audrey, ignore Mark. Or, if you want to distract him, ask him about tennis."

"I want to hear if you're dating anyone," Coop murmured, leaning in so close, Audrey could feel the warm swoosh of his breath in her ear.

Good grief. Am I actually getting goose bumps? she thought. *This is ridiculous. I'm like a schoolgirl with a crush on the inappropriate bad boy. This must stop. Now.*

"No, I'm not dating anyone," Audrey said calmly. "I'm running a business. That doesn't leave much time for romance. I have been thinking of getting a dog, though."

This caused an amused rumble of laughter.

"The girls have always wanted a dog. They swear up and down that I won't have to lift a finger, and that they'll do everything. Walk it, clean up after it. But I know better. They'll lose interest within two weeks, and I'll be the one standing outside in the pouring rain, huddled under an umbrella, trying to convince the dog to pee," Fran said.

"Fran is more devious than she looks," Will said, smiling at his wife. "She got the girls a betta fish and told them that if they looked after it, we'd talk about getting a dog."

"What happened?" Jaime asked.

"I don't think three days passed before the pair of them lost all interest in the fish. And, just as I predicted, I was the one who had to feed him and clean his bowl and do pretty much everything," Fran said.

"You make it sound like you slaved over that fish," Will said, laughing. "Didn't he die after a week?"

"Yes. Clearly the pet store sold us a geriatric fish. It was very cynical and wrong of them," Fran said darkly. "And, anyway, I've never had the greatest track record keeping fish alive."

"I think it's good for children to grow up with pets. I had a chocolate Lab named Hershey when I was a kid, and I loved him to pieces. I just want to wait until Ava and Logan are a little older before we get a dog," Jaime said.

"I didn't know you were interested in getting a dog. Emily's been asking for one for ages, but her mother's allergic. Or claims she is, although I always suspected that my ex-wife just doesn't like animals," Mark said.

"What sort of a person doesn't like animals?" Leland asked.

"Exactly. I did say my ex-wife," Mark said. Then, turning back to Jaime, he said, "Maybe we should look into getting her one to keep at our house."

Jaime buttered a roll. Without looking up, she said, "Like I said, I think we should wait until the kids are a little bit older."

"Why wait? You just said that it's good for kids to grow up with pets," Mark said.

"It's a big decision. I don't want to rush into it right now," Jaime said.

"I just think—" Mark began.

"Can we talk about this later please?" Jaime asked, her tone sharp.

Audrey wished she hadn't brought up the topic of dogs. She had only been trying to deflect Mark's intrusive question about the status of her love life. It was turning out to be one of those prickly sort of nights. She remembered them from her married days. Tempers frayed, conflict threatening to flare up out of nowhere, and over nothing.

Coop lightly touched her shoulder. "Looks like you've started a fight," he said.

"No, she hasn't," Jaime said. "I'm sorry. I'm just a little cranky tonight. Ava was up half the night."

"Why? Is she sick?" Fran asked.

"No. I don't know what's going on with her. She's been getting up three, four, even five times a night. I keep waking up to the sound of heavy breathing and then when I open my eyes, her face will be an inch away from mine," Jaime said. "Sure, go ahead and laugh, but it keeps scaring the hell out of me. And then I can't fall back asleep, because I'm waiting for her to come in again."

"Luckily, I manage to sleep through this," Mark said.

"That's because she never does it to you! She always comes to my side of the bed," Jaime said.

Mark smiled what Audrey knew he probably thought to be his most charming smile. "I struck a deal with Ava. If she lets Daddy sleep, I'll buy her a pony when she's older."

"I once had a divorce case come before me where the couple had drawn up a premarital contract ahead of time about pretty much every aspect of their marriage in great detail—who would do what around the house, even who would get up with the kids at night," Leland said.

"What? Who would put that in a premarital contract?" Fran exclaimed.

"And who got the job of getting up with the kids? Because that's the worst," Will said. "Fran always made me do it. I didn't get a full night's sleep for five years straight."

"You are such a liar!" Fran said. She turned to Jaime. "I swear, men have a genetic ability to sleep through middle-of-the-night summons from their children."

"Under the terms of the premarital contract, the wife was supposed to take care of all child-related tasks, unless she'd secured an agreement from the husband ahead of time to cover for her," Leland said.

"That's not misogynistic or anything," Fran said, rolling her eyes.

"Well, yes. The contract was the husband's idea. He struck me as being a bit controlling. It's not a surprise his wife eventually had enough and filed for divorce," Leland said. "The contract also covered what sort of religious upbringing the children would have, how often they'd visit their in-laws, even how many times a week they'd have sex."

"I don't practice family law, but that sort of contract wouldn't be legally enforceable," Mark said.

"How many times a week were they obligated to have sex?" Will asked.

"That's the part he would be interested in," Fran remarked.

"If I remember correctly, it was three," Leland said, smiling.

"Wow," Will said reverently. "Three times a week? Maybe we should make one of those agreements, honey."

"Mark just said it wasn't enforceable," Fran said.

"Will, you're making Fran blush," Coop teased.

Audrey looked at Fran, who was sitting at the head of the table opposite Leland. Coop was right; Fran's cheeks were flushed. Actually, Fran was looking unusually pretty tonight, Audrey thought. She was wearing a red halter sundress that showed off her cleavage, and it looked as though she'd taken more care with her hair and makeup than usual.

"Can we please change the subject?" Fran asked. She reached for her wineglass, but ended up knocking it over instead. A dark red stain spread over the white tablecloth.

"Oh, no!" Fran said, staring at the stain in horror.

"Don't worry," Leland said. "It's just a tablecloth."

"But I've ruined it!"

"It's not ruined," Audrey said, rising quickly from her seat. "Leland, do you have any hydrogen peroxide?"

"There should be some in the medicine cabinet in the bathroom," Leland said.

"I'll get it," Coop said, also standing.

Audrey hurried to the kitchen, where she poured about eight ounces of liquid dish-washing soap into a glass measuring cup. She took the soap and a handful of paper towels back to the dining room, just as Coop returned with a brown plastic bottle of hydrogen peroxide. He handed it to Audrey.

"Thanks," she said. She added a cup of hydrogen peroxide to the glass cup, dipped a paper towel into the mixture, and then used it to dab the stain.

"Will that work?" Fran asked. She looked near tears. Her eyes were shining and she had flushed an even darker shade of scarlet.

"Every time. See? It's already coming out," Audrey said.

Everyone leaned forward to see. The stain was disappearing, leaving behind white, if wet, fabric.

"It's like magic," Will marveled.

"I've never heard of using hydrogen peroxide on wine stains before," Jaime said. "Where did you learn that trick?"

"I read it years ago in one of those housekeeping columns they have in the paper, and ended up clipping the column. Ryan was forever spilling glasses of red wine. He always got klutzy when he was . . ." Audrey stopped and swallowed. "Well, anyway. I managed to save a beautiful ivory linen tablecloth that had once belonged to my grandmother with this trick."

Even though the crisis had passed, Fran had her lips pressed tightly together and was blinking rapidly. Audrey squeezed Fran's shoulder gently as she returned to her seat, and tried to think of something to say that would make Fran feel better.

"Franny, do you know what I was thinking about the other day? That time that you, Will, and I went down to South Beach, and we convinced those tourists that Will was one of the Thompson Twins," Coop said.

Fran laughed, the tension in her face disappearing. "Oh, my God, I'd forgotten all about that. That was hilarious. Remember, they asked for his autograph?"

"Wait, what? The Thompson Twins?" Jaime asked.

"That eighties band," Fran explained.

"I couldn't believe they fell for it. Never mind that I was way too young to have been in that band—they must all be about twenty years older than I am—but I'm also not British," Will said.

"But then, right in the middle of the conversation, you realized that you were supposed to be English and started speaking with that awful fake accent," Coop said.

"Hey! It was not awful," Will said, affronted.

"Yes, it was. You actually said, 'Pip, pip, cheerio,' at one point," Fran said, giggling.

Audrey smiled and took a sip of wine. The mood around the table lightened considerably, as Will demonstrated his accent—Coop and Fran were right, it was truly terrible—and everyone laughed as Fran recounted how the tourists had asked for Will's autograph. She snuck a sideways glance at Coop, who was grinning, his teeth white against his darkly tanned skin. He had missed a spot shaving at his left jaw, leaving behind a small patch of blond hair, about the size of a dime. Coop's eyes flickered in her direction, and Audrey felt her heart give another involuntary jump. The laughter and talk grew louder and more uproarious around them.

"I'll go get the main course," Leland said, rising slowly.

Audrey glanced up at him. Leland looked happy, but tired. She wondered if hosting the dinner party had been too much for him. "Let me help you," Audrey said quickly, rising from her seat.

But even as she accompanied Leland into the kitchen, she could have sworn that she could still feel Coop's eyes on her. She experienced an odd mixture of exhilaration and terror at how pleased she was at the thought.

may

.. ..

MINI BLUE CHEESE SOUFFLÉS

MUSTARD CRUSTED RACK OF LAMB

WILD MUSHROOM POTATO GRATIN

ENGLISH PEAS WITH MINT

STRAWBERRY-RHUBARB PIE

COOP AND AUDREY MET for lunch at the Salty Dog the following Thursday. Coop hadn't planned to ask her out again, and yet somehow, as they were walking to their respective cars after dinner at Leland's house, he found himself blurting out an invitation to lunch. It was even more surprising when Audrey accepted. Now, Coop felt oddly nervous and wondered if he was sweating through his shirt. She, on the other hand, seemed annoyingly calm. Serene, almost.

"Would you like some wine?" he asked.

Audrey hesitated. "I really shouldn't. I have to go back to work." Then she seemed to shrug off this reservation. "Actually, I'd love a glass of Chardonnay."

Maybe she is nervous, Coop thought. He hoped so. He didn't want to be the only one.

When the waitress appeared with two glasses of ice water and hot rolls wrapped in a white napkin, Coop ordered a bottle of Chardonnay from the Russian River Valley in California. He wasn't normally a white wine drinker, but the Salty Dog was known for its seafood. The Chardonnay would be a good match.

He and Audrey both studied their menus in silence, while the waitress returned with the wine. He ordered the snapper special, and Audrey opted for the scallops.

"Do you like the wine?" Coop asked.

Audrey took a sip and nodded. "Very good," she said.

Coop figured they could either ignore the awkwardness between them or address it outright. "I was surprised you agreed to have lunch with me," he said.

"I was, too," Audrey said. "I meant to say no, but then . . ." She shrugged. "I don't know what happened. The 'yes' just sort of popped out."

Coop gave a comical pump of his fist. "I've still got it! Wait, I shouldn't even joke about that around you. You already think I'm conceited."

"Yes, I'm not sure how you're able to get dressed in the morning," Audrey said. Her expression was solemn, but there was a glint in her eye that Coop liked.

"Why's that?" he asked.

"How do you get your shirt on over such a swollen head?" She grinned.

Coop shook his head. "I walked into that one. Anyway, why didn't you want to go out with me before?"

"Fran told me about your . . . proclivities," Audrey said delicately.

"Proclivities? Jesus. I'm almost afraid to ask. Did she say anything about rubber underwear?"

Audrey laughed. She had a nice laugh, Coop decided. Deep and heartfelt.

"No, but now I'm actually worried," she said.

"What exactly did Franny say?" Coop asked.

"She said you date a lot," Audrey said.

"So?"

"A *lot*," Audrey said.

Realization dawned. Fran had made him out to be some sort of a playboy. Which annoyed him more than it should have. He'd dated a fair number of women, but surely that was normal for any forty-five-year-old man who'd never been married. It hardly seemed the sort of information that should be used against him.

"What else did Franny tell you?" Coop asked, not at all sure he wanted to hear the answer, especially when Audrey seemed to hesitate. He sighed. "Just tell me."

"It's not a big deal." Audrey shrugged. "I'm not into relationships, either."

"Not into relationhips? Is that what Fran said about me?"

Audrey nodded and raised one shoulder in a half-shrug. "It's not that bad."

"I'm not saying it's bad, but it's just not true. Franny doesn't know everything about my personal life, you know," Coop said.

"Really?" Audrey's eyebrows rose. "When was the last time you were in a relationship?"

Coop had to think about it and realized he couldn't remember. Samantha? No, he'd dated Vanessa after Samantha. How long ago had that been?

"Well, when was the last time *you* were in a relationship?" Coop asked, feeling suddenly defensive.

Audrey didn't hesitate. "My husband," she said.

"But that was what? Five years ago?" Coop asked.

"He passed away seven years ago," Audrey said.

"Then I've been in a relationship more recently than you have," Coop said triumphantly.

"It's not a contest."

"Of course it is. Especially if Fran is going around telling people I'm some sort of an unreliable bounder," Coop said.

Audrey laughed. "I don't think she actually used the term *bounder*."

"From what you've said, she implied it," Coop said.

Before Audrey could respond, the waitress appeared with their salads, offered freshly ground pepper, and then departed.

"What happened?" Audrey asked, spearing the mesclun mix with her fork.

"With what?" Coop asked. He'd ordered a wedge of iceberg dressed with creamy blue cheese, and was busy cutting the lettuce into edible bites.

"With your last relationship," Audrey reminded him.

"Oh, right. Vanessa. We dated for a few months and then things just sort of fizzled out," Coop said. He shrugged. "It happens."

"That's not exactly a long-term relationship," Audrey said.

"Not a one-night stand, either."

"I think your standards might be a little low."

"Really, because I was just thinking yours might be a bit too high," Coop said, which made Audrey laugh. "I almost got engaged once."

"You did? Really?"

"Your disbelief is so flattering," Coop said dryly.

"What happened?"

"Well, ah . . ." Coop wished he hadn't brought it up.

"Spit it out," Audrey said.

She seemed to be enjoying his discomfort, Coop thought. And he had to admit, he was enjoying amusing Audrey, even if the conversation was not personally flattering. When Audrey smiled, a small dimple appeared in the corner of her mouth. Coop was quickly becoming obsessed with it.

"Her name was Samantha. She gave me an ultimatum.

We had to either get engaged or we were through," Coop said.

Audrey grinned, waiting for the punch line. "And?"

"And we broke up," Coop confessed. "But I almost went for it, I swear."

Audrey laughed again, and Coop held up the wine bottle. "More wine?"

THE REST OF LUNCH passed by in a pleasant haze as they chatted. Between the wine and Coop's easy manner, Audrey actually started to relax. She could feel the tension in her shoulders loosen, and found herself smiling more.

Coop charmed her with a story about his boyhood obsession with fire trucks, thanks in part to the location of a fire station down the block. One night, when he was six, he snuck out of bed, crept down the street, and climbed up into the cab of a fire truck, left unlocked by a forgetful sergeant. When his parents discovered his empty bed, they panicked and called 911, and the excitable operator dispatched both the police and the fire department to his house. An on-duty fireman found Coop curled up asleep on the vinyl bench seat, and gave him the treat of his life by taking him home in the fire truck, complete with the lights flashing and siren wailing.

Audrey found herself admitting that her girlhood ambition had been to be a professional ice skater. And despite the fact that there wasn't an ice rink in her small Florida hometown and that she'd never actually ever been ice skating, she was undeterred. She was convinced that, given the chance, she'd be an Ice Capades star. Every Saturday afternoon, when ice-skating competitions were aired, she'd stand in front of the television, pretending her T-shirt and shorts were a satin and sequin short gown, and she'd twirl and jump around the room.

And then, at some point, long after they'd finished their lunch and were lingering over the last of the wine, Coop's fingers had lightly brushed Audrey's forearm. Audrey had suddenly become consumed with lust. It seemed unreal, and yet, there was no getting around it. She wanted Coop. Badly.

After that everything happened quickly. Audrey left her car behind at the restaurant—she was too light-headed to drive—and rode with Coop in his truck back to his condo. No sooner were they inside—Audrey barely had time to register the large shaggy dog which nosed at her knees, until Coop pushed him aside, muttering, "Not now, Bear"—then Coop reached for her. Suddenly, Coop's arms were around Audrey, and they were kissing. Clothes were shed. Coop was leading her back to his bedroom. They were falling together on an unmade bed.

What am I doing? Audrey wondered, suddenly swamped by a wave of panic.

But then Coop kissed her again. And for a long while, Audrey didn't think of anything at all.

AS SOON AS IT was over—Coop rolled on his back, his eyes closed, his breath shallow—Audrey's panic returned This was a terrible idea. She'd been celibate for over a year. And now here she was, thoughtlessly, hell, practically *drunkenly,* jumping into bed with a man she barely knew.

Audrey couldn't help remembering the first time she'd slept with Ryan. They'd met their senior year of college at the University of Florida and had dated for over a month before going to bed together. And even then, she'd had long, heartfelt discussions with Fran over whether that was moving too fast.

Ryan. God, I just cheated on Ryan, Audrey thought, suddenly flooded with guilt. But, no, that was ridiculous. Ryan had been dead for seven years. And she hadn't felt this sort of guilt when she'd slept with the handful of other men there had been in the past seven years. Why was that? Maybe because she'd never lost her composure, not even for a moment on those occasions. With Coop, it had been the complete opposite. Sleeping with him hadn't even been a conscious decision, but a spontaneous event that had seemed entirely out of her control.

"How are you doing?" Coop asked sleepily. He rolled toward Audrey, and slung an arm over her torso. She instantly felt claustrophobic.

"I have to go," Audrey said, sitting up abruptly.

"What?" Coop opened one eye to peer at her. "Why?"

"Work," Audrey said. "I have to get back to the spa. I told Lisa she could go home early." The lie slipped out before she had time to think it through. There was really no reason for her to rush back. Lisa was scheduled to be there until five.

"What time do you have to be back by?" Coop asked.

What time had they left the restaurant? Audrey wondered. "Two-thirty."

Coop leaned over and picked up a small alarm clock from the bedside table. "It's three."

"Oh, no," Audrey said, jumping up with alarm. It was as if the lie had suddenly become the truth, and she really was worried about being late for work. "Where are my clothes?"

She didn't wait for his answer, but followed the trail of clothing that started at the foot of the bed and led all the way to the front door. The shaggy brown dog reappeared, wagging his tail and looking at her expectantly. Audrey buttoned her blouse with shaky hands and wiggled into her pencil skirt.

"You missed one," Coop said. He had appeared in the doorway to his bedroom, still stark naked, his blond hair rumpled.

"What?" Audrey asked defensively.

"A button," Coop said.

Audrey looked down. He was right, the front of her blouse was askew, none of the buttons in their proper buttonholes. Coop stepped toward her.

"What are you doing?" Audrey asked, alarmed. Somehow, being this close to him while she was dressed and he was naked seemed even more intimate than sleeping together had.

"Helping," Coop said calmly. He unbuttoned her blouse, and then buttoned it up properly. "There."

"Oh. Thanks," Audrey said.

"Happy to oblige," Coop said. He peered down at her. "Are you okay? You seem a little stressed out."

"I'm fine. I just hate being late," Audrey said.

"Why don't you call work and let them know you're on your way," Coop suggested.

"No, that's okay. Could you take me back to my car?"

"Sure. Where did I put my keys?" Coop asked, looking around, his hands on his hips.

"They might be in your pants pocket. Which you might also want to consider putting on before we leave," Audrey suggested.

"Oh, right," Coop said, looking down with surprise, as if he'd forgotten he wasn't wearing any clothes.

They were both quiet on the drive back to the restaurant. When the silence became too awkward to bear, Audrey cleared her throat and said, "It's warm out today." And then immediately wanted to slap herself on the forehead. The weather? Could she bring up anything more inane?

"Would you like me to turn the air conditioner on?" Coop asked courteously.

"No, thank you," Audrey said, just as politely.

We have officially turned into Chip 'n' Dale, she thought.

After what seemed like an agonizingly long trip—Audrey was fairly sure they hit every red light between Coop's condo and the Salty Dog—Coop pulled up next to Audrey's car.

"Thanks," Audrey said. She busied herself collecting her bag, getting out her keys, putting on her sunglasses.

"Anytime," Coop said, his voice edged with irony.

Audrey turned to look at him. "I meant for dropping me off," she said.

"Oh, right. Me, too." Coop smiled. "What are you doing for dinner tomorrow night?"

"Dinner?" Audrey blinked. She was no longer the least bit drunk, but her brain felt like machinery that had been rusted through, the wheels and cogs frozen in place.

"Yes. The meal that comes at the end of the day. After lunch, but before bedtime."

"Thanks, I know what dinner is."

"I wasn't sure. You seemed confused. What do you think? We can go out, or I can cook. Get some practice for when it's my turn to host the dinner party club," Coop said.

Audrey knew what she thought: It was a truly terrible idea. Right now, all she wanted to do was to get away from Coop, from the sheer physical presence of him, and retreat to somewhere cool and quiet until her head started working properly again.

"No. I don't think so," she said, so intent on fleeing that she was more abrupt than she meant to be. She risked a quick look at Coop and saw the hurt clouding his eyes. "Look, it's just . . . I meant what I said earlier. This is a bad idea. I don't think we're well suited."

"I thought we were suited just fine," Coop said, his eyebrows arching.

Audrey felt her cheeks grow hot. "I think we should just be friends," she said, knowing that this was the oldest, lamest line in the history of old, lame lines. And tacky, too, considering they'd just slept together.

Coop nodded coolly, his face like stone. "Right. Friends. I guess I'll see you around, then."

"Yes. At the next dinner party club," Audrey said. She climbed out of his truck and escaped before she could do any further damage.

"WHAT'S FOR DINNER?" RORY asked. She hopped up on one of the tall stools by the kitchen counter to watch Fran chop a pile of cilantro.

"Fish tacos," Fran said.

Rory made a face. "Gross."

"I thought you liked fish tacos."

"No, Iris is the one who likes them. Or she used to. She's a vegetarian now," Rory said.

Fran's knife stilled and she looked at her younger daughter. "Since when is Iris a vegetarian?"

"I don't know." Rory shrugged, unconcerned. "A few weeks."

"Why is this the first I'm hearing of it?" Fran asked.

Another shrug. "You didn't notice she hasn't been eating meat?"

"I thought she was just being difficult to be difficult. I didn't realize it was a lifestyle choice," Fran said. She sighed. Now, on top of everything else Iris-related she had to worry about, she also had to make sure her older daughter didn't become anemic. "Don't some vegetarians eat fish?"

"Don't ask me," Rory said cheerfully. "Can I have a hot dog for dinner?"

"Sure," Fran said distractedly. "We're grilling the fish anyway, so throwing a hot dog on the grill will be easy enough. Coop will be here any minute."

"Coop's coming over? Awesome," Rory said.

Will wandered in. He was dressed in his oldest, most stained shorts and a T-shirt that read NEVER FORGET under a picture of a dinosaur.

Fran looked him over critically. "Is that what you're wearing?"

Will looked down at himself in surprise. "Yes. Why?"

"Because we're having company," Fran said.

"Isn't it just Coop?" Will asked. "Since when did he count as company?"

"Yeah, Mom, why are you so dressed up?" Rory asked.

"I'm not dressed up. This is just really comfortable," Fran said defensively.

Fran thought, not for the first time, that it must be easier to have sons than daughters. Boys were so much less critical, especially when it came to their mothers. And she wasn't about to admit to either her husband or daughter that she'd bought the blue knit maxi dress that very day.

The doorbell rang.

"There's Coop now," Fran said. She felt a nervous flutter and smoothed her dress down.

"I'll let him in," Rory said, scampering out of the kitchen. A moment later, Fran heard the front door opening and Rory's enthusiastic greeting.

"Coop's here," Rory announced, bouncing back into the room. Coop trailed in after her.

"I come bearing fish," Coop said, holding up a cooler. "Caught fresh this morning."

"Excellent," Will said, taking the cooler from him.

"He gets the fish, you get the wine," Coop said, handing Fran a bottle of Chardonnay and kissing her on the cheek.

"You didn't have to bring wine, too," Fran protested. "You brought the fish."

"But you're cooking it for me. That's a trade I'll always be happy to make," Coop countered.

"Can I get you a beer?" Will asked.

Will and Coop both had beer, while Fran opted for a glass of Coop's Chardonnay, which was crisp and buttery. Fran put out blue tortilla chips and a bowl of guacamole she'd made earlier.

"What have you been up to, Coop?" Fran asked, as she wrapped corn tortillas in foil.

"The usual," Coop said. "I've been out on the boat a lot."

"Can I come fishing with you again?" Rory asked.

"Anytime," Coop said, smiling at her.

"I hope we see a shark again," Rory enthused.

"Again?" Fran asked, turning to her younger daughter.

Coop made a throat-slashing gesture at her.

"Oh, sorry, I forgot I wasn't supposed to say anything about that," Rory said sheepishly.

Fran looked at Coop, eyebrows raised. "Shark?" she said.

"Just a very small one. It was sniffing around the boat, hoping to snag a snapper off my line," Coop said.

"Why do I suddenly have a vision of Jaws leaping out of the water and snatching Rory off your boat?" Fran asked.

"Come on, honey, that practically never happens," Will said.

"And the shark would be much more likely to eat me. I'm sweeter than Rory," Coop teased. Rory punched him playfully in the arm. "Ow! Yikes, how does such a little girl pack such a punch? Did you take up boxing?"

Rory held up her fists, rolling them like a boxer. Coop held up his hands and laughed.

"I'm officially scared," he said.

Iris wandered into the kitchen. Her long dark hair was ironed stick straight, and her eyes were ringed with heavy black eyeliner. Her jeans were so tight, Fran wondered how she could walk in them. Or breathe for that matter.

"Hey, Coop. I didn't know you were here," Iris said.

"Hey, gorgeous," Coop said, grinning at her. "Are you still hard at work breaking the hearts of all the boys at your school?"

"You know it," Iris said, smirking.

"That's my girl. Just like I taught you," Coop said, holding up a hand for Iris to slap.

"Iris, where did you get those jeans?" Fran asked. "I haven't seen them before."

"Duh." Iris rolled her eyes. "Where do you think? The *mall.*"

"Iris," Will said sharply.

"What?" she asked.

"Don't *duh* your mother," he said.

"That sounds like the title of a rap song," Coop said. He crossed his arms over his chest, striking a rapper's pose, and began to sing: "Don't duh your *mother*, if you want me to be your *brother*."

Everyone laughed, except for Iris, who put her hands over her ears.

"Mom, make him stop," Iris begged.

"I have no control over him," Fran said.

Will got in on the action, providing a background rhythm for Coop's rap. "Pah pah *pah* pah pah *pah* pah *pah*."

"So listen to me, *guv'nor*, don't be rude to your *mother*," Coop rapped on.

"Guv'nor?" Fran repeated. "You don't hear many *guv'nors* in modern rap. In fact, you don't hear many *guv'nors* outside of *Mary Poppins*."

Coop paused, mid-rap. "What else rhymes with *mother*?"

"*Judger?*" Rory suggested.

Coop tried it out. "Don't duh your *mother*, or else I'm going to be a *judger*."

"I don't think you should give up your day gig," Will said.

"Absolutely not," Iris said, giggling.

Fran looked around at her family. Happiness fizzed up around them, their faces bright, laughter filling the room. When was the last time she'd heard Iris giggle? It had been so long, she couldn't even remember. It was Coop, Fran realized. His just being there made them all light up.

"No hot date tonight, buddy?" Will said, slapping Coop on the shoulder.

"No, not tonight," Coop said.

"Let me get you another beer," Fran said. She took one

out of the fridge, and then closed the door with her hip. She handed Coop the bottle. "Have you been seeing anyone lately?"

"Not really," Coop said.

Good, she thought, although she smiled sympathetically.

"I did take your friend out once, but it was pretty much a disaster," Coop continued.

Fran could feel the smile freezing on her face.

"My friend?" she repeated.

"Yeah, your friend. Audrey," Coop said.

"You and Audrey went out? On a date?" Fran asked.

She swallowed back the urge to pump Coop for details. When had he and Audrey been out? Where had they gone? Why hadn't Audrey mentioned it to her? And, most important, what had happened between them?

"It didn't go well," Coop said.

"Why didn't you like Audrey?" Rory asked.

"I did like her. I mean, I do like her. She's just not so crazy about me," Coop said. He grinned at Rory. "Shocking, right? I mean, who wouldn't love me?"

"Did you rap for her?" Iris asked. "That might explain it."

Coop laughed.

"Coop, come out to the garage. You have to see Iggy," Rory said, tugging at Coop's arm.

"Who's Iggy?"

"The battle bot Dad and I are building," Rory said. Coop allowed himself to be led off, followed by Will and even Iris. Fran was left alone in the kitchen, still trying to process this bombshell.

Coop and Audrey had gone out together. On a date.

Obviously, it hadn't been a success. Coop had made that

clear enough. Maybe there wasn't any chemistry between them, Fran thought hopefully.

But if that was it, Fran thought, *why didn't Audrey mention anything about it to me?*

THE NEXT MORNING, WILL wheeled his lawn mower over to Leland's yard. He'd mowed three passes before Leland came out onto his front porch, walking slowly, and waved him down. Will turned the mower off.

"What in tarnation are you doing?" Leland asked.

"You sound like Yosemite Sam from *Looney Tunes*. Are you going to call me a *wascally wabbit* next?" Will asked.

"I don't want you mowing my lawn," Leland said.

"I know. That's why I didn't ring your doorbell and ask permission before I started," Will said.

"Just because I'm old, doesn't mean I can't kick your ass," Leland said. "I have a cane, you know. And I'm not afraid to use it."

"I had nothing better to do than wander the neighborhood with my trusty mower, looking for lawns that need mowing," Will said.

"Fran put you up to this, didn't she?" Leland said.

"She might have mentioned something about it," Will said.

Leland sighed. He looked older, Will thought. And he was using his cane more than he had in the past.

"I know the lawn is getting to be too much for me," Leland admitted, which in itself was shocking. Leland had always taken great pride in his yard, and that he did all the work on his own. "But there's no need for you to do it. I'll hire a lawn service."

"No way," Will said. "They'll bring those heavy mowers in here, chop up your grass, and before you know it, you'll have bald patches all over the place."

"So? That way the lawn will match my head," Leland said.

"If I don't mow your lawn, Fran will kill me. Do you really want that on your conscience? Me dead. Fran in jail. Our children orphans."

Leland looked truly distressed. Will sympathized. The limitations imposed by aging must be hellish. One door after another closing on you, all the while knowing that you'll never be able to open it again.

"I'll tell you what. You can consider me your lawn service. And for my payment, you can make me a sweet tea," Will said, knowing full well that Leland always kept a pitcher of iced tea in the fridge.

Leland finally acquiesced, nodding. Will returned to his mowing, wondering why he felt so guilty.

Leland's yard wasn't large; it took Will only thirty minutes to mow it. He turned the mower off, and Leland reappeared, moving slowly without his cane and under the weight of a tray, which he set on a wicker table between two rocking chairs.

"Perfect," Will said, joining Leland on the front porch. He sat in one of the rocking chairs and accepted a glass of cold tea. There was also a plate of oatmeal raisin cookies, which Will helped himself to. "I hope you didn't bake just for me."

"No, I whipped these up this morning," Leland said. "I was going to bring some over to you-all after lunch."

"I'll just eat our share now. Save you the trip," Will suggested. He patted his round stomach. "Although I'm supposed to be cutting back. Fran's been on my case ever since Christmas, when I was asked to take on the role of Santa at the girls' school."

"Never a good sign," Leland agreed. "Fran's gotten so thin. How much weight has she lost?"

"I'm not sure. I know she's been buying a lot of new clothes lately," Will said. He tried to remember the last time he'd seen his wife naked and couldn't, which was actually a bit disturbing.

Leland looked sharply over at Will. That was the thing about Leland, Will thought. He seemed ancient, his body stooped and shrunken, his face as lined and veined as old leather. But it would be a mistake to suppose that old age had turned him dithery. His mind was as clear as ever.

"I had a very good marriage," Leland began.

Will nodded. "I wish we could have met your wife."

Leland continued, as though Will hadn't interrupted. "But like any marriage, we had our ups and downs. When you're with someone for such a long time, it's easy to start taking them for granted. To stop seeing them when they're right in front of you."

In his surprise, Will swallowed the piece of cookie in his mouth before he'd finished chewing it. It caught in his throat, causing him to cough and his eyes to water. He reached for his iced tea, and took a few hasty gulps.

"How do you do that?" Will asked, once he'd regained his composure.

"Do what?" Leland asked.

"Sometimes it's like you read my mind. Fran said you do it with her, too. Are you a witch doctor? Do you sacrifice goats in your backyard and stick pins in voodoo dolls?"

Leland laughed. "I've never sacrificed a goat, but I'll take the Fifth on the voodoo dolls."

"Seriously, what's your secret?"

"I think it comes from my years on the bench. I got good at reading people," Leland said. He shrugged modestly. "Sometimes what people don't say is more important than what they do say. I had to be careful, though, to only make my judgments on what was on the record."

"Yeesh," Will said. "Makes me glad I'm a humble city planner. The most responsibility I have is to figure out where the next traffic light should go."

"Every job has its upsides and its downsides," Leland said.

"Unless you're a crack whore. There's no real upside there," Will joked.

"Satisfaction in a job well done?" Leland suggested.

"I suppose there's that."

"Anyway, as I was saying, every marriage goes through lulls. Periods when you're not as connected. The thing is, you can't bury your head in the sand and pretend it's not happening. You have to deal with it before—" Leland stopped abruptly and cleared his throat.

"Before what?" Will asked.

"Before one of you does something stupid," Leland said.

Will shook his head. "I would never cheat on Fran, if that's where you're going with this."

"You never know what you might do. Or what Fran might do for that matter. Those feelings of loneliness, isolation, of being underappreciated can be powerful," Leland said.

"Fran and I have been married for a long time. I've never come close to cheating on her. And I know her well enough to be sure that she wouldn't do that to me," Will said. The whole conversation was making him uneasy. He liked Leland and was happy to help the older man out—to mow his lawn or move a bookshelf for him. But that didn't mean Leland had an open invitation to probe into his marriage.

Leland shrugged. "I've been kicking around for a long time. The one thing I know for sure about people is that they have an infinite capacity to surprise you."

"Sure, I can see that. But I know Franny," Will said. He put down his drained glass and stood. "And speaking of Fran, I'd better get home. She has a whole list of chores she wants me to take care of this weekend."

Leland's smile was a little sad, Will thought. He felt another pinch of regret. Why was he rushing off like this? What would have been the harm in letting the old man dole out his marriage advice? It probably made him feel wise and still useful.

"Thanks for the iced tea," Will said awkwardly.

"No, thank you for all your hard work," Leland said. "It is very much appreciated."

"We're always happy to help out," Will said. "And thank you for your advice. About not ignoring the lulls. I'll keep it in mind."

COOKING HAD ALWAYS SETTLED Audrey's nerves. So much so that Ryan used to joke that he always knew that if he could smell freshly baking bread when he walked in the door, he was in trouble.

She'd baked a lot of bread during that last year of her marriage, Audrey thought. Baguettes, country loaves, tea breads. Her arms had gotten toned from punching down so much dough. And when she'd gotten bored with bread, she'd baked dozens of cookies studded with chunks of chocolate, pans of brownies, towering cakes iced with swirls of cream cheese frosting.

But as soon as the memory had flickered into her consciousness, she pushed it away. Why was she thinking about that now? What was the point?

Standing barefoot in her kitchen, wearing her favorite striped men's pajamas and her hair caught back in a barrette, Audrey tried to refocus her attention on the recipe for rack of lamb, which she would be serving the next night when she hosted the dinner party club. She'd made rack of lamb plenty of times before—it was always a safe, elegant option for dinner parties—but this was a new recipe. It required crusting the lamb with a mixture of mustard, panko, and herbs.

This will be the best main course we've had yet, Audrey thought with satisfaction.

The dinner party club wasn't a competition. At least, not officially. But everyone secretly wanted to outdo the others. Audrey could tell that Jaime had been annoyed that everyone had raved over Fran's short ribs, more than they had over Jaime's individual filets en croûte. And although Leland's chicken had been perfectly cooked, there was a general sense of pleasure that his was not a hard dish to compete against. Fran was definitely winning so far, but Audrey was convinced that her lamb would top Fran's ribs.

The only downside to preparing lamb was that there wasn't much that could be done ahead of time. She had already diced the parsley and rosemary, and picked up the lamb from the butcher. She was pairing the lamb with a heavy potato gratin—the sort of dish that made you gain weight just by looking at it, but that was always a big hit—and that, too, was something she had to do tomorrow.

I'll make the strawberry-rhubarb pie, Audrey decided. That's a good Friday night project.

She retrieved the strawberries and rinsed them well in a colander before slicing off their green stems and cutting each berry in half. She dumped the cut strawberries in a large bowl, and then, after first cutting it into quarter-inch chunks, she added the rhubarb. Audrey measured out sugar, vanilla, and tapioca into the bowl, and, as a final touch, added some lemon zest, which the recipe didn't call for, but which always made pie taste better.

Audrey left the filling to sit, while she turned her attention to the pastry. She pulled out the heavy base of her food processor and fitted it with its plastic bowl and metal blade. There were two rules when it came to making the perfect pie crust. First, you had to use the coldest possible ingredients. And second, you couldn't overwork the pastry, which was always a danger when you used the food processor. Some pastry chefs insisted on using just butter or just shortening in their pie crusts, but Audrey had always found that a mixture of the two worked best, a one-to-three butter-to-shortening ratio.

She measured out first the dry ingredients, then the fat, into the bowl of the food processor, and pulsed it with quick on-off motions, until the mixture resembled coarse crumbs. Then, a few tablespoons at a time, she dribbled in chilled water, taking care to only pulse three times after each addition.

When the pastry was mixed, she turned half of it out

onto her special marble pastry slab and rolled it into an irregular circle with a French pin roller. She had to coax the pastry off the marble—it wanted to stick—but finally was able to transfer it whole into the waiting pie dish. She poured the strawberry-rhubarb mixture into the dish, and then began to roll the second round of dough. This time, she cut the pastry into quarter-inch lengths, which she braided lattice-style on top of the pie. Once it was done, and the edges were tucked under and crimped, Audrey brushed a little cream onto the top crust to ensure it would brown nicely.

Pies were particularly satisfying desserts to prepare, Audrey thought as she popped the pie into the oven. Unlike cakes, which sometimes fell for inexplicable reasons, pies mostly came out the same every time you made them. The only wild card was the fruit. If it was too bland or too ripe, the quality of the pie would suffer.

As the pie cooked, filling the house with its delicious hot fruit scent, Audrey poured herself a glass of wine and took it into her small living room. She sat cross-legged on the white couch and turned on the television. A few moments later, after scrolling through the four hundred channels and finding nothing to watch, she turned it off.

What was it going to be like seeing Coop tomorrow? she wondered, and felt a now-familiar shiver that always seemed to pass over her when she thought of him. The last time she had seen him, he'd been naked. Well, not the very last time—not when he'd driven her back to her car—but right before that. He'd held himself over her, absorbing his weight with his arms, his long muscular torso stretched out over her. . . .

No, she told herself. *No, no, no. I am not going to think about that. If I think about it now, I'll end up thinking about it tomorrow night when I see him. Then he'll know what I'm thinking. And what if everyone else senses the tension between us and figures out what happened? It would be nothing short of mortifying.*

Luckily, the phone rang at that moment.

"Hey, it's me," Fran said when Audrey answered.

"Hi," Audrey said.

"Where have you been? I've left you a bunch of messages," Fran said accusingly.

"I know, I'm sorry. I've been busy," Audrey lied. Well, the being busy part wasn't a lie—work always kept her busy. But the truth was, she had been avoiding Fran. She didn't want Fran to find out about her lunch date with Coop, and she was afraid that the whole debacle would somehow come out. Fran would want to know all the details—which Audrey was very much against sharing—and would give her all sorts of unsolicited advice.

Although that's just silly, Audrey thought. *I'm not sixteen years old. I'm perfectly capable of having a conversation with a friend without talking about a guy.*

"I can't believe you didn't tell me you and Coop went out on a date!" Fran said.

Audrey winced. *Uh-oh.*

"How did you find out about that?" she asked.

"How do you think? Coop told me. Although," Fran added, with what Audrey considered to be unnecessary belligerence, "I was really surprised that I had to hear about it from him instead of from you."

Audrey bristled, both at Fran's tone and implication. Just because she and Fran were friends, and Fran and Coop were friends, that didn't mean she was obligated to tell

Fran every single detail of her relationship with Coop. Not that she had a relationship with Coop, Audrey quickly amended.

"I didn't know I had to report in," Audrey said coolly.

There was an awkward silence, broken by a long sigh from Fran.

"I guess I just came across like a total bitch, huh?" Fran asked.

"You were a bit aggressive," Audrey agreed.

"I'm sorry. I guess I've been feeling a little hurt that you didn't feel like you could confide in me," Fran said.

Audrey took a sip of wine and considered this. Why hadn't she wanted to tell Fran? She wasn't entirely sure.

"We just had lunch together. It was fine. There weren't any fireworks," Audrey lied.

"That's too bad. Was it awkward?" Fran said.

Audrey started to feel guilty for not being more forthcoming. During those bleak, gray days after Ryan died, Fran had been a godsend. She'd accompanied Audrey to the funeral parlor and made the decisions that, in her fog of grief, Audrey had been incapable of making on her own. And then later, after the funeral, when everyone but Audrey had been ready to move on with their lives, Fran had called every morning to make sure Audrey was getting up out of bed, showering, eating. That she was getting on with the minutiae of living her life.

"Honestly? Coop makes me nervous," Audrey said, only just realizing at that moment that it was true. "I'm never sure how to act around him."

"I know I'm going to sound like a mom when I say this—I can't help it, I *am* a mom—but why do you need to act like anything? Just be yourself," Fran said.

"That's just it. When I'm around him, I start feeling unsure of myself."

"You do? Really?"

"Yes, me. Why does that surprise you?"

"You're the most self-assured person I know."

Audrey laughed. "I am not. Just when it comes to work. In every other area of my life, I'm a mess."

"No, you aren't. Even your lipstick is always perfectly applied," Fran said. "It's actually really annoying."

"If that's true, then why, whenever I'm around Coop, do I turn into a pod person?"

Fran laughed. "A pod person?"

"Yes. It's like my body is inhabited by some completely different being. I get prickly and argumentative. And it's like I suddenly have the hormones of a thirteen-year-old girl," Audrey said.

"Oh, *really?*" Fran said. "I know all too well what thirteen-year-old hormones are like."

Audrey flushed and took a quick gulp of her wine.

"Anyway, the date was a disaster. You were right. Coop and I would be hopeless together," Audrey said. "But I was thinking, maybe you were also right that it's time for me to start dating again."

"I never get tired of hearing the words *you were right,*" Fran mused. "I especially like them when they're followed by *and I was wrong.* Can you say that?"

"*Anyway,*" Audrey continued, "I don't think it was just Coop. It was me, too. I don't know how to date anymore, or even how to act around men. I'm out of practice. Actually, I'm not even sure if that's true. I don't think I ever knew how to do this."

"What are you saying? You want me to set you up with someone you can practice dating with?" Fran asked.

"Maybe," Audrey said, considering this, and seeing the genius in the idea. "That way, when I do meet someone I'm really interested in, I'll be prepared."

"But what if you like the man you're supposed to be practicing on?" Fran asked.

"I won't."

"How can you be so sure?"

"Because I'm not ready," Audrey said.

"You know you sound completely nuts, right?" Fran said.

"I do?"

"Yes."

"I think it's a very sensible plan. Practice makes perfect, right? I just need to practice how to date," Audrey said. "Can you think of anyone you could set me up with?"

"I don't know. I'll have to think about it. Believe it or not, I don't know many men who would fit your dateable-but-only-for-practice criteria," Fran said dryly. "Wait, actually, I can't believe it, but maybe I do know someone who would be pretty much perfect."

"Who's that?" Audrey asked eagerly.

"Did I ever introduce you to Kenny? He works with me."

"Is he a physical therapist, too?"

"Yes. He's a little older than we are, in his fifties, and divorced. He's very nice, very pleasant, flirty, but not aggressive. The only thing is he's not super attractive."

"That doesn't matter," Audrey said. "This isn't about attraction. It's about practice."

"So you keep saying. Anyway, consider yourself warned: He's vertically challenged. And his ears stick out," Fran said.

"I won't wear heels," Audrey promised. "And I won't stare at his ears."

"They're not freakishly big. I mean, he's not Dopey from *Snow White and the Seven Dwarfs*."

"Good to know," Audrey said. "Why don't you bring him tomorrow night?"

"What? To the dinner party club?"

"Sure. Why not?"

"Won't it be weird to have us all hanging around for your first date?"

"No, I think it would ease the tension. If things don't go well, we'd both have other people to talk to," Audrey said.

"And what about Coop?"

"What about him?"

"Won't it be awkward to have a date with another man right in front of him?" Fran said.

Audrey felt a twinge of discomfort and wondered if Fran was right. "We just went out the one time. It's not like we had an ongoing relationship," she said defensively. "Besides, there's no harm in asking, right? This guy—what did you say his name is? Kenny?—he might not even be able to come. It is last minute."

"Okay," Fran said, sighing. "I'll call him. Just . . ." Fran's voice trailed off.

"What?"

"I just hope you know what you're doing."

"Don't worry. I do," Audrey said, with much more confidence than she actually felt. The truth was, she had no idea what she was doing. Or why she was insisting that Fran bring her a date for the dinner party club the next night. She suspected that it all had something to do with seeing Coop again for the first time after sleeping with him. Kenny—short

Kenny, who she was now, thanks to Fran, picturing as an older, grayer version of Dopey—was going to be her armor tomorrow night.

JAIME OPENED HER EYES. The room was unusually bright. Sun streamed in through the edges of the closed plantation shutters.

What time is it? she wondered, her mind still groggy with sleep. She couldn't remember the last time she'd woken to a sunlit room. Ava had always been an early riser and rarely slept past five.

Jaime lifted her head and peered at the clock resting on her bedside table. Eight forty-five.

That's impossible, Jaime thought, sitting up. *How can it be so late?*

Mark's side of the bed was empty and as neat as usual. He was an abnormally still sleeper, frequently falling asleep while lying on his back—like a vampire laid out in a coffin—and then staying that way for the whole of the night. In stark contrast, Jaime was constantly restless, turning and shifting and wrestling with her pillows. Her body fought sleep, and she rarely got more than four or five hours even on one of the rare nights when Ava didn't wake her up every few hours.

Jaime got up, pulled on her favorite black yoga pants, and headed downstairs, following the wafting aroma of bacon and the sounds of clinking dishware, to find her family. They were in the kitchen, all still wearing their pj's, seated around the table and eating pancakes. Three faces turned to smile up at her as she entered.

"Hey, everyone," she said.

"Mama," Ava said, smiling sweetly. Her hair was twisted on top of her head in a tiny pigtail, like Pebbles Flintstone.

Logan had just stuffed a whole pancake into his mouth and his cheeks were sticking out like a chipmunk's. "Pancakes," he said thickly, through his full mouth.

Jaime suppressed her instinct to tell him not to talk with his mouth full. "I see that," she said, dropping a kiss on the top of Logan's head, before turning to smile at Mark.

Her husband was wearing a navy blue T-shirt and blue plaid pajama pants, and hadn't yet shaved. A shadow of dark, prickly hair covered his jawline. Mark smiled back at her.

"I thought you could use the extra sleep," Mark said.

"I definitely could. Thank you," Jaime said. "And you made pancakes. I'm impressed."

"Sit down, I'll get you a plate," Mark said, standing.

Jaime sat while Mark set her a place. Ava leaned toward her, and Jaime kissed her sticky face.

"We're going to have to hose you off in the backyard," Jaime teased her daughter, who giggled.

"Here you go," Mark said, setting a mug of coffee down in front of Jaime.

"I could get used to this," Jaime said. "Sleeping in late, my breakfast made, coffee served to me."

"You might want to try my pancakes before you decide to put me in charge of breakfast on a regular basis," Mark said.

The pancakes did look misshapen, but Jaime wasn't about to complain. She happily served herself from the serving platter, adding a strip of bacon.

"What do you think?" Mark asked after she'd taken a bite.

The pancakes were floury and undercooked in the middle. "They're great," Jaime lied.

Mark beamed at her, clearly pleased with himself.

"I thought you could use a break today. I've been working late all week, and spending a lot of time at the club with Emily. You've been on your own here a lot," Mark said. "Why don't you take the morning off. Go do something fun."

"Like what?" Jaime asked, confused by this sudden and bizarre transformation of her husband into the perfect man.

"I don't know. Go for a walk on the beach. Or get your nails done. Or go to the mall. Do whatever it is you girls like to do," Mark said.

"I wouldn't mind getting a pedicure," Jaime said. "And Nordstrom is having a sale."

"Perfect. A pedicure and shopping. Sounds like your perfect day," Mark said.

"Pea-cure!" Ava chirped. She adored having her nails polished, especially in lurid shades of green and blue.

"Not today, angel," Mark said, gently but firmly. "Your mama needs some time off."

Ava's lower lips protruded and began to quiver.

"I'll put polish on your toenails when I get home," Jaime promised, heading off tears.

"Poirple?" Ava asked hopefully.

"Purple," Jaime agreed. She turned back to Mark. "Are you sure? I assumed you'd be taking Emily to the club today."

"No, it's fine. Em had a sleepover party last night. I'm sure the girls stayed up all night, and she'll go back to her mom's house and crash," Mark said.

Jaime remembered how awful those overnight parties were. No one ever slept, riding late night sugar-highs into inevitable squabbles and hurt feelings. And in the morning, everyone's nerves were raw with exhaustion. She dreaded the day Ava would be old enough for sleepovers.

"You're right, Em will probably be too tired to see straight," Jaime said sympathetically.

"I told her that if she took a nap this morning and was up to it, I'd take her over to hit some balls later. If you get back in time," Mark said casually.

"Sure," Jaime said, nodding.

"Great," Mark said, rubbing her shoulder. "Do you want some more coffee?"

"No, thanks. I'm going to shower and get going before you change your mind," Jaime said, swallowing one last, tough bite of pancake and standing.

"Why would I change your mind?"

"You just might after you attempt to de-stickify those two," Jaime said, nodding at their offspring. Ava was rubbing her hands all over her syrup-covered plate and then clapping them together. Logan—who carbo-loaded like a long-distance runner—was still happily stuffing pancakes into his mouth. Mark looked at the children and his expression shifted to one of concern.

"Too late to back out now," Jaime said, laughing, and quickly retreated to take a shower and get her morning out started.

AUDREY LIVED IN A small cottage, set back from the road, with a long porch and a flowering poinciana tree in the front yard. Coop considered pulling in to the driveway, but then decided to park on the street, just in case he needed to make a quick getaway.

Coop had given considerable thought to skipping the dinner party altogether. It was going to be awkward seeing Audrey again, and he'd never fully embraced the whole din-

ner party club concept. It was the sort of thing married couples did when they'd reached the point in their relationship
where they were too bored to spend another Saturday night
alone together in a restaurant.

But if he didn't show up, Audrey would naturally assume
he was avoiding her. Why this should bother Coop, he had
no idea. Maybe it was just a perverse unwillingness to cede
any ground—even the dinner party club—to her.

Coop steeled himself as he walked up to the front porch
and knocked on Audrey's front door. When the door opened,
Coop was relieved to see Fran standing there. A momentary
reprieve from having to face Audrey.

"Hi. Are you the hostess for the evening?" he asked, kissing Fran on the cheek. She kissed him back, although her lips
landed just below his left ear.

"Whoops, sorry about that. Oh, no, I got lipstick on you,"
Fran said, looking flustered. She rubbed at the spot with her
thumb.

"You can get lipstick on me anytime you want," Coop
said, grinning at her.

It was the sort of teasing flirtation he and Fran had always
engaged in. He'd pretend to hit on her, Fran would make one
of her smart-ass jokes back. It was all perfectly innocent.

Except that Fran didn't make a smart-ass remark. Instead,
she looked into his eyes and murmured, "Do you really mean
that?"

Coop stared at her, confused and suddenly a little freaked
out. *Jesus,* he thought.

"Hey, Coop," Will said, appearing behind Fran, a bottle
of beer in one hand.

"Will! Hey! How are you, buddy?" Coop said, louder and
more enthusiastically than he meant to.

Will looked confused. "Fine. Why are you yelling? And why are you standing on the doorstep?"

Coop cleared his throat. "No reason. Sorry." He stepped into the house and held up the bottle of wine he'd brought. "Where's our hostess?"

"She's in the kitchen," Fran said. She hesitated and exchanged an uneasy look with Will. "But there's something you should know. . . ."

"What's that?" Coop asked. He had a premonition that he didn't want to hear whatever it was Fran was about to say.

But before Fran could spit it out, a man Coop had never seen before walked into the room. He was short—very short, probably no taller than five foot five—and had thinning dark hair that highlighted a pair of prominent, Prince Charles ears. He wore a short-sleeve blue plaid shirt tucked into khaki pants, and had a cellphone attached to his belt. The guy looked pleasant enough, but Coop was naturally suspicious of anyone who wore a cellphone holster.

"Hi, I'm Kenny Stabler," he said, approaching Coop with an outstretched hand.

"Nice to meet you," Coop said. "I'm Coop."

"Just Coop? Like Cher or Madonna?" Kenny asked.

"That's right," Coop said, nodding his head. "Minus the pointy bra and sequin costumes."

"That's not what I hear," Will said.

"Have you joined the dinner party club?" Coop asked. The idea annoyed him. Decisions about club additions should be made by the whole Table for Seven Club, not *ex parte*.

"No, I'm just crashing for the night," Kenny said.

"Kenny works with me," Fran explained.

"It's a blind date," Kenny said confidingly.

"A blind date?" Coop repeated.

"Yeah, I know. Pretty terrifying, huh?" Kenny said. "But Franny did me a solid. Audrey seems great."

Coop looked from Kenny to Will—who was studiously staring down at his feet, as though there was nothing more fascinating in the world than his well-worn penny loafers—to Fran.

Fran forced a smile and said, "You know me. I always love playing matchmaker."

"Yes. I did know that about you," Coop said, wondering if there was any way he could make a run for it. He'd been at Audrey's house for all of five minutes and was already dreading the rest of the evening.

There was a knock on the door. As they were all standing in the hallway, Will simply reached out and opened the door, startling Jaime and Mark who—clearly not expecting such a quick response to their knock—were standing very close. Mark had his hand on the small of Jaime's back and her face was tipped up toward his.

"Ahem," Will said.

Jaime and Mark started apart and turned to see Will, Fran, Coop, and Kenny standing there. "Oh, hi, everyone," Jaime said, blushing.

"We decided to all come and greet you at the door. En masse," Will said.

"So I see," Jaime said.

The group shuffled around the small foyer to make room for Jaime and Mark, who were now holding hands, their fingers linked loosely together. Coop was pressed back against a narrow console table so as not to rub up against either Kenny or Fran—right now, it was debatable about which alternative would be more embarrassing—when Audrey appeared, looking nonplussed.

"Hey, everyone. Why are you all standing in the foyer?" she asked.

Coop was annoyed at the frisson of excitement that shot through him at the sight of her.

"Yes, we deserted Leland in the living room," Fran said. "Everyone, move that way."

As the group went into the living room, Audrey greeted the Wexlers, hugging Jaime and allowing Mark to kiss her on the cheek, and then turned to Coop—the last one left in the entryway.

"Hi," Audrey said. She was wearing a simple black sheath dress, but instead of her usual high heels, she had on black patent flat sandals.

"Hi. For you," Coop said, handing her the wine and brushing his lips against her cool cheek. Then, while he was close enough to not be overheard, he murmured, "Are those shoes supposed to make you shorter or to make him seem taller?"

"Thank you for the wine," Audrey said stiffly, ignoring his crack about her shoes. "That was very thoughtful."

"I'm a very thoughtful guy," Coop said, winking as he passed by her, immensely pleased at her discomfort.

But his victory was short-lived. Although thankfully the group didn't linger long over drinks and quickly moved to Audrey's small dining room, dinner seemed to drag on interminably. Audrey was distracted and uncharacteristically disorganized, and there were long gaps in between the courses. The salad course was delicious—the mini cheese soufflés perfectly complemented the tarragon-flavored vinaigrette—but then everyone grew so hungry waiting for the lamb, that they ate too much bread and drank too much wine, and when the lamb finally appeared, they were so hungry they devoured it without stopping to savor the flavors.

Conversation was stilted, too. Jaime and Mark were being oddly lovey-dovey with each other and seemed like they'd rather be on their own than out in a group. Coop was avoiding looking at or speaking to Fran, as much as he could get away with it, fearing another weirdly charged interaction. Fran, in turn, was quiet, and not at all her usual animated self, and Will kept glancing uneasily at his wife. Audrey was flustered. Only Kenny seemed unaware of the tension, chatting easily with Leland about a cooking show they both watched, with Mark about junior tennis tournaments, and with Jaime about the dramas of toilet training. Despite his natural antipathy toward Kenny, Coop had to admit that Kenny seemed like an okay guy.

Still, Coop didn't get the feeling that there was much of a spark between Audrey and Kenny. They chatted about the benefits of massage therapy in patients recovering from sports injuries, which was apparently Kenny's specialty as a physical therapist. Kenny lavishly praised the rack of lamb and strawberry-rhubarb pie. Audrey smiled and said all of the correct, polite things in response. But they weren't leaning toward each other, or finding excuses to touch, to brush against each other. In fact, Audrey seemed much more interested in Leland's story about how two women in his garden club—both widows—were competing for his attention.

"You're the hot stud of the garden club?" Audrey teased him.

"They keep bringing me casseroles," Leland said in a melancholy voice.

"And that's a bad thing?" Mark asked.

"There's only so much tuna casserole a man can eat before it gets depressing," Leland said.

"Maybe we should tip them off that the way to his heart

is bacon," Audrey said, laughing. Then, when she saw Kenny's confusion, she shook her head. "Sorry. It's an inside dinner-party-club joke."

At one point, when Audrey was taking a stack of dishes out to the kitchen, Coop caught Kenny looking at Audrey's backside with frank, open admiration. Coop was seized with the sudden urge to take his fork and drive it into Kenny's hand, but decided that might be a bit of an overreaction and wouldn't go unnoticed by his dinner companions.

"Next month we're meeting at Coop's," Fran said, putting down her fork after taking only a bite of her pie. "And I was going to suggest that after that we take off the rest of the summer and then start up again in September."

"Why's that?" Will asked.

"We're going to my parents' for two weeks in July," Fran said.

"Oh, God," Will said, draining the rest of his wine.

"And Mark and Jaime normally go up north in August. And I'm sure other people will be traveling, too," Fran continued. "It'll be hard to find one Saturday a month when we'll all be able to attend."

"That's true. Emily has a bunch of tournaments this summer. We're going to be away nearly every weekend," Mark said.

"That sounds like fun," Fran said to Jaime.

"Oh, I'm not going to most of them. Mark will just take Emily on his own," Jaime said.

"You'll come to some of the tournaments, though, right?" Mark said, touching his wife's arm.

She smiled at him. "Of course. And when we start up in September, it will be our turn again."

"Sounds good," Will said. "Leland?"

"I'm going on a cruise," Leland announced.

"You are? I didn't know that. Where are you going?" Fran asked.

"Alaska," Leland said. "I've always wanted to go."

"And you're going by yourself?" Jaime said. "Won't you be lonely?"

"Haven't you been paying attention? Leland's been fighting the ladies off. He has his choice of the local widow pool to keep him company," Will said.

"I like traveling alone," Leland said.

"So do I," Audrey said. "It's so freeing. You can do whatever you like, whenever you like, without having to worry about whether your traveling companion is having a good time."

"But you also don't have anyone to share the experience with," Jaime said.

"Maybe it's like dog people and cat people. People who like to travel alone and people who like to travel with others," Audrey suggested.

"I'd love to try traveling on my own sometime," Fran said.

"I thought you hated traveling alone," Will said, turning to his wife.

"Not at all. Why would you think that?" Fran asked.

"Probably because you've told me that. On several occasions."

"You must have misunderstood me," Fran said.

Will was looking at her oddly, as though Fran had just announced that she was taking up cannibalism.

"I've always wanted to go backpacking through Europe," Fran said defensively.

"But you can't read a map. And you get lost here, in

town," Will said in a teasing voice. "How would you possibly navigate yourself through countries where you don't speak the native language?"

"I can read a map!" Fran said crossly.

"Can't a person be both a dog person and a cat person?" Kenny asked.

"No," everyone said together.

"But I had a dog growing up. Now I have a cat." Kenny shrugged. "I like both."

"You can like both. But you have to prefer one to the other," Fran explained. "If you had the choice of living with a cat or a dog—and you didn't have to concern yourself with the details about how big your house is, or the hours that you work, or anything like that—which would you choose?"

"I don't know," Kenny said, shrugging. "They both have their pluses and minuses."

"I think you're definitely a cat person, Kenny," Coop said.

"How can you tell?" Kenny asked.

"Oh, I can just tell these things," Coop said. He grinned at Audrey, who shot him a sharp, warning look. "No, I can't really. It's just that you chose to get a cat. That must mean you prefer them."

"I didn't choose him. He chose me. He showed up on my doorstep one day and pretty much never left," Kenny said. "What does that mean?"

"It means you're a very nice man," Audrey said. "Now, who wants another slice of strawberry-rhubarb pie?"

AUDREY KEPT HER COOL until her guests had left, including Kenny, who had seemed reluctant to leave with the others. But she insisted that she didn't need help with the dishes and accepted his invitation to lunch the next week, mostly because she couldn't think of a way to say no without hurting his feelings. It didn't escape her attention that she hadn't had any similar problem with hurting Coop's feelings. But Coop was different, she decided. He needed to be taken down a few pegs.

Coop. Audrey scrubbed at the roasting pan—the meat juices were caked on the bottom, forming a substance so hard and resistant, NASA could use it to patch space shuttles—and wondered what the hell his problem had been. Okay, so maybe she wouldn't have liked it if he had been the one to show up to the dinner party club with a date. But she couldn't believe that her having done so would really affect him. It wasn't like he was in love with her. If anything, his ego was probably bruised.

The phone rang. Audrey checked the caller ID, which flashed a local number without giving a name. Probably a cellphone, she thought, and considered not answering it. But then she wondered if it was someone who had been at the dinner party calling, looking for belongings accidentally left behind.

"Hello," Audrey said.

"He's not the guy for you," Coop said, his voice deep and warm in her ear.

Audrey leaned back against her kitchen counter and wrapped one arm around herself.

"And how would you know that?" Audrey asked.

"He has a cat. That's all I need to know," Coop said.

"What is it with you and cats?"

"I don't trust single guys with cats. It's not normal. Do you know what sort of guys have cats?"

"Do tell."

"The kind who buy pre-distressed jeans and call themselves metrosexuals," Coop said.

Audrey laughed. "I thought you were going to say the kind of guy who murders his mother and buries her body under the floorboards of his house."

"You got that kind of a vibe off Kenny, too?"

"No. I did not get the feeling that Kenny's a sociopathic killer. He seems like a perfectly nice man."

"And what sort of a grown man goes around being called Kenny?" Coop countered.

"He can't help what his name is," Audrey said.

"He could go by Ken. But Kenny? I never get when grown men want to be called Kenny, or Bobby, or Billy. Why not just have everyone call you Pee Wee and be done with it?" Coop asked.

"Pee Wee?" Audrey felt guilty laughing at this—Kenny *had* been a perfectly nice man—but couldn't help herself. "Come on. Pee Wee is much worse than Kenny. And maybe he didn't want people making Ken doll jokes."

"I don't think he's in any danger of being confused with a Ken doll. For one thing, Ken doesn't have ears like that," Coop said. Then, his voice growing softer, he said, "Do you want me to come back over and help you with the dishes?"

"I've already done them," Audrey said.

"Even better," Coop murmured.

Audrey tried to ignore the physical effect these words had on her. It was what had gotten her in trouble the last time.

"No," Audrey said. "I don't think that would be a good idea."

"That's too bad," Coop said. "Lamb is an aphrodisiac."

Audrey burst out laughing. "I think you're thinking of oysters."

"I like oysters, but red meat is much sexier. It's much more primal."

"I'm hanging up now," Audrey said.

"Take it from me—real men do not own cats."

"Good night."

"Good night. I'll call you tomorrow."

"Are you asking me or telling me?" Audrey asked, annoyed at how pleased she was. Especially since he probably wouldn't even call.

Coop laughed. "I was telling you. You can always screen my call if you want."

"I just may do that," Audrey said.

"I guess we'll find out tomorrow," Coop said. Audrey could tell that he was smiling, too. "The suspense is already killing me."

"I'm hanging up now," Audrey told him.

"You got that coming over to help you with the dishes was a euphemism for having sex, right?"

"Yes. Shockingly enough, it wasn't that subtle."

"Just wanted to make sure."

"Good night."

"Talk to you tomorrow."

june

· · ··

GREEN SALAD WITH WHITE BALSAMIC
VINAIGRETTE

STEAMED LOBSTERS WITH
MELTED BUTTER

POTATO SALAD

KEY LIME PIE

A WEEK AFTER THE MAY dinner party, Fran was still jittery with excitement. Something had passed between her and Coop. A charge. A frisson. Whenever Fran thought of it, she felt a shudder of excitement, a delicious sensation she distantly remembered from younger days, when a crush ran his hand down her back or brushed the hair away from her face.

At first, Fran had wondered if the moment had been one-sided. But Coop had been uncharacteristically quiet for the rest of the evening, which made sense. If he was having feelings for her—the wife of his oldest friend—of course it would bother him. Just look at what happened that day on the boat, all those years ago.

The question was, what was she going to do now?

I can't do anything. I'm married. I would never cheat on Will, Fran kept telling herself. But then, a minute later, she'd think, *But I have to find out if Coop is having the same feelings that I'm having. I have to see him. And I have to do it alone, not when Will and the girls are around. But when? And what will I say?*

These thoughts swirled around and around, refusing to dislodge themselves. Coop hovered in her consciousness while she packed lunches and vacuumed, and even while she was working with one of her physical therapy patients. He was quickly becoming an obsession, which was both exhilarating and exhausting.

What do I do? I can't do anything. But why can't I? Will, that's why. But Will and I barely even touch anymore, much less have sex. Aren't I too young to already be a celibate, to have all of my life's passion behind me? Fran wondered, as she chopped tomatoes for the chicken Cobb salad they were having for dinner. She always added extra avocado and blue cheese and dressed it in a tarragon vinaigrette.

"Bye, Mom."

Fran looked up to see a flash of black pass by the kitchen door.

"Iris?" she called out. "Where are you going?"

"Over to Hannah's," Iris called back.

Fran heard the front door open. "Wait! Come back here," she said.

"I'm going to be late!"

"Then you'll be late," Fran said.

Iris huffed, but closed the door and returned slowly, reluctantly to the kitchen. Fran looked at her daughter and recoiled.

"What in God's name did you do to your hair?" she asked.

Iris rolled her eyes, which were rimmed with thick black kohl liner. Her bangs had been inexpertly cut. They were far too short—ending an inch above her eyebrows—and had been curled under, probably to disguise the uneven ends.

"I cut it," Iris said, on the defensive, as usual.

"But it's . . ." Fran had been about to say *it's awful,* but stopped herself. It was hard enough being a teenage girl as it was, and she didn't want Iris to feel self-conscious. Then again, she had to know it didn't look good. "Did you cut it yourself?"

"Yes. And I like it like this," Iris said.

It's just hair. It will grow back, Fran told herself.

"In the future, let me know when you want to change your style and I'll take you to the salon," Fran said.

Iris just shrugged and picked at her dark purple nails. "Can I go?"

"No. Go wash your face first," Fran said.

"What! Why?"

"Don't raise your voice, young lady. You're not going out of the house with that much eye makeup on," Fran said. She had a flash of déjà vu, and it suddenly occurred to Fran that she'd had nearly the same conversation with her own mother when she was a teenager.

Great, Fran thought. *I really have turned into my mother.* And suddenly she felt decrepit, and a million miles away from the girl wearing the blue bikini who Coop had come close to kissing all those years ago.

"I'm just going over to Hannah's. Why does it matter if I'm wearing eye makeup?" Iris said.

She has a point, Fran thought. *What harm is there in a little eyeliner—okay, a lot of eyeliner—if she's just doing her math homework? Sure, Hannah's mother will judge me for letting her out like that. Then again, Hannah's mother wears her hair too blond and her shorts too short, so who is she to judge anyone?*

"Okay, fine, go," Fran said.

"Really?" Iris looked unsettled at the easy victory.

"You're just going to Hannah's? You two aren't going to the mall or out anywhere else?"

"No, we'll be at her house the whole time," Iris promised.

"Okay, good. Call me if you change locations," Fran said.

Iris looked like she couldn't believe her luck. "Okay, bye," she said, turning and hurrying out of the house before Fran could change her mind.

The phone rang, and Fran picked it up. "Hello?"

"Fran, it's Jaime." She sounded half-hysterical, and one of the children was wailing in the background. "Is Iris there?"

"Hey. No, she just left. Why, what's wrong?"

"Logan shut his hand in the door. I need to take him in for X-rays, and I can't get hold of Mark, and I need to find someone to watch Ava," Jaime said. The cacophony of screams in the background got louder. Jaime sounded like she was on the verge of tears herself.

"Oh, no, poor Logan. Don't worry, I'll be right there."

"Thank you so much," Jaime said. "You're a lifesaver."

"Just give me five minutes," Fran promised.

WHEN MARK GOT HOME, Jaime was in the middle of reorganizing their closet. It had suddenly occurred to her that she really should organize her clothes so that they hung not just by season and by type—skirts with skirts, jackets with jackets—but also by color. As soon as Ava and Logan had gone to bed—without argument, for once, as they were both too exhausted from the trauma of the day to fight sleep—she'd headed upstairs to tackle the project, and was still in the midst of the reorganization when Mark appeared at the closet door, looking confused.

"What are you doing?"

Jaime, who was sorting her jeans—white to light rinse to dark rinse to black—glanced up at him. His face was flushed with a healthy sheen, as though he'd been out in the fresh air.

She wondered if she looked as tired and hollowed-out as she felt. Her eyes were sore from the steady trickle of tears, her neck was stiff, and her head was buzzing with echoes of Logan's cries. She supposed she should have put some thought into what she was going to say to her husband.

"I'm reorganizing the closet," she said. "Where have you been?"

"Work, the tennis club. Why? Is something wrong?"

"You never called me back. I left you a bunch of messages. But you never called me back," Jaime said.

Mark took a step toward her, concern flickering. "What happened? Is everyone all right? Logan? Ava?"

"They're both fine. At least, they are now. Why didn't you answer your phone?"

"It ran out of power. I didn't notice until I went to check my messages on the way home from the club."

"I've been trying to call you for six hours. You didn't notice your phone was out of power that entire time?"

Mark shrugged. "No. I've been too busy. Are you going to tell me what happened?"

Jaime turned her attention to her shirts. White, white, pink, yellow, blue, pink and blue striped. She hesitated, and then switched the pink and the yellow around, so that it was pink, pink and blue stripe, blue. Much better.

"Jaime?"

"Logan shut his hand in the bedroom door," Jaime said without turning around.

"Aw, poor guy."

Jaime looked over her shoulder at her husband, underwhelmed by his reaction. "I had to take him in for X-rays."

"Seriously?"

"Yes, seriously."

"Did he break anything?"

"No. But he was really upset. He was in quite a bit of pain," Jaime said. "And I couldn't get ahold of you, so Fran had to come over and watch Ava while I took Logan to the doctor."

"I told you, my phone was out of power."

"I tried calling you at work, too. April said you were out of the office."

"I had a client meeting," Mark said. "And then I was at the club."

"And I tried calling the tennis club. They said you weren't there," Jaime said, turning to look directly at her husband for the first time. She wanted to see how he reacted to this news.

This was as close as she'd ever come to asking him outright if he was having an affair. Mark frowned, and, Jaime thought, looked confused.

"But I was there. Em and I were playing on the back court. Maybe the girl in the office didn't know we were there. You can't see that court from where she sits," Mark said.

"She seemed pretty sure you weren't. She wouldn't go check, even when I said it was an emergency."

Mark shrugged. "She probably just couldn't be bothered to get up off her ass. I'll say something to Becky about it."

"No, don't. The girl in the tennis club isn't the problem. The problem is that you were out of touch in the middle of a family crisis," Jaime said. She folded her arms over her chest.

"Don't you think you're overreacting?" Mark said. He sighed and rubbed his temples. "It really wasn't an emergency, was it? Did Logan really need to have X-rays, or were you just overreacting? You tend to do that whenever the kids get even the smallest bump or bruise."

Jaime was aware that Mark was engaging in what she always liked to call his lawyer arguing tactic. Rather than discussing *why* he had been out of contact for such an extended period of time—and the effect this had on his family—he wanted to instead go on the attack, challenging her decision to take Logan to the doctor. Rather than defend the indefensible, refocus the argument. But even though Jaime knew what Mark was doing—and knew that she should keep him on point—she was infuriated at this challenge to her judgment. Mark hadn't been there. He hadn't seen Logan screaming with pain. Not just fear—although, of course, he had certainly been scared—but in actual pain.

"How can you say that I was overreacting, that it wasn't a crisis, when you weren't even here?"

"Kids shut their hands in doors all the time. I know Emily did it once or twice when she was little, and we never took her for X-rays." Mark shrugged out of his sweaty T-shirt and tossed it on top of the laundry hamper.

Jaime's throat grew thick with anger and tears stung in her eyes. She blinked, willing herself not to cry. It always happened when she was angry, and then Mark would accuse her of trying to manipulate him with tears.

"Logan's hand turned red and began swelling. I called the pediatrician's office and spoke to Dr. Hung's nurse. She was the one who told me to take Logan in for X-rays. She said that kids his age have soft bones that are easily damaged," Jaime said.

"But she hadn't seen Logan at that point, right? She was basically just giving you the worst case scenario. Look, I'm not criticizing you," Mark said.

The hell you're not, Jaime thought.

"I know you did what you *thought* was right. But if Logan's fine—and he is fine, right?—well, then, you just got yourself worked up over nothing," Mark said.

"I am *not* worked up over nothing! I'm upset because you weren't there when I needed you," Jaime said.

"I told you, my phone was out of power. It's not like I was deliberately avoiding you. I was at work," Mark said.

"And at the tennis club," Jaime said.

Mark's face hardened. "Is that what this is about? You don't like me spending time at the club with my daughter, so you manufacture a crisis so you have something to be angry at me about?"

"Manufacture a crisis?" Jaime echoed, staring at her husband in disbelief. "Do you think I *wanted* Logan to shut his hand in the door?"

"No. But you might work what's basically a minor household incident up into a major drama just to try to make me feel guilty. I mean, how bad could it have been if you're now cleaning out the closet?" Mark asked.

Jaime could feel her grip slipping. Tears brimmed in her eyes, causing her vision to go blurry. "I'm not cleaning, I'm organizing. Because it makes me feel better. Calmer. And you weren't here, so you don't know how bad it was. But I'll tell you—it was horrible. Logan was screaming in pain, and I didn't know what to do."

Mark's expression softened. "That must have been very scary."

"It was." Jaime drew in a ragged breath. "And I kept trying to call you, and you wouldn't pick up."

"Because my phone was out of power."

"But I didn't know that. I just couldn't get you, and I needed you. We needed you," Jaime said.

Mark leaned forward, pressing his forehead against hers. "I'm sorry I wasn't here. I'm sorry my phone was out of power."

This was nothing short of a major victory. Mark never apologized for anything. Jaime could feel her anger ebbing, soothed by his admission that he had let her down. Or, at least, he'd come as close to admitting that as he ever would.

"And now you think I'm being some sort of a drama queen," Jaime said, sniffling. It occurred to her that sobbing uncontrollably tended to reinforce Mark's view of her as a drama queen, but she couldn't seem to stem the flow of tears. It had been such a long and difficult day.

"No, I don't. I just said that because I felt like you were attacking me," Mark said. Jaime leaned against him, too tired to stay angry.

"I didn't mean to attack you. I was just so scared. What if Logan had been seriously hurt? I couldn't bear it," Jaime said. A shudder went through her as she remembered Logan's wails of pain. Just the idea of him being seriously injured made her sick to her stomach.

"I couldn't, either. Thank God he's fine." Mark kissed the top of her head. "Is there any wine?"

"Yes. I opened a bottle earlier."

"Great, I could use a glass. Can I get you one?"

"Sure, thanks," Jaime said, giving him a watery smile.

It wasn't until after he'd walked out of the closet, whistling softly, that Jaime realized he'd never explained why he—the man who was practically surgically attached to his phone—had failed to notice it had been out of power for hours.

AUDREY LAY ON HER back with the sheet pulled up to cover her breasts and stared up at the ceiling fan, which was turning so slowly she could count each rotation. One, two, three, four, five. It was oddly hypnotizing. She could almost forget that she had, yet again, ended up in bed with Coop on her lunch hour. And this time, they hadn't even gotten to the lunch part of the date.

"You're being very quiet. What are you thinking about?" Coop asked.

Audrey turned toward him. Coop was lying on his stomach, his head resting on folded arms.

"What am I thinking about?" Audrey snorted. "Please."

"What?"

"Your entire gender lives in terror of what the response to that question might be," Audrey said.

Coop grinned at her. *He has an annoyingly sexy grin,* Audrey thought. *I really need to stop letting it have such an effect on me.*

"I think I just disproved your thesis. I am a man, this is real life, and I am interested in hearing what you're thinking about. Especially if it's along the lines of, 'Wow, Coop is a beast in the bedroom. I never knew sex could be so damn good.' "

Audrey giggled and then thought, *Did I really just giggle? I'm lying naked in bed, with a man I hardly know and now I'm giggling. Nothing good can come of this.*

"Not even close," Audrey said.

"No? Damn. Well, I know it's not anything along the lines of, 'I'm not the sort of woman who does this.' Right?"

"Why's that?"

"Because that would be a cliché."

"But people think in clichés all the time," Audrey argued. "That's what makes them clichés."

"You're avoiding the question."

Audrey shrugged, then grabbed the sheet before it fell away. "I'm not the sort of woman who does this."

Coop groaned and buried his face in his pillow.

"But I'm not," Audrey said. "This feels . . . I don't know. Weird."

Coop looked back up at her, shaking his head. "Weird. Great. That's just the review I was hoping for. 'How's Coop in bed?' 'Well, actually, he makes me feel weird.' It's what every guy wants to hear."

"Who am I supposedly having this conversation about your sexual prowess with?"

"I don't know. Isn't that what women talk to each other about?"

"Not in my experience."

"Really? I thought there was an entire television show about four chicks sitting in a coffee shop talking about their sex lives."

"*Sex and the City*. Which is, by the way, a fictional show. And what I meant by the weirdness is that this"—she waved an arm around, encompassing the bed, the room, the sunshine streaming in through the tilted blinds—"is out of my comfort zone. I normally spend my lunch hour eating a turkey sandwich at my desk."

Coop kissed her shoulder. "I think we can do better than that," he murmured.

"Seriously? I thought men your age needed a longer rest period."

"Ouch. Just for that . . ."

Coop pushed himself up on his arms and loomed over Audrey who shrieked and said, "Wait, no, you're going to have to feed me first. I'm starving. And then I really do have to get back to work. I have a business to run. I can't spend all day lolling around in bed with you."

"Pity," Coop said, but he got out of bed and pulled on first a pair of blue striped boxer shorts and then his faded blue Levi's. He glanced at Audrey, who was admiring the effect of a tanned male torso. "Come on, lazybones. Let's go rustle up some lunch."

"Are we going out?" Audrey asked, sliding out of bed. She felt suddenly shy of her nudity, and turned her back to him as she dressed.

"No, I'll cook."

"Can you cook?"

"I sure hope so. I have the whole dinner party club coming over in three days."

"What are you making, anyway? You haven't emailed out your menu."

"Am I supposed to do that?"

Audrey, now fully dressed, turned to face Coop. "Everyone usually does. But it's not like we have club bylaws or anything. Aren't you going to put on a shirt?"

"I wasn't planning on it," Coop said. He grinned. "Why? Does the sight of my bare chest distract you?"

Audrey rolled her eyes. "What are we having for lunch?"

"I'm going to make you the best cheeseburger you've ever had in your life," Coop said.

"Big talk. But can he deliver?"

"Watch and learn, sweetheart."

Coop headed toward the kitchen. Intrigued, Audrey trailed after him. His apartment was small and spartan, and the kitchen was just off the living room. Bear, who had been sleeping on his rectangular hunter green bed in the living room, stood, shook himself, yawned widely, and padded into the kitchen after them.

"Where are you going to put everyone for the dinner party?" Audrey asked. There was a small square table in the living room, which doubled as Coop's desk, but it wouldn't seat more than four, and there wasn't room to extend it.

"You'll see," Coop said.

"Why all the mystery?"

"I like to maintain an element of surprise at all times," Coop said. He rummaged through the fridge and pulled out a package of meat wrapped in white paper. "Here's my first secret: Butcher Bob's secret blend."

"Butcher Bob?" Audrey repeated. "That sounds like a character from a kids' cartoon."

"He's my meat guy."

"You have a meat guy?" Bear nosed at Audrey's knee, and she leaned over to rub his head.

"Sure. Don't you?"

"No."

"You should. Everyone needs a good meat guy," Coop said.

"I'll keep that in mind," Audrey said.

She leaned against the counter and watched Coop work. He formed the meat into three round patties, and then seasoned each patty on both sides with sea salt and freshly ground black pepper.

"Three?" Audrey asked.

"One's for Bear," Coop explained.

Audrey smiled. Bear planted himself at Coop's feet and stared intently up at the counter, as though willing one of the hamburgers to zoom off of the plate and right into his mouth. He licked his chops and began to pant.

Coop washed his hands, got out a skillet, and set it on the burner to heat up. Audrey could tell by the way he worked in the kitchen—competently, with an economy of movement—

that he was comfortable there. It was surprisingly sexy. Ryan had never cooked. He always joked that he was even incapable of making toast. But as soon as this disloyal thought flitted into her head, Audrey felt a twinge of guilt.

Why do I keep comparing the two of them? she wondered.

"And here's my second secret," Coop said, reaching into the fridge again. He held up a package of bacon. "Something near and dear to Leland's heart."

"Bacon burgers? That sounds—" Audrey began.

"Amazing?" Coop interrupted.

"I was going to say completely decadent. But, yeah, it also sounds pretty amazing."

"It's going to sound even better when you see what else I'm putting on them," Coop said, pulling out a triangular package of cheese with the air of a magician pulling off a master trick.

"Blue cheese?"

"And not just any blue cheese. This is Maytag blue cheese. The very best," Coop said. "What do you think?"

What Audrey thought was that consuming a blue-cheese bacon burger in the middle of the day was about as out of character for her as having a nooner. But as soon as the bacon started to sizzle, her mouth began to water and she realized that she was suddenly craving a hamburger.

Coop cooked the bacon until it was crispy, then drained most of the grease from the pan, leaving behind a tablespoon. He added the meat patties to the pan, letting them sizzle in the fat, and flipped them after a few moments. Coop then added shavings of blue cheese to the patties and tented the pan with tinfoil.

"So the cheese will melt," he explained helpfully.

"Is there anything I can do? I'm just standing here," Audrey said.

"You're being decorative." Coop ducked from Audrey's swat. "No, I've got it under control."

Coop used a spatula to move two of the burgers from their pan to freshly sliced Kaiser rolls, garnished with lettuce and thick slices of tomato. He put the third burger in a plastic dog bowl, and set it on the ground for Bear, who attacked the food as though he hadn't eaten in days.

"Lunch is served," he said.

"Should I set the table?"

"No, it's a nice day. Let's go outside. What would you like to drink? Iced tea? Or would you prefer a beer?"

"Actually, a beer sounds great," Audrey said.

Coop handed her a bottle of Guinness, got one for himself, and then they headed outside. The patio ran the length of the condo, and had a lovely view of the Intracoastal river. Like the rest of Coop's apartment, the patio was sparingly decorated. There was a single lounge chair, a round table covered by a striped umbrella, two bistro chairs, and several palm trees in terra-cotta pots. Audrey and Coop sat at the table.

"Cheers," Coop said, and they clinked their beer bottles together.

"What a great view. I would live out here," Audrey said.

"I practically do," Coop said. "I have my coffee out here every morning. Dig in and tell me what you think."

Audrey had to open her mouth wide to fit the burger in. It was heaven. The meat was perfectly cooked and superbly enhanced by the smoky bacon and creamy blue cheese flavors. Juice dripped down, and Audrey had to lean forward, before it covered her shirt.

"Oh, my God," she said, when she had swallowed and could finally speak.

Coop grinned. "Told you. Best burger you've ever had, right?"

"It seriously is. Amazing."

"Nothing beats a good burger. If I were on death row, awaiting my execution, a bacon cheeseburger would definitely be on my last meal list," Coop said.

Audrey had just bitten into her burger, which was inconvenient, as she now started to laugh.

"You could have anything in the world, and you'd choose a burger?" she said. "Not that this isn't fantastic. But I think if it were me, I'd go for seared foie gras."

"No, I'm a burger man. Although I'd want it served with deep fried onion rings and a chocolate shake." Coop sighed with pleasure at the thought. "And a chocolate brownie for dessert. The fudgy kind. Vastly preferable to cakey brownies."

"Agreed. But the brownie should be à la mode with coffee ice cream." Audrey was getting into the exercise. "And topped with hot fudge sauce and toasted pecans."

They grinned at each other. It was one of those practically perfect moments—good conversation, good food, a beautiful view. So, of course, it only made sense that things immediately went downhill.

"I think I'm going to have to disagree with you on the coffee ice cream. I'm a vanilla man myself," Coop said.

"You wouldn't feel that way if you'd tasted the coffee ice cream I had when I was in Cape Cod. It was at this place called Four Seas Ice Cream and was seriously the best I've ever had," Audrey said.

"That seems like a long way to go for a cone," Coop said.

"I don't know, it was really good. But we went there for—" Audrey began and then stopped abruptly.

Coop looked at her questioningly. "For?"

Audrey swallowed and looked at her half-eaten burger, her appetite suddenly gone.

"Ryan and I spent two weeks on the Cape for our honeymoon," she said.

"What part of the Cape? I've been to Martha's Vineyard a few times," Coop said conversationally, clearly oblivious to Audrey's uneasiness.

"Let's talk about something else," Audrey said.

"What did your husband do?" Coop asked.

"I meant, let's talk about something other than Ryan," Audrey said.

Coop took a swig of his beer. "Why?"

"Because it makes me uncomfortable," Audrey said.

"Why?" Coop asked again.

Audrey's discomfort quickly morphed into irritation. "Because I don't want to talk about him, that's why."

"Don't you think he's something we should be able to talk about?" Coop asked.

"No. I don't."

"Why are you getting so upset?"

"I'm not upset," Audrey lied. "I just . . . look, it just feels weird enough to be here with you. Talking about him with you makes it worse."

Coop studied her. "You think it's disloyal to discuss your late husband with me?"

Audrey could feel her shoulders tensing up.

"Maybe. Are you trying to say that I should be over it by now?"

"I didn't say that."

"You didn't have to. People always assume that grief should have a time limit. Like it's some sort of equation. X amount of time equals no more grief. But it doesn't work that way."

"How does it work?" Coop asked.

"It's a process," Audrey said.

"A process. Okay." Coop regarded her. "Is part of that process that you're going to feel like you're cheating on him every time you're with me?"

Audrey opened her mouth, ready to deny this. But instead, she found herself saying, "I don't know. Maybe. Look, I don't want to talk about it."

Coop nodded, taking this in. He took a sip of his beer. "What if I want to talk about it?"

"It's not up to you."

"That's not actually how a relationship works. Even I know that," Coop said. "We both get a say in what we talk about."

"This isn't a relationship. At least, it's not that sort of a relationship. And my late husband has nothing to do with you," Audrey said.

"It's my business that every time we're together, we seem to be having a great time, and then suddenly a shadow will cross over your face. And I can tell you're feeling guilty for being happy," Coop said.

Audrey shook her head.

"That's not true," she lied. "You don't know what you're talking about. Anyway, look . . . I like spending time with you. But this"—she waved a hand between Coop and herself—"this isn't serious. It's just a fling."

Coop sat back in his chair and picked up his beer. "A fling," he repeated and shook his head.

Audrey hesitated. "Isn't that what you thought it was?"

"As a matter of fact, no, I didn't."

Audrey felt her cheeks flush. *I'm being such a jerk,* she thought. *Further evidence that I'm terrible at this.* "I'm sorry if I hurt your feelings," she said awkwardly.

"I've been asked to go on a shoot that leaves out of the Bahamas," Coop said.

"Oh." Audrey blinked. "When?"

"I'd have to leave early next week and then I'd be gone for two months."

Coop looked at her, clearly waiting to see how she'd react to this news. Strangely enough, considering her insistence a moment earlier that their relationship was nothing more than a fling, Audrey's temper flared. He was giving her crap about not opening up and sharing with him, and all along, he'd been planning to skip town for two months and was just now telling her about it?

Audrey stared at Coop for a long, level moment. "How long has this plan been in the works?"

"I got the call this morning. The director they had slated to handle the shoot broke his ankle. I told them I'd think about it because I wanted to talk to you about it first." Coop shot an unfriendly look at Audrey. "But in light of today's discussion, I guess I'll just go ahead and take it."

Does he want me to beg him to stay? Audrey wondered, her own anger swelling. *Well, that's not about to happen.*

"Good. I think you should," Audrey said coolly.

"Okay, then," Coop said, his tone equally chilly.

"I should get back to work." Audrey raised her head, squared her shoulders, and turned, preparing to leave with as much of her dignity intact as possible. "And if I don't see you before you leave, have a nice trip."

"I'll see you Saturday," Coop said.

Audrey turned back. "Saturday?"

"The dinner party club."

"Right. See you Saturday," Audrey said. "Thanks for the burger."

And with that, she turned and strode out of Coop's apartment, wishing she'd managed to make her exit without tripping over the door jamb and also that she'd been clever enough to come up with a better exit line. The sort of zinger that Katharine Hepburn—wearing a fabulous trouser suit with padded shoulders—would say to Cary Grant, just before sweeping out of a room.

Somehow *thanks for the burger* didn't quite cut it, Audrey thought, clutching her car keys so tightly her nails dug into her hand. She'd have to have a better exit line than that ready for Saturday night.

"SHOULD WE BE AFRAID?" Will asked when Coop opened the door to Will, Fran, and Leland.

"Of eating the best meal of your life?" Coop retorted.

"Just so you know, if you give me food poisoning, I will sue," Will said, swatting Coop on the shoulder in greeting and handing him a bottle of wine. "I have no idea if this is any good, but it cost thirty bucks."

"Will!" Fran said. "You're not supposed to tell him how much you paid for the wine!"

"Why? I want to get credit for it," Will said.

"Hey, Leland," Coop said, shaking the older man's hand.

Leland handed him a bottle, too.

"Bourbon," Leland said succinctly. "The good stuff, to

have after dinner. Will and Fran drove me over, so I can in-dulge."

"I like the way you think," Coop said.

He began dispensing drinks—champagne for Fran and Leland, a beer for Will—and just as soon as he was done, the doorbell rang again. This time it was Jaime and Mark.

"Sorry we're late," Jaime said.

"It was my fault. I had to try on five outfits before we could leave," Mark said. "Oh, wait, no—that was Jaime."

Jaime rolled her eyes. "As if. I was ready ages ago. You were the one who insisted on showering at the last minute."

"I didn't want to offend our friends with my post-tennis stinkiness," Mark said.

"A fact that we are all grateful for," Coop said. "Come in and get a drink."

"Is everyone else here?" Jaime asked.

"Everyone but Audrey," Coop said, hoping he sounded more casual than he felt.

He hated to admit it—even to himself—but he was ner-vous about seeing Audrey again. Their last meeting had not gone at all as planned. He'd meant to tell her that he was going to turn down the directing job, that he was enjoying their time together too much to leave. But then she'd be-come defensive and prickly, and suddenly he heard himself announce out of nowhere that he had decided to take the job. It had all gone pear-shaped, he thought, remembering this favorite line of his mother to describe any situation that got mixed up.

Jaime handed over a bottle of Oregon Pinot Noir. "I didn't know what you're serving, but the wine store guy said this is versatile and goes with just about everything."

"Thank you," Coop said. "What can I get you to drink?"

He went to get wine for the Wexlers while they joined the rest of the small group in Coop's living room, munching on the cheese and crackers, watched intently by Bear.

"Come here, Bear," Fran said, and the dog sidled over to her, his whole body wagging. Bear hooked his nose over her knee while she stroked his ears.

"Where are we eating?" Mark asked after Coop had returned with his wine. The small dining table wasn't set.

"Out on the patio," Coop said.

He'd moved the patio furniture into his bedroom for the evening and rented a long table and chairs from a party supply company. They'd also supplied linens and dishware, which meant that he wouldn't have to deal with dirty dishes. He'd actually planned on having the dinner catered, too—that was the reason he hadn't sent the menu out ahead of time, as he and the caterer had been trading phone calls—but at the last minute, he changed his mind and decided to cook. Having it catered would have been cheating. Why it mattered, he wasn't sure, but for some reason it did.

The doorbell rang again.

"That must be Audrey," Fran said.

Coop went to answer the door, trying to ignore the fact that his palms were suddenly sweaty. It didn't help that Audrey was looking especially lovely. She had on her usual red lipstick and ridiculously high heels, which Coop found both silly and endearing.

"Hi," Coop said.

"Hi," Audrey said. She, too, held out a bottle in greeting.

"Thank you," Coop said.

"You're welcome."

"Would you like to come in?"

"Yes, please."

"Can I get you a glass of wine?"

"Yes, thank you. Red, if you have it."

They both sounded so stiff, and so formal, Coop almost laughed. This was the woman he had been tangled up in bed with a few days earlier, licking the saltiness of the sweat off her neck. She smelled amazing he noticed, as she passed by him into the apartment. He considered kissing her cheek in greeting, as he had with Fran and Jaime, but there was something in the set of her shoulders and the tightness of her mouth that kept him from leaning in.

"Audrey!" Fran called out.

Coop escaped for a moment to get Audrey's wine, while she headed into the living room to greet everyone. He poured himself a glass of wine, too, reminding himself that he had to keep his head clear if he was actually going to cook dinner.

"Thank you," Audrey said when he handed her the glass.

"Don't mention it. Cheers," Coop said, clinking his glass against hers. "Here's mud in your eye."

For a moment, Audrey looked as though she might laugh. But then Will came up—Audrey readily accepted *his* cheek kiss, Coop noticed resentfully—and said, "Couldn't you find higher shoes? Those are only, what? Four or five inches tall?"

"Five," Audrey said.

Will made a face. "That's no fun. You need to branch out. Go for a pair of those enormous platforms that drag queens wear."

"How do you know what kind of shoes drag queens wear?" Audrey asked.

"I'm a fountain of knowledge," Will said.

Coop laughed. "Make that a fountain of bullshit."

"That, too," Will said. "Or, better yet, Aud, you could start walking around on stilts."

"That would be an interesting fashion choice," Audrey said, turning away to greet Leland, who was sitting on the sofa next to Jaime.

"Why do women wear those things?" Will asked. "They look like torture devices."

"I don't know," Coop said, although as he admired Audrey's legs, he thought that might be the answer. He glanced at Fran, who was chatting with Mark. She looked over at Coop and gave him a surreptitious wink. Coop smiled back at her.

"Franny looks great," Coop said.

"Does she?" Will asked, glancing at his wife.

"You hadn't noticed? Jesus." Coop laughed. "And that right there is the reason I'm not married. Now if you'll excuse me, I have to go make some magic in the kitchen."

"Are you seriously going to cook?" Will asked. "I was hoping you were going to order in and try to pass it off as though you'd cooked it yourself."

"Like I would do something so devious and underhanded. I'm shocked you'd even think it," Coop said, shaking his head.

"Do you need any help, Coop?" Fran asked. "I did promise to be your sous chef."

"No, I've got it under control," Coop said.

He headed back to the kitchen, where he had a huge stockpot full of water already running on a gentle boil. He turned up the heat a bit, and then turned to the Styrofoam cooler that contained seven squirming lobsters. He had never cooked lobster before—much less a live lobster—and had to steel himself.

"Time to cowboy up," he told himself, picking up the first lobster. It waved its bound claws at him. "This is going to hurt me more than it hurts you. Actually, that's not true. But know that you're dying for a good cause."

"Are you talking to our dinner?" a voice said behind him.

Coop turned and saw Audrey at the door. She again looked like she was suppressing a smile.

"That depends on what you heard me say," he said.

"Something about dying for a good cause. And cowboying up," Audrey added.

"You may not want to be present for what I'm about to do," Coop said. "I don't want to offend your delicate lady sensibilities."

She took a sip of wine, studying him over the brim of her glass. "I think I can handle it."

Great, Coop thought. He was already nervous about the lobster slaughter that was about to take place, and now he had to do it in front of an audience.

"Go ahead," Audrey said, nodding at him.

Coop took a deep breath and took the lid off the enormous stockpot, purchased especially for the evening. Unfortunately, just as he was about to drop the lobster inside, it—perhaps sensing its fate—began to squirm.

"Ack!" Coop said, panicking. He dropped the lobster inside, causing hot water to splash out, and clanged the lid on.

"Good job," Audrey said dryly. "Way to cowboy up."

"Like you could do any better," Coop said.

Audrey set down her glass of wine, headed to the cooler, and, then—with a terrifyingly cold-blooded efficiency—she quickly transferred the six remaining lobsters to the pot, and replaced the lid. The lobsters let out an awful high-pitched screeching sound that made Coop's stomach turn.

"They're screaming," he said, swallowing hard.

Audrey looked at him in disbelief. "I thought you were supposed to be some sort of master fisherman? Lobsters can't scream. They don't have vocal cords."

"What's that noise?"

"I think it's steam being released from their shells, or something like that," Audrey said.

Coop contemplated if this was any less gruesome than screaming, and decided that it was. Slightly.

"I think I'm officially scared of you," Coop said. "You just committed six counts of lobstercide and seem completely unaffected by it."

This time, Audrey laughed. "You know that ground beef you cooked the other day came from a cow that was, once upon a time, alive and well and unaware of its future as a hamburger."

"That's different."

"How so?"

"Because I got that meat from Butcher Bob, already dead and wrapped in plastic," Coop said.

They smiled at each other, and for a moment Coop wondered if everything might be all right between them, after all. But then Fran stuck her head in the kitchen.

"What are you two doing in here? Coop, do you need any help?"

"There's a salad and a bowl of potato salad in the fridge. You could bring those outside," Coop suggested, hoping to get rid of her quickly.

But Audrey said, "I'll help you, Fran."

"Thanks." Fran opened the fridge and handed a large green bowl to Audrey. "Here's the potato salad. Does the green salad need dressing, Coop?"

"Yes. The dressing should be right there next to it," Coop said, watching Audrey depart with the potato salad.

Fran took out a Pyrex measuring cup that Coop had mixed the vinaigrette in and then covered loosely with Saran wrap. "You made your own dressing? I'm impressed."

"Thanks," Coop said. "I like to underpromise and over-deliver."

"Is that your personal creed?" Fran asked, twinkling up at him.

"No, my personal creed is Every Man for Himself," Coop said.

She whacked him playfully with a dish towel.

By the time the lobsters were steamed, and the melted butter divided into seven mini soufflé dishes, Fran had herded the dinner party club out to the patio. Coop thought the setup looked nice. The table was decorated simply with a row of votive candles—also provided by the party supply company—and you couldn't beat the view.

"Everything looks wonderful," Jaime said.

"Do you know what you need out here?" Fran said, surveying the table.

"What?" Coop asked, as he set the platter of lobsters in the middle of the table to general murmurs of approval.

"Twinkle lights," Fran said.

"Excuse me, what?" Coop said.

"Twinkle lights," Fran repeated. "Those little white lights that you string on your house at Christmas."

"I think it's safe to say that I'm not going to involve myself with anything called 'twinkle lights,' " Coop said. "It wouldn't be manly."

"If you were really manly, you wouldn't have to worry about whether or not things sound manly," Fran retorted.

Coop smiled. "Too true. Shall we eat?" he said.

Audrey chose a seat as far away from Coop's as possible—
On purpose? he wondered—and spent most of the remaining
evening discussing films with Leland. They both had a fond-
ness for small English period dramas, the sort of movies that
acted as instant Ambien on Coop. Every once in a while a
date would drag him out to see one, and he'd fall asleep ten
minutes into the film. Maybe this was another sign that he
and Audrey weren't meant to be. That, and the fact that she
didn't seem to like him very much.

Toward the end of the meal—which everyone said was
delicious, although Coop personally thought the potato
salad was too bland and the salad dressing too vinegary;
clearly he wasn't about to have a future as the next big celeb-
rity chef—Audrey and Leland seemed to move off the subject of movies and into relationships. Coop perked up and
turned away from Fran—who was flushed from the wine
and kept going on and on about some boat trip they'd all
taken together twenty years earlier—and tried to listen in on
what Audrey was saying to Leland.

"We talked about my meeting someone else before she
died," Leland said.

"You did?" Audrey asked. She was leaning toward Leland.
By candlelight, her eyes looked large and luminous.

"She said that her life was nearly over, but mine
wasn't, and that she wanted me to be happy and fulfilled. Of
course, at the time, I couldn't imagine ever meeting another
woman, much less falling in love with one. But Penny knew
that over time, I'd be ready to move on. She wanted me to
know that I had her blessing," Leland said.

"But wasn't that hard? I mean, she was *dying*. That must
have been awful enough. But to think of your husband with

someone else . . ." Audrey stopped abruptly, mid-sentence, as though suddenly worried that her words might upset Leland.

"That was just it. The idea that I would keep living gave Penny peace," Leland said gently.

"That's beautiful," Jaime said, twirling her wineglass by its stem. "And so romantic."

"Just so you know, when I die, you can date whoever you want," Mark said, leaning back in his chair. "But just make sure you do a background check on him before you let him near the kids."

"Somewhat less romantic," Jaime said.

"And yet ever so practical," Will said.

Audrey shook her head and shrugged. "I think your wife is a better woman than I am," she said to Leland. "I'd want to think that my husband would love me so much, he'd spend the rest of his life mourning my loss."

"At the risk of sounding like an old fart, that's your youth speaking. Yes, your youth," Leland repeated, when Audrey snorted. "When you get a bit older, it becomes less about sex and rock 'n' roll and more about companionship. Not that the sex can't still be quite gratifying," Leland added.

At this point, everyone at the table was listening in. There were a few guffaws at Leland's rock 'n' roll comment and then a general stunned silence.

"That's good to know. Here's to gratifying sex," Will said, raising his glass.

"To gratifying sex," a few others chimed in, also raising their glasses, and laughing as they did so.

"I should probably get going," Audrey said.

It was a clunky interruption, and six surprised faces turned toward her. Audrey flushed with embarrassment.

"Sorry," she said. "But I have to work tomorrow."

"On a Sunday?" Fran asked.

Audrey nodded. "We decided to expand our weekend hours in an effort to cater to working women who might not be able to fit in spa treatments mid-week."

"Speaking as a workingman, I can say I frequently have that problem," Mark said.

"I think it's a very smart idea," Jaime said.

"Thank you," Audrey replied, smiling at her.

"You haven't had dessert yet," Coop said.

Audrey looked at him directly for what seemed like the first time since the lobstercide.

"Thanks, but I really have to get going," she said.

Coop stood. "I'll see you out," he said.

Audrey looked like she wanted to object, but then—possibly realizing that there was no way she could do so without looking awkward or possibly even rude—she changed her mind and nodded.

He followed her to the front door. His head was buzzing slightly from the wine and aftereffects of the rich food. Bear had been dozing on his bed, but as they walked through the living room, he jumped to his feet, gave his furry body a firm shake, and trotted after them.

When Audrey reached the door, she turned. Coop didn't know what to expect. Best case scenario, she'd throw herself at him, kissing him deeply while knitting her hands in his hair and murmuring in his ear that her early departure was just a ruse to lure him away from the others, so they could have a quickie by the front door.

This did not happen.

"Thanks for dinner. Everything was wonderful," Audrey said.

"Thank you for coming," Coop said.

"Thank you for having me."

They seemed to have fallen back into their Chip 'n' Dale politeness routine.

"Look, I'm . . ." Coop paused, searching for the word. He remembered girlfriends of yore criticizing him for not being able to apologize. "I'm sorry if I upset you."

Audrey's face seemed to close. Her expression hadn't exactly been welcoming before—her eyes had been wary, her features a mask of polite diffidence. But suddenly, all friendliness seemed to vanish.

"Okay. I'm sorry if I upset you, too," she said coolly.

Coop understood at once that this was not a real apology. For one thing, she didn't sound sorry. She sounded pretty pissed off. And second, he hadn't been upset. Irritated, yes, but she was the one who had stomped off that day.

"I wasn't upset," Coop said.

"Oh, right. Okay, then," Audrey said.

Ah ha, Coop thought. Further proof that her apology had been bogus: She was clearly annoyed at this denial. If she'd really been sorry for upsetting him, she would have been glad to learn that he wasn't upset.

"I'm leaving Monday for the Bahamas," Coop said.

Audrey nodded, one curt bob of her head. "Have a good trip."

"Thanks. I'll call you when I get back," Coop said.

"Okay, whatever," Audrey said.

Coop knew he should leave it there, on somewhat less-than-completely-hostile ground. But for some reason, he couldn't.

"Whatever?" he repeated. "Whatever, I should call you, or whatever, you'd rather I left you alone?"

Audrey's nostrils seemed to flare, and she pressed her lips together. Finally, she swallowed and spoke. "There's not much point, right? I think we both know this—whatever it is—has run its course."

"Okay," Coop said. "If that's what you want."

"That's just what it is," Audrey said, her manner prickly enough to make Coop miss the earlier Chip 'n' Dale politeness, no matter how awkward it had been.

"Well, then," Coop said.

Audrey opened the door, and walked through it. "Bye," she said. She leaned over and patted Bear on the head. "Bye, Bear." Bear's tail thumped against the ground. Audrey looked back up at Coop. "Thanks again for dinner."

"Don't mention it," Coop said.

She didn't.

ONCE THE DOOR HAD closed behind her, Coop headed toward the kitchen, under the guise of getting out the dessert—a key lime pie he had bought from a local bakery, but had no plans of trying to pass off as his own work—but really more to process what had just happened.

Yes, he was disappointed. Part of him had hoped that the conflict between Audrey and him would have passed, that they would pick things up where they'd last left off. Or, at least, where they'd last left off just before the fight. Maybe she'd even stay the night.

Apparently not.

Coop shook his head, as he lifted the pie out of its white box. And his ex-girlfriends had thought *he'd* had intimacy issues. Compared to Audrey, he was Mr. Relationship.

You should be glad for the clean break, Coop told himself. In fact, it was a good thing he'd be leaving town for two months. Even if he was tempted to call Audrey, it was hard to make calls from a boat in the middle of the Atlantic Ocean.

"A nice clean break," Coop said out loud, dishing pieces of pie onto small white plates. And hopefully, by the time he got back, Audrey would be completely exorcised from his thoughts.

WILL DIDN'T REALIZE HE'D fallen asleep until Fran kicked him.

"Ouch," he said.

"You're snoring."

"How can I be snoring? I wasn't asleep."

"Either you were snoring or there's a rhinoceros in distress somewhere in the room."

"I love it when you flatter me like that," Will said, curling toward her.

Fran squirmed away. "Don't."

"Why not? I just want to cuddle."

"Because you'll fall asleep on top of me and snore in my ear."

Will rolled back to his side of the bed.

"Did you have fun tonight?" he asked.

"Mmm," Fran said.

"What?"

"I don't know. It was an odd night."

"I didn't think so. Everyone seemed like they were in good spirits," Will said.

"What do you think about Mark and Jaime?"

"What about them?"

"I get the feeling that Jaime isn't happy. Do you know

what I mean? She and Mark weren't really interacting that much. They talked to everyone else, but not to each other."

"I didn't notice. Has she said anything to you?" Will asked.

"No. She won't talk about it with me. You know what she's like. Everything's fine. Always perfect. Although she was pretty pissed off at Mark last week, when Logan was hurt and she couldn't track him down."

Will shrugged. "It's a hard time. Their kids are young, they're probably not getting a lot of downtime. Or sleep."

"Maybe," Fran said.

"I actually thought Audrey seemed a little off," Will said.

"Yeah, that was weird how she left so early," Fran said.

"I think there might still be something brewing between her and Coop," Will said.

Fran turned toward him. "Why do you think that?"

"Just the way they were acting around one another. Like they were trying too hard not to notice one another."

"That could be residual awkwardness from their bad date," Fran said.

"I don't think so. Coop kept staring at her when he thought no one was looking."

"No, he wasn't," Fran said.

"Why are you so against the idea of the two of them getting together?" Will asked. He put his hands behind his head. "I thought you liked Coop."

"I love Coop. You know that."

"Then, why are you being so weird about him and Audrey getting together?"

"I'm not." Fran rolled away from him again. "They didn't hit it off, remember? Anyway, maybe it's a good thing the dinner party club is taking the summer off. It will give them a chance to get a break from each other. By the time we start up again in September, the awkwardness between them will have passed."

Will moved closer to Fran, now feeling more awake than he had a few minutes before. He stroked her back, the way she'd always liked. In fact, once upon a time, this would be enough to make her purr with happiness and roll back toward him. Now she just lay there, still as stone, tolerating his touch.

"Is something wrong?" Will asked.

"No, nothing."

"You've just been . . . distant lately."

"Have I? I'm sorry," Fran said.

She continued to lie with her back to him. Will stroked her back, still hopeful that it might lead somewhere.

"Honey, do you mind? I want to go to sleep," Fran said.

Will withdrew his hand.

"Good night," Fran said, her voice muffled in her pillow.

"Night," Will said. He closed his eyes, wondering when they had stopped kissing each other before going to sleep.

"And try not to snore, okay?"

"Believe it or not, I don't actually have control over what I do when I'm asleep," Will said. He sighed and turned away, and tried to stay awake until he heard Fran's breath slow into the steady rhythm of sleep.

september

. . . .

SPINACH SALAD WITH GRAPEFRUIT AND
RED ONION

CHICKEN RILLETTES

CHICKEN LIVER PÂTÉ

SLICED BEEF TENDERLOIN WITH
HORSERADISH MAYONNAISE

CREAM PUFFS

*J*AIME FELT LIKE SHE'D been standing at the kitchen counter forever. The travertine tile floors were beautiful, but probably not the most comfortable choice they could have made when they redid the kitchen. She picked up one foot and rested it on the other as she diced carrots. She'd already chopped cupfuls of garlic, onions, celery, and thyme.

"Is this a new kind of yoga?" Mark asked, coming into the kitchen. "One that involves standing on one leg while you chop vegetables?"

"Are the kids asleep?" Jaime asked. The nighttime routine was usually her job, but this was her only chance to cook without having little ones underfoot. Mark had stepped in and helped out. For once.

No, Jaime chided herself. *He's been much better about helping out lately.*

"I seriously doubt it. However, they are in bed."

"Faces washed, teeth brushed?"

Mark slapped himself on the forehead. "I knew I was forgetting something! No, I'm just kidding. I'm not completely incompetent, thank you very much. But I think whoever wrote *Brown Bear, Brown Bear* was a sadist."

"Eric Carle."

"Right. He was probably abused as a child, and to get back at his parents—and all parents everywhere—wrote the most mind-numbing collection of children's books ever to be published."

"I sort of like *Brown Bear*. You can get a rhythm going with it," Jaime mused. " 'Brown bear, brown bear, what do you see?' "

Mark gave her a dark look.

"Hey, I'm a fan of anything that doesn't have Elmo in it," Jaime said.

"What are you making, anyway?" Mark asked, taking in the vast piles of minced vegetables.

"Chicken rillettes," Jaime said.

"Right. And what exactly is that?"

"Potted chicken. That sounds weird, I guess. But basically, you braise a chicken, then shred it, and mix it up with butter, herbs, and a vegetable-infused broth, and then you put it in jars to sit for a few days," Jaime explained.

"That sounds like a lot of work. The kids would probably be just as happy with hot dogs," Mark said.

"This isn't for the kids. It's for the dinner party club."

"Are we still doing that?"

"Yes. We just took the summer off, remember? Everyone's coming over here on Saturday. I decided to shake things up. Instead of serving an entrée, I'm going to do all small plates," Jaime said.

She had thought that her small plates idea would be elegant and impressive. However, she was already having second thoughts about it. It was actually easier to do one main dish than lots of little ones. But at least the rillettes could be prepared completely ahead of time. All she'd have to do on Saturday was decant the potted chicken into a pretty bowl and slice up some crusty French bread to serve with it.

She glanced up at Mark, to see what his reaction to her brilliant idea—minus the extra work—was. He was looking at her with a mixture of guilt and wariness.

"What?" she asked.

"This Saturday? As in three days from now?"

"Yes. Emily doesn't have a tournament this weekend. I checked the calendar before I scheduled dinner," Jaime said quickly.

"No, I know she doesn't. But she's going down to take a clinic in Boca this weekend. I was going to go with her," Mark said.

"And you were going to tell me this when?" Jaime asked, feeling a flash of the old irritation.

Things had been going better recently between her and Mark. They'd taken Logan and Ava to the South Carolina coast for two weeks, and for the first time in a long time it had felt like Mark had been really present. They took the kids to the beach every day, where they splashed around in the ocean and hunted for shells, and ate fresh seafood and farm corn for dinner every night. It had been a magical time.

The only sour note came when Jaime hired a photographer to take a picture of the four of them at the beach. She envisioned Mark and Logan wearing white button-downs and khaki shorts, and she and Ava in matching Lilly Pulitzer dresses, their family looking like something out of a magazine. The perfect family on the perfect vacation.

"We can use it as our Christmas card photo," Jaime enthused.

Mark had stared at her. "But Emily isn't here. We can't take a family photo without Emily."

Jaime now closed her eyes, remembering the resulting argument. She hadn't meant to exclude Emily—who had been invited on the trip, but chose instead to go to Spain with Libby. She'd just gotten carried away at the idea of a family portrait of the four of them. But even when she'd backed off the idea of using it as their Christmas card photo—which she'd done immediately, with a heartfelt apology—Mark had still refused to participate. Jaime ended up going alone to the photo shoot with the kids, but the photos hadn't turned out well. She wasn't even going to bother having them framed.

"I was going to tell you as soon as I'd opened up a nice bottle of wine and talked you into having a glass," Mark admitted. "Is there any way we can postpone the dinner party club?"

Jaime shook her head. "No way. Everyone's coming, and I've already spent a fortune on food."

"Let me call Libby. Maybe she can take Emily," Mark suggested.

"Good idea," Jaime said. She smiled at Mark. "Thanks."

He kissed her cheek and then fished out his ever-present phone and hit a button.

"Hey, it's me. I need to talk to you about Emily's schedule this weekend," Mark said into the phone.

He wandered off toward the living room, speaking in the calm, level voice he always used when talking to Libby or one of his more difficult law clients. Jaime turned her attention back to her rillettes. When the last of the chopping was done, she set her heavy, cherry-red Le Creuset Dutch oven on a burner and poured in a dollop of olive oil. Once the oil had heated she put a whole five-pound chicken inside, and rotating it every three to four minutes, browned the chicken on all sides. She scattered the chopped vegetables and herbs around the chicken, and after they had softened, added a cup of white wine. Once the alcohol had burned off, she finally added six cups of low-salt chicken broth, brought it to a boil, and then moved the chicken pot to the oven, so the chicken could braise for an hour.

By the time she was shutting the oven door, Mark had returned to the kitchen, looking grim.

"Is Libby taking Em?" Jaime asked.

"Yes, but she's not happy about it," Mark said. "She said it's my weekend to have Em, and if I'm not going to honor our custody agreement, maybe it was time we revised it."

"Are you serious?" Jaime asked. Mark nodded. "But you spend all sorts of time with Em. Libby can't seriously question your commitment to that child."

"She's just steamed because she has to cancel a date she had planned for Saturday," Mark said. He opened the refrigerator door and got out a bottle of beer.

"I'm surprised she was willing to do that," Jaime said. In her experience, Libby rarely if ever inconvenienced herself.

"She wasn't at first. I said that of course we wanted Em for the weekend as usual, and that she's always welcome here, that this is her home. However, I wouldn't be able to take her down to Boca." Mark shook his head and twisted the top off his beer. "Libby said she didn't want Em to miss the clinic—which, I agree, would not be ideal—and so she said she'd take her. She just wasn't happy about it."

Jaime blinked at her husband. It was so rare that anything came before Em's tennis practice. She couldn't help wondering if Libby's reaction played a part.

"Thanks," she said, giving him a hug. Mark squeezed her back and then released her.

"Don't thank me too quickly," he said.

"Uh-oh," Jaime said. "What's going on?"

"Libby wants to revisit the subject of homeschooling Emily."

"I thought you'd decided against it?"

"We did, for this year. But if Em starts playing more national tournaments, we'll eventually reach a point where homeschooling her will make more sense," Mark said. He kissed Jaime's forehead. "Don't worry. We'll deal with it when the time comes."

"Just do me a favor," Jaime said.

"Anything."

"Talk to me about it before you make any decisions. Okay?"

"Of course. I always do," Mark said, patting her shoulder.

WILL WAS AT HIS workbench, putting the final touches on his newest Rammer combat bot, which he'd christened Brutus. Iggy had suffered an ignominious defeat at the last combat bot competition down in Boca in July and Will had brought him home in pieces in a cardboard box. Undeterred by the loss, Will had immediately commenced work on Brutus. This time he planned to give him a much heavier shell. He hadn't had much of a chance to work on it over the summer, but there was a tournament in Miami next month, and he had every intention of winning. Or, at least, of not getting his ass seriously kicked.

"Hey, Dad," Rory said. "What are you working on?"

"Just putting some finishing touches on Brutus. What do you think?" Will presented the robot with a game-show-hostess hand flourish.

"Very cool," Rory said. "He's sort of cute."

"Cute? I don't want him to be cute," Will exclaimed. "I want him to look like a lean, mean, robot-killing machine."

Rory giggled. "He looks sort of like R2-D2. Only flatter. Like R2-D2 would look if he got flattened in one of those car smooshers."

Will scrutinized the robot. "Maybe he does a little," he admitted. "Anyway, I thought you were supposed to be helping me with him."

"I was going to, but Mom said I had to do my math homework," Rory said, making a face.

"I guess it's all about priorities. What's more important, Brutus or your math? No, I'm just kidding. Obviously, homework comes first," Will said hastily. He had seen the gleam of opportunity in Rory's eyes. "And that's the story I'm sticking with if you try to tell your mom that I said you could skip your homework."

Rory slumped onto the stool next to his, and watched Will work.

"Did you know Iris has a boyfriend?" she asked after a few minutes. Will could tell that although she was feigning a casual air, Rory was thrilled to pass along this juicy gossip.

Will set down his screwdriver and looked at his younger daughter. "She does?"

Rory nodded and grinned. "His name is Xander."

Surely Iris was too young for a boyfriend, Will thought. He thought back to when he was thirteen, and remembered that although couples might announce that they were "going out," they rarely even spoke to each other at that age. At most, they might go to the movies with a group of other thirteen-year-olds.

"They're going to a party together on Friday night, but you and Mom aren't supposed to know," Rory continued.

"What? Why not?"

"Because Mom said Iris isn't old enough to date," Rory explained.

"Oh, right. Good," Will said, glad that Fran was on top of the situation.

"Iris is going to tell you she's sleeping over at Hannah's house, but really, she's going to meet Xander at the party," Rory said.

Will wondered if the pain in his chest was from anxiety, or if he was actually having a heart attack.

"How exactly did you come by this information?"

"I listened at the door when she and Hannah were talking about it. You know, that whole glass to the door thing doesn't really work. You can hear much better if you just put your ear right up against it. Anyway, I thought you should know. By the way, Xander's a senior."

Will now understood how it was possible to age ten years over the course of a few minutes. He had a feeling he was supposed to tell Rory off for eavesdropping on her sister, but decided this was not behavior he wanted to discourage.

"Do you know where the party is?"

"It was supposed to be at some kid's house—somewhere where the parents were out of town—but then they decided to have it out at the sandbar instead, so they'd be less likely to get busted," Rory said.

Will sighed and stood up. The sandbar was a strip of beach located in the middle of the Intracoastal Waterway and accessible only by boat. Clearly, Brutus was going to have to wait. Protecting his thirteen-year-old's virtue from drunken senior boys partying at the sandbar took priority.

"Where are you going?" Rory asked.

"To talk to your mother about locking the two of you up until you reach the age of majority," Will said wearily.

"What did I do?"

"Nothing yet. But you'll be thirteen someday, too. Go do your math homework."

It took Will a few minutes to find Fran. She was standing

in their walk-in closet, which was jam-packed with clothes and shoes, along with winter coats, boxes of holiday decorations, rarely used sports equipment, and a mismatched set of luggage.

"What are you doing?" Will asked.

"Going through my clothes and throwing out what doesn't fit anymore."

"Are you sure that's a good idea? What if you gain the weight back?" Will asked.

Fran gave him the sort of look that would shrivel the balls of a lesser man.

"I mean, it's great that you've lost so much weight," Will said quickly. "You look amazing. But maybe you should put the stuff you can't wear anymore in storage. You know. Just in case."

"Just in case I lose all control and start pigging out on jelly donuts and chili cheese fries?" Fran asked.

"That's right," Will said. Then, seeing that rather than placating Fran, his words seemed to make her angrier, he said, "Look, it's nothing personal against you. It's just that a lot of people who lose weight tend to put it back on eventually."

"Did you want something? Because as much as I'm enjoying this conversation, I'm a little busy at the moment," Fran said, grabbing an armful of jeans and khaki pants.

Will was momentarily diverted. "Why do you have so many pairs of jeans?"

"Because that's what my life has become. Wearing scrubs to work and jeans to the grocery store," Fran said wearily. "I don't exactly have a lot of invitations to social events that require slinky cocktail dresses."

"You could wear a cocktail dress to the grocery store. Maybe it would start a whole new trend," Will said.

Fran smiled reluctantly. "Or I could get a BeDazzler and BeDazzle all of my scrubs with rhinestones."

Will grinned back at her and gave her shoulder a quick squeeze. They'd been in what felt like a holding pattern lately. Fran didn't seem unhappy necessarily, but she was still distant and distracted. And quiet. She'd been unusually quiet. Her chatter had been the background noise of his life for so long that the silence unnerved Will.

"None of these fit anymore," Fran said, dumping the assorted jeans and pants onto the bed with great satisfaction. "And besides, they're mom jeans, which I will never wear ever again. From now on, I'm only going to wear sexy, cool jeans. So out they go."

"We have to talk," Will said.

"Don't worry, I'm not going to go crazy buying stuff."

"This isn't about clothes. It's about Iris. And it's pretty serious."

This got his wife's attention. She stopped sorting through clothes and looked up at him. "Oh, God. What did she do?"

"Nothing yet. But Rory just told me that Iris is going to a party on Friday night. At the sandbar. With a boy named Xander," Will said.

"No, she's not. She's sleeping over at Hannah's house on Friday. . . ." Fran began, then stopped. Her eyes narrowed as the pieces fell into place. "You have got to be kidding me. Is she seriously going to try to pull the whole I'm-only-pretending-to-sleep-over-at-a-friend's-house-while-really-going-out-with-a-guy lie on us? I'm going to kill her. Then I'm going to ground her forever."

"Can we ground her for something before she's actually done it?" Will asked.

"Of course. Why couldn't we?"

"I thought you had to commit a crime before you could be punished for it."

"This isn't the American judicial system. It's a totalitarian dictatorship," Fran said, putting her fists on her hips.

"Wait, who's the head dictator? You or me?" Will asked.

"Who do you think?" She raised her voice. "Iris! Get in here!"

"What?" Iris called back.

"Right now!" Fran bellowed.

Iris appeared in the doorway, her arms crossed and her expression disgruntled.

"What?" Iris asked.

"Don't *what* me, young lady," Fran said.

"I don't even know what that means," Iris said, rolling her eyes heavenward.

Will decided this would be a good time to back up his wife.

"It means you should be more respectful when you speak to your mother," he told his daughter. Iris sighed and tossed her hair, but remained silent.

"You said you're sleeping over at Hannah's on Friday night?" Fran asked.

Will, who was watching his daughter closely, thought he saw a flicker of apprehension pass over her face.

"That's right," Iris said.

"If I call Hannah's mother and ask her if you're sleeping over, she'll know all about it?"

Now Iris definitely seemed on guard. "I don't know. I don't know if Hannah's told her yet," she said.

"Shouldn't Hannah ask her mother for permission before inviting friends to spend the night?" Fran asked.

Iris shrugged. "Hannah's mom is always cool about it."

It was a misstep, Will thought. What Iris meant—without actually coming out and saying it—was that Hannah's mother was cooler than Fran. This tactic didn't work with Fran at the best of times, much less when she knew her thirteen-year-old daughter was trying to bamboozle her.

"Why don't we have Hannah over here instead," Fran said smoothly.

"No, that's okay," Iris said quickly, alarm flashing in her eyes.

"Why not?"

"Because . . ." Iris was clearly groping for a credible reason. "I already told Hannah I'd sleep over at her house. It would be weird to change the plans now."

"No, it wouldn't. I'll tell you what. I'll call Hannah's mom now while I'm thinking about it," Fran said, picking up her cellphone.

"Mom! No!" Iris said, but Fran waved her off. Will looked on, half-amused at his wife's feint and half-sick that his daughter was lying to them so brazenly.

"Kim, hi, it's Fran. Good, how are you? I was calling to see if it's all right with you if Hannah sleeps over here on Friday. Oh, really? You're going to Tallahassee for the weekend? I see. No, another time. Thanks, Kim. Bye."

Fran hit the off button on her phone and looked at her daughter with raised eyebrows. "Hannah's mom said they're going to Tallahassee for the weekend."

"They are?" Iris asked. She shrugged. "I guess Hannah didn't know that."

"That seems unlikely, considering they're going to be there because Hannah's choral group is giving a performance," Fran said. She crossed her arms and looked levelly at her older daughter. "Are you going to tell the truth now, or are we going to keep this game going?"

"I don't know what you're talking about," Iris said. She was still trying to pull off her favorite sullen teenager act, but there was an edge of hysteria to her voice now that undermined the effect. "It was just a mix-up. Hannah probably meant next Friday."

"Oh, really? Is there a party at the sandbar next Friday, too?" Fran asked.

Iris's eyes went wide, and her mouth dropped open. Will was glad to see this. It meant his daughter wasn't as accomplished a liar as he had started to fear.

"How did you know about that?" Iris gasped.

"It's my job to know these things," Fran said coolly.

"Our job," Will said. He was mildly irritated that Fran wasn't giving him credit for being the one to find out what Iris was up to. Okay, so Rory really deserved the credit for that, but whatever.

"I can't go to the party?" Iris asked. Her voice was thin and high. Tears weren't far off.

"Of course not. Consider yourself grounded for the indefinite future," Fran said.

"For what? I haven't done anything yet!" Iris said.

"You lied to us," Will said.

"That's only because I knew you'd never let me go to the party if I told you about it!"

Fran let out a bark of laughter. "Of course you're not going to that party."

"Why not? All of my friends are going!" Iris said. She stamped her foot, which, Will thought, made her look like she was six years old again and demanding to know why she couldn't keep a miniature pony in the backyard.

"I highly doubt that, unless they're all planning on sneaking out, too," Fran said. "No parent in their right mind would let their freshman daughter go to a beer party at the sandbar with a bunch of senior guys."

"This is so unfair," Iris moaned. "Why can't you trust me?"

"We'd be more likely to trust you if you didn't lie to us," Will said. "Just a thought."

"You're grounded for one month. No going out, no having friends over, and no cellphone," Fran said.

"God, you're ruining my life!" Iris said. She stormed off, and a minute later, her bedroom door slammed shut.

Will sighed and looked at his wife. "Are you going after her or should I?"

Fran shook her head. "No, let her sit and stew in her room." She turned her attention back to the pile of clothes on her bed. "This may be the last peace and quiet we'll get for the next month. I swear, grounding her and taking away her phone is going to be more of a punishment for me than her."

Will stepped up behind her, and wrapped his arms around Fran. She relaxed against him for a moment.

"Just think. Only four more years until she goes to college," Will said.

Fran groaned and covered her face with her hands. Will laughed and kissed the top of her head.

COOP STOOD IN THE shower, luxuriating in the feel of the hot water streaming down over his body. The shoot had gone well, but two months on a crowded boat that carried both the ship's crew and a full camera crew meant they'd all had to rough it. Showers had been a luxury. When he'd scrubbed what felt like a layer of grit off his body, he finally turned the taps off and briskly toweled himself dry.

Coop shaved carefully, while Bear looked on. He was lying on the bath mat, his furry head resting on his paws. The unmistakable odor of unwashed dog wafted up from him.

"Don't think you've escaped. Tomorrow is bath day for you," Coop told him.

Bear—who knew the word *bath*—slunk out of the bathroom, glancing back with a worried expression.

"Coward," Coop called after him.

It was Table for Seven night. Two months ago, after he'd fulfilled his hosting obligation, Coop had had every intention of dropping out of the dinner party club. It was, he'd decided, a hassle he didn't need in his life. That went for Audrey, too. She had serious issues, and Coop had never had a masochistic streak when it came to women.

But then he'd gone away for two months. And despite the many distractions—the gorgeous aquamarine water, the frequent sightings of schools of dolphins, a sexy brunette photographer named Giselle—thoughts of Audrey kept drifting into his mind, no matter how firmly he tried to push her away. He even considered calling her, but cell reception on the ship was spotty. He would have had to place the call from the ship's bridge with the ship's crew listening in.

He'd gotten back in town that morning and had planned to call Audrey as soon as he'd gotten settled in. But then he checked his email and saw that tonight was dinner party night. Even better, he'd thought. It was always easier to rekindle a romance in person than over the phone. He'd called Jaime and double-checked that he wasn't too late to RSVP, and she assured him that he was more than welcome.

Coop dressed casually in khaki shorts and a white button-down shirt that showed off his tan.

"How do I look?" he asked Bear, who, caught between his desire to be near Coop and his terror of baths, had compromised by sitting at the bathroom door. "Will she be impressed?"

Bear's ears pricked up, and he began to pant. Coop took this as a sign of approval.

On his way over to the Wexlers' house, Coop stopped at the liquor store to buy a few bottles of Spanish wine. Jaime had said they were having tapas, so it seemed in keeping with the theme of the evening.

"Hello," Jaime said, when she opened the door to Coop. He kissed her cheek in greeting, and she accepted the wine. "Come on in. Everyone's in the living room."

Showtime, Coop thought.

"How was your trip? Fran was just telling us that you've been out to sea for two months," Jaime said.

"That's right. We docked in the Bahamas this morning and I took a flight into Fort Lauderdale," Coop said.

"What were you shooting?" Jaime asked.

"Dolphins, mostly. The documentary is about the complexity of their social networks. But we got some great shark footage, too," Coop said.

"That sounds very exciting," Jaime said, leading him into the tasteful beige living room.

The whole group was there. Fran and Will, Mark, Leland. But Coop's eyes sought out Audrey, who was sitting on the sofa next to Leland, looking radiant in an orange wrap dress. She looked up at Coop, and he could see the same apprehension and excitement he was feeling mirrored in her face. He smiled at her, trying to silently communicate how happy he was to see her.

"Coop! I thought I heard your voice." Fran was at his side, smiling up at him. He leaned forward and kissed her, and then shook hands in turn with Will and Mark, who were standing with her. Then he turned, ready to greet Leland, and, finally, Audrey, when he realized he was suddenly face-to-face with Kenny. Short, balding Kenny with the big ears.

"Kenny Stabler," Kenny said, sticking out his hand for a firmer than necessary handshake. "We met before at one of these shindigs. You're Coop, right?"

"Right," Coop said. He withdrew his hand.

"Your surprise appearance has been all anyone here can talk about," Kenny said with a smile.

"Not me. I'm more excited about the pâté Jaime has promised us," Will said, thumping Coop on the shoulder.

"We weren't expecting you back in time," Fran said. "I thought you weren't due until sometime next week."

"We got in a few days earlier than planned," Coop said. He tried to look calm and collected, and not give away how annoyed he was at Kenny's presence. Was he here as Audrey's date again? And if so, how the hell had that happened?

"You'll have to come over and see the girls. Rory's grown about a foot since you left," Fran said.

"And Iris has started lying to us and sneaking around with boys. It's a phase we're particularly enjoying," Will added.

"I'll come over and see them tomorrow," Coop said.

"Hi, Coop."

Coop turned to see Audrey standing beside him.

"Hi," he said, hesitating for a few beats too long before he leaned over and kissed her cheek. She smelled like clean hair and expensive perfume.

"How was your trip?" she asked.

"Good. Long, but good," he said.

Kenny stepped next to Audrey and slid his arm around her, his hand at her waist. Coop registered this, his eyes flickering down and then back up to Audrey's face. She looked uneasy, he thought, and Coop wondered if she was embarrassed by Kenny. Or maybe it was having past and present lovers meet. This, the thought of Kenny sleeping with Audrey, instantly made Coop feel queasy.

"Hi, Leland," Coop said, turning away from the sight of the happy couple to shake the older man's hand.

"Good to see you back," Leland said. "Franny was worried you'd been lost at sea."

"I think Fran watches too many movies. And old episodes of *Gilligan's Island*," Coop said.

"Hey, can I help it if *The Perfect Storm* seriously freaked me out?" Fran called from across the room.

"Are you still obsessed with bacon?" Coop asked Leland.

Leland chuckled. "You haven't been gone that long, my boy."

"Really? It feels like I've been gone forever," Coop said. He couldn't help a rueful glance in Audrey's direction. Kenny still had his arm around her. The only small comfort Coop could take was that Audrey wasn't leaning toward Kenny or murmuring in his ear.

Leland followed Coop's gaze and looked thoughtful. "I wouldn't worry too much about that if I were you," he said quietly.

"No?" Coop asked, so startled at this comment he forgot

to deny any interest in the budding relationship between Audrey and Kenny. He wondered how Leland had figured out that he and Audrey were—or, at least, had been—involved. Did everyone at the dinner party club know? Did Kenny?

Leland shook his head slightly. "Definitely not," he said.

"Here's your drink," Jaime said, appearing at Coop's elbow. She handed him the vodka and tonic he'd requested.

"Thanks," Coop said. He wanted to pursue his conversation with Leland, but knew it was impossible while everyone was there. He had to content himself with nodding his thanks at Leland, who was still looking thoughtful.

"I WANT TO HEAR more about your trip, Coop," Fran said, once they were all seated around the Wexlers' dining room table, eating a spinach salad studded with sweet chunks of grapefruit.

Fran was feeling a little light-headed, both from the wine and proximity to Coop. She'd forgotten how physically imposing he was. Even the hair on his arms—bleached blond from hours spent in the sun—fascinated her. She wanted to run her hands down his arm, to feel the texture of his skin against her fingertips.

"Big deal, Coop swam around with some sharks. That's nothing compared to what I faced down this summer," Will said.

"Which is what?" Jaime asked.

"Disney World," Will said grimly. "Apparently, in August, all of Europe heads to Florida and makes a beeline for Disney World."

"So? What do you have against Europeans?" Audrey asked, smiling at him.

"Nothing, right up until they make me have to wait an hour to ride Space Mountain," Will said. He smirked. "Speaking of which, I have the best vacation photo ever of Fran riding Space Mountain."

"Please tell me you didn't bring that with you!" Fran exclaimed.

"I wish I had. It's great," Will said.

"You were able to take a picture of her? How? Isn't that the ride that's really dark?" Jaime asked.

"They take the photo while you're on the ride, and then sell it to you on your way out," Will explained. "And as soon as I saw the one of Fran, I knew I had to have it. She has her eyes shut and is screaming in terror."

"For good reason," Fran said.

"You're afraid of roller coasters?" Mark asked Fran, looking incredulous.

"It's a normal thing to be afraid of," Fran said defensively. "They make those rides for little kids."

"They go really fast and turn you upside down. The whole thing is terrifying," Fran said.

"Actually, Space Mountain doesn't turn upside down," Will said.

"Are you sure? I could have sworn I was upside down at one point. It was when I started screaming," Fran said.

"Positive," he said. "And you were screaming before the ride even began. You started when they were just checking your seat belt."

"I can't help it if I have a deeply ingrained sense of self-preservation," Fran said.

"I don't blame you. I hate roller coasters, too," Jaime said, standing to collect the salad plates.

"Do you need help?" Fran asked, standing.

"Sure, you can help me bring out the tapas. You all got my email, right? Instead of making a main course, I made several small plates," Jaime said.

"Show-off," Fran teased her.

"I'll help, too," Audrey said. She looked around at the men. "Don't all hurry to get up and help us out."

"Cooking and cleaning is women's work," Will said, grinning at her.

"Watch out, Will," Kenny said. "Audrey will stab you with her stiletto. Those things she walks around on are lethal weapons."

"I HAVE SOMETHING TO tell you guys," Fran said, keeping her voice low, once the three women were alone in the kitchen.

"What?" Jaime asked.

"I'm leaving Will," Fran said. A burst of nervous excitement cascaded through her. It was the first time she'd said the words out loud.

Audrey had been stacking salad plates in the sink. Jaime was taking the chicken rillettes out of the refrigerator and peeling back the plastic wrap that covered the serving dish. But at Fran's words, both friends turned and stared at her with matching, dropped-jaw expressions.

"What?" Audrey asked.

"Fran," Jaime said, reaching out and touching Fran's shoulder.

"It's okay. I mean, I'm okay. This is what I want," Fran said.

"What's going on? Is Will . . . is he . . . ," Audrey began, but couldn't seem to complete the thought.

Fran shook her head. "He's not cheating on me. At least,

not that I know of. But, no, I seriously doubt it. Infidelity is not in Will's nature."

"Then *why?*" Audrey asked.

"It's something I've been thinking about for a long time. I'm just not happy. Will's not happy, either. He spends all of his time in the garage, completely checked out of life."

"Have you talked to a marriage therapist?" Audrey asked.

"No. We have in the past, but it was a waste of time and money. The truth is, we're just not in love with each other anymore," Fran said. Her initial burst of excitement faded at the bleak reality. "We lay in bed every night, side by side, like we're brother and sister. I can't remember the last time we kissed, much less the last time we made love. It's not like we fight all that often, but it's not like there's anything else there. We just stagnate."

"You're friends, though, right? I always thought Will was your best friend," Audrey said.

Fran felt sadness wash over her. "Maybe at one time. But it's been so long, it's hard to remember. Now he's just the guy who sits in the garage, ignoring everything that's going on in our lives."

"But a separation? That's a really big step," Jaime said.

"I know, trust me," Fran said. She paused to take a sip of her wine, and then leaned back against the counter. "And I know it seems sudden to you two. But trust me, I've been thinking about it for months. About how we can't keep going on like this. Without passion, without any spark between us. We both deserve more."

"But why can't you rekindle that spark with Will?" Audrey asked. "Spend time together, go out on dates, meet him at the front door wearing Saran wrap."

Both Jaime and Fran laughed.

"I've never seen how wearing Saran wrap is supposed to be sexy," Fran said.

"It seems like it would be hot," Jaime said. "Not sexy-hot, but just hot."

"And hard to get out of," Fran added.

"I'm serious. Maybe if you try harder—if you both try harder—you can get back what you once had," Audrey said.

"I have tried. We've tried. But how can I make myself feel something for him that I don't? Whatever we once had, it's just . . . gone," Fran said, shaking her head.

"So, you're giving up?" Audrey shook her head. "Just like that, you're giving up?"

"It's not a matter of giving up."

"You just announced you're leaving your husband of, what? Seventeen years?" Audrey continued.

"Sixteen next July."

"Fine. Sixteen years. You're leaving a sixteen-year marriage because you're *unhappy*. Do you have any idea how selfish that sounds?"

Fran blinked. She'd expected surprise, shock even, at her announcement. But not anger. "Marriages end, Audrey. People fall out of love. It happens all the time."

It probably would have happened to you and Ryan, if he hadn't died so young, she wanted to add, but managed to stop herself.

"What about Iris and Rory? Have you thought about how this will affect your daughters?" Audrey demanded. Her face was flushed, and her eyes were narrowed into two angry slits. Fran almost took a step back from her. She had never seen Audrey this angry, and certainly never at her.

Jaime, who had been listening in what seemed to be shocked silence, said, "I think what Audrey is saying is that this is a big decision. It's not something you should rush into."

Fran crossed her arms, as though this would repel her friends' disapproval. "Do you seriously think this is some sort of a whim? Of course I've thought about it. I haven't thought about anything else for months. I know that the girls will be upset for a little while. But I think it will be better for them to eventually see that it's important to have passionate, loving relationships in life. That when it comes to love, they shouldn't settle."

"Bullshit," Audrey said.

"Excuse me?" Fran asked, staring at her.

"I said, *bullshit*. Kids don't care if their parents are happy or not. All they care about is if they're together."

Fran suddenly remembered this very sentiment stated in a conversation they'd had, months earlier, when they'd been talking about Allison Hart and her divorce—which, Fran had recently learned, had been finalized over the summer. Fran also remembered how disgusted she had been with Allison—with her affair, with how she had frittered away her family's stability. *Is that how everyone is going to view me?* she wondered.

"I don't know. I think that if the parents are fighting a lot, and there's a lot of tension in the house, the kids might actually be relieved to not have to live with that anymore," Jaime said.

"I thought you said that when your parents divorced you would have preferred they stay together than be happy," Audrey said.

Audrey had always had an annoyingly good memory.

"Did I say that?" Jaime asked, her brow creasing. "I guess so. But I was a kid then. With a kid's perspective. If Will and

Fran are in turmoil . . ." She trailed off with a wave of one hand.

"But Will and Fran aren't fighting. Are you?" Audrey asked, cutting her eyes at Fran.

Fran shook her head. "No."

"No," Audrey repeated. "Fran's just going to tear her family apart because she's bored."

Fran's shock at Audrey's anger fell away, quickly replaced by a white-hot fury that pressed in her chest and burned at her throat.

"I didn't say I was *bored*. I said I was *unhappy*. There's a big difference," Fran said, spitting out the words. "But I guess I shouldn't be surprised by your reaction. You've always overly romanticized marriage."

"No, I haven't!" Audrey's arms were crossed now, too, her body language mirroring Fran's.

Jaime stood off to the side, glancing nervously at the swinging doors that led off to the dining room, clearly worried that they might be overheard. Fran glanced in that direction, too, but thought they were safe—the men's lively voices and laughter were muffled through the doors. If she couldn't hear what they were saying, they certainly couldn't hear her.

"You always talk about marriage as though it's some sort of fairy tale. And they lived happily ever after. But they don't always. And I would think you, of all people, would know that," Fran said.

"What is that supposed to mean?" Audrey demanded.

Fran shook her head. "Do you seriously not remember what it was like when you were married to Ryan? Or have you deluded yourself into thinking that you had a happy marriage?"

Audrey flinched as though Fran had slapped her, and the blood drained from her face.

"You don't know anything about my marriage," Audrey whispered.

"I know that Ryan was an alcoholic. I know that it was normal for him to start drinking at lunchtime and not stop for the rest of the day. I know that there were nights when he didn't roll in until two or three in the morning, and you had no idea where he was," Fran said.

Even in her anger, Fran knew she was crossing a line. But she couldn't seem to stop herself.

"You've never even admitted that the reason he probably died that night was because he'd been drinking. People don't just drive into overpasses. At least sober people don't," Fran continued.

"Fran," Jaime murmured. She touched Fran's arm. "That's enough."

"Yes. That's enough. I know my husband better than you did. I know what his faults were. Just because I don't talk about it, doesn't mean I didn't know what was going on. But, unlike you, I would never have thrown away my marriage. I would have fought for it. Fought for him," Audrey said. She gave Fran a long, level stare. Fran felt something between them break away. A fault line cracking open.

The doors to the kitchen swung open, and Mark and Kenny came in.

"You're taking a long time. We thought you might need some help," Mark said.

Mark seemed oblivious to the tension in the room, but Kenny's eyes sought out Audrey and he frowned with concern.

Audrey turned to Jaime. She was still very pale and her red lips were set in a thin line, but when she spoke, her voice was composed. "Thank you for having us over, Jaime, but I'm afraid we're going to have to leave early."

"Leave? But we haven't had dinner yet," Mark said. He slung an arm around Jaime's shoulders. "Jaime's been slaving over the food for days. You have to try the roulettes."

"Rillettes," Jaime murmured.

"Right. Rillettes. You have to try the rillettes," Mark said.

"No," Audrey said abruptly. She looked at Kenny. "I'm sorry, I have a terrible headache. Would you mind taking me home?"

Fran stood back, her arms crossed, her head still buzzing with anger, as Audrey and Kenny made a quick departure— Audrey collecting her bag from the living room, Kenny returning to the dining room through the swinging doors to make their excuses to Coop, Leland, and Will. Jaime turned and looked at her reproachfully.

"Maybe you should go after her," Jaime said softly.

"No," Fran said. She shook her head in defeat. "Just let her go."

"What's going on?" Will asked, pushing through the swinging doors with Coop in his wake. "Kenny just came in and said that he and Audrey are leaving. What's that about?"

Fran looked at her husband's round, boyish face. His cheeks were flushed—a by-product of the wine, Fran knew, drinking always made him turn red—but his eyes were bright and inquisitive as he looked at her for more information. She gave him a warning look, one that was meant to communicate, *Not now, I'll tell you later.* Will nodded, and she knew he'd understood. They'd always been able to have complete conversations like this, without a word ever being spoken. Maybe all married couples did, after years of practice negotiating the minefields of children and in-laws.

Fran's throat suddenly felt thick and sore, and tears stung at her eyes as she pictured herself in the life she'd have post-Will. Living alone in a small, neat house, spending her evenings reading quietly, cooking meals for one. She thought she'd be okay with the solitude, and having the girls with her half-time, and even the inevitable fallout among their friends, like what had just happened with Audrey. But she realized—maybe for the first time, really realized—that it would mean giving up the intimacy of a husband. Someone she could exchange one look with and communicate an entire conversation.

But then she looked at Coop—who, if possible, was looking even more sexy than usual; he had lost weight on his trip, and was lean and darkly tanned—and she felt a rush of excitement when his pale eyes met hers. She'd never have that stomach-swirling feeling again with Will, or turn jelly-legged when he kissed her. How could she go through life never feeling that again? Even if Coop wasn't her future—and even in her most lust-filled fantasies, Fran knew he probably wouldn't be—there was at least the chance of something else. With someone else. The chance of a life that was exciting and full of passion. Something other than the vanilla pudding life she was now living.

Will tilted his head to one side. "You okay, Franny?" he asked.

Fran nodded. "I'm fine," she said, hoping she sounded more brisk and in control. "Let's eat."

october

. . ..

ANTIPASTO

SAUSAGE AND MUSHROOM RISOTTO

ROASTED BEET AND
BITTER GREEN SALAD

CHERRY-APRICOT COBBLER

$\mathcal{J}$ AIME FELT UTTERLY RIDICULOUS, sitting in the front seat of her silver SUV, hiding behind a pair of enormous sunglasses. Why was she trying to disguise herself? It wasn't like Mark wouldn't recognize her car if he spotted it.

"Mama, what are we doing?" Logan asked in his high, breathy voice.

"Why don't you put your head back and close your eyes?" Jaime suggested. Ava was already napping, her plump cheeks sweetly slack, her well-loved stuffed frog, Hoppy, in her limp arms. But Logan was fighting sleep. He rubbed at his eyes and was starting to grow fretful.

"I want to go home," he whined.

"We'll go home soon," Jaime said soothingly.

"But the car's not moving," Logan said. He wiggled in his seat, thrusting his chest forward, as though this action alone could get the car started.

"Shh, keep your voice down," Jaime said, sotto voce. She didn't know why she bothered. Once Ava was asleep, nothing woke her. A marching band could parade through her room, crashing cymbals and banging drums, and Ava would sleep right through it.

Suddenly she saw a black Lexus sedan pull out of the parking garage. Jaime slouched down in her seat, hoping Mark wouldn't see her across the street, idling in the parking lot outside a strip mall that was home to a frozen yogurt shop, a barber, and a psychic who advertised tarot card readings. But Mark didn't glance in her direction. Instead, he signaled and turned right, driving smoothly away.

Her heart racing, Jaime put her car into gear and drove slowly after him.

"Yay, we're moving," Logan called from the backseat.

It was easy to make him happy, Jaime thought. A cookie, a hug, a car headed home. He'd always been a sunny child. Ava was the one who was quick to tears, quick to pout. Mark had nicknamed her Drama when she was still a newborn and never seemed to stop fussing.

What would he say if he knew I was following him to find out where he goes in the afternoon? Jaime wondered. *Drama would be the least of it. He'd probably accuse me of being paranoid, crazy even, to suspect that he might be cheating.*

It was true, Jaime still didn't have any hard evidence that Mark was being unfaithful. If anything, things between them had improved over the past few months.

And yet . . . and yet. Sometimes she'd look over at Mark when he was sending a text, his fingers flying over his phone, and she'd catch something in his unguarded expression. Excitement, maybe. Or anticipation. *Who was he texting?* Jaime wondered. Was it Sarah?

Jaime finally decided to tail Mark, and see just where he was really going when he claimed to be at the tennis club. She knew she might be wrong—she *hoped* she was wrong—but she had to find out for sure.

Jaime drove after Mark, staying far enough back that he wouldn't spot her. She was actually too far back and almost missed it when he made first a left-hand turn, and then a quick right. Luckily, she managed to hang with him.

Mark took another left just past a car wash, and Jaime

followed. The terrain out the window changed from commercial spaces to the green manicured lawns of gated communities. They were only a half-mile or so away from the tennis club now—it seemed that's where Mark was headed, after all—but Jaime hung with him, just in case he took a sudden turn into one of the subdivisions. But no, he didn't put on his turn signal until the drive of the tennis club came into view, and then he turned into the parking lot. Jaime turned, too, counting on a bank of palm trees to hide her from his view. She needn't have worried. Mark got out of his car and retrieved his tennis bag from the trunk without looking in her direction once.

"Daddy?" Logan chirped from the backseat. He kicked his feet against the back of her seat. "There's Daddy!"

"Shh," Jaime said automatically, even though it didn't really matter. There was no way Mark would be able to hear Logan.

"I want to see Daddy!" Logan announced.

Ava stirred behind him, her eyes blinking sleepily. "Daddy?" she said.

Worried that her children would somehow will Mark's attention in their direction, Jaime was about to ditch the surveillance. But then a woman crossed the parking lot toward Mark, her back to Jaime's SUV. *Was this the woman her husband was having an affair with?* Jaime wondered. But, no, almost as soon as the thought crossed her mind, causing her heart to skitter nervously, Jaime saw the woman clearly. It was Libby.

Mark leaned over to hug Emily, while Libby stood back, her arms crossed. Mark's ex-wife was wearing a chocolate brown shawl draped artistically around her shoulders and her curly hair blew a bit in the wind. Once Mark and Emily broke apart, Libby rested a hand on her daughter's shoulder and said something that caused Emily to skip off toward the tennis club. Mark and Libby trailed after her at a more sedate pace, chatting.

Jaime suddenly realized how very stupid she'd been. Mark wasn't having an affair. All the times he claimed to be going to the tennis club, he had been telling the truth. He was just what he appeared to be—a man so devoted to the daughter from his first marriage and so intent on keeping her world intact that he was willing to spend time with his disliked ex-wife.

And rather than admiring him for his dedication, and loving him for being such an attentive father, Jaime had let herself sink into a fog of jealousy. She was jealous of the time he spent away from her, jealous of what she perceived as his favoritism for Em over Ava and Logan, and even jealous of Em's pretty young tennis coach, even though Mark had never given her one reason—one real reason—to doubt him.

What kind of a person am I? Jaime thought, thoroughly disgusted with herself. *I've been consumed with jealousy and pettiness. In fact, I've officially turned into the evil stepmother.*

"That's it. I'm done," Jaime said out loud.

"Done?" Logan parroted from the backseat.

"That's right. Mommy has been very, very silly. But she's not going to be silly anymore," Jaime said.

Both children giggled at this.

"Silly Mommy," Ava said.

"Come on, let's go home," Jaime said. She put the car into drive and made a three-point turn. "Maybe we can make cookies."

Logan cheered enthusiastically at this. Ava swung her chubby legs and hugged Hoppy to her chest.

"Can we make sugar cookies?" Logan asked.

"Let's make chocolate chip," Jaime suggested. "Those are Daddy's favorite."

IT'S BEEN A LONG DAY, Will thought as he made his way through the garage—too tired to do more than send a glance in the direction of Brutus, who had been languishing on the workbench, ignored for weeks—and headed into the house. He listened for a moment, wondering if he would, yet again, be walking into a gale-force family drama. Iris shouting at Fran and then storming off to her room, slamming her door behind her. Rory in tears because she'd failed another math test. Fran short-tempered with everyone and coldly distant to him. But amazingly, the house was quiet.

Will headed into the kitchen. Fran was there, sitting on one of the high stools, studying a cookbook. Will leaned in to kiss her; Fran turned her head, offering up her cheek. Will dutifully bussed her cheek, remembering back to the early days of their marriage, when he'd occasionally arrived home from work to find Fran waiting for him in their bedroom, dressed in sexy lingerie.

"How was your day?" Fran asked absently, still paging through the cookbook. Then, without waiting for his answer, she said, "We're hosting the dinner party club this month, and I can't decide what to make. What do you think about Indian food?"

"I love Indian, but not everyone else may," Will said.

"Hmm, maybe you're right. I can't decide what to cook," Fran said.

"How about Italian?" Will suggested. "That's always a big hit. You could make meatballs or lasagna."

"Yawn. I want to do something spectacular. Jaime's tapas were a big hit. It's going to be hard to follow," Fran said.

"I thought the idea was for everyone to get together and share a good dinner," Will said. Since dinner didn't seem to be imminent, he retrieved a bag of pretzels from the pantry and tossed a handful into his mouth.

"You thought wrong. The idea is to win," Fran said.

"Have you talked to Audrey?" Will asked, trying to keep his tone casual.

He had no idea what had transpired that night in the kitchen, but it was obvious Audrey and Fran had had a falling out. Whenever Will tried to probe into what exactly had happened between them, Fran just shook her head, pressed her lips together in a tight line, and said she didn't want to talk about it.

"No," Fran said. "I'm sure she won't come, though. We'll have to rename ourselves the Table for Six group."

"Or invite someone else. Maybe Coop will want to bring a date," Will suggested.

Fran looked up sharply at him. "Why? Is he seeing someone?"

"Not that I know of. But this is Coop we're talking about," Will said.

Fran bit her lip and inhaled deeply. She seemed to be working up to saying something.

"We need to talk," she said.

"Oh, God," Will said, feigning horror. "That's a statement rarely followed by good news."

Fran didn't smile. She just looked at him with an expression that suddenly frightened Will.

"Are the girls okay? Where are they?" he asked anxiously.

Fran blinked. "Relax, they're fine. Rory's at soccer practice, and Iris is at Hannah's house. I think they're working on a project for school."

Will nodded. "Good," he said, although his stomach felt tight and sour. He had the distinct feeling that he didn't want to hear whatever it was Fran planned to tell him.

"I think you know I haven't been happy," Fran said.

"You haven't seemed like yourself lately," Will said.

"I know. My temper always seems to be at the breaking point. I hear myself snapping at you and the girls, and I hate the way I sound," Fran said.

"Maybe you need to take more time for yourself," Will suggested.

"That's exactly what I was thinking, too," Fran said.

Will nodded, the tension knot in his stomach finally starting to relax. "You should have a spa day. Or maybe you and"—he was about to say Audrey, but then remembered just in time about their falling out—"your friends could go away for a weekend. You could go to Sanibel or Miami Beach."

"Actually, I was thinking of a more . . . significant change," Fran said.

"What?" Will asked. He shook his head. "I don't understand."

His phone began to ring, and even though he was starting to get the feeling that this was a very important conversation, and one that he very much needed to stay engaged in, he glanced down at the caller ID out of habit. "It's Iris."

"You'd better answer it," Fran said.

It was the unspoken parent code. Children could be ignored when they were safely at home, badgering you to buy them something or for more TV time. But calls from children when they were away were always taken.

"Hey, Iris," Will said. There was a slight pause, and then a ragged intake of breath. Will tensed. "What's wrong? Are you okay?"

"Can you come get me?" Iris asked.

"Of course. I'll come right now. Where are you?" he asked.

She was crying now, and Will could barely understand what she was saying. "I'm at the police station."

AS SHE AND WILL drove to the police station, Fran felt numb.

"What did she say?" she asked again.

"I've already told you everything," Will said.

"Tell me again."

"She said she was at the police station and asked if we'd pick her up. I said yes. Then she hung up."

He sounded too calm, Fran thought, but then wondered if he was feeling numb, too.

"But *why* is she at the police station?"

"I don't know. Trust me, I'd tell you if I did," Will said.

They lapsed into silence. Fran began to chew on a fingernail, a bad habit she'd had since childhood. Normally when she did this, Will would reach over and gently pull her hand down, reminding her to stop. But now he let her gnaw away, not saying a word.

When they got to the police station—the outside of which was painted in bright Caribbean pinks, blues, and greens, as though these colors would disguise the sobering business conducted within—Will pulled in to a spot in the mostly empty lot. He sat for a moment, perfectly still, while Fran fumbled with her handbag.

"Are you leaving me?" Will asked suddenly.

Fran's stomach made a nauseated lurch. "I don't think this is the best time to talk about it," she said.

"No, I need to know now. Are you leaving me?" Will's hands were still on the steering wheel, and the car was idling.

"I think . . . , " Fran started, then stopped, sucking in a deep breath to summon her strength. Her mouth felt very dry, and her throat was so tight, the words barely squeezed out.

"I think we should consider separating."

Will sat silently, his hands not moving from the wheel. Fran glanced over at him, wondering what he was thinking. But Will seemed frozen, not even blinking.

Finally, not able to take the silence for one moment longer, Fran said, "Are you okay?"

Will finally turned toward her. His eyes were glittering with unshed tears. Will, who she'd never seen cry before, not even when his mother had died. For the first time, Fran felt the weight of what she'd done. And it was unbearable. She loved Will, even if she wasn't *in* love with him anymore. She didn't want to hurt him. And yet, she didn't see any way that she could avoid it.

"This isn't any kind of a life," Fran whispered. "We never make love. We never even kiss. It's like we're roommates. Good friends, comfortable with each other, but that's not a marriage."

"I guess that's the difference between us. When I tally up everything we have going for us—our life together, the girls, our house, everything—I think that outweighs all of the bad," Will said.

"Can you honestly say you're still in love with me?" Fran asked.

"Yes," Will said instantly. Then, after a painful beat, he said, "But I take it you don't love me."

"Of course I love you," Fran said. "I'll always love you. But this, what we have together"—Fran made a circular gesture with one hand— "it's not enough for me. Not nearly enough. We've talked about it before, but nothing ever changes."

Will absorbed this blow, flinching as though her words were physically painful.

"Is there someone else?" he asked.

Fran thought of Coop, of the way she could barely breathe when he was close by. She had no idea if he felt the same way—in fact, she seriously doubted whether any feelings he might have for her were as strong as hers for him—but in an odd way, Coop didn't really matter. He wasn't the issue. It was the promise of Coop, or of someone else. Someone that Fran could love completely and without reservation. Someone who, when he touched her, would make her want to fall into his arms, all languid eyes and jellied limbs.

"No," she said. "There's no one else."

"Are you moving out?" Will asked.

Fran suddenly felt overwhelmed by the magnitude of this conversation. In all the times she'd pictured them discussing the dissolution of their marriage, she'd never thought it would take place in a car. Parked in front of the police station. With Iris waiting inside for them.

"I don't know. I mean . . . we don't have to make a decision about that right away," Fran said. "I was thinking we should wait until after the holidays. I don't want to spoil Christmas for the girls."

Will stared into space. "So, what? We're supposed to pretend everything's fine until then?"

"We have a lot of experience with pretending everything's fine, don't we?" Fran said, her lips twisting in a bitter smile.

"No, actually. I really thought we were happy," Will said quietly.

The smile vanished from Fran's face. There was nothing, not one single thing, humorous about this situation.

"I'll sleep on the couch for now," she offered. "And we'll take some time to figure out how everything else is going to work."

"No, I'll sleep on the couch," Will said.

"I don't mind."

"Yes, you do. Your back will start to bother you," Will said. He hesitated. "What are we telling people?"

"Nothing, yet," Fran said. "I don't want the girls to hear it from someone else first."

Will nodded. "I suppose we should cancel the dinner party."

"What? Why?" Fran asked.

He finally turned to stare at her. "You want to go ahead with it?"

Yes, Fran thought. *Yes, I want to go through with it.*

She'd only seen Coop the one time since he'd gotten back in town. Part of her—the sensible part, she assumed—had hoped that his absence from her life these past few months would make it easier to get over the fantasies she'd been having about him. But if anything, it had been just the opposite.

"I think we should. It will be fun," Fran said.

Will looked incredulous. "Fun?" he repeated.

"It could be," Fran said, feeling defensive.

"You don't think we might be just a little distracted by whatever is going on with Iris?" Will gestured to the police station. "Not to mention the fact that our marriage is apparently falling apart?"

"I've already invited everyone over."

"So uninvite them."

"No," Fran said. She shook her head. "Then we'll have to say why, and the entire thing will be a huge drama, and I don't want to do that."

Will sighed. His face—usually so youthful—suddenly looked years older. "Fine, I don't want to fight about it. Do what you want, as usual. Let's go in and get Iris," he said.

Will and Fran walked into the police station together, both of them silent. The building was new and everything was clean and shiny in an industrial way. At the front desk—the reception area, Fran thought, before realizing that this was ridiculous, it was a police station, not a hotel—a uniformed officer took their names and told them to take a seat in the empty waiting area. The room was decorated with maroon chairs made out of the sort of indestructible plastic that would probably survive a nuclear holocaust, and fake ficus trees in basket planters. Posters on the wall warned against DUIs and listed the warning signs of drug addiction.

"It's so quiet," Fran said.

"I guess six o'clock isn't the rush hour for criminals," Will said.

They lapsed into silence again. After they'd been waiting for about ten minutes, another officer—also in uniform—came out to the waiting room.

"Mr. and Mrs. Parrish?" she asked.

Fran's heart gave a sickening lurch, as she and Will stood. It reminded her suddenly of the time when she was pregnant with Rory, and the ultrasound tech had become concerned that the baby might have a heart defect. She'd been referred to a fetal medical specialist for a type II ultrasound. And even though everything had turned out fine, and Rory was born healthy with a beautiful, strong heartbeat, the wait to find out what the specialist was going to say had been excruciating. She and Will had sat in a waiting room not unlike the one they were in now, clutching hands, united in their terror.

"Come right this way," the officer said, after introducing herself as Selena Rodriguez.

She led them to a room with a long table flanked by more indestructible plastic chairs and a long mirrored window along one wall.

"Oh, my God," Fran said, recognizing the setup from the police detective shows she watched. "Is this an interrogation room?"

Officer Rodriguez smiled. She was short and plump, with kind eyes and pretty long, dark hair. "It's just a convenient place for us to talk," she said.

Fran nodded. She and Will sat down on one side of the table, their backs to what Fran assumed was a one-way mirror, and Officer Rodriguez sat across from them, placing a folder on the table in front of her.

"What has Iris done?" Fran asked.

Will elbowed her gently. "What has she been accused of doing?" he corrected her.

Fran flushed. Of course she shouldn't talk as though her daughter's guilt was a foregone conclusion. She'd seen practically every episode of *Law & Order*.

"Iris was pulled over on US-1 for speeding," Officer Rodriguez said.

"Wait, *what*?" Fran asked. "Iris was *driving*?"

The policewoman nodded. "The officer asked to see her license, but she said she didn't have one."

"That's because she's thirteen," Fran said.

"She finally admitted that, which is why she was brought down to the station."

Fran's mouth gaped in a horrified O. She glanced at Will. He seemed composed, but she could tell by how pale he'd turned that he was equally stricken.

"Whose car was she driving?" Fran asked.

"It belongs to a boy named Alexander Hitchens," the officer said.

Xander, Fran thought furiously. *Iris's so-called boyfriend, who I still haven't met.*

"What happens now?" Will asked.

"Iris broke several laws. She was underage, operating a car without a valid license, speeding. The underage charge alone is a second-degree misdemeanor, which can carry a five-hundred-dollar fine and up to a sixty-day jail sentence."

Fran gasped, as a vision of Iris dressed in an orange coverall with the jail cell doors sliding shut behind her swam up in her thoughts. *"What?"*

"But that's very unlikely. It's more likely that you'll be able to work out a plea agreement with the state attorney. Iris will probably end up having to do some community service hours."

Fran rubbed a hand over her face. She wished Will would put his arm around her, but he sat as still as a statue.

"I'll go get Iris," Officer Rodriguez said, standing. "She's pretty shaken up."

"She better be," Fran said, crossing her arms over her chest, as though that would keep her fury from erupting.

"Thank you," Will said.

Once they were alone, Will looked at Fran. "You need to calm down," he said.

"We are in a police station. Picking up our daughter. Because she was driving some older boy's car. Even though she doesn't have a driver's license," Fran said, biting the words out.

"I know where we are."

"She could have been killed. She could have killed someone else."

"I know," Will said again. "But I still don't think you should lose your temper."

"If there has ever been a time and a place to lose my temper, this is it," Fran said.

"We have to take Iris home and deal with her there. In private," Will said.

"I already know how we're going to deal with it. She's grounded forever. No cellphone, no Facebook, no sleepovers, no contact with friends," Fran raged. "And she's going to pay back every last cent of the fine."

"No contact with friends? How are you going to manage that? She'll see her friends at school," Will said.

"No more school, then," Fran said.

Will's eyebrows went up. "So, what, you're going to homeschool her?"

"If that's what it takes," Fran said.

"I see. And what about your job?"

Fran opened her mouth, about to say that she'd quit if she had to, if that's what it took to keep their daughter on the straight and narrow, when suddenly she remembered— she was about to become a single mother. She'd said she wanted a trial separation, but she and Will both knew what that really meant. Divorce. She stared at her husband. He looked back at her, sad resignation stamped on his face.

The door opened and Iris walked in, shoulders slumped

and arms wrapped around herself, with Officer Rodriguez right behind her. Iris's cheeks were red and splotchy, and her thick black eyeliner was smudged. She looked younger than her thirteen years and even more vulnerable. When she saw her parents, her face crumpled.

"I'm so, so sorry," Iris wailed.

Will and Fran both stood, the legs of their chairs scraping against the industrial tile. Fran's anger drained away. Will was right—there would be a time for Iris to face the consequences, which would be swift and tough. But for right now, Fran was just thankful that her daughter was safe. She opened her arms, and Iris stepped into her embrace, and sobbed unrestrainedly on her mother's shoulder. A moment later, Fran could feel Will's arms going around them both.

"You both must hate me," Iris said, her words thick with tears.

"Shh," Fran said, stroking Iris's hair. "It's going to be okay. Everything's going to be okay."

AUDREY SAT AT HER desk, going over the monthly payroll. Her mind kept wandering, though. It touched on Coop, skated over to Kenny—who had unsurprisingly begun to make noise about wanting to take their relationship to a new, physical level, which was something she didn't think she could go through with—and finally landed on Fran, which caused her anger to simmer up again, black and foreboding.

How dare she, Audrey thought for the thousandth time since the night of the Wexlers' dinner party. How dare Fran tell her she'd been deluded about the state of her marriage. Yes, Ryan had a problem with alcohol. But Audrey was sure they would have worked through it. Unlike Fran, she would never have given up on her husband.

It was all just an attempt to deflect Fran's own marital deficiencies, Audrey decided. Fran was looking for any excuse to justify ditching a perfectly good marriage, just because boredom had set in. *How selfish can you be?* she thought scornfully. Fran was going to upset everyone around her, especially her daughters, all because she didn't still get weak in the knees when Will walked in the room.

"Grow up," Audrey muttered out loud.

"Excuse me?" Lisa asked.

Audrey looked up, startled. She hadn't noticed Lisa passing by her office. And now the young woman was looking surprised and a little hurt.

"Sorry, I didn't mean you," Audrey said. "I was talking to myself."

"That's not a good sign." Lisa grinned. She had clear ivory skin, spattered with freckles, shiny dark hair, and bright green-blue eyes. The fact that she didn't live a particularly healthy lifestyle—she ate junk, never exercised, and freely admitted that she fell asleep with her makeup on more often than not—didn't matter. Her glowing appearance was good marketing for the spa. "Why do you need to grow up? You're the most grown up person I know."

Audrey flapped a hand at her. "Not me. I was thinking about someone I know."

"Who? That hot guy who had the pedicure to impress you?" Lisa asked.

Audrey blinked, taken aback. "What?"

"You know. James Bond."

"James Bond?"

"Yes. The guy who looks like the actor who plays James Bond," Lisa said.

"Are you talking about Sean Connery?" Audrey asked, bewildered.

"Is that his name?"

"That's the name of the actor. He's Scottish, I think. In his seventies, I would guess," Audrey said.

It was Lisa's turn to blink in confusion. "Huh? I'm talking about the guy who plays James Bond in the movies."

It suddenly occurred to Audrey that Lisa was young enough—and, yes, it had to be admitted, *dim* enough—not to realize that the James Bond movie franchise was forty years old.

"Okay, which actor are you talking about? I have no idea who plays James Bond these days," Audrey said.

"His name is Craig something. No, wait—it's Daniel Craig."

"I know who you're talking about. You think Coop looks like Daniel Craig?" Audrey asked, oddly buoyed by the idea. She could see the resemblance. Not in their features necessarily—Coop's features weren't as chiseled, and his eyes didn't droop at the corners, but now that she thought about it, they did have the same sort of roughly hewn sex appeal.

I slept with someone who looks like James Bond. Audrey was pleased at the thought. Okay, not the real James Bond. But the actor who plays him.

Then Audrey remembered. She wasn't seeing Coop anymore. She was dating Kenny. Short Kenny with the protruding ears. Kenny, whose touch made her shrink away.

Lisa nodded enthusiastically. "Yeah, totally," she said. "He was hot in, like, a raw way. Do you know what I mean?"

Do I know what you mean? Audrey thought. *Yes. I know exactly what you mean.* She tried to banish the stomach quiver that thoughts of Coop always set off.

"I really need to finish the payroll," Audrey said.

"Okay," Lisa said good-naturedly and strode out of the office, a bounce in her step. Audrey could picture her, ten years from now, with a brawny, big-shouldered husband and four cheerful children, all of them excellent soccer players and solid C students.

Audrey attempted to refocus on the payroll. But for some reason, her thoughts kept wandering back to the last Easter before Ryan died. They weren't particularly religious, so Easter had never been more than a chocolate bunny sort of holiday for them. They'd been invited to a party at a childless friend's house, where an Easter egg hunt had been planned. Only instead of finding chocolate-filled eggs, they'd searched for miniature bottles of vodka and gin and individual-sized packets of aspirin. The party had been one of those social occasions where everyone was drinking too much. Suddenly, out of nowhere, Ryan had appeared stark naked, except for a pair of fake fur bunny ears.

"Say hello to Peter Rabbit," he'd said, his speech slurring slightly. He then proceeded to hop around, a carrot stuck out of his mouth like a stogie, while the women scattered out of the way, lest he attempt to hop up against them.

Audrey had tried to pretend that it had all been planned, and that she was in on the joke. She'd laughed loudly and played along, as though it were all hilarious. But it wasn't funny. Not at all. It had been mortifying, and she'd been furious with Ryan, who passed out that night in the middle of the resulting argument.

Yes, his drinking had been getting out of hand. *Would*

their marriage have survived? Audrey wondered, suddenly doubting her earlier conviction that it would have. How many nights, weeks, months would Audrey have been content to fall asleep by herself, never sure of when Ryan would roll home from the neighborhood bar? He'd acted as though it was all very British—"I'm stopping by the pub," he'd say, in an affected English accent—but that didn't make it less dysfunctional.

Audrey shook her head, trying to dislodge these depressing thoughts. What was the point? What difference did it make now?

Focus on the payroll, she told herself, shaking her head again, as though that would dislodge the unpleasant thoughts swirling around inside. Payroll now. Breaking up with Kenny later, because obviously there was no way she was ever going to sleep with him. And after that . . . well, she'd deal with that when she had to.

WHEN WILL ANSWERED THE door, he looked pale and wan, as though he'd recently been sick.

"Jesus, what happened to you?" Coop asked as Will stood aside so he could enter the house. "Have you been on a diet?"

Will shook his head. "No." He looked down at himself. "I guess I have lost a little weight," he said. He sounded strained. In the distance, Coop could hear the sound of dishes clinking and someone laughing.

Coop stared at Will. "You okay, man?"

"Sure," Will said. He hesitated, and then looked back over his shoulder. "Things have just been a little rough around here lately. We've had some trouble with Iris. And, well . . . Fran and I are having some issues, too." He closed the door.

"Should I go?" Coop asked, sticking a thumb out and pointing back toward the door. "Maybe this isn't a good time for you to be hosting the dinner party club."

"No, no. You have to stay. Fran's been cooking all day. In fact, I shouldn't have mentioned anything," Will said.

Coop wondered if he should press Will further. But in all the years they'd been friends, they never really talked about weighty, emotional issues. It wasn't what men did. They talked boats and sports, would even discuss politics occasionally. But you never asked one of your friends how his marriage was going. It just wasn't done.

While Coop deliberated whether he should break with tradition and ask Will for more details on what was going on, Will turned, and, waving Coop to follow him, said, "Come on back. Everyone's in the kitchen."

They headed toward the kitchen and as they approached, the voices and cooking smells became more pronounced. Coop braced himself for facing Audrey and Kenny. But neither was there. Fran, Jaime, Mark, and Leland looked up at his entrance.

"Coop! I didn't even hear the doorbell," Fran said, beaming at him.

He kissed her on the cheek. She looked like she'd lost more weight, too, but—unlike Will—it suited her. Her skin was glowing and her eyes, as they met his, were bright and laughing.

Coop greeted everyone, also kissing Jaime, and shaking hands with Mark and Leland.

"The men outnumber the women two to one tonight,"

Leland said. He was perched on one of the kitchen stools, looking especially spry. A gardenia was stuck in the button-hole of his blue blazer.

"Those are never the sort of odds I like," Coop said.

Leland laughed. "That makes two of us."

"Where's Audrey?" Coop asked, hoping he sounded more casual than he felt.

"She's not coming," Fran said. "Do you want a glass of wine?"

"Is she out of town?" Coop asked.

Fran and Jaime exchanged a meaningful look.

"Audrey's decided to drop out of the dinner party club," Jaime said delicately.

"What?" Coop goggled at her. "Was it because of me?"

Fran and Jaime stared at him with twin expressions of confusion.

"Why? What did you do?" Fran asked.

"Nothing," Coop said quickly. "I just . . . I thought from the way you said it. Never mind."

"Fran and Audrey had a falling out," Jaime explained.

"Jaime," Fran said sharply.

Jaime glanced up, startled. Her expression quickly turned sheepish. "I didn't say why," she said.

"I feel like I'm missing something," Coop said.

Mark put his arm around his wife's shoulders. "That's be-cause they're talking in women code."

"We are not," Jaime said, but she smiled at him and leaned back against his shoulder.

Coop desperately wanted to know more—Why wasn't Audrey coming? Was she that desperate to avoid him? And was she still dating Kenny?—but Fran and Jaime seemed to have entered into a silent pact not to talk about Audrey. Instead, Jaime launched into a discussion of falling house prices while Fran turned and began the risotto, which momentarily distracted him. Coop had always been partial to risotto.

"What are you putting in it?" he asked, as Fran diced up an onion with a large kitchen knife.

"Didn't you get the email I sent out with the menu?"

"Um, maybe," Coop said.

"That was convincing," Fran said. "It's sausage and mushroom risotto." She showed him a white bowl, containing the already cooked sausage and mushrooms. The mixture was scented with thyme and oregano.

"It smells fantastic," Coop said.

"Thanks," Fran said.

She finished with the onions, and moved on, diced four plump cloves of garlic. She melted a stick of butter in a large pot, and dumped the diced onion and garlic in to sizzle in the butter, stirring the mixture with a rubber spatula. She looked up at Coop under lowered eyelashes.

"Are you watching me?" Fran asked.

"I've always wanted to learn how to make risotto," Coop said. "I order it whenever I'm out and it's on the menu."

"I know," Fran said. This time, there was a teasing lilt to her voice and she tilted her head to one side. She looked at him meaningfully. "That's why I'm making it."

What was up with her lately? Coop wondered uneasily. He glanced at Will, wondering if he, too, was noticing his wife's behavior. But Will, still looking morose, was chatting with Jaime, or, rather, listening to Jaime while she talked at him about the trials of finding a good nursery school.

"Maybe I should go see what . . . ," Coop began, having

no idea how he was going to finish the sentence. Listen to Mark bore on about his daughter's latest tennis triumph? Ask Leland for dating advice? But Fran stopped him.

"No, don't go. I'm about to start pouring the rice in, and then I basically have to stand here and stir for the next twenty-five minutes," she said.

"That long? Wow. You're really committed to your risotto," Coop said.

"That's how you make it," Fran said, adding Madeira wine and chicken broth to the pot. They began to simmer, and she added the Arborio rice, stirring the mixture vigorously. "Stay and keep me company while I stir."

"Okay," Coop said. He leaned against the counter, folded his arms, and watched Fran stir the risotto in a brisk, clockwise motion. He wondered if every cook stirred in one direction, or if some changed directions. Maybe it was one of those personality indicators, like having a preference for the toilet paper hanging over rather than under the roll.

"Are you seeing anyone?" Fran asked.

"Not at the moment," Coop said.

"And why's that?" Fran asked. "I know it's not for lack of interested women. You always have quite the following." She ladled some hot broth, which was simmering in a sauce pan on the stove, and added it to the risotto.

"I don't know about that," Coop said.

This time, the look Fran gave Coop was not at all flirtatious. In fact, it was the same old Fran he had known for years looking at him with exasperated disbelief. "What's this? Since when did you start acting humble?"

"I've changed my ways," Coop said. "I pretty much had to after my ex-girlfriends ganged up on me and accused me of being cocky. It was ugly."

"It must have been if it turned you modest," Fran teased him. She was stirring the risotto so vigorously, her cheeks had flushed again and a loose curl bounced against her temple.

"Have you heard from Audrey recently?"

Fran's smile faded, and her face closed off. "No."

"I thought you two were good friends?" Coop said.

Fran shrugged. Coop wondered if Audrey had told Fran something about him—about what had happened between them—and Fran was reluctant to divulge any confidences to him.

"Is she okay?" he asked quietly.

"Why wouldn't she be?" Fran asked, looking at him, her expression a mixture of defiance and confusion.

"No reason. Never mind. I'm going to head to the restroom," Coop said, and then, when he returned to the kitchen, he joined Will and Jaime's mind-numbingly dull conversation about pre-primary schools. Luckily, it was short-lived, as Jaime took over keeping Fran company while she stirred, leaving Will and Coop free to talk fishing.

"I think we're just about ready to eat," Fran said twenty minutes later. "Why don't we move to the dining room."

The dinner party guests obligingly tripped off to the dining room, and once everyone was seated at the table, Will held up a bottle of wine.

"How is everyone doing on drinks? More wine, Leland?" Will asked.

Leland smiled and held out his glass. "Please. Empty glasses always depress me."

"That sounds like one of those sayings that should be embroidered on a pillow," Fran said, laughing, as she came in with a platter of antipasto and a loaf of warmed rustic Italian bread.

Coop wondered again at how cheerful Fran seemed, and the stark contrast this made to Will's pallid and somber demeanor.

As the antipasto platter was passed around, Leland, seated to Coop's right, looked at him sternly and said, "What is the story behind Audrey's absence?"

Coop shook his head and shrugged. "I have no idea. I know as much about it as you do."

Leland continued to look at him. It reminded Coop vividly of being a kid hauled up in front of the principal.

"I think these dinner parties are good for Audrey," Leland said censoriously. "She spends too much time on her own. That's not good for a woman like her."

"A woman like her? What does that mean?" Fran asked, frowning.

"Some people are happier on their own. But I think those types are rare. Most people are social beings. They need to be out, around other people, having fulfilling relationships," Leland said.

"I think that's true," Jaime chimed in. "I read an article a while back that said people who are involved in organizations are happier than people who aren't. It doesn't matter what it is—a church, a sport, a book club."

"A dinner party club," Mark said.

"Exactly," Jaime said, nodding at her husband.

The conversation shifted into a discussion of clubs. Jaime said she also belonged to a book club, and Mark joked that he might be a Free Mason, but wouldn't be able to tell them if he was. Leland used the cover of this conversation to turn to Coop and quietly say, "You need to make things right with her. That's not the sort of woman you should let get away."

Coop was starting to feel exasperated. "I don't know

what you think I've done, but trust me—I'm not the reason why Audrey isn't here," Coop said. As he spoke, he wondered if this was in fact true. After all, he'd never known that so many of his ex-girlfriends carried such resentment about how things had ended. But that was just it, Coop thought—*he* hadn't broken up with Audrey. *She'd* ditched *him*. And then ran off with Kenny and his cellphone holster.

"Why would Audrey not come because of Coop?" asked Fran, who was sitting at the head of the table on Leland's other side.

"She wouldn't. I'm sure it has nothing to do with me," Coop said. He shrugged, feeling defensive.

"Hmm," Leland said, clearly not buying this.

Fran sighed. "Okay, I didn't want to get into it, but it really has nothing to do with Coop. Audrey's not here because she and I had an argument. A bad one, actually. I think it's the end of our friendship."

"No, it's not," Jaime protested. She slid a sidewise glance at Will, which Coop found odd.

"Anyway, I know it's awkward, but let's just try to move on," Fran said. She turned to Coop and smiled. "How's your new project going? Are you still in the process of editing the dolphin footage?"

Fran served the risotto, and they segued into small talk. Mark updated them on his daughter's tennis career, of course, and Jaime and Fran lamented the lack of a good local bakery, while Will stayed mostly mute, coming to life for only a brief period when the bakery discussion turned to which restaurant in town made the best brownies.

"Margaret Davies," Leland said suddenly.

Coop looked at him, feeling vaguely uneasy. Was this early stage dementia? Leland had seemed a bit off all evening. He asked Jaime twice what her children's names were, and seemed confused when Fran handed him the bread basket.

"Do you want some more water?" Coop asked, brandishing the pitcher.

"Margaret Davies made the best carrot cake. It was so spicy and moist," Leland said, his voice dreamy.

An uneasy silence fell over the table. Leland's eyes were unfocused, and his speech was slightly slurred. He seemed to be listing to the right. Coop poured water into Leland's goblet.

"Have some water," Coop urged the older man.

"She was a beautiful woman, too. Those long, long legs that seemed like they went straight up to her shoulders. My wife never forgave me for Margaret. Not really. I wish she had. You should forgive the people you love, especially when they're so sorry. And I was so sorry," Leland continued. His voice began to slur.

Coop looked at Will. "Stroke?" he mouthed.

"Maybe we should call 911," Will said.

Suddenly, Leland slumped forward, crashing into the table. Jaime gasped, and Coop and Fran both jumped to their feet.

"Call 911!" Coop yelled.

Will sprinted off to the kitchen to retrieve the phone. With help from Fran and Mark, Coop got the elderly man out of his chair, and laid him down on the floor.

"Do you know how to do CPR?" Fran asked him.

Coop nodded and began to check for vital signs. Leland wasn't breathing, and his eyes were open, staring unseeingly up at the brass chandelier. Trying to remember the CPR class he'd taken years earlier, Coop blew two deep breaths into Leland's mouth and then began to do chest compressions on Leland's thin chest. *One, and two, and three, and four . . .*

He counted to thirty, then stopped. Leland still wasn't breathing.

"An ambulance is on the way," Will said.

"Let me help," Fran said.

She positioned herself at Leland's head and took over blowing deep breaths into his mouth. Coop began another series of chest compressions.

"Come on," Coop said through gritted teeth. "Come on, Leland."

It felt like forever until the ambulance arrived. He and Fran worked together. Breaths, compressions, breaths, compressions. The others stood by silently, watching. Coop and Fran kept at it, right up until emergency rescue services arrived. And even after the EMTs took over, attempting to revive Leland with a portable defibrillator, Coop continued to count in his head. *One, and two, and three, and four . . .*

Come on, Coop thought, trying to focus all of his willpower onto the elderly man. *Come on. Wake up.*

But in the end, nothing any of them did helped. And Leland never did wake up.

november

...

BLUE CHEESE AND BACON DIP

PÂTÉ DE CAMPAGNE

BACON-WRAPPED DATES

FONTINA CHEESE, CARAMELIZED ONION,
AND BACON TART

GRILLED ASPARAGUS WITH GOAT CHEESE
AND CRISPY BACON

AUDREY THOUGHT THAT LELAND would have liked his funeral. It was so unlike Ryan's funeral had been. There, everyone had been white-faced with shock, and when his best friend from their boyhoods began sobbing during his eulogy, there hadn't been a dry eye in the church.

Leland's funeral was an entirely different affair. He had led a good long life, and his mourners were teary, yes, but more inclined to celebrate the man they had known and loved. One of Leland's old law clerks—now a man in his fifties—flew in from Illinois to give the eulogy. He talked about how Leland had tasked him with picking him up every morning and driving him to court. He'd thought this was a regular duty for law clerks, and only found out years later that Leland had enlisted his services as a chauffeur because the Judge—that's what the clerk and countless others called him, the Judge—had adored the clerk's sporty red convertible.

The Leland these people had known was both different and yet the same as the Leland the dinner party club had grown so fond of, Audrey mused. The people from his previous life had known Leland when he was a man of consequence—a judge, a husband, a father. But the things they said about him—how funny he was, how thoughtful, the interest he'd taken in their lives—were exactly like the retired Leland that the Table for Seven Club had known.

Sitting in the church pew, Audrey checked her program

and had a jolt of surprise. Coop was scheduled to speak. She hadn't thought Coop was particularly close to Leland. All of the other speakers—Leland's two sons, his old law partners, his former clerks—had known Leland for years. As far as she knew, Coop had met Leland at the same time she did, back at the first meeting of the Table for Seven Club, less than a year ago. Audrey craned her neck around and scanned the congregation, looking for Coop's sun-bleached head. She saw him standing near the back—every seat in the church was filled—and her heart gave a little skip. Audrey had thought she had grown immune to Coop and any attraction he held for her.

Apparently, she was wrong.

The law clerk finished speaking, and everyone clapped politely. Coop strode to the front of the church, and took the clerk's place at the lectern.

"Hi, there," Coop said, leaning in close to the microphone. "I'm Preston Cooper. I didn't know Leland as long as many of you did, but in the time I did know him, Leland impressed me as the rarest of men, in that he was someone who actually understood other men."

There was a titter of laughter across the congregation. Audrey watched Coop intently, her hands fisted so tightly, her nails left marks on the skin of her palms.

"I don't mean that in a Tim Allen, *Home Improvement* sort of way," Coop said. "Where the men grunt like apes and wait around to be civilized by the womenfolk. What I mean is that Leland had a habit of assessing a situation and the people involved, and delivering a piece of advice that was so on point, I wondered at times if he was some sort of a psychic."

There was another spattering of laughter. Apparently,

the Table for Seven Club members were not the first people in Leland's life to take note of his intuitiveness.

"Just before he passed away—the very night, in fact—Leland gave me some advice." Coop paused, and looked directly in Audrey's direction. She felt her face flush, and shrank back in the pew, certain that everyone was staring at her. "And like everything that Leland said, I realized, upon reflection, that he was right. Very right. And I was so very wrong." A heavy man in the front of the church guffawed loudly, which caused another ripple of tittering. Coop smiled wryly. "I see I wasn't the first person to benefit from Leland's keen insight. But that's a good thing. I can't think of a better legacy than to have people grouped around your coffin, remembering you for the positive influence you had in their lives.

"So, Leland, know this: You left us all too soon. Nearly everyone sitting here benefited from your wise advice. And it is to our great detriment that we will have to go without it from now on." Coop paused and smiled sadly. "We'll miss you."

Coop replaced the microphone to its holder on the lectern while applause rang out. Audrey sat still as could be, trying to make sense of what had just happened.

THE REMAINING MEMBERS OF the Table for Seven Dinner Party Club gathered at Audrey's house the night of the funeral for a special meeting in Leland's honor.

Audrey had offered to cook, but everyone wanted to contribute, so in the end, they decided to put together a potluck buffet, which they christened Bacon-alia. Fran and Will brought dates stuffed with blue cheese and wrapped in bacon and chocolate bars studded with bacon that Will had found at Whole Foods. Jaime made pâté de campagne, a country pâté seasoned with brandy, which had, she explained, been cooked in a layer of bacon, removed prior to serving. Audrey set out an onion, cheese, and bacon tart and a platter of grilled asparagus sprinkled with goat cheese and bacon. Coop brought a blue cheese and bacon dip.

Once they had filled their plates and sat at the table—a seventh place had been set in Leland's honor—they raised their glasses to the empty chair and said, "To Leland."

"I just wish we had thought to do this for him when he was here to enjoy it," Fran said sadly, looking at her plate. "An entire meal of bacon. He would have been thrilled."

Jaime patted her arm. "I think wherever Leland is, he would definitely approve," she said.

"Leland's sons look just like him," Mark said.

"Really? Weren't they both over six feet tall? And Leland was so short. I wonder how tall his wife was," Jaime said.

"No, I know what Mark means," Audrey said. "They both had his eyes. And the younger one—" she paused, trying to remember his name.

"Peter," Coop said.

"Right, thank you," Audrey said. She glanced at Coop, then looked quickly away. "He had Leland's nose and ears."

"His ears? Really?" Will said.

Audrey nodded. "Exactly the same."

"I didn't notice," Will said.

"What do you think Leland meant when he said his wife never forgave him?" Jaime asked.

"Let's not talk about that," Fran said sharply.

"Why not?" Jaime asked. "I think Leland wanted to talk about it that night."

"He wasn't in his right mind," Fran said.

"What are you all talking about?" Audrey asked. It was the first time she had directly addressed Fran since their fight.

Fran seemed so surprised by Audrey speaking to her that she answered, despite her unwillingness to discuss the subject. "Just before Leland died, he was talking about a woman who used to make him carrot cake," she said.

"He said her name was Margaret," Jaime said.

"And from the way he was talking about her, it was pretty clear that they'd had an affair," Fran said reluctantly.

"Really?" Audrey said. She leaned back in her chair. "Wow. I always got the impression that Leland adored his wife."

"He did adore her," Fran insisted. "I don't think we should remember him for a mistake that he obviously regretted."

"And he was talking about his wife at the end," Jaime said. "He said that he wished she'd forgiven him. I think she was really the one who was on his mind at the end, not the cake woman."

The group fell silent, remembering how awful that night had been. One moment Leland had been there, and the next he was gone.

Audrey shivered. "I feel terrible that I wasn't there," she said, wrapping her arms around herself.

"There was nothing you could have done," Will said gently. "Coop and Fran gave him CPR, and then the EMTs came and used the paddles on him."

"You gave him CPR?" Audrey asked, looking at Coop.

"Coop was great," Fran said. "The rest of us were shell-shocked when Leland collapsed, but Coop just jumped right in and started trying to revive him."

A shadow crossed Coop's face. "Obviously, I didn't do enough."

"That's not true. You did everything you possibly could have," Jaime protested.

"Is that why Leland's sons asked you to speak at the funeral?" Mark asked.

Coop nodded. "I told them it wasn't necessary, that I didn't do anything heroic, but they insisted."

"No, I like that you spoke. It's good that his friends and family knew he was loved and appreciated during his retirement years," Fran said.

"And seriously, Coop. Leland was an old man. It was just his time," Will said.

Coop shrugged away these soothing words and stared down at his plate. He hadn't eaten much.

He's taking this so hard, Audrey thought. Her hand lifted—why, she wasn't sure, maybe to reach out to him across the table, to touch Coop's hand—but she stopped herself, and folded her hands in her lap.

"I like what you said at the funeral," she said instead.

Coop looked at her, his eyes meeting hers for the first time that day.

"Thank you," he said quietly.

Audrey felt a sudden urge to get away for a moment.

"I'll go get another bottle of wine," she said, standing. "We seem to be low on both red and white."

"I'll help you," Fran said.

Audrey was about to protest, but then shrugged and said, "Okay, sure."

Fran followed Audrey back to the kitchen. Audrey pulled a bottle of Chardonnay out of the refrigerator and set it on the counter, next to several bottles of red. She tucked her hair behind her ears, and set about opening the bottles with a corkscrew.

Fran watched her silently for a moment. Then, finally, she said, "I'm not sure why you're so angry with me."

"I love Will. I love the two of you together."

Fran nodded. "I know. And I understand that the end of a marriage affects people outside of the marriage. But it really hurts me that you haven't even tried to understand my point of view."

"I think I've always seen you and Will as perfect for each other. And if the two of you can't make it . . ." Audrey shrugged. "Maybe you're right. Maybe I do tend to idealize marriage. I'm sorry I was hard on you."

"Thank you for saying that," Fran said. "I did sort of drop a bombshell on you."

"Yeah, it was a bit of a shock. But, to be honest, I think I was angry because you seemed almost happy about it," Audrey said.

"I don't know if happy is the right word. It's going to be hard, I know that. But things haven't been great in my marriage for a long time now. I know everyone thinks Will is the greatest guy in the world—and in some ways he is—but he's not the most attentive husband. And that's hard. I want to be with someone who adores me. I think I deserve that," Fran said.

"Will adores you," Audrey protested.

Fran shook her head. "I know he loves me. And I love him. But we're not lovers anymore, and we haven't been for a long time."

Audrey hesitated. She didn't want to get into another fight with Fran, not now that they were just making up. But she also didn't think she'd be a very good friend if she didn't at least try to talk Fran out of what was a huge mistake.

"Do you think maybe you have an unrealistic picture? In

any relationship, the passion eventually fades. Hopefully it never fully goes away, but those shivery, exciting feelings you have when you first fall in love never last," Audrey said.

Fran shrugged, turning away, and Audrey knew that this was not a point she was willing to concede.

"Just think about it, okay?" Audrey said.

Fran nodded. "Okay."

"What happens now? Do you have a plan?"

"We're going to stay together in the house until after Christmas. But that's about as far as we've gotten. I've tried to talk to Will about the details, but, well . . ." Fran ran a hand over her face and closed her eyes briefly. "I'm having a hard time getting him to discuss it."

"I'm sure he's devastated," Audrey said.

"I don't know why he would be," Fran said.

Audrey frowned. "Maybe because his world is falling apart? His marriage, his family? Of course that would upset him."

"The only thing Will cares about is sitting out in the garage, working on those damn robots," Fran said with heat. She shook her head. "Sorry. Ignore me. I'm still in the bitter phase. Hopefully it will pass soon. Anyway, let's talk about something else. How's it going with you and Kenny?"

"It's not. I ended it," Audrey said.

"I'm not surprised. I didn't get the feeling there were a lot of fireworks between you," Fran said.

Suddenly, Audrey's eyes filled with tears. She set down the bottle of wine she'd picked up and pinched the top of her nose, trying to stop them from flowing.

"Oh, my God, are you okay?" Fran said, stepping closer and putting a hand on Audrey's arm. "I had no idea that things were so serious between you and Kenny! Were you in love with him?"

"Of course not," Audrey said. The tears started streaming down her face, and her chest heaved with sobs.

"I'm confused," Fran said, shaking her head. "Why are you so upset?"

"I don't know. This keeps happening." Audrey lifted both hands, fingers splayed, and gestured to her tear-slicked face. "Ever since Leland died, I keep bursting into tears for no reason."

"That's understandable," Fran said. "You were fond of Leland. But you know he had a long, full life, right?"

"That's just it. I don't think I *am* crying for Leland. I mean, I'm sad that he died, of course, and I'll certainly miss him. But for some reason, I keep thinking of Ryan."

"Oh," Fran said and fell silent for a moment, as she considered this. "Do you think that your feelings of grief over Leland's death are somehow dredging up similar feelings for Ryan?"

"No, I don't think that's it. I mean, it wouldn't make sense, would it? Leland was a nice man who I was fond of. But Ryan was my husband. It's not the same at all," Audrey said. She picked up a paper towel and dabbed at her eyes. "Good thing I put on waterproof mascara."

"Then, what do you think is going on?"

"I think . . . well, I think part of it is that I'm sad Ryan didn't get to have the sort of life Leland had. I kept thinking that at the funeral today, about how everyone there seemed to want to celebrate Leland. At Ryan's funeral, everyone was in shock. All anyone could say was what a waste it was," Audrey said. She stopped and swallowed back another sob, which she could feel pressing upward in her chest. "And it *was* such a waste. Ryan was this smart, handsome, funny man. He had it all, and he just threw it all away." She looked at Fran. "He'd been drinking that night."

Fran nodded. "I thought he probably had been."

"Yeah, well this was Ryan." Audrey gave a humorless laugh. "The odds were always pretty good that he was drinking. And you know what? The worst part about it is that he didn't just throw away *his* life. He threw away *our* life together. The children we never had. The holidays, and the memories, and the family vacations. He just crumpled it up and tossed it away."

"Do you think his accident was . . . ," Fran began, but then stopped.

"Do I think it was suicide?" Audrey asked. Fran nodded. "No. But he was basically playing Russian roulette. He drank and drove all the time. It didn't matter how many times I asked him not to, or how many business cards of taxicab companies I stuffed into his wallet. And I can't tell you how many nights I went out, driving around, trying to find which bar he was at, so I could take him home."

"You did?" Fran asked, looking surprised.

Audrey nodded. "I've never told you that before?" She shrugged, and shook her head, then dabbed at the tears that had started flowing again. "He was always drunk and I was always covering for him. Not exactly the stuff that healthy marriages are made of."

Fran wrapped her arms around her friend.

"At least I think we know why you can't stop weeping," Fran said.

"Why? Because I'm just now realizing how stupid I've

been? I was stupid to stay in my marriage while Ryan was alive and stupid to pretend to myself and everyone else that we were happy together," Audrey said bitterly, turning away and folding her arms.

"No," Fran said gently. "That's not it. I think you're sad because you're just now grieving the real Ryan. Your real marriage."

Audrey was silent for a few minutes. Her sobs had quieted, and the tears had slowed. "Maybe you're right," Audrey said.

"It's bound to happen once in a while," Fran said.

Audrey smiled weakly. "How awful do I look?"

"You look perfectly fine. Just a little teary. But no one will notice. Or if they do, they'll think it's because of Leland's funeral. It has been a sad day, after all," Fran said.

"I suppose we should go back in. They'll be out of wine by now, and wondering what's taking us so long," Audrey said.

Fran threw her arm around Audrey's shoulders and squeezed her.

"You're going to be fine, you know," Fran said.

"Despite all evidence to the contrary?" Audrey asked, with an ironic laugh.

A FEW NIGHTS AFTER Leland's funeral, Fran drew in a deep breath and knocked on the front door of Coop's condo. She could hear Bear's nails scrabbling over the tile inside, and a moment later, the door swung open.

"Hey, Franny," Coop said. "What are you doing here?"

He was wearing a gray T-shirt and well-worn khaki

shorts. Coop hadn't shaved that morning, and now, at seven o'clock at night, his chin was thick with blond stubble. Fran, already nervous, felt her heart give a few extra leaps.

"Hi," Fran said. "Can I come in?"

Coop looked puzzled, but he held the door open and said, "Of course. I was just getting a beer. Do you want one? Wait, you don't like beer."

Fran smiled, pleased that he remembered this about her. "No, I'm not a beer girl."

"Let me see what else I have." Coop led her to the tiny galley kitchen and rummaged around in the cupboard. "I have a nice bottle of Cabernet. And I think I have some Grey Goose in the freezer."

"A glass of wine would be great," Fran said, petting Bear's head. He sat on her feet and panted happily.

She wouldn't have minded vodka, glugged straight from the bottle. However, this was not the time to lose her head.

Coop poured a glass of wine and handed it to Fran.

"Cheers," she said and clinked her glass against his beer bottle.

"Let's go outside," Coop said, leading her back to the patio.

Fran followed him, Bear at her heels. They sat down at the round table, in comfortable mesh-backed chairs. In the distance, the ocean roared softly, rumbling as the tide rushed in. The scents of the beach—salt water and something slightly fishy—filled Fran's nostrils. She imagined living in an apartment by the sea. So different from a suburban household. And so much more freeing. Fran breathed in deeply and sipped her wine. It was, of course, delicious. Coop had always had fabulous taste in wine.

"I bet you were surprised to find me on your doorstep," she said.

Coop tipped his head to one side and shrugged. "Actually, not completely surprised."

The breath caught in Fran's chest. "Really?" she asked.

Maybe this would be easier than she had thought. Maybe rather than having to be the one to broach the exciting but incredibly uncomfortable topic of the feelings she'd developed for him, Coop would save her the trouble by announcing how he felt about her.

Coop nodded, and for a moment, Fran thought he somehow knew what she was thinking, and was nodding along to say, yes, he had feelings for her, and yes, it would be incredibly awkward considering his relationship with Will, but like her, he knew they couldn't be ignored.

But then he continued.

"I've been worried about Will," Coop said, taking a swig of beer and looking at her closely.

"You have?" Fran asked cautiously. If he was about to declare his feelings for her, this was an odd way to lead in.

Coop nodded. "He didn't seem like himself the night . . . well, the night that Leland . . ."

He seemed unable to continue. Fran understood, shivering a little, even though it wasn't chilly out. The sun was setting, wreathing the western sky in ribbons of orange and red. And for a moment, the night of Leland's death loomed up, swamping them both with emotion. Fran felt like something had lodged in her throat, and she swallowed hard, trying to keep her tears at bay. Coop brushed something out of his eyes.

A tear? she wondered.

"It's been tough," Fran said.

Coop nodded. "And then again, seeing him after the funeral. Will didn't seem like he was in a good place."

"No," Fran said. "He hasn't been in a good place."

"He said you guys were having some issues, and something was going on with Iris, but he didn't go into details. I figured that was why you stopped by," Coop said.

Fran froze. She kept her face in a neutrally pleasant expression, and moved her wineglass to her mouth, but the whole time, an alarm was going off in her head.

He thinks I'm here to talk about Will. He thinks I'm here to get his advice as Will's friend, Fran thought, and for a moment, she had to bite down on her lower lip to keep from breaking out into hysterical laughter.

"That's not why I'm here," she said abruptly.

"What?" Coop asked, wrinkling his brow.

"I'm not here to talk about Will. Well, not to talk about him directly. It concerns him, I guess. But not in the way you think," Fran said. She realized that she was babbling and took another sip of wine, hoping it would help her to compose herself.

"What are you here to talk about, then?"

Fran hesitated. Coop looked sexily rumpled sitting there in the hazy evening light. He had a very physical presence, taking up his space unapologetically. She tried not to stare at the flat of his tanned neck, which she had spent so many hours fantasizing about kissing.

"Franny?" Coop asked. He frowned again and leaned forward. "Are you okay?"

Fran nodded and took in a deep breath. *It is now or never,* she thought. It had taken all of her nerve to drive over to Coop's apartment. She might as well get it out.

"The thing is," Fran said. Her mouth suddenly felt bone

dry, as though all of the moisture had been sucked out. She craved a glass of ice water, but thought it best not to delay this any further. Instead, she took a sip of her wine, her hand shaking. "I have . . . well, I have feelings for you."

There. The words were out. She waited, her nerves vibrating with tension, as she anticipated Coop's reaction. He looked at her, apparently clueless.

"What do you mean?" Coop finally asked.

Fran's stomach seemed to fold over on itself. Part of her wanted to say, *No, never mind,* and scuttle back to her car. But she forced herself to stay calm and finish what she had come here to do.

"The thing is," she said again, wondering when *the thing is* had become her big lead-in. "I think . . . well. I think I'm in love with you." She stopped abruptly, not believing she'd actually just said it out loud.

Coop stared at her, apparently absorbing the weight of these words. She looked back at him, half relieved that she'd had the nerve to go through with it after all and yet half terrified at what his response would be.

Coop had gone very still and behind him, the sky had darkened. Fran leaned forward and placed a hand on his forearm. She'd read somewhere that touching someone's forearm made them more likely to do what you wanted. She waited and watched as realization dawned on Coop's face. His pale eyes widened.

"Oh, Christ," he said. He shook his head slowly. "Oh, Franny."

"I've felt this way for a long time. Pretty much since you moved to Ocean Falls. Although actually, that's not entirely true. I think I've been in love with you for years. We've always had . . . well, I don't know how to explain it. A connection. Haven't you sensed that, too?" Fran knew she was babbling, but seemed unable to stop herself. Coop's arm felt hot under her hand, but now that she was touching him, she didn't dare move it. Coop leaned forward, and Fran wondered if he was going to kiss her. She felt almost sick with excitement, and her heart was beating so hard in her chest, she was amazed Coop couldn't hear it.

Coop's hand closed on hers.

This is it, Fran thought, thrilling at his touch. *This is it.*

But then she realized that he was gently moving her hand away. Away from him.

"No, Franny," he said softly. "No."

A starburst of embarrassment exploded inside Fran. She closed her eyes, trying to block out Coop, to block out everything that had happened in the last twenty seconds.

"It's not that I'm not flattered," Coop said.

"Don't," Fran said.

Fran opened her eyes and allowed herself one long, level glance at Coop. He looked embarrassed. She closed her eyes again and shuddered. There was nothing, absolutely *nothing,* worse.

"I should go," Fran said. She set her wineglass down with unnecessary force—it was a miracle the glass didn't shatter—and stood. Coop caught her arm, stopping her.

"It's not that I don't think you're lovely. I do. I always have," Coop said.

Fran hesitated, suddenly unable to turn away until she heard the rest of what he had to say. "But?"

"But you're married," Coop said. "To Will."

"What if I wasn't?" Fran asked.

Coop rested a hand on her shoulder. And for a moment, Fran wondered if he was going to kiss her, after all. She'd imagined the scene so many times. Coop's pale unfathomable eyes searching out hers, the palm of his hand against her skin.

"It wouldn't make a difference," Coop said gently.

Fran stepped back, and Coop's hand fell away from her. She swallowed hard and tried to focus all of her will on not crying in front of him. The danger signs were already there—her throat felt thick and pinched, her lips were quivering, tears burned at her eyes.

"I have to go," Fran said, turning away.

"Wait," Coop said.

Fran shook her head and began walking on leaden legs, heading for the front door. She knew Coop was following after her, although thankfully he didn't try to touch her again. She couldn't take any more of his kindly, commiserating pats.

"You don't have to go," Coop said, just as Fran finally—mercifully—reached the door.

Fran took a deep breath, willing away her tears. She had one last chance to get out of there still clutching the tattered remains of her dignity. Miraculously, when she turned to face Coop, her eyes were dry and her voice was surprisingly steady.

"I think it would be a good idea if we didn't see each other for a while," Fran said.

Coop leaned back against the wall and crossed his arms in front of his chest. "Okay. If that's what you want."

"It is. And I'd also appreciate it if you didn't mention any of this to Will," Fran said.

"Of course not," Coop said.

"Thank you," Fran said.

She pulled open the door and walked out. The good news

was that she didn't look back, not once, to see if Coop was watching her. The even better news was that she waited until she was safely in her car before she started to cry.

WILL WASN'T SURE HOW he felt about anything anymore. It was like he'd been in a fog for weeks. One thought kept coming back to him, over and over again, until it had become a sort of mantra: *I thought we were happy.*

And we were happy, Will thought, as he sat at his workbench, shoulders hunched with misery, fiddling with the motor on his combat bot, Brutus, getting him ready for the upcoming competition in Miami. He didn't care at this point whether he won or lost, but Rory was enthusiastic about their chances, and he didn't want to let her down.

He and Fran hadn't told the girls yet about the looming separation, but their daughters were not stupid. It had not escaped their attention that Will was sleeping on the couch, and that their parents were avoiding spending time together when possible.

Rory didn't say much about it, but she had started sleepwalking again, which she hadn't done in years. Will had to believe that it was a manifestation of the stress.

Iris was more forthright.

"What's going on with you two?" she asked sharply one night after dinner. Will had politely offered to do the dishes, and Fran had just as politely thanked him. Iris had turned on Will. "Why aren't you and Mom speaking?"

"We are," Will lied.

"No, you aren't. You never talk anymore. Are you getting a divorce?"

Will's eyes had slid to Fran, waiting to see what her response was. Fran shook her head.

"No, of course not," Fran said briskly. "You'd better go get started on your homework."

But Iris hadn't been convinced. Will didn't blame her. The problems in their marriage were taking up too much house space to ignore.

The door to the garage opened. Will glanced up, expecting to see Rory, who had promised to come help him with Brutus when she had finished her math homework. But instead, it was Iris. She was wearing a black and gray striped cardigan and dark too-tight jeans.

"Hi," she said. "I didn't know you were home."

"I got back a few minutes ago," Will said. "Where's Rory?"

"She's in her room," Iris said. "Where's Mom?"

"Out," Will said. The word felt as heavy as a rock in his mouth.

Iris pulled the cuffs of her sweater down over her hands and she stood with one foot twisted over the other. Will felt a wrench in his heart. Iris always wanted to look older, act older, dress older, but sometimes she still stood and moved like the little girl she had once been. It always made him want to pull her into a bear hug, to whisper in her hair that there was no reason to rush, that growing up took time, but he knew that she would just pull away and roll her eyes, often adding a "Da-*ad*," the word drawn out into two contemptuous syllables.

"Do you, like, need some help?" Iris asked. She nodded at Brutus. "You know. With your robot thingy."

"Seriously?" Will asked.

Iris nodded.

Will frowned. "Come over here and let me see your head," he said.

"What?"

"Come on, I need to make sure you haven't suffered any recent head injuries."

Giggling, Iris stepped closer. Will peered at her head, looking at each side.

"I don't see any obvious bumps or blood. But you do have a lot of hair. What's your name? Who's the president? How many fingers am I holding up?" Will asked, making a V sign with his fingers.

"Dad," Iris said, still laughing. "I'm fine. Stop being such a goofball."

"I'm a dad. Being a goofball is part of the job description. Anyway, what's prompting this sudden interest in Brutus?" Will asked.

Iris looked blank. "Brutus?"

"My combat bot," Will said, pointing to the robot with a game-show-hostess flourish. "Iris, meet Brutus."

"He looks different from the other robots you've made," Iris said.

Will nodded. "I thought it was time I went into the ring with some power behind me. Ka-pow!" Will karate-chopped the air. "Are you really serious about wanting to help?"

"Yep," Iris said.

"Excellent. Take a seat." Will patted the stool next to him. "You can hold the motor casing, while I tighten these screws."

They sat side by side, working quietly.

"Can I ask you a question?" Iris said.

"No, I can't get you an early parole on your grounding sentence," Will said. "Sorry, kiddo."

After her driving stunt, Iris had been grounded for two months, including a ban on all phone and socializing privileges. Because she was a first time offender, the district attorney had arranged a deal where Iris had to perform two hundred hours of community service and in return, her record would be expunged. Three days a week after school and all day every Saturday, Iris worked at the local animal shelter. She walked dogs, cleaned out cages, basically did whatever the shelter employees needed her to do. At first she hadn't been enthusiastic, but after the first few weeks, it seemed as though she'd started to look forward to her time at the shelter. Just last week, Iris had brought home a flyer for a course that taught volunteers how to train Seeing Eye dogs.

"It's not that," Iris said.

"No? That's good. Your mom and I have been really proud of how you've been working so hard on your community service hours," Will said.

Iris's head bent forward, her hair falling in two curtains on either side of her face.

"Really," Will said, patting her back.

"I can't believe I got caught," Iris said suddenly. "Hannah and Ashley drive all the time, and they never get caught. I do it once and end up getting arrested."

Will hated these types of conversation. He knew that, as a concerned parent, he should immediately contact Hannah's and Ashley's parents, and repeat what Iris had just said about their joyriding. He also knew he'd never do it. In the past, this was the sort of thing he'd tell Fran, and let her handle. She was hooked into the mom network, and after years of serving on the PTA and manning bake sale tables, Fran knew the lowdown on every family their daughters' friends came from.

Will suddenly had the uneasy sensation that this, his willingness to dump anything uncomfortable relating to the girls into Fran's lap, had contributed to her discontentment with their marriage. He suddenly remembered the advice Leland had given him over the summer—about how he shouldn't take Fran for granted, about how important it was not to let the connection between them fray.

When was the last time I took Fran out to dinner? Will wondered. *When was the last time we went away for a weekend, just the two of us? Is that why she's leaving me, because I've lost the ability to connect with her?*

He'd always rationalized that money was tight. He didn't earn a high salary, and they had two daughters in private school. They somehow managed to get by, but never actually got ahead.

Then Will remembered their younger days, back when they were first married. They'd had even less money then. But they had found ways to get away, ways to be together. They'd taken picnics to the beach, spent weekends camping, Will had given Fran spontaneous back rubs.

"What's, like, going on with you and Mom?" Iris asked, startling Will out of this uneasy realization. "And don't tell me everything's fine. I know it's not."

Will put down the pair of pliers he'd been holding. "No, it's not," he admitted.

"I knew it," Iris said, although any triumph she felt at being right quickly gave way to worry. "Is everything going to be okay?"

"This—well, this problem—it's between your mother and me. It's not something I can talk about with you," Will said.

"Why not? Rory and I are part of this family, too. If you guys get divorced, it will affect us," Iris said.

Will wanted to tell her that no one was getting divorced, that everything would work out, that everything would, in fact, be fine, but even as he opened his mouth to speak, he knew the words wouldn't come out. The truth was that he had no idea what was going to happen. And he didn't want to lie to Iris.

"I don't know what's going to happen," Will said instead. "But no matter what, your mother and I love you and Rory more than anything in the world. Nothing will change that."

Iris's eyes filled with tears. "So you *are* getting a divorce."

"I didn't say that," Will said.

"Yeah, but that's what parents always say when they're getting a divorce. About loving the kids still. Well, it's just a crock. If you really loved us, you'd stay together. You'd make things work," Iris said.

"Iris," Will said, reaching out an arm to put around her thin shoulders.

But Iris shook him off. She jumped to her feet. "Don't," she said. And then she turned and ran out of the garage, leaving Will alone in the dim light.

He rested his elbows on the workbench and put his face in his hands. He had not handled that well. Iris was at such a difficult age, and Rory wasn't far behind. And now, on top of all of the usual struggles teenage girls faced, they'd have to deal with this, the dissolution of their family, as well.

"I screwed up," Will said out loud.

"What?"

Will started. In his fog, he hadn't heard the back door open, hadn't heard Fran come in behind him. And these days, it was rare for her to seek him out. They had only short, businesslike conversations about bills to be paid, the children's schedules, household tasks.

"Nothing. I mean . . . actually, it wasn't nothing, I think I just handled something with Iris badly." Fran moved closer to him, her arms wrapped around her body. Will peered at her in concern. "Have you been crying?"

Fran shrugged. But it was clear, she had been crying. Her eyes were red and her face was puffy. Red tear streaks stood out against the pale of her face.

"Are you okay?" Will asked.

Fran shrugged, said, "I'm fine," and then burst into tears.

Will stood quickly and moved toward Fran. He folded her into his arms, and she buried her face in his chest. She cried for a long time, heaving, body-racking sobs. Her breathing gradually slowed, and finally the sobs shuddered to an end.

"I got your shirt all wet," Fran said, her voice muffled against Will's chest.

"It's okay. It'll dry," Will said.

"And I got mascara all over it," Fran said, leaning back a little to inspect the damage.

Will pulled her close again. "I'll throw it out."

"Don't be nice to me. I don't deserve it." Fran's voice was muffled again.

"Of course you do."

"No, I really don't." Fran leaned back again and looked up at him. "After everything I've put you through. I've been so stupid. I almost walked away from our marriage. I almost . . . well, I did something stupid."

Fear slashed through his stomach, hot and sickening. He didn't want to hear whatever was coming next. Fran was about to tell him she wanted to come back. That was all he wanted to hear. That their marriage would have a second chance. He didn't want any of the details of why she'd come to this decision.

"You've changed your mind about leaving?" Will asked.

"Yes. Unless you want me to leave. Which I would totally understand, after everything I've put you through."

Will closed his eyes and breathed in deeply, inhaling the essential Franness of her. And then he asked the question he had to ask, no matter how much he didn't want to know the answer.

"What were you doing at Coop's tonight?" he asked.

Fran stiffened in his arms. "Did he call you?" she asked.

Will shook his head. "I followed you."

"You *followed* me? Why?" Fran stepped back. Her face was pale and vulnerable. Dark circles under her eyes stood out like bruises.

"I wanted to find out if you've been having an affair," Will said.

And then he waited.

Fran looked at him. In each moment that ticked by, Will felt his world falling down around him.

"I haven't. Not exactly," Fran said.

Will waited, but she didn't go on. "What does that mean?" he finally asked.

Fran sighed. "It means that I wanted to have an affair with Coop. He turned me down," she said flatly.

Will looked at her for a long moment. He could hear his breath, loud and ragged, in the quiet night. Fran looked back at him, her eyes large and somber, her makeup smeared. But Will barely noticed this. Mostly, what he thought as he stared down at her, was that he did not know his wife.

Then he turned and walked away from her, heading into the house.

"Will," Fran called after him.

Will didn't turn back. He'd spent weeks wondering what

he could have done differently, what he could still do to keep his marriage together. And now, for the first time in their life together, he was no longer sure that he still wanted to be married to Fran.

COOP PUSHED OPEN THE door to the Seawind Day Spa, set- ting off the chime of a bell. The aroma of rosemary and olive oil and something else—*Patchouli?* he wondered— enveloped him. The cute but ditzy receptionist was behind the desk.

"Hi, there," she said when she saw Coop. She smiled flir- tatiously. "You're Audrey's friend. The mani-pedi guy."

"Right. The mani-pedi guy. Just what I've always wanted to be known as."

The receptionist giggled. "What's your name again?"

"Coop."

She smiled at Coop, showing off lots of large white teeth. "I'm Lisa."

Coop had the feeling that Lisa would be thrilled if he popped a biceps for her. Or asked for her number. And he had to admit, there was a time when she would have been exactly his type. Young, beautiful, vapid.

"Is Audrey here?" Coop asked.

"If you want another pedicure, I can book it for you," Lisa said helpfully.

"No, thanks," Coop said. He grinned, taking care not to hit her with his most charming smile. There was no reason to punish the girl. "I was just hoping to talk to Audrey, if she has a free minute."

Lisa shrugged in a good-natured way. "I'll go check," she

said. "She might be in a meeting. That's what she pretends, sometimes."

Coop wondered if he should mention to Audrey the obvious deficiencies in her receptionist's job skills—hitting on potential clients and/or business contacts, an inability to lie convincingly about her boss's schedule—but decided that when it came to Audrey, he had enough complications to deal with without getting into her staffing issues.

Lisa got up and sashayed to the back of the office. She was wearing a very short plaid skirt that showed off her very long legs. Coop made a valiant effort not to notice.

I do not ogle receptionists. That is not my way. Or, at least, it isn't anymore, he thought.

She reappeared a few minutes later.

"Audrey will be right out," she said.

"Did you give her my name?" Coop asked.

"Mmm-hmm. I said that there was a Carson waiting to see her. Oh, and that you were a repeat customer," the brunette said.

"It's Coop."

"Oh, well. Too late now," Lisa said.

Audrey's appearance was heralded by the clicking of high heels against hard floors.

"Lisa, have you called to confirm tomorrow's appointments yet?" Audrey said as she rounded the corner into the waiting room. She saw Coop and came to an abrupt halt.

"I can, like, call, but people always say they're coming in, even if they aren't," Lisa said, clearly dubious that such phone calls were worth her time.

"Hi," Coop said.

"Hi," Audrey said.

She looked beautiful, if a bit flustered. She was wearing a red blazer, a black and white striped shirt, dark jeans, and—as usual—black pumps with very high heels.

I love her, Coop thought. He knew it absolutely. It was like a spotlight shone down on her, highlighting the crown of her head, the angles of her cheekbones.

Coop opened his mouth. He wasn't sure what he meant to say—declarations of love, perhaps?—but instead, what came out was, "What is it with you and high heels?"

Audrey frowned and looked down at her shoes. "What?"

"Why do you always wear such high heels?" He had absolutely no idea why he was going on about her shoes.

Stop it. You're being a jackass, he told himself.

"Is that why you came here? To ask me about my footwear?" Audrey asked. She crossed her arms.

"Um, no. About something else actually." Coop glanced at Lisa, who was watching them with frank, wide-eyed curiosity. "Maybe we can go somewhere a little more private?"

"Don't mind me," Lisa said, flapping a hand. "Just pretend I'm not here."

Coop had to swallow back his laugh. And, for a moment, he thought that Audrey was also trying not to grin. However, when she spoke, her voice was cool. "Let's go to my office."

Lisa looked disappointed.

"Don't forget the calls," Audrey reminded her.

"Oh, right," Lisa said without enthusiasm.

Coop followed Audrey back to her office.

"Is it wrong that I continue to employ someone I have absolutely no faith in?" she said once they were inside her office, and the door was firmly closed.

"Yes," Coop said. "But I'm sure she has her good points."

"I'm sure you noticed all of her good points," Audrey said darkly. "She doesn't exactly keep them hidden."

Coop wasn't about to fall for that one. "She seemed like a very nice girl," he said lamely.

Audrey snorted and sat down behind her desk. "What can I do for you?" she asked.

"This is all very businesslike," Coop said, sitting in one of the chairs opposite her desk. It wasn't exactly the reception he was hoping for, but then again, maybe it was unrealistic to expect Audrey to strip off her clothes and fold herself onto his lap.

"That's me. I'm all business," Audrey said.

Coop had a flashback to Audrey in his bed, arching up under him, but decided that mentioning this distinct lack of businesslike behavior might not be in his interest at the moment.

"How was your trip? I never got a chance to ask you about it," Audrey said.

"It was a mistake," Coop said. He wished they weren't having this conversation in an office, across a desk, but didn't want to squander the opportunity. "I shouldn't have gone. I should have stayed and worked things out with you instead."

Audrey's hand, which had been playing with the pen, stilled. "I told you to go."

Coop smiled. "I've never been one to do as I'm told."

When Audrey spoke again, her voice was gentle. "It wouldn't have changed anything. You and I . . . we're just too different. It would never have worked."

This was not what Coop wanted to hear. His feelings were hurt and the childish retort came out before he could stop it. "And you and Kenny are?"

"No. We're not seeing each other anymore."

Although Coop welcomed this piece of information, he was still stung by Audrey's lack of enthusiasm over his admission that he'd been wrong to leave. Still, he decided, he might as well make his case.

"You and I were great together. You just need to give it a chance. To give me a chance," Coop said. He hesitated. "The thing is, I think . . . I mean, I don't just think it, I know it . . . but here's the thing . . . I love you."

Audrey's eyes seemed to grow darker and larger, and Coop found that he was holding his breath. He flexed his hands over his thighs, amazed to find that his palms were sweating.

"Thank you," Audrey finally said.

Coop swallowed. "Thank you?" he repeated.

"Yes. That's a lovely thing to say."

"Is that all you have to say?" Coop asked. It felt like there was a balloon inflating in his chest. Only no, not a balloon—which was soft and elastic—but something harder, that made it difficult to breathe.

"It's just . . . I can't. I can't be in love right now," Audrey said, her voice barely louder than a whisper.

Forget the balloon. Coop felt like he'd been punched in the stomach. He actually had to remind himself to start breathing again. In all the times he had imagined this moment, he had never, not once, thought she'd first thank him—what the hell was that?—and then turn him down. And while some of his ex-girlfriends might chalk that certainty up to his innate cockiness, that wasn't it. The truth was, he truly did love Audrey. And he thought she might just love him back.

Clearly, he had been wrong.

"Okay, then," Coop said. He stood, feeling a little shaky.

"Wait," Audrey said, standing, too, and quickly moving around her desk toward him. She put a hand on his arm. "It's not you. It's me." She closed her eyes and shook her head. "Jesus, now I am talking in clichés. But this really is about me. I don't trust myself enough to be with someone else right now. Does that make sense?"

"Not really, no," Coop said, glancing at the door and wondering if he should just make a run for it.

"I need to figure out why I'm so bad at relationships. And until I do, getting involved with someone . . . with you . . . it wouldn't be fair. Not to you, and not to me."

"That sounds like a firm, definite no," Coop said, trying to keep his tone light.

Audrey's eyes softened, and her grip on his arm tightened. "I'm so sorry."

Coop nodded stiffly and swallowed. "I am, too," he said. Then he gently dislodged her hand from his arm, stepped around her, and walked out of her office.

JAIME WAS JUST FINISHING changing Ava's diaper, when she heard her cellphone.

Crap, she thought. She'd left her phone in the kitchen.

"Let's hurry," she said to her daughter, stretching the diaper tabs to close them, and making a mental note to look into early toilet training. Who knew, maybe Ava would turn out to be a baby prodigy and pick up the idea quickly. It was unlikely. Logan, almost four, still hadn't mastered the concept.

Jaime plucked Ava off the changing table, which she had

outgrown, and, tucking her daughter on one hip, hurried across the house. She managed to grab the phone right before it went to voice mail.

"Hi, Jaime, it's me." It was Emily calling from her cellphone. She sounded upset.

"Emily? Why aren't you in school?"

"I *am* in school." Emily was definitely upset. In fact, it sounded like she was in tears, or close to them. "Something terrible's happened, and I can't get ahold of my mom."

"Calm down. Take a deep breath," Jaime said. "What's going on?"

"Today's my presentation on the early pioneers, and I left all of my stuff at home on my desk," Emily wailed.

"Can't you just ask your teacher if you can give your presentation tomorrow instead?"

"No way! Mrs. White is so mean. She'll make me give the presentation today, even if I don't have my notes and visual aids. And then she'll fail me! You have to bring them to me. Please, Jaime," Emily begged.

"But you said they're at your mom's house? How am I supposed to get them?" Jaime asked. She suddenly pictured herself trying to crawl into Libby's house through a window and getting arrested for breaking and entering in the process.

"There's a spare key hidden by the front door. It's under the sundial," Emily said. "*Please,* Jaime. Practice went so late last night, and Coach Sarah made me run wind sprints. And then I had to stay up past midnight to finish my presentation and I overslept this morning, and Mom made me rush to get to school on time, and I forgot it," Emily wailed. "I swear, if you bring it to me, I'll never ask you for anything ever again."

Jaime hesitated, but then sighed. "Where exactly is this key hidden?"

"Thank you, thank you, thank you!"

JAIME LOADED AVA AND Logan into the car. Ava was rubbing her stuffed turtle against her face. Logan had brought along three Thomas the Train engines with him, but was worried about the ones he'd left at home.

"Mommy, I need Percy," Logan said.

"Don't worry," Jaime soothed. "Your trains will be fine. We're almost at Emily's house."

"I thought our house was Emily's house," Logan said.

"This is Emily's other house. Where her mother lives," Jaime said.

"I want two houses, too," Logan said.

Ignoring this, Jaime said, "Once we get there, we're going to run into the house, pick up something for Emily, and then drive it to her at school." Jaime glanced in the rearview mirror and groaned inwardly. Ava had fallen asleep. It meant that the already Herculean task of herding the kids from the car to the house, back into the car, then into the school, then back to the car yet again would be made even more difficult by the heavy weight of a sleeping child. It was one of life's mysteries: Sleeping children always weighed more than awake ones.

Jaime pulled in to the driveway of Libby's large home with its stunning view of the Intracoastal and found herself staring at Mark's car. She felt a stab of irritation. Had Emily also called Mark and asked him to pick up the forgotten history presentation? And if so, why hadn't she called back to tell Jaime he was getting it?

"Typical," Jaime muttered.

Jaime pulled out her cellphone to call Mark to confirm that he was in fact bringing the school project to Emily before she bothered to unload the children.

The phone rang four times and then went to voice mail. Jaime tried again. This time, the phone rang only twice before it went to voice mail.

Did he just reject my call? Jaime wondered, her irritation growing tenfold.

Then, suddenly, Emily's voice came back to her. *I can't get ahold of my mom.*

Libby wasn't answering the phone, not even for her daughter. And now Mark wasn't answering his phone. And his car was parked in front of his ex-wife's house.

Suspicion trickled down Jaime's neck like cold water. *No way,* she thought. There was no way Mark would ever have an affair with Libby. He couldn't stand his ex-wife. They always made an effort to remain polite for Emily's sake, but when Mark and Jaime were in private, Mark rarely had a positive word to say about Libby or his marriage to her. He thought she was selfish and demanding, said that she had always put her needs ahead of his and Emily's.

But then Jaime thought of all the late nights Mark spent at the tennis club, all of the weekend trips he took with Emily. Libby went sometimes, too. Jaime had never thought much of it—they were both committed to Emily's tennis career, and besides, they always traveled separately and, of course, stayed in different hotel rooms.

Didn't they?

No, Jaime thought. *No way.*

Then again. The weekends away would have given them plenty of opportunities to be alone together. When she wasn't playing, Emily always spent most of the tournament weekend off with her girlfriends, hanging out by the pool or in the hotel coffee shop.

Jaime turned her ignition off. She glanced back at the kids. Ava was still asleep, but Logan was wide awake, kicking his chubby legs up in front of him.

"Come on, we have to go inside for a minute," Jaime told him.

"Carry me?" Logan asked hopefully.

"I can't carry both you and your sister. You're going to have to walk," Jaime said, wishing she could leave them in the car, but knowing it was probably a bad idea. Logan was perfectly capable of unhooking the straps of his car seat, climbing into the front seat, and putting the car into gear. Just the mental picture of the SUV rolling down the driveway, out of control with both of her children inside, gave Jaime the chills.

Jaime could feel her heart beating hard and fast, as she climbed out and retrieved the children from the backseat. With Ava heavy in her arms and Logan's small hand in her own, Jaime made her way slowly to the front door. The whole way, Jaime kept hoping the door would open, that Mark would come out with Emily's school project in hand.

On the front step, Jaime hesitated, wondering what she should do. Ring the bell, or retrieve the hidden key and let herself in? If she rang the bell and waited to see if anyone answered, she might never know what was really going on. Mark might have an excuse for why he was here, why he wasn't answering his phone. Then again, if Mark and Libby were having an affair, did Jaime really want to walk in on them, both babies in tow?

Jaime pressed the bell and waited. No one came to the

door. Jaime pressed the bell again, this time leaning on it for longer. The third time, she hit it repeatedly, not caring how obnoxious this was. And the obnoxious behavior was rewarded: Footsteps echoed inside, and a moment later, the door opened. Libby was standing there, wearing white shorts and a man's striped button-down shirt.

It was Mark's shirt. One of the striped, French-cuff shirts Jaime bought him for Christmas the year before, ordered specially from London. This one was yellow and blue. She had a very clear memory of Mark pulling it out of the closet that morning. He'd said that the dry cleaner had used too much starch, and Jaime had promised she'd mention it the next time she went in to drop off the laundry.

Jaime's skin suddenly felt too tight, and she struggled to focus her eyes. It felt like she was looking through a telescope, where Libby was at the same time right in front of her and yet very far away. She wondered, distantly, if this was what a nervous breakdown felt like. And then, with Ava's heavy bulk to remind her, she remembered that she was a mother, and therefore couldn't afford the luxury of a nervous breakdown.

"Hi, Libby," Logan said, waving.

Libby was standing very still, her hand still frozen on the doorknob. She gave no indication that she'd heard Logan.

"Where's Mark?" Jaime asked. She was shocked at how calm she sounded. As though it were a common occurrence for her to stumble upon her husband and his ex-wife in the sort of intimate situation that ended up with Libby wearing Mark's shirt.

"Mark?" Libby asked. She shrugged and tried to feign surprise. "Why would he be here?"

She's seriously going to try to brazen this out? Jaime thought. While wearing Mark's shirt, with his car in the driveway? It was almost funny. Or else, it would be if it weren't so horrific.

Ava was heavy in her arms, and Jaime tried shifting her daughter without waking her up.

"Please tell him I'd like to see him," Jaime said. Libby opened her mouth as though to protest, and Jaime added, "And you might want to give him his shirt back before he comes out."

Libby looked down at her shirt, and then back up at Jaime.

"He isn't happy, you know," Libby finally said. Her voice was quiet, but without contrition. In fact, she seemed almost defiant, as though daring Jaime to deny it.

"That's funny. He always told me he wasn't happy when he was married to you," Jaime said. Her cool tone was belied by the tears that were welling in her eyes. "Isn't it interesting how we keep believing him? Actually, it's not really interesting at all. It's tragic, considering there are three children involved."

"Mommy, when are we going home?" Logan asked, pulling at the hem of Jaime's shirt.

Libby looked down at Logan, as though she was just now seeing him and Ava. Her face went pale and slack, and she suddenly looked like she might be sick.

"I never stopped thinking of him as my husband. Even after we divorced. Even after he married you. And when this happened . . . it just seemed right. Like we were hitting a reset button," Libby said.

Libby reached out to touch Logan's head, but Jaime said,

"Don't." The word was almost a growl, and Libby's hand fell away. Logan looked up at his mother, clearly startled by how ferocious she sounded.

"Lib? What's going on?" Mark's voice called.

"Daddy?" Logan asked in a clear, carrying voice.

"Mark, can you come out here please?" Libby asked.

Mark appeared at the door. He was—thankfully—dressed, wearing a tennis jacket and shorts. Jaime wondered if he kept clothes at Libby's house. *He probably does, the bastard.*

"Oh! Hey, honey, what are you doing here?" Mark asked.

He had clearly decided to take the same tack as Libby and pretend that there was nothing unusual about his being at his ex-wife's house in the middle of the day, when he was supposed to be at work. Still, all of the color had drained from his face, and his eyes were moving shiftily from wife to ex-wife and back again.

"Daddy!" Logan said, his small face lighting up. He ran to Mark, who scooped him up in his arms.

"Hey, squirt," Mark said, hugging Logan. "What are you guys doing here?"

"Emily asked me to come by and pick up the notes and visuals for her history presentation," Jaime said. She was still amazed at how calm she sounded and wondered, distantly, if she was in shock.

"She did?" Libby asked. "She left her presentation at home?"

"Yes," Jaime said.

"Why didn't she call me?" Libby asked.

"You were apparently too busy to answer your phone," Jaime said, raising her eyebrows.

Recognition dawned on Libby's face, and she blushed and looked away.

"Oh. Right," Libby said.

Mark looked back and forth between them again. "This is an odd coincidence. I stopped by to go over Emily's tournament schedule with Libby," he said, affecting the same breezy tone. "Too bad Emily didn't call me, I could have saved you the trip over."

Jaime stared at her husband, and decided that she officially hated him. In fact, all of the very characteristics that had first attracted her to him—his dark eyes, the sexy thin lips, the square jaw—were now the things she hated the most about him. Well, his face, and the fact that he was a lying son of a bitch.

"Mark, she knows," Libby said wearily.

But even then, Mark wasn't ready to drop the act. "Knows what?" he asked. "That we're meeting to discuss Em's schedule?"

Libby gave him the sort of irritated look that Jaime again thought might have been funny, had this all not been happening to her. She wondered if, like her, Libby was finally seeing Mark for the sort of man he was. Standing there with his young son in his arms, lying glibly.

"She knows about *us*," Libby clarified. She gave Logan another uneasy look. "Maybe Logan should go up to Em's room, so we can talk? And you can put Ava down in . . ." Jaime was sure that Libby had been about to say, *my bedroom*. But, as if remembering what had just happened in that bedroom, she quickly substituted, "the guest room."

"I want to go to Em's room," Logan said, looking delighted at the idea. He adored Emily, and although she was very sweet to her younger siblings, this affection did not stretch to allowing them unfettered access to her room and its precious belongings.

"No," Jaime said, raising a hand. "We're going to leave."

"You shouldn't drive while you're upset," Libby said.

"I'm fine," Jaime said. She looked at Mark, who was pale with shock and looking almost lost, as though he couldn't figure out what to say or do. "Or I will be. Come on, Logan. Let's go home."

december

.. ..

a tasting menu

SEARED FOIE GRAS WITH A RED WINE
AND SOUR CHERRY REDUCTION

SEARED DIVER SCALLOPS WITH
BLOOD-ORANGE SAUCE

VEGETABLE TERRINE

SLOW BAKED DOVER SOLE

DUO OF BEEF

CARAMEL AND SEA SALT ICE CREAM

*T*HE DECEMBER MEETING OF the Table for Seven Club was canceled. Audrey called Fran and Jaime and invited them to meet her for dinner at the Lemon Tree on the night the club would have met. The restaurant was owned by one of her regular clients, Heather, and her husband, Juan, who was the chef.

Audrey arrived at the restaurant first. Heather greeted her warmly, and sat her at a large corner table. Audrey sipped a glass of ice water while she waited for the others to arrive.

Fran got there next, looking wan and wearing a yellow dress that didn't suit her.

"Sorry," Fran said, sitting down across the table from Audrey. "One of those nights."

"It's okay. Jaime's late, too," Audrey said. "Is everything okay?"

Fran looked defensive. "Why wouldn't it be?"

"You look tired," Audrey said.

"That's probably because I'm exhausted." Fran pulled out her cellphone and began frantically scrolling through her text messages. Apparently not finding what she wanted, she dropped the cellphone on the table, and raised a hand to the waiter.

"I'd like a glass of the house Merlot, please," Fran said.

"I thought we might order a bottle," Audrey said.

"Sure," Fran said. "Whatever you want."

Audrey waited for Fran to cancel the glass of Merlot. When Fran didn't call back the waiter, Audrey prompted. "Do you still want the glass?"

"What?"

"If we're getting a bottle, do you still want the glass?" Audrey asked patiently.

"Oh, right. I guess it's too late now," Fran said, as the waiter appeared with her glass of wine.

Audrey stared at her friend, wondering what was going on. Fran seemed distracted and possibly even depressed. She looked terrible, too. Her skin was sallow and there were dark circles under her eyes.

"Are you okay?" Audrey asked, leaning forward across the table and touching Fran's hand.

"Hi, sorry I'm late," Jaime said, arriving at the table out of breath.

"Hi, Jaime," Audrey said, smiling up at her.

Fran glanced up and frowned. "Jesus, what happened to you?"

"There is a right and a wrong way to take that," Jaime said, sitting in the empty seat next to Fran.

"You look like you've lost fifteen pounds since the last time I saw you," Fran said.

Fran was right. Jaime had always been slim, but now she looked positively emaciated. She was, as usual, perfectly groomed—her blond hair sprayed into place, her makeup perfectly applied, her pink Lilly Pulitzer dress setting off her tan skin—but her eyes had a sad, haunted look and her face was hollowed out.

Audrey looked from one friend to the other, and finally said, "Okay, you two, what's going on?"

Jaime and Fran exchanged uneasy looks.

"Actually, I do have some news," Jaime said.

"Me, too," Fran said, with a deep sigh.

"Okay, hold on. I think we're going to need some wine before we get into it. Or at least, Jaime and I still need wine," Audrey said, gesturing for their waiter.

"Give me two minutes, and I'll be ready for a refill," Fran said.

Audrey ordered a bottle of Chardonnay from Sonoma County, which the waiter promptly brought back to the table. He uncorked the wine, and poured a glass for Audrey, who took a sip, although she was now so worried by her friends' general weirdness that she barely paid attention to the wine. She nodded to the waiter to go ahead and pour for the table.

"Have you had time to look over the menu?" the waiter asked, once the wine was poured.

"I have, but they haven't," Audrey said. "But I was going to suggest we try the tasting menu. Heather recommended it."

"Fine with me," Jaime said, pushing her menu to the side, and looking relieved to have the burden of making a decision lifted.

"Me, too," Fran said.

Once the waiter had left, Audrey raised her wineglass. "Cheers," she said.

"Cheers," the other two said, and they clinked their glasses together in a dispirited way.

"What's going on with you two?" Audrey asked again.

"You go first, Fran," Jaime said.

"No, you," Fran said.

"You've had a head start on the wine," Jaime said, nodding to Fran's mostly empty glass of red.

"And I need at least another glass before I can get into it," Fran said.

"Me, too," Jaime said.

"Oh, for God's sake. One of you had better start talking!" Audrey said.

"Why don't you start, Audrey," Jaime suggested. "Tell us your news."

"I don't have anything to share. It's the same old with me. Work, work, and more work."

"How's Kenny?" Jaime asked.

"We're not seeing each other anymore," Audrey said.

"That's too bad. I liked him," Jaime said. "Although I guess he wasn't the most exciting guy in the world."

"Exciting is overrated. But Kenny and I didn't even have basic chemistry." Audrey shrugged. "I've told you before, I'm not cut out for romance."

"That's not what Leland said," Fran said.

"That's right. I forgot about that, with everything that happened," Jaime said.

"What are you two talking about?" Audrey asked.

"The night Leland died—right before he died—he said something about how you weren't the type of woman who should be alone," Fran said.

Audrey stiffened. "I think I've been getting along okay," she said.

"He didn't mean it as an insult. Just the opposite. I thought what he was saying was that you were the sort of person who would love well, and it would be a shame not to share that with another person. Isn't that how you took it?" Jaime looked at Fran for confirmation. Fran nodded.

"How did my love life—or lack of a love life, I should say—become the subject of the dinner party conversation?"

Audrey asked. This idea, that the others had been talking about her, made her uneasy.

"It wasn't," Jaime said. "Leland said something about it to Coop. We just overheard him."

"He said it to Coop?" Audrey asked more sharply than she intended.

Jaime nodded. "I got the feeling that Leland wanted to test out his matchmaker skills on you and Coop." She smiled for the first time that evening and gave Fran a sly glance. "Didn't you get that impression, Franny?"

Fran shrugged. "I don't know about that."

"Really? I thought Leland was being so obvious! I thought he was basically telling Coop to ask Audrey out," Jaime said.

Audrey could feel her face flush red, and she stared down at her wineglass.

"I guess that just goes to show that no one's right all the time. Not even Leland," Fran said.

Jaime cocked her head to one side. "Why's that?"

"Coop and Audrey went out on a date once. They didn't hit it off," Fran said.

"Seriously? I didn't know that," Jaime said, looking at Audrey.

"Actually, it was a bit more involved than that," Audrey said.

"What?" Fran asked, finally looking focused and alert. "What does that mean?"

"I guess you could say that Coop and I had a bit of a fling," Audrey admitted. She took a sip of her wine. "Although I'm not sure how Leland figured that out. I wonder if Coop told him?"

"You had a *fling* with *Coop*?" Fran asked, staring at Audrey. "I don't blame you. He's really sexy. What happened?"

Jaime asked, her eyes round with interest. She took a sip of her wine and nibbled at a piece of buttered bread.

"Excuse me, ladies." Their waiter appeared again, brandishing a tray with three small spoon-shaped bowls. "An *amuse bouche* from the chef to start your meal. This is a Thai lobster bisque." He set the bowls down in front of them, said, "Enjoy," and whisked off again.

"Mmm," Audrey said, after tasting the soup. "This is excellent."

"Audrey!" Fran said. Audrey looked up, surprised by the sharpness of Fran's tone. "What happened with you and Coop?"

Audrey sighed. "Honestly, I wish I hadn't brought it up. I don't really feel like talking about it."

"But you did bring it up, so now you have to give us the details," Fran said.

"No, she doesn't," Jaime said, glancing curiously at Fran. "Although, of course, we'd very much like to hear them, if you want to tell us."

But Audrey was looking at Fran, frowning. "Fran, what's going on?"

"What do you mean?"

"I mean, every time Coop's name comes up—especially in connection with me—you start acting weird," Audrey said.

"I do not!"

"Yes, you do. First, you told me he was gay. Then you basically told me he was a male slut. Then you insisted that he and I would have nothing in common. And now you look completely pissed off," Audrey said.

"I'm not pissed off. I just don't know why you've never

mentioned this fling before," Fran said. Her face flooded with color, and she looked away.

"Do you have feelings for Coop?" Audrey asked quietly.

"Why would you ask me that?"

"I've wondered whether you might have a crush on him," Audrey said.

"Yeah, I actually wondered about that, too," Jaime interjected.

"You did? You both thought that?" Fran asked.

Jaime nodded. "You get really animated when he's around."

"Oh, God," Fran said. Her cheeks flushed. "I do?"

"Yes," Jaime and Audrey said together.

"Great. That's just great. I'm officially mortified," Fran said.

"But is it more than that? More than a crush?" Audrey asked.

Fran didn't respond. Instead, she sipped her wine, while still staring fixedly at the bread basket.

"Fran?" Audrey said gently. "Is that why you've been so against him and me getting together?"

"You're not together though, are you?" Fran asked. "You said you had a fling. As in past tense."

Audrey cleared her throat, knowing that what she was about to say might hurt her friend. But she didn't see any way around it. "Actually, it was in the past. But Coop came to see me recently. I told him that I didn't think it would work between us. But since that day, I haven't been able to stop thinking about him. And I've been wondering if I pushed him away because I've been afraid."

"Afraid how?" Jaime asked her.

Audrey lifted one shoulder. "Like I said, I'm bad at relationships. I don't have a good track record when it comes to
picking good guys. But I don't want to go through life like
that, afraid of becoming involved with someone. It's no way
to live," Audrey said.

"You're right, it's not," Jaime said. She squeezed Audrey's
hand. "You deserve to be happy."

But Audrey was looking at Fran, who still seemed intent
on not making eye contact with her. "What do you think,
Fran?"

"Of course I think you deserve to be happy," Fran said.

"No, I know that. But what if being with Coop is what
makes me happy? How do you feel about that?" Audrey
asked.

Fran finally looked at her then, and Audrey could see the
pain in her friend's face. "Does he make you happy?"

Audrey nodded. "Yes," she said simply.

"Then you should be with him," Fran said. Her eyes glit-
tered with tears.

"Franny, what's going on?" Audrey asked, leaning forward.

"It's nothing," Fran said. "Excuse me."

Fran got up so quickly her wooden bistro chair nearly
toppled over. She fled in the direction of the ladies' room.

"Should I go after her?" Jaime asked anxiously.

"Give her a minute," Audrey said, knowing that if it were
her, she'd want the chance to compose herself—to get the
tears under control, to be able to speak without sobbing—
before anyone attempted to comfort her.

The waiter arrived with their first course and cast a concerned look in the direction of Fran's empty chair.

"It's okay, she'll be right back," Audrey assured him.

"Here we have a nice foie gras with a sour cherry reduction," the waiter said, setting the three small plates down. He refilled their wineglasses, draining the last of the bottle. "Would you like another bottle?"

"Yes, please," Audrey and Jaime said together, and then looked at each other and laughed.

"I think tonight the wine counts as medicinal," Jaime said.

"I agree. Although we may be taking a taxi home," Audrey said. "Unless we can talk Mark or Will into coming to pick us up."

The smile vanished from Jaime's face. "We won't be calling Mark."

"Uh-oh," Audrey said. She realized it was the first time Jaime had ever opened up to her. Maybe they were friends, after all. "What's going on?"

"Let's wait until Fran gets back, so I only have to say it once," Jaime said. "So, you and Coop, huh?"

"Maybe. I don't know if he's still interested," Audrey said.

"I thought you said he wanted to get things started again?"

"He did. But that was a few weeks ago. And I turned him down. I don't know if he'll want to give me another chance," Audrey said.

"Just tell him how you feel," Jaime said. "Tell him what you told us."

"I don't know if I'm ready for that," Audrey said.

"You just said you didn't want to go through your life being afraid," Jaime said.

"Baby steps," Audrey said. "First thing is to identify the problem. Then I'll work my way up to doing something about it."

Fran returned to the table at the same time the waiter arrived with their fresh bottle of wine. She sat down and waited for him to open the bottle and depart. Fran's eyes were red, but she otherwise looked composed. The tears were gone, and she'd freshened her lipstick.

"Sorry about that. You didn't have to wait for me to eat," Fran said.

"Are you okay?" Audrey asked.

"I will be." Fran smiled weakly. "I guess I'm going to have to explain, aren't I?"

"Only if you want to," Jaime said. She tasted the foie gras and closed her eyes. "Oh, my God. This is heaven. It's like meat butter."

Audrey laughed. "Meat butter. That sounds like something Leland would say." She sampled her foie gras and sighed happily. "Forget men. Maybe I should focus my attention on mastering charcuterie." When neither Fran nor Jaime laughed—in fact, they both became unusually quiet, like a pair of hermit crabs snapping back into their shells—Audrey looked at them, bewildered. "Okay, you two. Spill it."

Jaime drew in a deep breath and put down her fork. "I might as well tell you. Mark and I are getting a divorce. He's been having an affair with his ex-wife."

Fran's mouth gaped open, and Audrey inhaled audibly.

"How did you find out?" Fran asked.

"I found them together at her house," Jaime said.

"You suspected something was up?" Audrey asked.

"No, I had no idea. I went over to Libby's house to pick up a school project Emily needed. And I found them there together." Jaime swallowed hard, but remained composed. "Libby answered the door wearing Mark's shirt."

Fran and Audrey both gasped.

"No!" Fran said.

"Are you serious?" Audrey asked.

"Unfortunately, yes, I am serious. I've asked Mark to move out, and I've already hired a divorce attorney," Jaime said.

Fran shook her head, looking amazed. "You seem so together."

"Do I? Well, that's funny, because I feel like I'm falling apart," Jaime said. She paused, as a shudder of pain passed over her features. For a moment, Audrey thought Jaime might cry, too, but she took a deep breath and pulled herself together. "I've gotten so used to pretending everything's going to be okay—you know, for the kids' sake—that maybe I've managed to delude myself into believing it."

Fran put an arm around Jaime's shoulder and squeezed her.

"You'll get through this," Fran said.

"I know. I'm going to be fine. It's Ava and Logan that I'm worried about. Divorce is so hard on children," Jaime said. Her voice broke, and she looked near tears again. She held her wineglass out to Audrey. "More Chardonnay, please."

Audrey poured wine into Jaime's glass, filling it almost to the top. Jaime smiled weakly.

"Is there any chance you and Mark can work things out?" Audrey said, wondering if she would be able to forgive a straying husband.

"Could you?" Jaime asked, echoing Audrey's thoughts.

"To be honest, I don't know. But some couples manage to get past affairs," Audrey said.

The foie gras was so excellent that despite the difficult conversation, all three managed to clean their plates. The waiter whisked away the empty dishes. If he noticed how traumatized first Fran, and now Jaime, looked, he was tactful enough not to say anything.

Once the waiter had departed, Jaime leaned forward to answer Audrey's question. "I might be able to forgive a one-night stand. Something that happened while he was drunk and out of town. But a long-term affair with his ex-wife?" Jaime shrugged helplessly. "I don't see how we get past that. I could never trust him again. And it's not like he can cut off contact with Libby, even if he wanted to. There's Emily. They'll always be connected through her."

"The same way you'll always be connected to Mark through Ava and Logan," Audrey said.

"And to Libby, too. Don't forget, her daughter is Ava and Logan's sister. It's such a mess," Jaime said. She shook her head. "I've always hated the term *divorcée*. It makes my skin crawl. But that's what I'll be from now on—a divorcée."

"I may be right there with you," Fran said.

"Are you still thinking about leaving Will?" Audrey asked. She tried hard to keep all judgment out of her voice, but it was difficult.

"No. But now he's thinking of leaving me," Fran said. She smiled without humor. "This is quite the night for bombshells."

Audrey and Jaime stared at Fran.

"Why would Will leave you? He adores you," Jaime said.

"He used to adore me," Fran corrected her. "Now he can barely stand to look at me."

"What happened?" Audrey asked.

They were interrupted again by the appearance of the waiter with their second course.

"Seared diver scallops in a blood-orange sauce," the waiter said, setting down the three small plates.

"Oh, yum, I love scallops," Fran said. "I wish I was the sort of person who stopped eating when they're in a crisis. I swear I just get hungrier. I've put on seven pounds in the past three weeks."

"Fran, stop stalling and tell us what's going on," Audrey said.

"Oh, my God, you have to try this," Fran said, infuriatingly. She pointed to her scallops with her fork.

Audrey sighed, but took a bite. "Wow," she said, as the flavors exploded in her mouth. The smooth buttery scallop, chased by the bold citrus of the oranges.

"I know, right?" Fran said. Then, catching Audrey's look, she said, "Okay, fine. I guess Coop will probably tell you anyway, so you might as well hear it from me."

Audrey felt a shiver of misapprehension. That sounded ominous. Had something happened between Fran and Coop? And suddenly Audrey wasn't at all sure she wanted to hear what Fran was about to say.

"Tell me what?" Audrey asked cautiously.

"I pretty much threw myself at Coop," Fran said flatly. "And he turned me down, so nothing happened. But Will found out about it. And, as you can imagine, he's furious."

Audrey felt like she'd spent the entire night staring open-mouthed at her friends, and now found herself gaping once again, this time at Fran. Jaime was staring at Fran, too, although her eyes were narrowed.

"You cheated on Will?" Jaime asked. There was a sharp edge to her voice. Audrey realized that Jaime was probably not in a forgiving mood when it came to infidelity at the moment.

"Actually, I'm only guilty of attempted adultery. Like I said, Coop turned me down," Fran said. "And between the humiliation of being rejected and my husband threatening to leave me, I think I've been punished enough."

"Sorry," Jaime said quietly. "I didn't mean to sound judgy."

"No, I deserve your judgment. I would judge me, too," Fran said. She pushed her curls back from her face and sighed unhappily.

"How did Will find out?" Audrey asked.

"Believe it or not, he followed me to Coop's apartment," Fran said.

"Why?" Audrey asked.

"He wanted to find out if I was having an affair. If that's the reason why I told him I wanted to separate," Fran said.

"Was it?" Audrey asked.

"Well, I wasn't having an affair, so technically no. But I had convinced myself that I was in love with Coop. That I would be happier with him than I could ever be with Will. So I guess I was cheating on him emotionally, in a way."

"Do you still want to leave Will?" Jaime asked.

Fran shook her head. "When Coop turned me down, it was like I suddenly woke up to reality for the first time in months. I realized I was pretending this entire relationship was taking place—or about to take place—when it couldn't have been further from the truth. And I finally saw how stupid, how incredibly stupid, I'd been. I don't want to lose Will. I was just bored and looking for some excitement. I was such an idiot."

"But you didn't actually cheat," Audrey said.

"Not for lack of trying," Fran said.

"But it's really not the same thing," Jaime said. "Trust me. There's a big difference between finding out your spouse is interested in someone else and finding out that they've slept with them."

"I don't know if Will's going to be able to forgive me after everything I've put him through," Fran said sadly.

"Your marriage is stronger than that," Jaime said.

"You just said that you wouldn't be able to forgive Mark," Fran said.

"Did you miss the part where I said he was *sleeping* with his *ex-wife*? That's a little different than having a crush on someone."

"And did you miss the part where I said I asked Will for a separation and then tried to seduce Coop?" Fran asked. She glanced at Audrey, as if suddenly concerned how this would go over. "Sorry. I didn't know you were involved with him."

"I know. Don't worry," Audrey said. She sighed and sipped her wine. "Wow, we are in good form tonight. Is it the curse of the Table for Seven Club? Two marriages on the rocks, one floundering romance, and one . . . well, one Leland." Audrey felt a pang of sadness.

"The dinner party club had nothing to do with it. Mark didn't screw around with his bitch of an ex-wife because of our dinner party club," Jaime said.

Fran's eyes widened and she gave a brief clap. "Bravo. I don't think I've ever heard you swear before. I'm impressed."

"I swear all the time," Jaime said.

The other two looked at her, eyebrows raised.

"In my head," she clarified. "Hey, I have two children under the age of four. My life is G-rated." She shrugged. "Maybe that's why my husband decided he needed to fuck someone else."

The waiter appeared at just that moment with the next

tray of small plates. At Jaime's words, he stopped dead and looked horrified.

"Oh. Sorry," Jaime mumbled.

"This is a therapy group. We're working out some anger issues," Fran explained.

"Very good," the waiter said, somewhat stiffly. Jaime giggled and then coughed to cover it up.

"What are we having next?" Audrey asked the waiter.

"A vegetable terrine," the waiter said, setting down the plates. Each contained a pâté, made up of three layers—one red, one green, one white. Then he checked the bottle of wine, and distributed the remnants among the three glasses. "Would you like another bottle of wine?"

"Yes," all three women said at once. And then they started laughing. It was the sort of half-drunk, hysterical laughter that once begun is hard to stop. The waiter made a hasty retreat, muttering that he would bring them another bottle immediately. This just made the three laugh even more, until Jaime had a coughing fit and Audrey's eyes began to tear up.

"We," Fran said, "are officially a mess."

"To us," Audrey said, raising her glass.

"To us," the others said, and they clinked their glasses together before feasting on the vegetable terrine.

JAIME WAS LYING IN bed, reading her latest book club selection, when Mark came in. His hair was ruffled and he looked unusually somber.

"Are you sure about this?" Mark asked.

He'd already carried out three suitcases of belongings. Only a garment bag with his suits was left, slung over the back of a linen upholstered wing chair. Jaime had asked him to move out all of his things after the children had gone to sleep. She had told them that Daddy would be living some-where else from now on—Mark had taken out a lease on a sterile furnished condo with a view of a golf course—but she thought that actually seeing him move his belongings out of their house would be more traumatic for them. Maybe she was deluding herself, but the one thing she was slowly learning through this mess was to trust her instincts.

Jaime put her book down and looked at Mark.

"About your moving out?" she asked. He nodded. "Yes, I think it's for the best."

Jaime realized she sounded stiff and cold. But it wasn't like there was a Martha Stewart guide on how to make sepa-rating from your cheating bastard of a husband a Good Thing. And besides, trying to create the perfect life had not exactly paid off for her so far. Why not add a bit of her own emotional mess to the pile?

"I'd be willing to go to marriage therapy," Mark said.

Jaime stared at him, wondering if he had any idea how obnoxious he sounded. As though consenting to marital therapy was some huge favor he was willing to throw her way.

"Thanks, but I think I'll pass," Jaime said.

"But what about Logan and Ava?"

"What about them?"

Mark sighed. "Do you really think splitting up our family is in their best interest?"

"Did you think of that when you were fucking Libby?" Jaime asked.

Mark flinched at the expletive, which gave Jaime a rush of

pleasure. *Good,* she thought. An ugly act deserves an ugly word.

"I wasn't thinking," Mark said. "It was a mistake. An enormous mistake."

"Are you apologizing?" Jaime asked.

"Yes, of course," Mark said.

"Because it didn't sound like an apology. 'It was a mistake' is not the same thing as 'I'm sorry.' Which you have yet to say to me."

Mark walked over to where Jaime lay in the bed, the blankets pulled around her like armor, and sat down on the edge of the mattress. He took her hands in his and looked at her earnestly.

"Jaime. I'm so, so sorry. I'm sorry about everything. If I could go back and undo it, I would. I love you. I love Logan and Ava. I love our life together," Mark said, his tone humble and his expression earnest. "Is that what you want to hear?"

Tears flooded Jaime's eyes, hot and salty.

"No," she said, her voice harsh. "What I want is for none of this to ever have happened. And unless you are capable of building a time machine, so that you can go back and not have an affair, then we are done. Over. Through. And don't you dare throw our children's happiness at me. If you cared about them, if you cared about me, you would never have done this in the first place."

Mark looked anguished. "I know how stupid I was. But please give me another chance. I won't bring up the kids if you don't want me to, but please give me another chance for us. For our family."

He looked at her pleadingly. And for a moment, Jaime wondered if she was doing the right thing. Divorce was hard on everyone, especially the children. It was messy and expensive and often destructive. And Mark had offered to go to marital counseling, which was completely unexpected. It was the sort of thing he'd always scoffed at in the past.

And yet . . . and yet. As Jaime looked at this man, her husband, she realized that nothing would ever be the same between them again. Even if they went to counseling, even if she found a way to forgive him—something she wasn't at all sure she'd be able to do—she'd always be wondering in the back of her mind if he was going to do it again.

"I'm sorry, Mark," she said, her voice as gentle as his had been a few moments earlier. "Our marriage is over. But I would really like to work with you to find a way to divorce that doesn't cause any extra trauma to our children."

Mark's face hardened. Jaime recognized the stony fix of his features; it was exactly how he had looked every time she had offered an opinion, or—even worse—a criticism of his relationship with Emily.

"Fine," he said, standing abruptly. Mark turned and picked up his garment bag, slinging it over his shoulder. "If that's what you want."

"None of this is what I wanted," Jaime said.

"You know, you aren't exactly blameless yourself."

Jaime's mouth fell open. "Are you saying it's my fault you had an affair?"

"There were a lot of problems in our marriage."

"Like what?"

"Your attitude toward Emily, for one."

"I love Emily," Jaime said.

"You've always resented her. Do you think I didn't notice?"

"That's not true. I resented the fact that you have never invested as much time in Ava and Logan, but that has nothing to do with my feelings toward Em," Jaime insisted.

"Bullshit," Mark said. "And do you think it's easy being married to someone who expects—no, *demands*—perfection at all times? The house, the kids, me—we all have to live up to your unrealistic expectations. People aren't perfect. Kitchens get messy. Kids spill juice. Husbands make mistakes."

Jaime gaped at Mark for a few beats, before being able to splutter, "That's not what this is about! This isn't about my mistakes—it's about yours!"

"They're not unconnected," Mark said.

"That's just a typical lawyer's argument. You can't win the argument, so reframe it. Well, I'm not playing this game with you anymore. Just go. Seriously. Leave," Jaime said, hurling the words at him.

But long after Mark left, and Jaime lay there, listening to the house vibrate with silence, she thought of what he'd said to her. *If that's what you want.*

"None of this is what I wanted," Jaime said again, her mouth twisting. "None of this."

WHEN FRAN ASKED WILL to have lunch with her, she half-expected him to say no. He'd been icily distant for weeks, leaving rooms when she entered, giving curt answers to any questions she posed to him, continuing to sleep on the sofa.

"This can't go on," Fran finally said to him one evening, after the girls were in bed. "I found Rory sleepwalking again. And Iris has been having stomach pains. You and I need to sit down and talk. We need to figure things out."

Will had hesitated, but finally nodded. "Do you want to do this now?" he asked.

Fran felt a stab of fear. It was one thing to worry that Will might leave her; it was another thing to get confirmation.

"No," she'd said, chickening out. "I'm too tired right now. Let's talk about it tomorrow. Over lunch. I know. Let's go to the Café Rouge." It was a small French bistro, a favorite locale for their rare date nights. Fran held her breath, waiting for Will's answer.

But just when Fran was sure Will was going to refuse, he'd shrugged and given a stiff half-nod, and said, "Sure. I'll meet you there tomorrow."

And then he'd retired to his couch-bed and ignored her for the rest of the night.

Fran agonized over what to wear. She wanted to look pretty, but—considering the circumstances of their estrangement—didn't want to look too suggestive. Excessive cleavage might just remind Will that she'd thrown herself at his best friend. But she also didn't want to show up in her work scrubs. Fran finally decided on her favorite dark rinse jeans and a peacock blue cashmere sweater that Will had given to her for Christmas a few years ago, which she packed in a bag, so she could change at work.

She arrived at the Café Rouge first. The waiter recognized her from their previous visits and seated her in a private booth, near the back of the restaurant.

"Would you like anything to drink while you wait for your husband?" the waiter asked.

Fran hesitated. She had a feeling that if she ordered wine, she'd end up glugging down too much, and right now she needed to keep a clear head.

"Iced tea, please," she said.

The waiter brought her the tea, and Fran had nearly emptied the entire glass before Will arrived, looking flustered.

"Sorry, I'm late," he said, sliding into the booth across from her. "There was a meeting at work that ran way over, and I couldn't get away."

"It's fine," Fran said, although the wait had been agonizing. For a while, she'd wondered if he was going to stand her up.

Will picked up his menu and scanned it. "What are you having? I've never had lunch here before."

"I haven't, either," Fran said. "But I thought the quiche sounded good. Roasted red pepper and feta."

Will nodded. "I think I'll have the steak sandwich with pommes frites."

"That sounds perfect. I'll have the same thing," she said, putting down her menu.

The waiter appeared and took their order for the steak sandwiches. They waited in silence while the waiter went to get another iced tea for Fran and a Coke for Will.

When they both had their drinks in front of them, Fran took a deep, shaky breath, and said, "I'm so sorry."

Will nodded, staring down at his Coke. "I know you are," he said. "And I appreciate that."

Fran felt a rush of hope. "Can you forgive me?" she asked.

Will looked up at her, and the expression Fran saw there caused her blooming hope to wither and blow into dust. Even despite the lack of passion in their relationship, she'd always known Will adored her. It had shone from him, even when he was exasperated or under the weather. But now, as he looked at her, his eyes were blank.

"I don't know if I can," Will said.

Tears pricked at her eyes, but Fran blinked, determined

not to fall apart. *Look at Jaime,* she thought. She had kicked Mark out of the house, hired a divorce attorney and a part-time nanny, and next week was starting back at the realty office where she'd worked before her marriage. And despite all of these seismic changes, Jaime was taking the whole thing in stride. No, it was more than that—she seemed to be coming into her own, both toughening up and relaxing the over-the-top expectations she'd always put on herself. When Fran had stopped by Jaime's house for a glass of wine a few nights earlier, there had actually been dirty dishes in the sink.

"Dirty dishes?" Fran had said, her eyebrows shooting up to her hairline. "I think you're going to have to turn your Little Miss Perfect badge in."

Jaime had shrugged, lifted her glass of wine in a toast, and said, "I think I can live with that."

"That's my girl!" Fran had said.

There was the occasional crack in this tough facade. That same night, Jaime had gotten a little weepy when she reported Logan's offhand comment about seeing Emily's mom when he was visiting his dad.

"I guess they're still seeing each other. It's like he can just slide from one marriage to the next, and then back again," Jaime had said.

"You know you're better off without him," Fran said.

Jaime shrugged. "No doubt. But it's still disturbing. It's like he wants to pretend our marriage never took place, and just go back to the way things were. Mark, Libby, and Emily. The perfect little family."

"Except that he can't erase it. There's Ava and Logan now."

"That's the one good thing to come out of this mess. Mark's actually spending more time with them, now that he has to plan when he sees them." Jaime sighed, and tossed her long hair back over her shoulders. "And he is a good dad."

"When he's not fucking his ex-wife," Fran amended.

"Exactly," Jaime said, and they'd both laughed.

Now, sitting across the table from Will, wondering if her marriage was truly over, Fran hoped that she could channel some of Jaime's bravado.

"The thing is . . . I didn't actually cheat on you," she said.

Will's face hardened. "Not for lack of trying," he said, the words a whiplash.

Fran held up her hands in a sign of surrender. "Granted. And I was completely wrong to do what I did. And if it makes you feel any better, I made an absolute fool of myself."

"No, it doesn't really."

Fran suppressed the urge to sigh. "What I'm trying to say is that in the end, nothing happened. I didn't have an affair."

"But you wanted to," Will said.

Fran nodded. "Yes," she said. There was no point denying it. That was exactly what happened. She had wanted to have an affair. In a sense, it *had* been an emotional affair, even if Coop hadn't been an active participant, simply by the amount of emotion and energy she'd put into thinking about him. She'd been ready to walk out on her marriage, on her family for him. "I am very sorry. I would promise that it will never happen again, but I know my word isn't worth much to you right now."

"No, it's not."

"But I love you. Please tell me we can fix this," Fran said. Tears filled her eyes again, and this time she couldn't blink them back. They welled up and spilled over her lashes.

Will looked at her and then down at his Coke.

"It's not like I'm completely blameless. You were un-happy for a long time. I should have seen that," Will said.

"I should have talked to you about it," Fran said.

"And I should have been investing more energy into our marriage," Will said. "If I'd spent as much time working on us as I spend on my combat bots, maybe we wouldn't be in this situation."

"Oh, God, no, that would be annoying," Fran blurted out. Then she gave a shaky laugh while wiping her eyes on her sleeve. "I couldn't stand that much quality couple time."

A corner of Will's mouth turned up. "Okay, half as much time."

"Maybe a quarter," Fran compromised.

"I don't spend that much time working on the bots," Will protested.

"Will. You have a disturbingly large army of combat ro-bots in our garage. All of which you've built by hand," Fran said.

"Maybe it's time for a new hobby," Will said.

"No . . . no. You just need to be you," Fran said.

She was about to reach across the table, to put her hand on his, but the waiter chose that moment to arrive with their steak sandwiches. Fran leaned back to make room for the plates, and then there was an extended wait while the server asked if they wanted fresh ground pepper on their sand-wiches (an odd question, Fran thought, considering they hadn't yet tasted them), and if they needed anything else. When he finally accepted that they were fine and departed, Will seemed distant again. He dipped a pomme frite in the small dish of ketchup, and popped it in his mouth. He had always been a fries-first kind of a guy, Fran thought. She liked to eat her food together, alternating bites of sandwich and fries, while Will would often polish off entire side dishes before moving on to the entrée. In another, less strained time, she would have remarked upon this to him, and he would pretend that it was a criticism and act offended, all the while enjoying there was someone who cared enough to notice his idiosyncrasies.

Instead, she said, "Is there anything I can do to make it up to you?"

"What do you think about seeing a marriage counselor?" Will asked carefully, not looking up from his lunch.

"Okay," Fran said, keeping her voice neutral. The truth was she hated therapy, and couples therapy in particular. "Do you think we need one?"

Will looked up at her. "Well, yeah. Don't you?"

"I'm willing to do whatever it takes," Fran said quickly. "But I just sort of hoped we could put this behind us. That we could move forward, with the understanding that I'll have to earn your trust again."

"And then what? What if six months from now, you feel like leaving again?"

Fran shook her head vehemently. "No. That was a terrible idea. Childish. I was just playing out this stupid fantasy I had of a different life."

"Well, that happened for a reason," Will said. "There must be something missing in your life that you were trying to fix."

Fran bit into her steak sandwich, quickly leaning forward so that the juices wouldn't drip onto her sweater. She barely tasted the food, but wanted a minute to think. Her plan for this lunch had been to throw herself on Will's mercy and beg for a second chance. But, at the same time, she knew he was right—she *had* been unhappy. That was something that probably should be addressed if they were to move on.

"I think what I was feeling—what I've been feeling for a long time—is that my entire life had become about working, and helping the kids with homework, and doing laundry. There hasn't been any excitement, any passion. Nothing to look forward to, other than more of the same," Fran said.

Will sat up, his back stiffening. "I work hard, too. And I do a lot to help out around the house," he said.

"I know. It isn't a contest. But I thought you wanted to know what I've been missing."

"Which is what?"

"This," Fran said, gesturing to the restaurant. "This is the first time we've had lunch together at a nice restaurant, just the two of us, in ages. And it took a crisis to get us here. I want to have date nights. I want to go on a vacation, just the two of us."

"You know money has been tight," Mark said.

"I know. I'm not saying it has to be all filet mignon and trips to Paris. We could go have a picnic on the beach, for all I care," Fran said.

"The problem with that is that it always sounds good in theory, but then sand gets in the food. And flocks of seagulls end up stalking you for leftovers," Will said.

Fran stared at him. "Really?"

"Sorry," Will said. "No, I do hear you. You want romance."

"I want you," Fran said. This time she did lean over the table and put her hand on his arm. "I want to spend time where it's just you and me. Time apart from the kids, and the household chores, and paying the bills, and the monotony of everyday life."

Will nodded. "Okay," he said. "That's something we can definitely work on."

Tears filled Fran's eyes yet again. "Really?" she said. "You're not going to leave me, then?"

Will put his hand on top of Fran's. And this time, when he looked at her, it was the way he used to. With love.

"Fran," he said gently. "You're my life. You and the girls. I couldn't live without you."

"I can't live without you, either," Fran said, now full-on blubbering. She used the crisp white napkin to wipe at her eyes and nose, while wondering, *What is it with me and crying in restaurants lately?* She held up one hand to Will, and with the other dug in her purse for her compact. "Wait, don't look at me. I know I'm all red and splotchy."

"You are. You're red, and splotchy, and you're snotty, too," Will said. He smiled at her, and Fran wondered if his eyes were extra shiny because he was tearing up, too. "But I love you anyway."

"You do?" she sniffled.

"I do," he said, and he lifted her hand and kissed it.

THE SUN WAS SETTING in ribbons of pink and orange as Coop steered his boat back toward the dock. It had been a good day out; he'd caught three red snapper early, which were now in the cooler, and then had spent the rest of the afternoon sitting in the sun with a beer, Bear at his side, contemplating his life. He had spent most of his adulthood doing exactly what he wanted, when he wanted. He'd dated more than his share of beautiful women, had professional success in a job he enjoyed, and had the love of a good dog.

This introspection led him to an inevitable conclusion: He had been the world's biggest schmuck.

He was forty-six years old, well past the age when most men married, had kids, bought a house. They carved turkeys at Thanksgiving and decorated Christmas trees and hid chocolate eggs for Easter egg hunts. They watched bad sit-coms tucked up on the couch with their wives' feet on their laps. They slowly lost the hair on their heads, and grew it back in their noses and ears, and displayed the pottery pencil holders their kids made them for Father's Day on their desks. Was it boring and unoriginal and suburban at times? Undoubtedly. But it was a life full of textures and memories, and—above all—a life filled with love.

That was the sort of life he wanted to have with Audrey, he thought. Unfortunately, she was even more damaged than he was. She was so hung up on her late marriage, she had yet to realize that her life was still going on.

"But what can I do? I can't force her to be with me," Coop said out loud.

Bear looked at him, adopted the pose of the concerned listener—his brown furry head cocked to one side, his eyes fixed on Coop.

"I know what you'd say if you could talk," Coop said. "You'd say I didn't exactly go all out trying to win her over. I mean, I did tell her I love her. But I didn't make the big gesture. I didn't hire a sky writer or propose during a nationally televised sporting event. I didn't even bring her flowers."

Bear's tongue unfurled from his mouth, and he began to pant.

"Yeah, I know. Audrey doesn't seem like the big gesture type. In fact, I'm pretty she she'd think sky writing was tacky. But most women like to be wooed, right? It just seems like there's a fine line between continuing to woo a woman who's turned you down cold—twice, no less—and stalking," Coop continued.

Bear yawned and lay down on the padded boat seat, his head resting on his paws.

"I hear you, buddy. I'm boring myself. And I'm also questioning my sanity, considering I'm looking for love advice from a dog." The dock came into view, and Coop drove slowly toward it, obeying the speed law and staying in the designated lane for boat traffic.

He basically had two choices. He could either take one more run at Audrey—and this time with a little more flair than just barging in on her at work and blurting out that he was in love with her—or let it go and move on. The first option was scary. But the second was worse.

"I guess I'll go with the big gesture," Coop said, although by now Bear was asleep, snoring softly, and thus unable to offer any more canine advice.

The question remained: What should he do? The person he would normally have gone to for advice was Fran, but that was out of the question for obvious reasons. He hadn't even been able to bring himself to talk to Will since the night Franny had come over and offered herself up to him. There was no way Will would find out about it—he sure as hell wasn't going to tell him, and he sincerely doubted Fran ever would, either—but Coop still felt guilty about it. He must have led Fran on without realizing he was doing it. Either that, or he just oozed sex appeal, which, now that he thought about it, was hardly his fault.

Where is all of this excessive, out-of-my-control sex appeal

when it comes to Audrey? Or is she somehow impervious to it?
Coop wondered.

Coop pulled up to the dock, cut his motor, and deftly jumped out of the boat to moor it to the dock. There were quite a few people milling around, who, like him, were coming back from late afternoon tours. Coop was too busy settling in his boat to pay them any attention.

"Hi," a voice said.

Coop looked up. He blinked. Audrey was standing there, a large black scarf wrapped around her shoulders to ward off the evening chill. She was holding a leash, at the other end of which was a familiar-looking bulldog.

"Nice dog," Coop said.

Bear jumped out of the boat, padded over to the bulldog, and gave him a thorough sniffing over, which the bulldog tolerated amicably.

"This is Winston," Audrey said. "He belonged to Leland."

"How did you end up with him?"

"Neither of Leland's sons could take him, so I offered. I'd been thinking about getting a dog, anyway. And he's good company, although he has an awful snoring problem."

"And you just happen to be out taking Winston for a walk on the dock?"

"No." Audrey hesitated. "I was looking for you."

"How did you know where to find me?" Coop asked.

"I asked the manager at your apartment building. Fred, right? Fred said that this is where you keep your boat," Audrey said. She frowned. "Actually, you should probably have a talk with him about it. He really shouldn't give out information about tenants to complete strangers."

Coop made a mental note to give Fred a very large tip at Christmas.

"I'll do that," he said. "But how did you know what time I'd be here? I had no idea when I was coming in, so there's no way Fred would know."

"I've been waiting."

"For how long?"

"A while."

"A long while?" Coop pressed. Happiness began unfurling inside of him.

"Define *long*."

"Hours?"

"Look, why does it matter?" Audrey asked. She was starting to look flustered, and she drew her black scarf around her.

"It's the big gesture," Coop said. "Waiting on the dock for a sailor's return." He grinned cheekily. "It's almost poetic."

"And I'm starting to regret it," Audrey said, rolling her eyes. She pointed over her shoulder. "Maybe I should leave you and your ego alone?"

"No, don't do that," Coop said, stepping closer to Audrey. "I was just coming to find you."

Her eyes were large and, in the waning light, so dark they almost looked black. Coop brushed her hair back from her cheek, and tucked it behind her ear. He took it as a good sign that she didn't bat his hand away.

"You were?" she asked softly.

Coop nodded. "I was coming to make the big gesture. It was going to either sweep you off your feet or get me arrested for stalking."

Audrey's lips twitched. "What was this big gesture?"

"I have no idea. I was going to improvise on my way over to your place," Coop said.

"Wow. That's really not at all impressive," Audrey said.

"No, it was going to be good. Like, climbing-up-the-side-of-your-building-with-a-bouquet-of-roses good," Coop said.

"That would probably land you in the hospital with a broken back," Audrey said.

"I see your point. Maybe I would have thrown stones at your window, and then when you came out, serenaded you," Coop suggested. He took another step closer to Audrey and put both hands on her waist.

"Can you sing?"

"Not at all."

"Hmm."

"I think you should be more supportive of my big romantic gesture," Coop said, leaning forward, so that his nose was only inches away from hers. Her cheeks were pink from the cool air and her lashes were very long.

"I think you should come up with a better idea."

"I could recite poetry. 'She walks in beauty like the night.' That sort of thing."

"Mmm, I like that," Audrey said. "How does the rest of it go?"

Coop hesitated. "Actually, I have no idea."

Audrey laughed. Coop leaned forward and kissed her. He felt Audrey relax into his arms, warm and light, a perfect fit. After a long, long time, he leaned back and looked down at her.

"Give me some time, and I'll come up with something better," he said. "Wait, I know. How about a trip to Paris?"

"I was going to suggest a bottle of wine and a nice dinner of whatever you caught out there today. But now that Paris is on the table, maybe I should set my standards higher," Audrey said, grinning up at him.

"You got it," Coop said. "All of it."

january

.. ..

SPAGHETTI CARBONARA

MIXED GREEN SALAD WITH
ROQUEFORT VINAIGRETTE

GARLIC BREAD

BLACK-BOTTOM CUPCAKES

I KNOW SPAGHETTI CARBONARA isn't exciting, but I thought we could all use some comfort food," Fran explained to Jaime and Audrey, as they watched her dice shallots.

"I don't see why we shouldn't start up the Table for Seven Club again," Audrey said. "Leland wouldn't mind us going on. In fact, I think it would make him happy to know that we were getting together once a month and eating bacon."

"Yeah, that would be a lot of fun for me," Jaime said. "Two couples and me. We could just rename it the Fifth Wheel Club."

Fran and Audrey both laughed, and Audrey said, "Trust me, I've been there."

"I know. I've only been single for, what? Six weeks? In fact, I won't even technically be single until my divorce goes through," Jaime said. She sighed, and took a sip of her champagne.

"What are you going to do about the house?" Fran asked.

"Sell it," Jaime said.

"Oh, no, that's too bad," Audrey said sympathetically. "You did such a beautiful job on it."

"Thanks, but even if I could afford it, it's too much work keeping it up. And now that I'm working again, time is not something I have a lot of. I think the kids and I will be happier in a smaller house. It will be more relaxing. More freeing," Jaime said.

"Good Lord, who are you and what did you do with my

friend Jaime?" Fran asked. "The type-A perfectionist we all knew and loved? And, to be honest, also hated a little."

Jaime laughed. "I was pretty obnoxious, wasn't I? You-all don't even know the half of it. I ironed my sheets. All of them, even the kids'. And I had a special labeled shelf for each size set."

"You did not," Audrey said.

"And how on earth did you have the time?" Fran asked.

"I did. I never let anyone see my linen closet, though, because I knew it would out me as being a complete freak," Jaime said. "And I never slept much. Although these days, I can't seem to stay awake. I went to bed at eight o'clock last night. Do you think I'm depressed?"

"You don't seem depressed," Fran said. "If anything, you seem more relaxed. Divorce clearly agrees with you."

"I don't know. I'm already tired of taking out the garbage. That was always Mark's job. And I've had some seriously bad days mixed in. But I think I am rallying. Or, at least, I'm trying to," Jaime said, raising her chin a fraction.

"I think once the word is out among the Ocean Falls bachelors that you're available, you'll be snapped up quickly," Fran said.

Jaime raised a hand, as though to ward off an evil wish. "Don't even say it. I don't ever want to get married again. Life is far, far simpler without a man involved. Even if it means having to drag the trash cans to the curb twice a week myself."

Audrey looked thoughtful and took a sip of her wine. "You feel that way now. But you may change your mind, eventually. Look at me."

Two heads swiveled to face Audrey, who was taking another sip of her wine.

"Um . . . do you have some news for us?" Fran asked.

Audrey tilted her head to one side, and then, realizing what Fran was asking, she burst out laughing. "Oh, God, no, I see how that sounded. No, Coop and I aren't getting married. At least, not anytime soon. I just meant that I always said I had no interest in dating again after Ryan, and life proved me wrong."

"You mean I proved you wrong," Fran said. She scraped the shallots into a dish with the blade of her chef's knife, and began to dice the pancetta.

"What are you talking about? You were against Coop and I in the beginning," Audrey said.

This was still a somewhat touchy subject that the friends danced around. But they were slowly trying to make it into a joke. The story would be, from now on, that Fran thought Coop was all wrong for Audrey, and yet they fell in love anyway. The part where Fran had thrown herself at Coop, and been rejected, would never be mentioned again, and eventually would be erased from the history of their friendship. Sometimes, a certain amount of amnesia was not only excusable, but necessary for friendships to endure.

"Yes, but I was the one who kept telling you to get back out there," Fran reminded her. She tossed her hair back, so that the loose curls hung down her back. She glanced at Jaime. "And it's way too soon to be bugging you about it—you need at least a year to eighteen months to get over your marriage before you're ready to see anyone seriously—but I'll eventually get on your case, too."

"I'll consider myself warned. But I doubt I'll ever get married again. I'll just have a string of hot, young lovers who all worship me," Jaime said, twirling her wineglass. "And take out the garbage for me."

"Mmm," Fran said. "That sounds . . ."

"Be careful how you finish that sentence. Your husband is now in the room," Will said, coming into the kitchen with Coop behind him.

"Oops," Fran said, but she smiled at Will, and he sidled up to her, slipping an arm around her waist.

"I was just showing Coop the battle bot Rory's building," Will said. He beamed. "It's her own design and everything. She takes after her old man."

"Will's turning into a stage dad," Fran informed the group, but she smiled up at him and he kissed her cheek.

"When are you two going to the Bahamas?" Audrey asked.

"At the end of January," Fran said.

"I didn't know you were going out of town," Jaime said.

"It was Will's Christmas present to me. We're only going for a weekend—it's all we could afford, and frankly, we're sort of terrified about leaving the girls for longer, anyway—but I can't wait. It's been a long time since we got away, just the two of us," Fran said.

"Good for you," Jaime said. "That's the one thing I think Mark and I did right. We were pretty good about putting time aside to take trips on our own. But my mom was always willing to come down and stay with Ava and Logan, so we didn't have to worry about that. Who's staying with the girls?"

"We are," Coop said indignantly. "And frankly, I'm a bit insulted that you're terrified of leaving the girls in Audrey's and my care. I am Rory's godfather, after all."

"Iris's godfather," Fran corrected him. "Audrey is Rory's godmother. And I'm not worried about them, I'm worried about you. You have to look after two hormonal girls and a puppy. I don't think you know what you've gotten yourself into."

Fran and Coop had both decided to pretend that the night when Fran went to his apartment didn't happen. They conversed easily, as they always had, although any flirtatious element that may have been there was gone. Coop didn't kiss Fran on the cheek when he saw her now, but that was probably all for the best.

"A puppy?" Jaime asked, looking around, as though she'd somehow failed to notice one in the room. "You have a puppy?"

"Didn't I tell you? I swear, we need to sit down and catch up," Fran said. "We got the girls a puppy for Christmas. A labradoodle. They named him Homer."

"After the poet?" Jaime asked, wrinkling her nose.

"No! After Homer Simpson," Fran said, laughing.

"I thought you said you would never get a dog," Jaime demanded. "Wasn't that one of the conversations we had at the dinner party club this year?"

"I did say that. But Iris has been volunteering at the animal shelter and helping to train assistance dogs, so I thought she had proven herself," Fran said, adding a healthy dollop of white wine to the frying pan. It hissed and gave off a plume of steam. "In fact, Homer came from the shelter. He was dropped off with his mother and littermates, and Iris fell instantly in love." Fran paused. "I'm just thankful that her first love is a dog and not a boy with tattoos."

"Where is he?"

"Upstairs with the girls, I think," Will said. He picked up the bottle of champagne. "Who's ready for a refill?"

"I am," Jaime said, holding out her glass.

"Me, too," Audrey said. She was sitting on one of the

high stools lined up by the kitchen counter. Coop moved behind her and rested his hand on the small of her back.

"Anyway, consider yourselves warned," Fran said. "But
don't even think about backing out on us."

"We wouldn't," Audrey assured her. She looked up shyly
at Coop. "Besides, we have a trip of our own to look forward
to this spring."

"Where are you two going?" Will asked.

"Paris," Audrey said happily.

"Oh, that's great. Thanks, guy. I finally surprise Franny
with a trip, and you find a way to one-up me," Will said to
Coop.

"Hey, I owed Audrey a big romantic gesture," Coop said.
"And all's fair, and all that."

"It's fine. I'd much rather go to the Bahamas than to
Paris," Fran said to Will, patting his arm.

"Then you're nuts," Will said, laughing.

Fran began to sauté the pancetta, and its bacony smell
filled the kitchen. Once the fat began to render, she added
the chopped shallots to the pan. Will got out the mixed baby
greens and put them in a big bowl.

"Hon, what else is going in here?" he asked.

"Red onion, goat cheese, and orange slices," Fran said.
"Do you need help?"

"Nope, I've got it," Will said.

"He's a new-age man. He cooks, he cleans, he's in touch
with his emotions," Coop teased.

"Oh, hush. You cook, too," Audrey said. "In fact, aren't
you going to tell everyone what I got you for Christmas?"

"Do I have to?" Coop asked.

"I got him a series of cooking lessons with Juan, the chef

at the Lemon Tree," Audrey said. "And don't let Coop fool you. It's exactly what he said he wanted."

"Well, after a year of exquisite home-cooked meals, I thought it was time I learned how to do something other than grill fish and make hamburgers," Coop said. He squeezed Audrey's waist, and the others wondered why she was blushing, but no one dared ask.

"Once he's had a few lessons, you'll all have to come over for another dinner party," Audrey said brightly. She smiled at Jaime. "And yes, you, too. You'll never be a fifth wheel with us."

"So the Table for Seven Club continues?" Will asked.

"I don't think so. Not officially, anyway," Fran said. "For one thing, we're five now."

"And for another, I don't think I'll be in a position to entertain anytime soon. I have a lot on my plate right now," Jaime added.

"No, I think we can do away with the monthly meetings," Audrey agreed. "But we can still get together for dinner now and again, right?"

"Absolutely," Fran said.

Jaime nodded her head, and Coop gave a thumbs-up.

Fran beat four eggs in a large Pyrex measuring cup, then stirred in grated pecorino romano and parmesan cheeses, salt, and freshly ground pepper. She drained the spaghetti, which had been cooking in a large pot of salted water, and added it to the frying pan for a moment, before removing the pan from the heat. She stirred the egg and cheese mixture into the pasta, while the others looked on. Fran took a fork, sampled the pasta, and looked up with a smile.

"Dinner is served," she said.

READ ON FOR

AN EXCERPT FROM

......

WHEN
YOU LEAST
EXPECT IT

...

by *WHITNEY*
GASKELL

ONE

INDIA

I'VE ALWAYS LOVED THE LIGHT BY THE OCEAN AT THE END of the day. Those magical moments, just as the sun is sinking low in the sky, when everything on the beach is cast in a rosy, golden glow. I raised my ever-present camera and snapped a few shots of Miles, Rose, and Luke as they played at the water's edge. The three of them had found a stick and were taking it in turn to throw into the water for Otis, our black and white border collie mix. He barked happily and plunged into the foamy white surf after it.

"Otis is going to smell like a fish after this," I said, lowering the camera.

Jeremy was in the middle of attempting to get the charcoals on the hibachi to catch fire. He looked up in Otis's direction and grinned. Jeremy had an appealing, open face with a high forehead, long chin, and oversized, Jimmy Durante nose.

"Maybe he's part fish. He's always loved to swim," he said, running a hand through his short red-brown hair until it stood up on end.

"It's good to see him active. His arthritis has been so bad lately," I said.

"Otis and I are both getting to be old men," Jeremy agreed. He sat back on his heels, admiring the charcoal, which was now smoking nicely. It had been a warm day—

typical weather for West Palm Beach in the late spring—but there was a breeze blowing off the water.

"Not so old," I said, dropping a kiss on the top of his head. I settled down on the plaid blanket we'd spread out over the sand, and began to rummage through the cooler.

"What gourmet delicacies are we cooking up tonight? Breast of duck in a sour cherry reduction sauce? Beef tenderloin with roasted shallots?" Jeremy asked, settling down next to me on the blanket. He lay on his back, his hands folded behind his head, and closed his eyes.

"Hot dogs," I said, holding up the plastic-wrapped package. "Followed by marshmallows."

Jeremy opened one eye and squinted at me. "God, I love you," he said reverently.

"Because I brought hot dogs?" I asked, smiling down at him.

"Partly because of the hot dogs. But mostly because of the marshmallows," he said.

"Not just marshmallows," I said. I rummaged in an oversized tote bag and pulled out a box of graham crackers and a six-pack of chocolate bars. "We're going to make s'mores. Your favorite."

"Will you marry me?"

"I'm already married to you."

"Good thing. A woman who serves me processed meat products and s'mores. What more could any man want?" Jeremy said. He sat up, propping himself on bent arms. "Should I call the wild bunch up here?"

"Give them a few minutes. The hot dogs still have to cook," I said, pulling a bunch of bamboo skewers out of the bag. I looked at them doubtfully. "Do you think these are long enough to roast the marshmallows on? I don't want one of the kids to catch fire."

"Yeah, we'd have a hard time explaining that to Mimi and Leo," Jeremy said.

"They'd never let us babysit again," I agreed.

The children belonged to my best friend, Mimi, and her husband, Leo. They were on a romantic overnight getaway to South Beach, so Miles, Rose, and Luke were spending the night with Jeremy and me.

"Are the coals hot enough?" I asked.

"They should be," Jeremy said, reaching for the shrink-wrapped package of hot dogs. He pulled the dogs out and, one by one, dropped them on the grill.

While the hot dogs sizzled, I got out paper plates, napkins, mustard, and a bag of potato chips. The children, sensing food was imminent, abandoned the stick-tossing game and ran up the beach toward us. Otis, soggy but triumphant, followed them at a trot, proudly holding the stick in his mouth.

"I'm starving," Miles announced, tripping just as he reached us. He tried to cover his embarrassment over this clumsiness by flopping down on the blanket, but his cheeks flushed red. Miles, ten, had recently gone through a growth spurt and was still getting used to his new longer legs and arms.

"You're always hungry," Rose said, daintily brushing the sand off her bare legs before sitting down cross-legged next to me. Rose, age eight, was our goddaughter. She was her mother in miniature—the same slanting dark eyes and full lips, an identical cloud of dark hair. The only traces of Leo were evident in her long nose and slightly squared chin.

"Look who's talking," Miles retorted. "Mom says that you eat more than you weigh on a daily basis."

"Liar," Rose said, but without much rancor.

Six-year-old Luke, who'd been unsuccessfully attempting to convince Otis to part with his stick, sat down next to his sister. He had a sturdier build than his lanky big brother and still had baby-rounded cheeks. His small, square feet were caked with sand. I considered brushing them off, but then decided it was a lost cause.

"What are you making for us?" Luke asked. He regarded me with large, suspicious brown eyes.

"Hot dogs," I said as I handed out plates with rolls and chips on them. "There's mustard here. Does anyone want ketchup? Or relish? I have chopped onions, too."

"Dinner is served," Jeremy said, setting a paper plate full of hot dogs down on the blanket. Miles and Rose fell on their dinners as though they hadn't eaten in days, but Luke frowned and poked his hot dog suspiciously.

"I don't like hot dogs," he said.

Otis perked up at this. He sat down at the edge of the blanket and stared meaningfully at Luke's hot dog.

"Yes you do," Rose, Miles, and I said in unison.

Luke was going through a stage where he claimed not to like anything served to him, including foods he'd happily eaten since he was a baby.

"I don't," he insisted.

"Just try a bite," Jeremy suggested.

Luke looked doubtful. Otis licked his chops.

"Hot dogs are really unhealthy," I said.

"They are?" Luke asked.

I nodded solemnly. "In fact, your mom probably wouldn't approve that I made them for you. I bet she'll be really mad at me when she finds out."

"That's okay, we won't tell," Miles assured me. I winked at him, and he grinned.

Luke was intrigued. He picked up the hot dog and took a microscopic bite. Deciding that it was acceptable, he took another, larger bite. Otis drooped with disappointment.

"Do you know what hot dogs are made of?" Rose said conversationally. "They make them out of—"

I cut her off before she could complete her thought. "It's probably better not to talk about it while we're eating."

Rose giggled. "But it's really gross," she said temptingly.

Luke looked up, his mouth full of hot dog. "What's gross?"

"I can touch my eyeball," Jeremy said quickly.

"Ewww!" Rose said, safely distracted.

"Let me see!" Luke said.

Jeremy—who'd worn contacts for twenty years—obliged, touching his right index finger to his eyeball.

"Don't you think you should wash your hands before you do that?" I asked.

"I want to try!" Luke said, stuffing the last of his hot dog into his mouth.

"I don't think that's such a good idea," I said, with a sudden vision of calling Mimi with the news that we were in the emergency room having Luke's scratched cornea tended to.

"Don't worry," Jeremy said, lowering his voice so Luke wouldn't hear. "When I first started wearing contacts, it took me forever before I could put the lens in without blinking."

Jeremy was right; there was nothing to worry about. As soon as Luke's finger was an inch away from his eye, his eyelid snapped shut.

"I bet you a billion dollars you can't do it," Rose said.

"You don't have a billion dollars, half-head," Luke retorted, trying—and failing again—to touch his eyeball.

Half-head? Jeremy mouthed at me. We both swallowed back laughter.

"I won't need it," Rose said smugly. "But you will."

Miles, the pacifist in the family, was rarely drawn into arguments with his bickering siblings. Ignoring Rose's taunts and Luke's attempts to touch his eyeball, he stood, pulled a Hacky Sack out of his pocket, and began kicking it.

"Are Hacky Sacks back in? I haven't seen one since high school," Jeremy said.

"My soccer coach says it's a good way to improve your

ball control," Miles said, shaking back his long hair. He'd talked his mother into letting him grow it out and was immensely proud of its shagginess.

"I used to be pretty good with a Hacky Sack," Jeremy said. He stood, and Miles passed him the ball. Jeremy kicked it once off his heel and sent the small beanbag flying. Miles chased after it.

Used to being the operative words," Jeremy said sheepishly.

"Let me try," Rose said, springing to her feet, always eager to join in a game.

Miles kicked the Hacky Sack to her, and Rose juggled it expertly before kicking it back to her brother.

"Good job, Rose," I said.

"She's better than me," Jeremy said.

"Rose is the star of her soccer team," I reminded him. "She gets more practice than you."

"Girls rule and boys drool," Rose crowed.

Miles passed the ball to Jeremy again, but Jeremy wasn't able to catch it and it fell to the sand.

"Whoops," Jeremy said.

"You just need some practice," Miles said supportively.

"Why don't you have kids, India?" Luke asked.

The question caught me off guard. It wasn't that I hadn't heard it before. Jeremy and I were in our mid-thirties and had been married for seven years, so I'd gotten used to being asked about our baby plans. Acquaintances at cocktail parties, clients of my photography studio, even cashiers at the grocery store. I suppose asking someone if they have kids is pretty harmless. Unless, of course, you happen to be infertile.

Normally, I give an abbreviated version of the truth: that we very much wanted a baby, and were hoping to get pregnant, but it hadn't happened for us yet. I never mention the grittier details—the extensive medical exams, the hormone injections, the failed IVF cycles. Repetition had made this little routine nearly painless.

But I hadn't been expecting to hear the question from Luke, in these idyllic surroundings, while relaxing with the kids. Instead of my usual, measured response, I found myself stuttering, "W-why do you ask?"

"It's just that if you had a kid, Jeremy would have someone to practice Hacky Sack with," Luke explained, as though it were the most logical thing in the world. Which, to a six-year-old, it probably was. "And I'd have someone to play with when we visit you," he added.

Jeremy looked sharply at me, his face etched with concern. I smiled at him, and shook my head slightly to let him know it was okay.

"If we did have a baby, it would be a long time before he was old enough to play with you. And by then, you probably wouldn't want to play with him, because you'd be so much older," I explained to Luke.

Luke considered the wisdom of this argument. "But I wouldn't be the youngest anymore. And I'd have someone to boss around."

"That's true," I said.

"If you had a girl, it would almost be like I had a sister," Rose said.

"Yeah, and if it was a boy, it would be like I had a brother," Luke continued.

"You already have a brother," Rose informed him, her voice dripping with sarcasm.

"Yeah, thanks, Luke," Miles said mildly, still juggling his Hacky Sack.

"Besides," Rose continued, "India and Jeremy are *my* godparents, not yours. So if they had a baby, it would be my sister or brother, but it wouldn't be yours."

Rose liked to lord her superior claim to Jeremy and me over her two brothers whenever possible. It had the desired effect now. Luke swelled with outrage.

"That's not true! Take it back!" he demanded.

"It is too true. Right, India?" Rose said.

Both kids looked at me, as though I were the referee. I tried to remember what Mimi did at moments like this, and had a vague recollection of her saying that if there wasn't actual bloodshed, she stayed out of sibling warfare.

"Okay, everyone simmer down. I promise that if Jeremy and I ever do have a baby, you can all be official big brothers and sisters. Yes, Rose, that includes Luke," I said. "Now, who wants to toast a marshmallow?"

WHITNEY GASKELL briefly—and reluctantly—practiced law before publishing her first novel. This is her eighth novel, all published by Bantam, and she lives in Florida with her husband and son. You can visit Whitney's website and read her blog at www.whitneygaskell.com.